Unfolding Souls

Unfolding Souls
Oman McCullough-Fuqua

Unfolding Souls

Edited by Susanna K. Green

Book Design by Madhouse Design, Inc.

Published by Sweet Nectar Publishing

ISBN: 978-0-9977022-2-4

This book is dedicated to all men and women who have survived any type of abuse. My character, Jamaica Gold, dedicates her love with all out freezer-burning emotions and bitter secrecy; defrosting hostile words she must express about her rapists. First, she dedicates breaking her silence to males and females who are still frozen in their pain, day and night. As I tell her story, my heart goes out to the wounded that are trapped inside their complex misery, afraid to live again. To all victims who are angry and in despair, Jamaica Gold's soul unfolds and shares with you her time of hostility and warfare.

With each word, I feel your cry for help; I've been there. Trust me, you're not alone. Understand that life repeats itself; we live in each other's shadows. We learn from each other's mistakes. I hope someone learns from Jamaica Gold. Whether you feel the abuse was your fault or not; no one deserves to be taken advantage of or exploited. In this book, I express how my character, Jamaica Gold, was raised to expose the abuse that could happen to any one of us.

In this commonly heartless and judgmental world, you've buried your pain, and life seems unfair. I'm not your judge, and this book is not for you to judge. Instead, be motivated to seek help. My character, Jamaica Gold, exposes skeletons that may be serious addictions in your present life. If you need to reveal any type of abuse or addictions, don't read this book alone, for you are vulnerable, unprotected, and susceptible to more abuse. Read it with someone that you trust.

You shouldn't be alone, and thereby, allow abuse to develop into mental or emotional illnesses. Abuse can grow hostile when ignored. Everyone has a spirit. Molesters and rapists exploit their victims with deep, dark, rough, and violent spirits that penetrate their victims and reproduce vile images and emotions in their victims' minds; however, life doesn't have to stay that way.

If you have experienced rape, acknowledge that your abuser has misled you. You're not a bad person, but the pain of abuse can make you feel and think like a bad person. It makes you suffer with a mindset of not being good enough or deserving of love. Pain is easy for you to accept and live in because it's your present state of mind. You don't have to work to find pain; you dwell in it, and some way, somehow, it continues to attack. Please remember, your pain is not about you; it comes from somewhere else. You're bearing someone else's pain that was put on you internally, physically or psychologically. It doesn't belong to you, and it doesn't own you. Don't give up trying to defeat it, and don't pass it on.

There are people in this world whose thoughts tell them that they are bad; some choose to be bad naturally, and others can't help themselves. If your inner thoughts are telling you that you're better than the person you and others envision, then believe that you are and choose to be that person. We are all worth more than what we perceive. My point for this book is to leave you with this: reliving the abuse over and over in nightmares of the abuse, abuses you more and delays the healing process.

Fight your way out of suffering a slow death; find strength in pain. Most of all, find a healthier you. Break the chain. Even in our darkest season, we sacrifice to plant seeds of love for the next generations. Our happiness comes from watching them grow, be healthy, and succeed in life.

Contents

Acknowledgements

To mom, Carrie Lee Muccular, (1925-1995) and dad, William Muccular, (1922-1996); thank you for the encouragement and unconditional love.

I thank my husband and soul mate of many years, LaMar Fuqua, for encouraging me to talk real talk in this book.

I thank my one and only daughter, Keshia Fuqua, you have grown into a beautiful woman that I love and adore. I love how you take care of my grandchildren. Thank you for loving me.

To my five living brothers and sisters, Clyde Muccular, Bill Muccular, Betty Davis, Diane Williams and Gary Muccular; thank you all for your love and support.

Special thanks to my brother, Vodie Lee Muccular (1948-2007). When he was dying, he told me to never stop writing and that people need to hear what I have to say. Vodie was the life of our family. His voice lifted our spirits. When he passed, it broke our hearts. After we buried him in California, I returned home to Louisville, Kentucky and began writing this book, I finished before April 12, 2008.

Special thanks to my one and only son, Dan De Andre Webster. There are many things about you that I love and respect, like how you take care of yourself and my grandchildren; you're so good at what you do. You have my heart and many more good qualities. Thank you for the love and respect that you have always shown me. You have always been there for me. I couldn't imagine my life without you. I love you, son.

Introduction

My name is Jamaica Gold. I'm 16 years old; born and raised in San Francisco California and this is how I evolved.

My dad, Ray Patterson was a Pastor. My mom, Irene Patterson was the first Lady of the church and house wife. She single-handedly turned the ghetto that we called home into one big loving family. To her, everyone was a work in-progress. They were both Texas natives'.

Dad always bragged about how he and my mom made four boys; Cool Willy, Toby Lee, Moe Joe, and Ray Jr. Seven girls; BJ, Jazzy Black, Sassy Girl, Lady Dee, and one set of twins Shlisa and Lisa that died days after they were born; and me, I was the baby in the family.

We were the Patterson's. Our house parties weren't like any other house party in the ghetto. We had church parties. Besides, my father and brother's music, there were plenty of other musicians hanging around; playing and singing old church songs with a rhythm that sounded like jazz. Those guys grew-up playing in the bayous of Mississippi and frequently came to visit. Our home was their home and in the morning, musicians would be lying in the four corners of the living room floor, sleeping.

Some people came to eat, sleep and rest. Others, they came for prayer, and to release their demons. Our house was alive with music and afterwards, the elders retired to the kitchen for homemade buttermilk cornbread, bread pudding, cakes, and pies. The small children would play musical chairs and I would sneak away to the back of the house and watch the older teenagers play my favorite kissing game, Spin the Bottle. I grew up wanting to be in love.

Early one morning, I had been out all night. I rushed up the stairs to my parents' house. As I put the key in the lock, I left my party life at the door. I stepped over our house guest sleeping on the floor, trying to make it into the bathroom in the hallway. I grabbed the doorknob and turned it. The door was locked. Our bathrooms were never empty.

I knocked on the bathroom door.
"Who's in there?"
My dad yelled, "Hey, girl!"

He called me girl because I was number eleven of eleven children and he couldn't remember all of our names.
"What'd ya want?"
"I got to use it bad."
"Go use my bathroom and don't wake up your mother," he yelled!

He doesn't want to be exposed by his wife this early in the morning, I thought to myself as I went around the corner to the master bathroom quietly running at full speed. I took a glimpse at my mother sleeping in bed. She appeared to be sound asleep. I ran right past her into the bathroom and closed the door. Yes! I made it. Now, if I could get out of here without hearing her mouth, it would be a miracle.

She's going to scold me for breaking curfew by staying out all night. At least I told her where I would be this time. So I won't hear her ask, 'where have you been' and say the one hundred year old line, 'we thought you were laying somewhere in a ditch dead'. I finished taking care of my personal business, and I was in big trouble. I walked out the bathroom slowly, being careful not to interrupt moms, sleep.
"You and your friend have been doing what married folks do," she said in a low, distressed voice.
"Excuse me, I thought you were asleep?"

"How do you think I can rest? You've been sexually active out there, living like you're married with a man that hasn't married you!"

"What are you saying?"

"I know he's been touching you down there."

"Excuse me; what?" I reacted, standing there shocked to death!

I didn't know what to say. I didn't know where she was coming from so I didn't respond. I tried to get out of there in a hurry.

"Come here!" She demanded.

"Oh no, there's more?" I thought to myself.

"When you're a virgin, your pee comes out in a straight line in a heavy pour. When you lose your virginity and let someone play down there, your pee comes out in a sprinkle and a tinkle."

She went on to explain. I couldn't believe what I was hearing. I felt violated.

"Look at me when I'm talking to you."

I couldn't look at her. She heard me use the bathroom, and now she knows all my business. Where did she come from? How did she know such things? I had been exposed; she's such a party-pooper. All my life, my mother exposed me and everyone that I had dated.

Our lives are precious. Every heartbeat is created to have compassion. Our mentality is meant to be concerned about one another's gifts and mental disabilities given at birth. In addition, there are mental and physical handicaps acquired after birth that we are all supposed to help each other defend. Yet, the fact remains, there are special qualities in each of us.

My mom informed me about the day that I was born. She heard a distinctive sound in my cry in the delivery room. I was born with a gift to touch people's hearts with singing or poetic voice.

Even though I grew up knowing my purpose here on earth—I had to survive the pain that life had in store, to perfect it. I had to learn to accept it, in order to live and work toward my potential. I would have to use my God given authority and the divine power that it holds to accomplish the lifelong job.

Moms' intuition and spiritual insight was always right. I must write this book. To whom it may concern. My story is an example and testimony about abuse. I talk about what can happen when you hold it in and allow it to capture you; how it can fester and grow into anger, revenge and more. This book is fiction, based on a true story—out of the box—in the world that I lived in, created to help heal the wounded soul. Jamaica Gold's life secrets unfold such things that most women die with.

Introduction of Woman

I'm pleasure that moves with talent
ALL Woman. Shining like Jamaica Gold
My eloquence rises; my essence continues to fill the air
Right-On, Woman, Right-On!
My shadow haunts the dreams of my man
(He is my baby, fully grown)
Yet to him, my love remains a mystery
Men study my every move
Wanting the opportunity to lie in this organized house
To taste and feel the true essence from a woman
The seeds I nourish will keep me alive
I have suffered in labor
Lost a multitude at birth
Cried out in pain from carrying
The human race in my womb
I have struggled and kept the faith
At the same time, demanding my rights in society
As an aggressive Woman
My life is significant; become aware of my Role
My skills build you up, nurturing you down to earth
Relaxing in intensity of gravity
My Universe!
True Woman Rhythm
Will sway, swing, and shake your world
With countless capabilities to rock and cradle your world
I am your highest high, your highest mountain to climb
Surrender your love to me, completely
Welcome to my saga, my evolving history
I am higher than I have ever been in position and dignity
I've proven myself, justified, authorized, and validated to suc-
ceed
In the many things that I have successfully accomplished
Bow down my King
You're in the company of majestic greatness
Her Majesty. the Queen Allure.
Praise me! I am your Morning Star

I have risen before the Sun
To brighten your day in so many ways
Love me and don't stop my growth
I have purpose!
Together, we have given humanity to the world
Love and cherish our union forever
Know this part of you for more than sex
I have much more to offer
Notice my life is laughingly happy
We shall laugh together
Don't spoil my smile, baby, I'll always be around
Talk my language, and you'll have no need to frown
My love, with or without you I will be happy
I will maintain!
Understand me, I am the Master's plan, His masterpiece
Realize my emotions are my Beliefs. Believe in what I am
Respect the way I live. Recognize the comfort I give you
Value and appreciate me as Woman
Do not be intimidated by my power, and I'll show you more
Remember, I am the focal point of life
Yes, I am seductive, except, I am not just a necessity of love
Face the reality; I have the power to change your life
With the ability to capture your thoughts
And the weapons to deal with your mind.

Chapter One
Against All Odds

At sixteen, I found out that I was three months pregnant, and my life changed forever. My mom's approach was firm. I would have to transfer to a maternity class at another school where my appearance wouldn't demonstrate a bad example for high school girls. I went to the new school feeling like I wasn't good enough for regular school. I walked around to get a sense of what the school had to offer. I was informed that the school offered rehabilitation for eccentric juveniles. I was surrounded by crazy students with real problems. I felt like I didn't belong.

I couldn't face the next phase of my life. I hated the school, and showing up there every day would be a challenge. I signed up for the natural childbirth class that started at noon the following Monday. I left there and went to the office at my current school. Instead of transferring my grades, I was handed a note and was told to go to each class and get my grades. I was to take them to the new school myself.

I first went to my sex education class. My teacher Mrs. Hall spoke to me.
>"Hello, Jamaica."
>"Hi, Mrs. Hall."

I walked over to her desk and handed her the note from the office. She looked at me with a concerned look. The news of my pregnancy surprised her. I got lost in her eyes.
>She laid the paper flat on the desk and interlocked her fingers, "How could you let this happen; did you listen to anything I've said?"

I wondered, if I were her daughter if the solution would be keep the baby, adoption, or abortion. Mrs. Hall, however, left that decision up to my family. She never said a word about my choices.

Mrs. Hall shook her head, "Take your seat until, I've summarized your grades."

As I sat down, I noticed that my baby's father, Taurus Smith, watched, but he didn't say a word. He's high yellow, five ten, and the star of the varsity football team. His devious behind had transferred into my class and he didn't know that I was pregnant. He looked at me while talking to another new student, who was about six four. He had to be the finest boy in school.

Mrs. Hall called me up to her desk. She handed me my grades, and I left the classroom. I went to clean out my locker. When I finished, it was lunchtime. I walked around until, I found my friends, Coco, Nicky, and JJ. We ate lunch and walked to the park. Even though today was my last day, I couldn't tell them I was pregnant and leaving school.

They were used to seeing me dance. Knowing the art of dance was our heart. If you saw the four of us on the street, we were dancing; if you saw us on the bus, we were dancing. On that day Coco and Nicky were dancing with me and JJ and some more girls sat laughing, being girls, having fun in the sun. We loved each other and shared everything. I didn't want them to know how my life had changed and make them cry. I wanted to see them enjoying life, even though, I wasn't. I wanted to leave on a happy note.

The fine guy I saw talking to Taurus walked up.

"Hi, my name is, Kenneth."

"Hi Kenneth," we all said in unison.

"I'm Coco."

"I'm Nicky."

"I'm JJ, the fine one, with straight A's."

We didn't know what he wanted or which one of us he was there for.

"I saw you in my sex education class; you like it?"

"Yeah, Jamaica right?

"Right! You remembered."

"Who wouldn't?" He winked at me and started rapping.

My girlfriends got excited. I wasn't impressed that a popular guy in school was attracted to me and offered to drive me home. I was pregnant. The bell rang, and he helped me up from where I had been sitting on the grass. My girlfriends went to their next class.

As soon as the park became empty, he put his hand on my thigh. I threw it off me, "Stop!"

My feet left track marks in the dirt as he grabbed me and dragged me by my coat across the park, "Kenneth, you're hurting me. Let me go!"

He stopped behind the bleachers, hurled me to the ground and tore my underwear off. My eyes bulged when I saw the size of his penis. I screamed while thinking, 'What is he about to do to me'? He climbed on top of me and my body effortlessly shook with fear. I couldn't control my hands. I felt my body fighting. All my senses separated and fought their own fight to help me survive. My mind fought him mentally. I won't let him break my spirit or my loving heart. I complimented myself, inwardly. I couldn't move physically until, the shock weakened, and I could comprehend that this was really happening to me.

Hurting badly, I shouted aloud, "Stop, I'm pregnant. You can't treat me this way. I'm not like this!"

My face immediately turned red from his backhand swing, "Shut up, bitch, before I hurt you real bad. I heard you've been giving it away, every guy in school been through you. Now, it's my turn!"

Who would spread such lies? I didn't understand. I was confused and distraught. I didn't know what the name meant, or

12

what a woman could do to deserve this type of treatment and name calling. I didn't know what a bitch did, or how she lived. All I knew was, she wasn't getting any respect around here. He threatened my life and left me lying there like trash on the ground with my underwear next to me.

> My brain told my mind to create poetry, "I was born to be in the light, raised to take over where my ancestors left off, taught to be proud of who I am. Until, I was beaten and dragged into the dark side. I was choked!"

He choked me and called me out by my name which my parents had so proudly chosen. I was lost from that light. I laid there feeling like nobody. I was the afterthought, the child who wasn't planned, but I was raised in a loving household. At that moment, I wished my mother's twins would have lived; then I would have never been born. How could a boy that fine represent such an ugly and sick human being? That was a brutal attack. I couldn't remember who I was before the assault occurred. That name he called me must have meant something really bad. In my mind, I had been mentally and physically abused.

I didn't want to think about what happened. His rage was unacceptable, and I couldn't stop thinking about it. Why was I being treated mean by boys? I wasn't thinking. I need to stop them so they wouldn't do this again to me or anyone else. Being raised as I was and if you were thinking at all, you're thinking, why did people think I was that bad person? What had I said or done that was so wrong? Why did I deserve such cruel and angry attention? This was personal pain.

I thought about me. Every love song I've ever heard and believed in played a symphony through my mind. I started frantically and wildly fantasizing, where was my true love, while digging my hands into the dirt and washing them as if they were dirty. How come my love hadn't rescued me out of this madness? My life was a bad, unspeakable dream, and I tried to treat it that way. Once you awaken from it, you would have forgotten all about it. I stood up. I put my underwear in the trash and suppressed the realization of it all.

As I boarded the bus for home, I was in a daze. For the first time, I didn't dance as I sat down. That was the day I lost all my ambitions and I lost my art of dance. Even though I knew damage had been done, I buried my pain. I knew that my ambitions were there, but I was detached from them; I had been misplaced.

The dark side of me awakened. I still had my spirit telling me that I could make it, to hold on, but my innocence had been taken to the last drop. I didn't want to go to Disney Land anymore; I felt like I had already been. While I was there, Mickey raped and murdered Minnie. Who cared? I'll never go to Disney World. After that ride, I felt very experienced and well-traveled. I was experienced at getting raped like an animal. My life was one big masquerade pretending that I was alright, when actually, I had become secretly numb in my world. Telling was not an option. If I tell one thing everything else has to come out. It was too much for my son to handle while growing up. I had x-rays and they came out fine.

I embraced real love from the men in my family. My dad, my four brothers, my granddad, uncles, and male cousins taught me not to hate all men. Because of them, I know there are decent men in this world. Knowing all of that doesn't stop the pain. In troubled times, grab hold to positive power around you and anything else that keeps you human. I was alone in the dark, I needed strength. The entire time of pregnancy I worried about my baby, wondering if he or she would come here mentally challenged with missing parts. My baby boy, who I named Little-Man, Mannie Smith, was born October, 1980. He weighed 8 pounds.

I wanted to confront my life. My reality was seven days old when I took him out for the first time. I delivered in time to make it to the third and final day of my family reunion with Little Man and my mom and dad. My parents were still trying to figure me out, acting as my bodyguards and didn't care if I liked it or not. They were terrified at the thought of me getting pregnant again—I was terrified of everything. Little Man was only days old and I was already exhausted from living life as a mommy.

Before my baby, I couldn't imagine being stressed-out; not the way I was feeling. I wanted to awaken from the nightmare and go back to correct the way things went down. My situation was unchangeable. This was some real grown up stuff, and I was not ready. I was having adult emotions. I was craving for things and it wasn't food. I didn't have an appetite. I lost the twenty-five pounds gained during my pregnancy. I thought it was my hormones in action but I was unsure about everything at that time.

Mom made sure I understood. Teen moms are forced to grow up fast or run from responsibility. When you make an adult decision like having a baby, you can't hide from the fact that you're a child having grown-up emotions and don't know how to have mature judgment. What she was saying was—I'm screwed! Whatever, to what mom was saying; I was happy to fit back into my clothes. My body felt human again. I didn't open up and tell her I was really unhappy with the way things were. I was depressed but I had hurt her and it didn't feel like the right time to tell her. I was definitely dealing with the unexpected. Back then they hadn't given postpartum symptoms a name. I wanted more to offer my son. I loved Little Man more than life.

How are we going to survive? Before I was sexually abused, I had dreams of becoming an author of some best-selling books, a great artist, and poet. Maybe hear my words in a song that would move people's hearts because they were written in blood, sweat and tears. Drowning in pity, I tried to concentrate on how I was going to make my dreams a reality. Put things into perspective—you know, set some goals, and stay focused on independence when I finished school. I couldn't keep my concentration. My motivation was gone, I didn't want to make any more bad decisions. I gave in to pity and shame and began feeling sorry for myself.

Unnecessary punishment; that was the story of my life. I was fortunate because I didn't get stretch marks. I lost my stomach, plus, I knew I was grown. My butt and breast were even more developed. At that point, I knew I had to wear a girdle to church. The girdle story came about one Sunday at a Women's Day Dinner at church. My mother, the first lady of the church, was conversing with the state mother and her husband. The husband thought that they were so immersed in their Jesus conversation that he could watch my behind walk across the floor. Just about the time they looked up and caught him gazing, everyone's reaction around me caught my attention. I looked back thinking, "What is the problem?"

The state mother's nose frowned-up so high, it went back into her face. Her nostrils flared wide enough to read what she thought and I was ashamed of her thoughts. Standing every bit of 6'3, I thought she was going to fall over backwards for sure. I wanted to be the one to holler, "Timber!" Even though my behind was innocent, I knew I was in big trouble. The state mother's figure was straight up and down. She would never understand that when you have hips and a butt, they've got to shift from one side to the other when walking. I was punished that day for having too much booty and sworn to a girdle for life. Anyway, I have an hourglass figure, the body of a woman and a bad reputation.

I had always felt important, like I was supposed to have a dreamlike life. Anyone in their right mind would dream of being me. I was feeling like life had served up the wrong plate of food for me. Some family members were passing my baby around and telling me how good we looked. Then there were those who didn't have anything good to say about me or my baby; they weren't saying anything at all—they were tongue-tied.

In my traditional, religious family, getting pregnant before marriage was shameful. There wasn't any big celebration at my home or anywhere else. My mom wouldn't allow that. There wasn't any baby shower with games, cake, and ice cream. I was on punishment, for having a baby, without being told I was on punishment. My friends called and asked if I needed anything. I told them, nope, but thanks anyway. Actually, I was depressed because I wanted pretty little baby clothes and toys for Little Man so bad, it hurt my feelings. How do I explain this to my friends?

"Oh yes," This is what I need—don't forget to hide it under your clothes. Try not to look happy when you walk through the door.
"Okay."
"Please don't blow it for me. I'm on punishment but I'm not supposed to know."

While I ponder, my three best friends and my sisters had gotten over their shock about the baby and brought Little Man something without asking. Other than that, there's basically nothing going on for my baby and me in my face. It's all behind my back. Gossip had gotten back to us and we were being discreet about it. My parents were refined about everything.

Cousin Retha, Ree-Ree for short, called me into the kitchen to introduce me to her new husband Don and his brother Troy, the best man at their wedding. The man would literally be my nightmare for the next four most shocking and stressful years of my life. At that moment, I was clueless as I listened to her boast, while looking at her wedding pictures.

During picture time, I sat at the kitchen table with them pretending I was as happy as they were pretending to be, knowing that I'm not. I was happy for her yet hurt that it wasn't me. How did she manage to get married before me? Troy was talking sweet nothings in my ear; literally saying, "Nothing, nothing, nothing," and I tried not to laugh out loud. Dad walked into the room looking with an expression that clearly said, "Get him out of your face, now!" Troy didn't care that my dad looked. I didn't care about what he was saying. Troy asked for my phone number right in front of my dad and called the next night. Could this be the man that will fall desperately in love with me and stay devoted to me only for as long as we both shall live?

I wanted him to be the one. He had crazy game, he rapped (Talked) to me all night long. He called it love at first sight. I called it very dominating and aggressive; like I'm someone he can manipulate and control. Here I am confused and feeling bad, I'm angry at life; thinking boys wouldn't take me seriously now that I have a baby. He threw this line on me, "I like the fact that you have a baby; that means you know how to take care of business and your man. If I were your man, I know you would take care of me. I'd take care of you, too," he told me in a sexy whisper. When you've been schemed, old folks say, "Yap, uh huh, he saw ya coming."

Troy approached me with plans to corrupt me with his deceitful mind but my parents raised me to be honest. He's the complete opposite of me. We're from two different worlds.

Things got critical. In my traditional, religious world, I had friends that were familiar with living in respectable and religious households, attending church at least four to seven nights a week. One friend named, Gabby, tall, dark, and talked way too much, told his mom I had a baby. When he told her he liked me a lot, she asked him, "Why would you want to be with a girl like that, Gabby? Your father and I have raised you better." He came back to me and exposed his mom. Doesn't he know that would hurt me? Get real. I have feelings. That was a type of prejudice toward my family that I don't need right now. I was raised the same way as he. She doesn't know anything about me or my life. Now I'm a tramp in both worlds.

All while growing up, it was like having two lives with two sets of friends. I didn't want my parents to know I was experiencing being judged at school and church. They already know how people are and have tried their best to protect me from these kinds of critical remarks.

Times were hard. When a child goes wrong, people blame the parents. I love my parents; they taught me values and principles that I was supposed to live by and I did honor and respect their values, until, now. I hated them for giving me a loving heart. Things had happened to me that had changed me. I didn't fit in their world anymore. It was my choice to either fight my way back to their way of life or leave it behind. My rebellious ways and making my own choices this young in life was making them look bad. That was what I was putting them through. It was not a good time for us.

I was bored with good and sweet. A sentimental friend from my same background rushed to my side to rescue me. I cared for him very much. His name was James King; all eyes, lots of hair, and the body of a black gladiator. He was tall, dark, and ready to rock my world. He was my first boyfriend for over a year. I met 'The King James' at church when I was fourteen and he was seventeen. He would pick me up from school and take me to the movies. I would let him hold my hand and he promised to never let it go. During the entire time we were together, I never let him touch me, and he kept his hands to himself. We had just had our first tongue kiss when all of the madness started to happen to me at school. When he found out I was pregnant, it broke his heart.

He asked me to marry him. He wanted to give my son his last name so he wouldn't be a bastard child. We were told that having a baby and not being married is called having a child out of wedlock. I know he meant well but that offended me because he didn't know my story. I wanted marriage. I loved James King but I was not in love with him. I was not getting married just for my life to be accepted. It was a hard question to answer— knowing he was in love with me.

I knew James King would be faithful. I also knew he wasn't ready or capable of taking care of a family at that time. My answer was 'No'. I thought to myself the entire time he was talking, "You would marry me and take me to your parent's traditional, religious household, then what?" James King fell in love with my innocence and I was not that person anymore. He cried, and then we cried together. He told me the other reason why he came to see me; that was the day he found out I was a victim of all the attacks.

He had heard rumors about me. King named names. There were a lot of boys telling these lies and King knew the innocent me and didn't believe one bit of it. After that day, I didn't see King anymore; he went into a deep depression. Both, James and Gabby, were momma's boys. They were both musicians and played and sang to me over the phone; we had fun times. They were sweet guys but I was bored with sweet.

I left my traditional existence to do my thing. Life as a good girl abandoned me and I was portrayed as a bad girl. I was not safe anymore; being hunted by boys like I was their prey. Hearing that I tried to trap my baby's dad, pushed me over the edge. It seemed lIke I was one of those girls that put out sex to get him and got pregnant to keep him. I didn't know about such things; my mind doesn't work that way. I'm too honest. I heard that Taurus said that he had sex with me because we were drunk and that had me down. All of the above was coming from people that I grew up with. I was crushed.

My so called friends, all talked about me behind my back. I am such a serious person and my life was a joke. I'm through with them all. Maybe, I would have gotten over the abuse faster if people weren't judging me out loud and all up in my business. My preference went from innocence and liking innocent boys, to bad girl and loving naughty, naughty, bad boys that would treat me good, of course.

I get pleasure from listening to this wanna-be-player rapping hard in my ear night after night. Since I'm a poet, I love words. Troy's a rhyme master of his rap. He seems to have experienced enough to have patience with me. I was fascinated with him, I had never heard such things, and I wanted to hang out with this man. Troy and I talked on the phone for six months. It took that long before I got up the nerve to say, 'yes' to a first date. That's because I knew he was crazy. Mom changed after I had Little Man. She wasn't so strict, I didn't have curfew, and I didn't have to sneak outfits or make-up out of the house anymore.

As I got dressed for my date, she said that I was getting too dressed up and my outfit would attract evil doers. I had on a green miniskirt and top, a rust colored leather jacket with different color suede patches, rust colored leather thigh boots that had platform suede wedge heels. She looked at me and explained that she raised us girls to be like her. When we got old enough to make our own decisions, hopefully, we would choose to be like her.

> "I never told you that my strict dress code and house rules were what would get you to heaven. I wasn't going to let the little things keep me out of heaven."

After the date, I asked Troy to come home with me to visit my parents because they really weren't properly introduced. He said, "Okay". He walked through the door and my mother took one look into his eyes, his costume, and his whole persona, and, after talking to him, she came to her conclusion. She walked into the bathroom where I was and asked me not to talk to him or date him anymore.

> Of course I asked, "Why Mom?"

"He practices witchcraft." She said, Meaning, he worshiped evil. He had been exposed. She turned and left the room.

She was too deep for me. I laughed it off. It doesn't matter to me anyway. I continued putting on more makeup to leave out with him. Even though I knew he was controlling to the point of telling me how he wanted me to act as his woman, it was a waste of his time. I acted like I wanted to act when I was with him. When we're alone, our private moments were very special to me. That's what I was after, the alone time, and didn't want to mess that up. I was happy I got a cool guy. I was living for the moment.

Troy's cold-blooded bad habits and characteristics had that edge. I liked the fact that this was our thing; it isn't anybody's business. What happened behind closed doors, stayed behind closed doors; I never thought for one minute he would treat me like he owned me in public. I ignored his lack of intelligence and enjoyed the chase. When it was just us, he was fun and exciting but, in public, he had a boring personality. He had an arrogant attitude and I often asked myself how could I be crazy about a conceited man? He ignored other people's existence. Troy acts like he doesn't need anyone. When he opened his mouth to speak he's patronizing, with a cool down to earth sarcastic voice which drove people crazy. He was too oblivious and people ignored him right back. In public you could tell he knew nothing about real life, love, or relationships.

Troy was a prisoner in a dark world he created for himself. He didn't understand anything outside his world. With an inability to listen or learn from decent people, he made life up as he went along. He speculates when it's something important he should know as an adult. He had accumulated unsympathetic wisdom (spirits with coldblooded habits he picked up here and there; from being in the wrong places and studying the wrong people).

I looked for love in all the wrong places. My weakness was a man that could make love expressing himself with words. This type of man is good one-on-one, for phone sex, and long-distant relationships. I wanted him to be my knight in shining armor.

Troy was so fake yet very entertaining. He lived in a dream world, acting like he was the star in a gangster movie. He tried to turn me into his gangster woman. I was a loving person with a big heart. I was quiet around unfamiliar people, I didn't speak unless spoken to. That was my personality, until, I got to know Troy. He wanted me to act mean toward everyone except him. There wasn't a cruel bone in my body. Even though, I made decisions that hurt the ones I loved, I was who I was on the inside. When my heart was troubled, I needed someone to hear me, understand me, and help me sort out this thing called life. Everyone kept laying down the rules. I shut them all out. I didn't want to hear them, I didn't care what they had to say, I needed my life back, and I needed Troy to be real. What I didn't need was Troy's fake entertainment.

My conscience was killing me. I knew I was doing wrong by being with Troy all the time. He was not giving me room to grow mentally. He was not the man I needed. I could never be happy with him; life was too difficult in his world. My life was hard enough. Troy made life seem much harder. People who are mentally poor will never have anything. Troy's love was too complex for me. I had never been around anyone with as many hang-ups, yet I was not strong enough to walk away; he gave me something else I needed. When I'm not with Troy, I cry myself to sleep and I knew it was my cry for help and I didn't allow anyone to hear or answer.

I was sixteen and totally confused. I wondered if there were any sixteen year olds that were happy. Anything is possible, even money can't buy happiness but it can make you comfortable in your misery. Even when you have money, you got to work hard to find your inner self. It's a struggle for everyone to surrender to maturity in life, to grow-up, to be a responsible, dependable person that people want to have around. I needed him to do what I wasn't doing for myself. I wanted him to do my job because I wasn't strong enough. My conscience told me to be independent but I couldn't find independence.

Troy and I both had lost touch with reality. In my dream world, I was starring in a movie. I was acting out the greatest love story ever told and he was my knight in shining armor. I always wanted a snazzy guy who I could talk to and walk hand-in-hand with. He wanted that too—with different motives in mind. Whatever he had to say, I heard him out but that didn't mean I agreed. Cool guys don't listen at all, they're stubborn to the bone. When you meet Mr. Wrong, it's best to get him out of your face fast, as my dad tried to get me to detect and I didn't pick-up on it. I refused to listen. I tried to be grown up. Today, I'm guilty of trying to mold Mr. Wrong into Mr. Right. I fooled around long enough for him to throw his best game down.

This was the sex life I wanted. I'm not buying the love he had to offer. I was caught up in a relationship with Mr. Wrong, on a head trip because I knew he would never be Mr. Right. I was in denial holding on to his merry-go-round that had me in worse constraints than my parents. His aggressive demands were like shock treatments to my mind, body, and soul. For what—the dream, the sex, room and board, the good times, or the high you get in a new relationship. My point! I was holding on to innocent childhood dreams and bedtime stories. I wanted a king. I wanted a decent loving relationship, and I wanted an upright love with a man who had a downright nasty addiction for corrupting me.

I chose the wrong man, as usual. Troy wasn't my king. I loved the attention when he took me shopping and sat there and watched me try on clothes that he and I picked out. The fact that he never put money straight into my hands was a turn off—he was cheap! He didn't trust what I would do with it. Would I ever be able to teach him anything? That love is trust and when you treat me, 'your mate', this way you are not building our relationship, you're tearing it down. My man had trust issues. He'd ask me out to nice restaurants and then order for me.

He stared at me while I ate, to see if I would make eye contact with anyone. He was like a child, amused with his favorite toy doll that he didn't allow anyone to touch, play with, or look at. I was at the point of having a conversation with myself, "Hey! Mr. Smooth-tongue-in-the-bedroom, we're a couple now. Okay, you got me. Let's be rational in public. I'm here with you. I'm human, you are human. Let's talk about something—how's the weather over there!" What hurt so bad was, I wanted to be deeply in love with the guy—but it was not going down like that; he lived in a different world without reality.

All women want to be desired. Women that say they're in love with a manipulative, controlling man are not being real. A woman keeps her guard up against a man that messes with her mind. When you see women in a relationship or marrying a man like this, she has her reasons and it's her choice to make. She may have love for the guy but she is not in love—maybe it's his money. Maybe, she's afraid of facing life alone and allows her relationships to confine her. When a real woman does not see anything appealing to fall for in a man, she starts looking for his potential and falls in love with that; well, if he has potential to become something. She starts to crave something about their relationship. Honestly, she doesn't even like him.

A real woman wants a man she can fall deeply in love with. A negative character stops her from falling. Some women are desperate enough to use this type of man to get what they want. Players and wanna-be-players often get played for what they possess. A manipulative man or woman who works hard for their possessions is worthy of their things; their behavior is not worthy of love. Women love money and ambition in a man. We like assertive men with a charming personality, with positive aggression that motivates his brain to get what he wants, who gives freely and doesn't buy love or force love, he lets his heart lead him. A man knows how to be in charge without controlling the way you think.

A woman thinks for herself. Women have power. However, the way we choose to use our power of choice is our business. Women that use their power to experiment are called sluts, whores, tramps, prostitutes, vag-hags, nasty, and the most popular term of all, bitches. These women will testify that the men that are defined as losers are the best lovers. These men are not choosy about whom they sleep with; they sleep with anyone that will put up with them. Women have made them very experienced lovers. As supernatural losers, they take time out just to learn women's wants and desires; it's their job to practice their rap to perfection.

There are women like myself, who don't mind teaching negative bad boys to be charming. We want to save our man. We actually believe we can change our man. We think we have the patience to help him to mature and take on a man's responsibility. We want the best of both worlds: money, looks, cool skills, and foreplay, enjoyable sex, and a passionate kisser. Sometimes we don't care what we have to put up with and it often sends us to an early grave. We take it too far and marry him and continue to teach him. When a man is capable of learning, you only need to tell him once and he will understand. If not, you become his mother in the marriage and the 'don't do this, and don't do that' takes its toll.

There isn't any man turned on by his mother. A man can only give what he knows. You don't allow him to do that and the hot sex will stop. All the lust and desire that brings romantic emotions, will stop. There are many ways to kill desire in a relationship, especially when it starts off on the wrong foot. Controlling men are bad tempered. Sooner or later, they resort to threats and violence. Troy was the prime example of Mr. Wrong. He was a supernatural lover that came from the heart, plus, a negative bad boy that doesn't give from the heart. Trust me, I was his possession; he didn't do anything for me, unless, he was going to benefit from it. I let him take advantage of me in most situations because that was his thing, not mine.

What I didn't know was, I was creating a monster. Troy was five years older than me, had a job as a prison guard, made good money for his age, had his own place, nice car and let me drive it once so far—he's selfish. I was working overtime, trying to teach him to lighten up, laugh a little. Love is about sharing everything. He seemed to have a lot going for himself—add a woman in the mix—he's exactly what women call a loser. I call it misled, lost, sick, or crazy because of the way he treated people. He's controlling especially with females.

Morals are vital in a man. We say people can't change morally. I believe they can, if their heart is in it. They will find their way to change by adapting and adjusting to some things to get along with society. All some men need is a good woman. Some let bad habits decide their future. They can't help themselves and a good woman won't do them any good. When you haven't been taught morals, life is more of a challenge because change comes hard for everyone.

First of all, with help, Troy's mind needed to be reprogrammed and that falls under the old saying, 'You can't teach old dogs new tricks.' Some people think, changing morally and growing into a mature adult is the same—but it's not; they just go together. You need one, in order to achieve the other. If you don't have any morals, it could stop you from maturing. Everybody gains knowledge as they get older. Before you can mature, you've got to find yourself. Just because you're getting older doesn't mean you're mature. Not everyone finds him or herself or gains the wisdom to mature in life; they struggle through and survive but always hanging on by a thread. Maturity is something we all should work to possess at some point in life.

Have you ever felt like a loser? Hypothetically, I ask you, have you wondered why people who are given the title stupid, dumb, or loser, and anything else that's beneath being human, are angry at the world? A defined loser is blinded by insults and blames everyone for their problems—mom, dad, sister, or brother, and people in general. The first thing you wanted to say when I asked that question is, who cares about their problems—I got my own, am I right? All their lives they hear that, plus you don't have a brain, you're not human, and you're so crazy. Even if you say to them, "You act like such a loser" all they hear is loser, loser, and loser. If you tell them they can't do one specific thing right, they say to themselves, I can't do anything right. They carry insecurities into their relationships.

Everyone seems to judge losers. Some losers physically hide themselves and become dwellers in dark places where nasty habits develop. Some losers mentally hide their thoughts and emotions from the world, so their intellect decreases, instead of increasing, as it should. Their ability to feel life and express love is missing. You can't be successful at something you know nothing about. The ones that act out are the ones that demand total control of everyone around them. While they appear to be strong and powerful, when we reject them, we are their painful reality, pushed away and denied the right to get close to them and we're their number one target when they strike back.

They would rather be alone, than with someone who stands their ground and fights. They prefer the company of pretenders, phonies turned out on some drug or alcohol, anyone that treats them superior; anything that stops their pain, they're there. The loser that can't be alone because they can't stand themselves is always somewhere causing trouble. There are so many loser types, society places them all in the same bag of defined losers looked upon as desperate humans who have a ruthless comprehension about life, love, and happiness. In a loser's mind of isolated illness, rejections turn into deadly viruses. When they are alone, living in their darkest misery, their only wish is to be someone else, so we can see that they are people, too. They go out and take what they want. They prey on us. They're all our problems because we are all here together. All of us have been a loser in some way at some point in life, so we should understand that some people deserve to be given a chance, but how do we know who they are? We're not all doctors.

Losers come in three categories. I haven't heard Troy blame anyone in particular for his ruthless ways. Yet he had lied to himself for so long, he had lied a phony into existence and that phony was strong in his convictions. He admitted he trained himself to be that way because of life's disappointments. He's so full of it. What kind of person admits to teaching himself to be a world-defined loser? Is that any different from being a born loser? My answer is yes. Born losers just deny, deny, deny. Surely, Troy loved just hearing his mouth make up some words. After I thought about what he said, I knew that it wasn't a lie. We teach ourselves bad habits all the time and we start young. I believe losers come in three categories: a first-class loser is a born loser, a second-class loser is self-taught, and a third-class loser is a person that's always caught up with a loser. All loser types fall under those categories.

Troy was not making mature connections for us to progress in life. I'm sure he had lots of problems that were not acceptable to many. He seemed to be trying to change for me. I saw effort. When you see someone making an effort that usually means that person is doing his or her best. People learn at their pace. People's efforts get better and sometimes change will occur. Repeatedly in life, Troy's best wasn't good enough. The results brought on his bad boy attitude. Troy had been called out of his name and looked down upon—it deeply manifested and he was not happy. He was fed up and mad at the world—that was our connection. He and I had that in common. We wanted to change something about us that we were not comfortable with. When I was alone, my biggest wish was to change the lies so people could see me for who I am. The rumor going around about me needed to stop because boys were attacking me for their own pleasure. I had my reasons why I couldn't tell anyone. A mother will do anything to protect her child. If I did tell, it will be their word against mine. Who was going to believe me—I got a baby. The immature connection Troy and I had been holding us back—but we refused to admit that fact to each other.

You've got to go back in order to move forward. After I had Little Man, I went back to regular school. All my siblings had graduated. Taurus, my baby daddy, he graduated with honors. He denied his baby and believed that I slept with lots of boys. I believed he was one of the guys spreading the rumors and that hurt. Taurus was long gone but because of those rumors I walked down the hallway and saw the varsity football team walking towards me.

As I tried to pass them, I noticed that they were forming a circle around me, saying things like, "Yeah, I heard you're giving it up now." "When do I get my turn?" "The quiet little church girl is having sex now." "Can I get some of that?" I wasn't saying anything. All I thought was, my life is over. I had tears in my eyes.

> One of my brother's friends said to them, "Look, can't you see you're embarrassing her; she's not that kind of girl."

They apologized and walked away. He clearly wanted to console me. I gave the impression that I didn't want to be touched. I never told Troy what I had been through or what I was going through at the time; Troy wouldn't be able to handle it either. Troy would have gotten his gun and killed everybody. I was happy that I had Troy to run to when forced to face my past; facing it was the only way to move forward.

Some people are turned off by falling in love and lovemaking. They fight the desire and never give love with anyone a chance because they're traumatized with the fear of being abused again. Other people are emotionally stimulated and have a promiscuous sex drive that even they don't understand. They don't know why they give in to it time and time again. After my worst attacks I didn't want anything to do with sex. I never wanted a man to touch me again in a sexual way—trying not to give up on love. I thought, 'Maybe love stories are just for TV; a real life love story wasn't meant for me. Maybe, love songs are just words and happiness, I would never see'.

After meeting Troy, I listened to him talk, I felt that my virginity had been physically and mentally taken by my abusers but psychologically, I was still a virgin, I hadn't had my chance to get emotional about love. I hadn't had that special moment every girl dreams of when losing her virginity. My virginity was taken. I had never felt a man's passion, or mine. I felt his and wanted my moment I had been cheated out of. I needed to be loved. I believe promiscuous people are searching for that moment. Some find it and some don't; others, get caught up in trying to find it again and again.

Troy became my magic man, moment after moment. He could always please me with sex, he loved my pain away. Troy made love to me in a way that allowed me to relax in my wildest dreams in another place and time. I knew it was just a temporary fix but I needed my fix over and over; it felt good to dream again. We had a bedroom love. I wanted the entire relationship to be drawn into the bond we celebrated in our bed. Troy had lived without intimacy in his life and so had I. We could have that now with each other if he could just identify with intimacy. It was important for us right now, we were both suffering. In reality, if I don't deal with these problems, pain would decide my future. Pain was an issue we shared and we would only be able to stand each other's misery for so long.

31

We were not soul mates. We were soul survivors that wanted the satisfaction to last always. Maybe then, I could feel the air that I breathed. I was numb. I wanted to walk outside and feel the sun shining on me again. In the bedroom he opened up and gave his heart completely. He was the perfect man. His anger turned into a love so passionate, it brought out things in me that I never imagined existed. I felt him; he fell into our bed with a bag of tricks. He was my sun; my "oh," so fortified psychotherapy. I loved when he laughed out loud with me in bed; it was the only time he laughed. This experience was far beyond my sexual fantasies. I never saw him so happy. When I first met him he didn't smile. In the bedroom his laugh and his smile were charming.

My first time, I was scared the night I officially chose to lose my virginity to him. It was the first time I felt my virginity take its natural course as a girl becoming a woman. The beginning of foreplay was wild, Troy had the gift of gab. He talked me through it, telling me to relax. I didn't know where my weak spots were—I was introduced as he found them all. I started thinking childish thoughts, remembering how I felt when I got my first talking doll; when I learned how to roller skate on my own; remembering, learning how to ride a bike on my own "Look, mom, no hands." That night, there were no words for what I was feeling. This first experience topped them all. My thoughts went from childlike to adult reality erotic dreams and making them come true. Loving each other was our drug to numb the pain. It was the only time we were good for one another.

It was the type of love that brought tears of joy. It was my life, my moment, and my first time. If it weren't for this gentle loving man keeping me satisfied, I don't know what I would have done. I felt like I was there for a reason, could this be love? I didn't move when we finished; I laid in his arms and listened to his thoughts. It was the only time he made any sense. He said things like, he wanted more to offer me, and he tried to accomplish something for us. He said that he needed me and couldn't live without me. He begged me to love him and he'd stay around for me. He never wanted anything or anyone the way he wanted me. I had never heard those words and when you hear those words for the first time, you believe whole-heartedly his love is true and your man's rap is real.

I knew and loved who he was in the bedroom; that was our real moments. I could never call a man with talent like that a loser. I could never think that I am better than any human, when we all have our imperfections and I had many. I know I'm worth more. I deserve more. I wish someday to have more. I had been badly wounded and I had him in my arms saying all the right things and I needed us to be real. We had each other that was all that mattered. I loved how this man caressed me and I felt like I was there to persuade him to open up his heart and let my love in. How can you save someone when you need to be saved? I have heard people say, "We rescued one another" and that's how I felt at that moment—but that was not the case.

Outside the bedroom, I didn't get a sense of freedom. His way of love couldn't set me free. I hadn't found the answers; I was worse off than I used to be. I continued to be angry for many reasons. For us to gain wisdom and knowledge of ourselves, the experiences in life and the things we go through are meant to happen to get our attention—shake us up, and awaken us that we can get serious about finding our purpose and reaching our goals. Sleeping with him was a painful wake-up call. After I gave my virginity away I wanted to feel complete, instead, I felt that I had committed a sin.

I didn't wait on the man of my dreams. My special moment was gone and will never come again. I had to look at what was hap-pening in a constructive way. I had to lie to myself to convince me that I was supposed to learn something from making bad choices. That's the only way I can survive my heartbeat beating to the beat of my throbbing pain, searching for the girl inside, fighting to have a teenager's life once again. I have to hold on to something positive and family was all I had. I am angry and I've been this way for too long. Whenever you see people in your family or someone around you growing and maturing, it gives you a reason to hold on to your dreams. It gives you someone to look up to and something to look forward to in life. They're teaching you by showing you that maturity is hard but possible. I keep telling myself since it exists in my family, I know my time will come. I pray that it comes while I am young. Everyone that's angry is in pain. If you don't have family or role models in life, you don't get that chance to dream. I believe everyone deserves it. Everyone has an angel to keep them on the right track and help them find peace of mind. If not, I could be your guardian angel and this story is dedicated to you. In this life; someway, somehow, your guardian angel will find you.

Post-it Note

Anger is Hate
They work together to turn you old and ugly.
They shut down the body and drain all energy.
When you're angry you forget to breathe normally.
Take deep breaths and try not to focus on your pain.
Anger takes away your motivation.
Hate eats away your insides—hindering
your mind from growth.
You don't develop with compassion.
You don't feel human kindness.
You're slowly dying—anger kills.
It could be why you're so stressed out.
And stress could cause heart attacks,
Eventually!
The dangerous lies people spread
about you does all of the above.

Troy became too much to handle. He loves me though my anger because our lovemaking was always overwhelming. I wished I could put him in a bottle marked, 'bedroom only' and share him with all women, just because we deserve to know ecstasy and when times get hard we are continuously thrilled. Time after time, we open our bottle of captive pleasures, escaping our problem and pleased to celebrate unleashed pleasures, to be loved this way, this much in one lifetime. He's much too much for one woman to handle.

Untamed love hurts. We were in for rude awakenings. Outside of our bedroom romance and hot sex rendezvous, he had devil-ish instincts. His arrogance wanted me to bow down and wor-ship his presence. He wanted my heart, body, and soul at all times by any means necessary. Our passion was out of control, way over our young heads, making all the wrong choices. To get what you want, you usually end up with less than you started with. I was surprised by my actions but most of all, afraid of the consequences they would bring.

There are many grown people trapped in abusive relationships. These relationships are one of the many generational curses passed down to us and to our children. I know young people are confused feel alone when it comes to relationships. They're doing more as young couples than ever expected; they're more experienced than we were at their age. I know they can't handle love mentally because I am writing from experience.

There is good-chemistry as well as bad-chemistry. Two abusive teenagers have bad chemistry. They're in a two-way abusive relationship. They're not talking about it—they find it normal. It's not normal when your relationship is a time bomb and you don't defuse the bomb. It's going to blow up and may cost you your life. You may not want to face it because someone will intervene and run the other person away. You're afraid that you can't make it on your own if they go for good. If you're strong enough to take the abuse, that same strength will take you a lot further in the world.

My point is that, grown-ups want young people to accomplish something in their youth; that they can grow-up with a sense of pride and purpose. Stop chasing life and chase after your life's dreams—life is short. Some people spend a lifetime chasing love, trying to find Mr. or Mrs. Right, or a good time. Some people meet their true love at a young age and must leave them for fame or work to achieve a profession. If that person is really your future, they will be your destiny no matter what.

Troy went from one extreme to the next, trying to keep me interested. He appointed himself the God of my world, seriously stressing me out, at times. He needed to be with me at all times to feel confident about us. I told myself, I was just having fun experimenting with having a man, going along with him because he takes me to cool places.

On the other hand. I really cared about him and wanted him to recognize his bad habits. I called them out from time to time to let him know I am aware. I wanted him to work on bettering himself, for him, and make our relationship healthy. I tried to save him and mend his broken heart, hoping he would mend mine. I don't want to give up on him, yet. Hoping his problems may be fixable, I'm not hopeful that mine could be. There are too many people involved and the numbers of men are growing. Blinded by sex, when will we awaken to the harsh reality—a good sex life is all we have and that wasn't enough for me.

California has beautiful parks and beaches and those are his favorite places to take me. He's a nice dresser; together our style was chic. When he dressed up like a player, with the pimp cane and the big hat, I encouraged him. I got right with him as his number one lady. I thought that we were only having fun; I love playing dress-up. He didn't have much of a life before me—he would put on an act like he gave up pimping women to be with me. He tells wild stories about his women. I checked into it. I asked his brother, Don, and the expression on his face alone answered my question. I knew there weren't any women, just another one of Troy's fantasies.

I found out some priceless information. I discovered that Troy's mother was killed in a car accident and his father married a woman half his age. Troy left his hometown as a teenager and never looked back. Troy was dealing with serious pain I had never experienced before.

I almost never go home, but when I do, boys chase me, wanting to sleep with me. I find myself fighting them off, once again. This time, it's an older man. He's heard the rumors about me and his dirty little mind schemed-up a plan to get his wife to ask my parents and me to Sunday dinner.

We arrived and twenty minutes later, he said, he forgot to get bread from the store—all a part of his plan that he thought for sure would work.

"Come on, Jamaica, let's go get bread."

"No, Jamaica stays here with us. You take your daughters to the store with you." My mother told him to his foolish face.

Only a foolish man would try to out-smart my mom. He had been exposed. I sat there too young to know that some men would go to the extreme to get what they wanted. His wife had to know how sick he was.

She was in the kitchen cooking up a big pot of denial. With a sprinkle of 'he loves me', and a dash of 'he loves me not'. The entire time he was coming on to me she was scooping, mixing and stirring. He didn't give up there. With bad boy thoughts dwelling in his devious juvenile mind, he had more dirty tricks up his sleeve. He asked someone how to find me—they told him where my parents lived. He drove up and down the street probably for weeks before he ran into me and pulled me over, acting surprised to see me, as if it wasn't on purpose or planned.

"Go park your car and come with me to pick up my wife for dinner."

I did what he asked. I didn't know what he was up to until, he drove to a hotel and parked.

"I'm not getting out of this car."

He tried to get me out of the car and I wouldn't get out. I was holding on to the door handle. He made advances, wasting my time and his. I guess he thought I was running around having sex with anyone.

On the way back to my car, he brought his family home some Barbeque, so he would have an alibi for where he's been. He tried to buy me off to make sure I wouldn't talk. I didn't want his bribe. I have heard of hush money—but hush food? He's cheap and pathetic.

> When he found out I wasn't who he thought I was, he dropped me off and asked, "Are you going to say anything to anyone? I love my wife and I don't know what I would do without her."
> "No," I answered.

He didn't know, I had my reasons why no one would find out. I wasn't trying to protect him, I was protecting me. That day, he had tried to pull the wool over my eyes also and it didn't work.

I thought of myself and what I needed. I ran to Troy, making the transition from my physically abusive world to Troy's world. Troy never met anyone that allowed him to be himself and still showed him love. All his life he has craved for someone like me, that can make him feel like a winner. I made him feel, and act like an ordinary family man working to become a powerful individual. I read, in a *Get Rich book* that, we think power is about how much we possess. Possessions are a natural commodity for powerful people. Power is having the ability to make things happen.

Ever since my love came along, Troy feels more powerful. I am his peace and confidence. He feels that he needs me to prosper. Love is power, and finding someone to love is like being pressured into taking challenging courses in school. If you knew they were hard before hand, you would have never taken them. You don't know what's coming next or what to expect and everything about it is demanding. Some of us are up to the challenge and others are looking to find an easy way out. Relationships are complicated; there isn't any easy way out. Not even for the people who take the 'easy' way out by walking out or running away. You will take that baggage to the next partner. Troy was on the run from past relationships and he had a lot of baggage, his life was going in circles.

Relationships are complex, like puzzles. They are hard to put together; sooner or later, you'll find out that there are pieces missing. You're always looking for something you don't have anymore. Parts have been hidden away, intentionally stolen, and you can't accept that they're gone forever. Good luck, trying to make it with a crazy person. You're living in denial. I find love to be mentally deceiving. You can laugh, cry, live, or die, all in the name of... love. We as people, have too many different meanings of what love is. We drive each other insane.

Many people say they have had love.
>Many say, "I don't know anything about love."
>Others say, "They're hopeful in finding love."
>It's the promiscuous ones that say, "I don't want anything to do with love."

People have so many points of view on love; they are the perpetrators, spreading confusion and heartbreak, among other things. They want sex so they stalk people that seem to need love most—desperate, die-hard romantics. We all have had encounters with someone that confuses sex with love.

What we all have in common is... we all crave love. We all assume that we are craving human love. Consistently, we think we have found it, but human love just doesn't seem to fill the void. Vulnerable people offer unstable passion. When you match that with true passion and compassion, you're going to deal with unpredictable emotions, like obsessive-compulsive disorders; that are going to become unbearable. People with the wrong chemistry can have good sex in common (opposites attract), but their relationships can turn into pure rage and destruction and still, they are committed to the search. With all our different opinions, love still makes our worlds go round.

Troy desperately wants my ability to love and to put love above life's disappointments and obstacles. He wants my power to forgive and most of all, my peace. He doesn't know that I'm going crazy on the inside. I haven't forgiven anyone. I'm trying to be strong for the both of us by keeping it to myself. I'm being selfish being in his life. I know he's not the man for me, he's not my peace. How is he going to take it when I've had enough?

Troy thinks I don't have any problems. I am a peaceful person but that doesn't mean, I'm at peace. My parents are my peace. Everything I represent, he is slowly draining from me. All the power in the world won't help him, if he's not smart enough to use it. He doesn't want me to face my problems. Facing them will make me strong enough to leave him. He never wants me to go home—because when I'm not around, Troy is insecure about us. Relationships are not his thing and he has no idea I know that. It takes two to fall in love.

This world exists because of love, yet, I believe only a small number of us have discovered real love or realized how big it is. Where real love is concerned, you can't do away with the term 'soul mate'. Our soul houses our spirit, which leads and guides us toward finding our true soul mate. Finding our true love is essential to our true nature; we are equipped for one another. It starts from the soul of every human. To recover and release anger problems permanently, face the problems that exist. Having sex to release anger helps us to get through the day. When the day is over, we're still an angry with a lonely soul.

Face the facts! The truth is that you won't have happiness with a soul mate, as long as you're angry. Soul mates share loving souls. True love develops and grows. A soul mate leads you to God and sets your soul free to love. Vow for better or for worse, for richer or for poorer, until, death do us part, and strive to honor that bond. Those vows were created because of our imperfections. Through the ups and downs and all of the breakdowns, we bear the break-ups and separations. All the changes that we suffer through, taking those vows of love are supposed to make us forgiving of one another.

Isn't it ironic, that, when one can't forgive the other, we have both broken our vows of love? The fact is, we all have our breaking points, limitations, and choices. Many of us don't listen to our soul. We choose to be alone because we can't have our way or get who we want. Everyone's soul mate is not rich but wouldn't it be nice if everyone's soul mate was perfect? Your soul mate can make a bad choice in the name of love. You can't stay mad at them because, in any circumstance, after the dust settles, they still make your soul happy and complete. There are people who are fearful of what true love means. Their fear makes true love unreachable for them.

Three other problems that hinder true love are... faith, trust, and being hurt. People would rather believe that love doesn't exist. It remains a mystery to them because they're looking to find it in each other before they find it in their own soul. Once you find it, you will know that love is bigger than life. Listen to your spirit, it teaches you how to nourish love and enjoy watching it grow. You have to work at keeping it, just like you would anything else worth having. You have to give up everything that comes easy and compromise; love is work. Once you realize that you possess it in your heart, you will always possess it. With everlasting belief that nothing about love is too hard when you give in to it, love is just a natural flow. Remember how hard it was to find love?

Commitment to love is what makes it easy; when you realize it's not about you, it's about us. Love, is the best high you'll ever have. True love is real love that stirs up confessions from one's heart. It's all about loving and supporting each other as soul mates and building a life together. And we are looking for the perfect mate. And around and around we go. Your soul mate may not be what you think they should be. Some of us are too choosy about love because you can't appreciate what you don't have. You can't identify love as a familiar comfort, an intimacy two spirits share. It's better than wham-bam, thank you ma'am, or entertaining a lover and having the hottest love affair.

A soul mate is a gift of true love. True love comes from a higher power of love within all of us that is our source and we are obligated to make the connection. When my heart beats—touching his—touching mine, Troy's livelihood showed and he listened. He noticed little things like, how a woman's heart beats slower than a man's. He falls to sleep to the rhythm of my heart. He admires my intelligence, the way I discuss things that most people can't talk about. In his mind, he owns my attributes. This is the right love for him. He believes he's making a true love connection with me. I had been taught that we had an obligation to find the Love of God within us, because God is Love. And He helps us to find ourselves. It takes two to fall in love and without God he doesn't know how to love me and make me fall deeply in love with him.

Three is not a crowd. He brings his best friend and roommate, Bay-Bay, with us everywhere we go. Both of them look good. Troy is shorter than me with heels on. He's light skinned with good hair, with a big natural. Bay-Bay's tall and dark-skinned with hair down his back. The three of us are inseparable right now. I wanted to believe that we were living our lives, no strings attached.

Troy asked me to move in with him. Well, personally, he makes me feel good. I act sexy around him. Mentally, I think we can work out our trust issues and get along. There is a difference between boys and men. He's not a respectable gentleman but he had written the bad-boy book on fore-play and sex. He is my first man. His sexy rap has no substance but his words are fluid love songs, playing softly in my ear. The songs are engraved in my heart, they portray me.

I knew I brought out the best in him. His body motions are for me; he moves his hands with masculine skills all for me. Physically, he speaks my language. Troy had rhythm under the black light. My black light lover giving his all to slow jam flings. The 'Isley Brothers' were rocking; 'Frankie Beverly', popping; he and I loved listening to the latest sounds. Candles and incense burning; our 'Love Jones' yearning, and I respect that he did it all just for me. I am not finished pleasing him. I'm not finished getting pleased. My answer to his question was, "Yes," When I was with Troy and high on drugs. I didn't care about God, my mom or whatever anyone else had to say. I didn't think about consequences. I moved in.

He was the antidote to my obsession. We had been fooling around for one year when I moved in. He has brought me out of my shell. I can't stop talking. He has brought out the rap in me. I am caught up and I can't come down. We worshiped each other. Throughout childhood, I was taught to worship God and love man unconditionally. Our arrangement is just what he wanted. Love is free and spontaneous. This isn't my kind of love coming from him. This is conspiracy to some kind of sick passion to exploit me. He didn't know what he was up against; thinking that he could handle me but I did. The values and principles my parents taught me will always be a part of me. He can take me away from my family. He can keep me away from my friends. He can't take away my principles; they're too far from his comprehension. Troy doesn't really know me. I am going against everything I've been taught to believe in. I left it all behind to be with him. I wasn't raised to live with a man without married. I'm in total disguise to live in his world. No one knows who I really am. Every time I get attacked or raped, I want sex. I have an addiction. I run to Troy. Only his love can satisfy my habit and calm me.

Chapter Two
Moving Out of My Parent's House

I was 17, the day I went home to get my son. Little Man turned one year old. His dad, Troy and I drove up at the same time. Little Man saw me from the front window and ran out of the house. I ran and met him halfway and got big hugs and kisses. His dad walked up and he met his dad for the first time. Troy leaned up against his car watching the three of us. They left together to celebrate Little Mans birthday. I'll never come between him and his father. He will grow up one day and see his father and me for who we really are. He'll be man enough to make decisions and come to conclusions, for himself.

Moving Little Man's bed and my things out of my parent's house is going to be hard. I knew my mother was going to make me face the reality of what I was doing and put me in check. I found out my parents had been looking for me. They told people that I kept running away from home. I was so busy doing my thing, I never thought of it as running away. I had to face that reality and it didn't feel good, and doesn't sound anything like me. I was numb. Mom reached out, but I was completely unreachable. I couldn't believe what I was doing. I had stopped thinking sanely. They didn't know the pain I felt.

> I have great parents that treat me good, all the time. As I packed, my mom ran behind me crying and praying, begging me, "please don't go."

I stopped. I didn't want to turn around and look at her, she reads eyes and she can feel your spirit. I knew I was badly hurting her, but I had been badly hurt. Before I got with Troy, I thought everyone outside of my surroundings was respectable, traditional, or a religious family, just like we were. I thought families watched TV together, to enjoy each other's company. I thought everyone said their prayers and went to sleep at night. I thought housewives stayed home and cleaned the house and got the children up every morning to feed them breakfast and send them off to school with lunch or lunch money.

They got up, had breakfast and went to work in the morning and came straight home after work. If there wasn't a housewife in the home that prepared dinner every day, the working mom or dad came home, cooked and set the table as a household, while enjoying their family quality time. At six o'clock in the evening, everyone sat down to dinner and discussed their day.

To me, home for everyone was sharing love. Making home-life comfortable. I didn't hear about people being abused in the home; it was kept secret. I didn't see it on TV. I didn't know what bad relationships were or how abusive they could become. I never saw anyone acting out or hurting each other. I just knew when something wasn't right.

My parents kept their anger and their problems private. Their secrets were kept to protect us; they didn't want to turn us against falling in love and committing to another. Their secrets produced in me, a woman that set out in life thinking, I could find a perfect relationship.

We weren't allowed to show anger. We weren't allowed to say, "Shut up!" No one argued or disagreed out loud. Troy was not that man. They should have fought in front of us and made-up in front of us, to let us know, that there isn't a perfect man or women; but, that doesn't mean to give-up and fall for a loser.

I had brought the wrong man into our lives. I couldn't allow myself to feel where she was coming from. I felt like I wasn't good enough to be her daughter. She was a virgin when she married my dad. I thought, parents are not perfect or equals in intellect. They can only teach you what they know; they can only give you their personal best. Never compare your parent's best to someone else's parent's best. All parents' finest qualities are at different levels. Get to know and understand them for who they are.

In this world, we have rules and regulations. That are made to live by, that are often broken, and we must reap the penalty. Our parents teach us their personal values and principles. When you value yourself, it teaches others to respect you; a principle that cannot be broken, it is who you are. Although, it can be disguised or hidden, if you don't stand up for who you are, you will reap the penalty. Principles represent your standard of living. It means, you believe in who you are and no one can change that about you. When you're older, you throw out things you don't like that your parents taught you and enjoy the good things like wisdom, knowledge, values, and principles.

I finally looked up, into her eyes. She looked into my eyes and she knew I was scared to death and didn't want to go with the man. I didn't want to be with him and I didn't want to be there, either. What she didn't know is that I felt like I didn't have any other choice but to go. I wanted to change my mind when I realized what I was doing to her. I watched her watch the man that was in a big hurry to take me away from her. She saw right though his handsome face and fancy clothes. She felt an evil force coming from this man that she didn't know very much about, and he had control of her baby girl. She could see that Troy had a problem with parents.

He had problems with his parents before his mother died. I can't imagine what would have gone down if my dad was home. As I walked out the door and down the stairs, my mom ran after me. She grabbed my left arm and pulled me back. He grabbed my right arm and pulled me towards him. My mom held on to my body with all her might, hoping I would push him away. I felt every drop of her heart and her mine. Troy pulled us apart and he and I got in the car. As we drove off, I looked at her.

She stood there heartbroken. Her beautiful eyes, heart and soul were crying, with her hands covering her face, too hurt and too ashamed of me to look up. I had run from a loving home that was stricter than the strictest. I had sold my soul to the devil, thinking, 'this is my life, this is my battle, and I got to fight it alone'. I didn't want to bring my family into my confusion. My mom didn't know. I believed that I ran to protect myself. I got a baby now. I got problems. I can't live with their rules and my problems.

Troy and my relationship was never the same after that day. We knew we had hurt my mom and dad. We were just smoking marijuana, talking to my mom every day, off and on, and crying. People have to know who you are to fall in love with you. If you haven't found yourself as a person whether you're a teenager or an adult, you haven't learned how to love yourself or anyone else. We were alleged lovers, wasting everyone's precious time. When you don't know about life, love, and who you are; you can't read into other people's intentions. You can't feel if the person you choose has lust or devotion. So, you end up settling for Mr. Wrong instead of waiting for Mr. Right, the one who will be infatuated with you. He will be devoted and committed to you only for as long as you shall live or need each other.

We don't know what the future holds. Some people grow in a relationship and some people stay the same; some people die on the inside. It is crucial to meet the parents, to see if there is life in them. Life represents growth, even if they're separated. In time, dating will teach you that if a man doesn't have respect for his mom, he doesn't know how to respect women. If a man said he respects his mom and he disrespects you and your mom, he's a liar. Unless he corrects the problem with counseling, there will be hard knocks, and counseling doesn't always work.

Building relationships takes time and patience. Many of us would rather be alone than learn or teach. I didn't know being with someone would be so hard. I never saw mom and dad angry; I never saw them lose their tempers about anything. My parents kept their anger and their problems private. Their secrets were kept to protect their children; they didn't want to turn us against falling in love and committing to another. Their secrets produced in me a woman that set out in life thinking I could find a perfect relationship. I was going to find a man that didn't get angry or loud, and didn't disagree.

Troy and I were lovers; we weren't talking; and I couldn't have a relationship by myself. I didn't care anymore. I was dead on the inside. My sister, Lady Dee, kept calling me. She said, I sound like Patty Hurst on the phone. I still can't leave him; I want to save him from himself. I know I can't stay with him forever and don't understand how can I live with a man that can tear my mom and I apart that way. I can barely stand myself right now. How could I let this happen? Now, I have this love/hate thing going on with him. We'll never be the same, this headache is too deep.

I'm stronger than I thought, when it came to men. Troy goes to work every day and leaves Bay-Bay here to watch me. He takes my son and me everywhere we want to go. One morning after Troy left for work, I got in the shower, minding my business. I stepped out of the shower, wrapped my towel around me, opened the bathroom door, and Bay-Bay stood there looking at me and I at him. As I walked to my room, he followed behind me and it seemed as if I walked in slow motion.

I walked into my room and closed the door behind me. I sat down on the bed, took the towel off and began rubbing my son's baby oil on my body. He opened the door without knocking and stood there, waiting for me to invite him in. OK, I am a fool for being here but far from crazy. I covered myself and asked him to leave. He turned away with a smirk on his face, like you know you want this. Later, I walked out of the room and into the kitchen. He came into the dining room area.

He struck a playboy lean on the counter.

"What is it with you and Troy? What do you see in Troy? He's shorter than you and he's very controlling. I don't like the way he treats you. You're special. You're not like the other girls we bring here, you're all woman. You take care of your man. He doesn't appreciate you, Jamaica. If I had a woman like you, I would."

I didn't say a word. I shouldn't have listened but I did. His words didn't sound like game, but they were. I felt he tried to win some kind of bet, that's why I stayed silent. He worshiped Troy and wanted to be like him. He went on to enlighten me. Maybe he tried to influence me to want him to express needing a good woman to love. He told me girls wanted him for his hair and his looks and they wanted to have his babies. He's crazy.

The entire time he talked, all I want to do was run my fingers through his hair. I had never seen a head of hair like that on a black man. I thought, 'get over here! Don't let any other heifers braid your hair, except me, with your fine self'! I never said a word out loud. I didn't look as if I was interested in what he was saying, it was too risky. He was testing me. I didn't want to dig any more ditches or burn any bridges. He wanted to see how far I would go as a woman. I'm here living with two men and I know my place as Troy's woman. A female should be able to be around the opposite sex in any situation without anything wild going down. There'll be no drama here. It's definitely a woman's obligation, to stop it from going down. Bay-Bay gave me respect for knowing that.

Post-it!

Your man's roommate will test you.
If you feel some attraction between you, get over it!
Don't trust him. Trust yourself
Only converse when need to, don't associate like
Hooking-up, hanging-out, or bonding.
Don't listen to his rap.
Don't lead him on
With flirtatious facial expressions and body language
Don't befriend him in private.
When you're alone,
No entertaining him with mind games like teasing,
Sex games and sex talk
No sex · no touching · no sharing · no secrets.
No partying festivities! No drinking together!
No getting high together!
Don't borrow · don't obligate yourself · don't owe.
Stay true to your man.
Know your man is worth fighting for.

The following day, I couldn't face Bay-Bay. My son and I left out alone and walked to the mall. When I left the mall and got back on the street, I noticed that I was being followed. I picked Little Man up and continued walking, until, I got to the traffic light at the intersection. I stopped and turned around to investigate. Troy had left his J-O-B. Troy and Bay-Bay were in the car spying on me. Troy jumped out the car, upset. In situations like this, you've got to weigh the pros and cons.

That incident was a wake-up call. Another reason why I don't need to be there. They picked us up and took us out to eat. When we got home, things were already bitter between us and Troy's stepmom kept calling. I wondered, why she was in town alone and where was Troy's dad? She asked him to go to the store and get tampons for her and she wasn't accepting no for an answer. It's obvious she's up to something. I picked up the phone and heard her undercover clue right away. It sounds as

51

he's her tampon to me. They're both up to something, she's after my man. That witch.

He left the house at night for her. "I was born at night, but not last night. I know what's wrong with this picture. She tried to break us up because she prefers to be with you rather than your father. You said, your father's been cheating on her. Now, she's playing payback. I know what I'm talking about. I know she wanted you when you first took me to meet her. You're the fool she's chosen to help her mess his head up. How can you let her play you against your own father? She crazy! You're crazy! All of you are playing dangerous games with your lives. She's going to make you and your father kill each other. You just wait and see what happens. You'd better recognize the game when it's in your face."

I can clearly see he's turned on by danger. He loved every bit of it. They got some kind of deadly sexual triangle going on. He once told me he wanted a woman that would kill for him or die trying. I'm not going to fight, or die, not for him. I'm certain, I won't hang around to see what happens. He started bossing me around, acting all cool and untouchable, laying down the rules, it was worse than being at home. He's not my parent.

Understand

I am woman independent.
I believe in real love
And understanding.
In a relationship
Without reality
There is no understanding.
Without understanding,
The relationship is not based on
Love.
Without love,
You are without strength.
Without strength,
You are weak.
To be weak
Is to be less than a man.
To be less than a man,
Is to be without woman.
Without woman,
There is no beginning.
Without a beginning,
You have no future.
Without a future,
You don't have me.

Chapter Three
Goodbye, Yes-Man

(I define a yes-man as a man that refuses to accept no for an answer) That night when he returned, I told him that I was leaving. He asked me to marry him. I said, "No," and I answered fast. He thought I was going to say yes. I am fed up with yes. I had let this man turn me out on sex and drugs, who knows what all I was smoking. He's growing marijuana right here in our bedroom. He had traveled all over the United States doing 'Lord knows what'. He thinks he got this little church girl for as long as his heart desires, but he is wrong. Troy can't fool me. I know what love looks like. If I say I do, he will change for the worst.

Troy found out he didn't have control over me when I answered, 'No' after he proposed marriage. That was the first time I used the no word in our relationship. That's the night I found out that a yes-man existed. It's going-down; better now than later. A yes-man blackmails his way through life; he cannot handle hearing the word 'No'. A simple, two-letter word brings out the beast in him and releases a totally insane person. He thinks he's being assertive, but don't get it twisted, his aggressive ways are over the top and exaggerated.

A yes-man will act the part of a good, down-home gentleman, as long as you let him walk all over you, answering, "Yes, baby" to his every command and jump when he says, jump. Don't even mention speaking, you haven't anything to declare to a yes-man. A yes-man uses his money to keep women in line. If he can't use his wallet to get her, she becomes a challenge and the game of threats begins. If he can't bribe her with things to possess her, he's intimidated. She'd better watch her back. When he can't use his cash to control her every move, he declares war. He comes in all ages, colors, shapes, and sizes and hangs in every social group and every class of men.

His arrogant, high n' mighty drama is self-centered. His interest is himself and his forever-bossy traditions are endless; like telling everyone what to do, when to do it, and how to do it, are exhausting. He will never admit that he's controlling. He's a proudly selfish and relentless man. When he does something for you, trust me, you're indebted to him. He will take your life, and then his, if he loses you or anything else he believes he owns. The bottom line is, you must live up to his expectations. If you take him on, he won't stop until, he destroys you. I didn't know all these things about him, until, I used the word NO.

Playing tit-for-tat wasn't planned. I told him, his roommate walked in on me when I didn't have any clothes on. I was hurt and it just came out.

"I don't need to be here with two men wanting me," I said.

It's not that he refuses to listen to reason; he can't hear logic. He thinks I told him because I wanted to hurt him for going out. For the first time, I saw his insecurities without the cool disguise. I'm looking at humanity's monster in the face, can't anyone tell me I created him by myself. Maybe, I did tell him to hurt him; either way, let the truth be told. I didn't lie! I wasn't wrong for telling him and I couldn't have picked a better time; he's crazy! There isn't any better time. I definitely learned that playing tit-for-tat with my man, using another man to get his attention, is dangerous.

I tried to get my point across. I had good reason for leaving before all this came up. Plus, I wasn't going to allow him to start leaving me at home at night, too. No way. Not after Bay-Bay expressed himself to me. For the first time, Troy thinks that he sees the monster in me. He's hallucinating. If I've got to fight, I am ready to fight for my life. Let's do this! I've had it up to here with his messy nonsense. He beat my butt thoroughly, like he was my biological father.

I waited to hear him say, "I brought you into this world, and I'll take you out." My heart had been broken before, but this time was different. This is a First experience. I have never been hit by someone that said they loved me. I didn't know it was possible. This was a penetrating, backstabbing pain; a deceitful and numbing pain that broke through my body, slowly and psychologically challenging. I was ready to fight. This beating separates the woman from the girl. He's an animal and he broke the part of my heart no other man had touched; it belonged to him only. I've been there trying to make it work and this is what I got.

You got to pay attention to whom you entrust your heart. This man was unfeeling. Once you love a man unconditionally, he could almost do anything and be forgiven, but not this. To me, love is much more than what he just demonstrated. I thought I could teach him by showing him what a woman's love is all about. My parents educated me with common sense. Tonight, Troy tried to beat it out of me. My point is, I couldn't fight him. Even though my brothers taught me how to defend myself, tonight, with Troy; my heart was too caught-up and over-involved in his lovemaking. I had given him my heart. I don't know how to act out anger. I will go off. I will make the man hurt me, or I him. He beat the little girl out of me and made me see the world differently.

I am conscious about leaving. Unconsciously, I had fallen in love with Troy's anger. When he got angry, I could see myself in his anger. I felt he was acting out my anger. I wondered if he had ever been the victim of sexual abuse. The bottom line is, I had a dangerous addiction. I was attracted to his temper, he was the coolest, angriest person I've ever seen. I'm not throwing myself to the dogs. I got to go; I'm sick enough. I'll never find myself here. I know the real me is buried under all my pain and I'm going to dig and dig to find me. To get out of that lifeless place, I said to myself, 'I'm beautiful, loyal, and honest. I cook well, keep the house clean, and I'm clean. I am a good, loving person filled with life. I am conscious about leaving and he is conscious about stopping me'.

I haven't been unfaithful. I haven't done him wrong. Why this is happening? I don't know. Even if I was in the wrong, a man should never lay his hand on a woman, for any reason. I am so through with him. What am I going to do? If I walk away right now, the question is, can my heart take a life that's all screwed-up, out of self-defense? I made my decision, stay and take it until, it's safe for my son and I to take our time and leave civilized. I have countless ways to get away from him. I will leave, and soon, because now it's all insults, assumptions, and interrogating questions.

"Did you do someone at the mall today?
"Is it your baby's daddy?"
"Are you doing my roommate when I'm at work?"
"What's going on with us?"
"Why won't you marry me?"
"You have never told me that you love me."

All day, every day, he's going insane. This is the man I would lay in the bed butt-naked for and wait for him to come home from work to pick up where we left off. He's right, I never told him I loved him. I have been showing him, love is an action word. I never told him, because he can't handle love and I'm certain he can't handle my love for him or my life situations. It's so much about me, he doesn't know and I can never tell him. Troy is now playing the blame game; blaming me for everything while he tries to redeem himself and I'm not falling for it. He's confused. He has stopped going to work, just to keep an eye on me.

What kind of mess is that? The three of us have been hanging out; Troy, Little Man, and I. It was time to do something for the two of us. One night, Troy and I went to an 'Isley Brothers' concert. It was nice. The brothers turned it into a rock & roll concert. I screamed when they began smashing their guitars; it was unexpected, I loved it. While the concert became more intense,

I'm totally in love with Troy. After the concert was over, I hated him more than ever. Troy couldn't comprehend how beautiful our love could be.

We are in a dangerous place. I'm never going to fall madly in love with him, not the way he is now. I don't know if he knows his abusive ways are the reason why. He blames it on everything and everyone these days. I'm his number one excuse for his violence. As we left the concert, he tried to hold my hand, acting like nothing bad has happened between us, like being crazy in the head is all in a day's work and he's proud of it. No one is the blame for his mess, but him. He's not done with me, yet. On the way home, we ordered Chinese food to go. As we're sitting at the dinner table eating, I notice that we have a lot of leftovers.

I called out to Bay-Bay, "Are you hungry? Come get some food."

He hollered back, "No thanks," and expressed gratitude to me for asking.

Troy is not done playing my big, bad boyfriend and before I could open my mouth again, I got hit on my thigh. It made a loud sound, but didn't hurt as much.

"You have gone too far. I'm abusing myself by being here and there's no way I am living like this any longer," I said.

I sat there in shock thinking, he promised he would never lay a hand on me again. I jumped up from the table, running. He ran after me because he wasn't done talking.

"See what you made me do? You're not here to take care of my roommate; your job here is to take care of me. This is my house; everything in it belongs to me. You belong to me."

He boasted like he really got something, he doesn't even have me. I'm sick in more ways than one. Hours later, I'm in the bathroom holding my stomach about to throw up China and he's in my face.

"Baby, I'm sorry. It won't happen again, you're my life," He cried.

He sounded like a no-good scratched record I wanted to throw away and resume my life. He hit me once and I fell for his apology and excuses. I thought I needed to call his bluff, but I didn't want to play those games anymore. I told him he had too many personalities for me to be in love with him.

"I am leaving your house and I am leaving you!"

In so many words. I stood up to him, but he didn't believe that I would ever leave.

That night, Troy messed up with me. What he didn't know was that he rescued me from something so bad and I ran to him, and had been running to him for years for him to take care of me. He never let me down, until, now. At this point, I've got to run from his abuse. I'm sick of running. I'm sick to my stomach. I'm scared, because I think I may be pregnant. I was in a bad relationship. If the woman wants to leave first, all hell is going to break loose. The man wants to work it out. He'll say, "I'll do anything, just don't go. I can make you love me, again. I'll make it up to you, girl."

If you don't answer right away, he'll say, "You'll never find anyone like me". He knows you can do better and he'll do anything to stop you from finding happiness elsewhere. Now, he wants you to play house, too. Most men are selfish and very deceiving. They lie to you. They lie to themselves. And, liars believe their own lies.

All men don't leave when they fall out of love. Some men, demote you lower and lower as you uncover their faults and deceitful ways. He knows he has messed up and showed his behind. He has broken your spirit and he doesn't like the fact that your eyes don't light up when you see him coming. Every time you look at him he has to make a run. He wants to go chase mischief because you make him feel small when you give him, 'the look'. That's the look he deserves and he knows what's coming next; the thought behind the look. You have opened your mouth and told him the truth about himself.

Some men keep you around just to dog you out. He'll put you down, while keeping his options open. He despises you for knowing who he really is. He'll tell you things like, "Baby you're the only woman for me," And, have you laying up loving him, wasting your life. Especially, women that are spending time dropping their dimes on him for food, clothes, and a gassed up ride. His sick mind is out there in your car, looking for another woman, or a man younger than you, that he thinks is going to love him unconditionally; the same way you've loved him. He never educated himself on how to show you some appreciation. Instead of learning how to have a meaningful relationship and try to better himself as a person, he will ruin life for his next victim.

Meanwhile, every time it comes to making love, all he wants is for you to sex him up and down and let him in and out your back door. When it comes to doing anything for you, your man got a stupid excuse for everything or he can't be found. The most famous excuse is, "Baby, I'll never cheat or leave; you're too good to me, but I got to make a run. I'll never find another woman like you. I don't want AIDs; I'm scared to have sex with any other woman," Trust me; he's going to lie, until, his hand gets caught in the cookie jar.

He is through loving you. When you hear him complain about why he's not making love to you or why he's not giving you a climax, he won't discuss anything because he's using you. Constantly talking about what he won't do with other women; claiming all women have a problem. Listen to me, he's their problem. When this type of man is not in love anymore, he doesn't work on falling back in love with you. He lacks common sense; he's not a responsible person. He's turned off forever. His past women have tried to change whatever it is about themselves that turn him off.

It's not them, it's him. He's turned off because you're turned off and he knows it's because of his past and present behavior. You're not the first woman that he has drained the life out of and you won't be the last. This type of man has to keep changing partners. He needs a woman that doesn't know what he's all about, that will believe in him and make him feel big. If you think that your eyes will light up again for your man, call his bluff. Play his game. Tell him, "Baby, let's work on it," as he did to keep you. Ask is it a medical term for his sexual problems, illness, or impotence.

Offer to go with him to the doctor. If you hear another explanation that sounds like a lie, he can't tell the truth. This type of man causes himself to be impotent, because of pride, sick nature and bad genetics. He doesn't want the relationship and he won't let it end before he finds comfort elsewhere. It's time to take your power back. No one should be able to make your decisions for you, but this one is long overdue.

When the lovemaking gets old; try different alternatives. What some men will do when the lovemaking gets old, is find a new. A good woman can keep an old love new all by herself, reminiscing about the way things were. She enjoys having 'Remember that time' over coffee or tea. This type of man can't remember the memories; he doesn't cherish his woman or time spent. While she's sipping tea, he's out buying a hot red sports car, dreaming of picking up a hot chick to match. A truthful man is about being true to his woman. Taking care of business and having peace of mind in his home. When the relationship gets old, he cherishes his woman and time spent together. He loves to reminisce. He will serve the coffee or the tea. He got what he wants and he's not going anywhere.

He deals with his home and woman peacefully. He's about the truth. He got it hard in this world and has to come behind men that don't believe in the truth. Once you have hurt a woman or man that has loved you unconditionally, it will haunt you, until, you die. There aren't any carefree tomorrows, not for you. It doesn't matter if it's your mother, sister, wife, or lover. It doesn't make any difference who you are and what you do. It doesn't matter how much money you make. You're not going to find peace of mind until, you make your peace with God. A true man is about taking care of business and building a foundation, not tearing it down.

Troy's threats have taken their toll on me. Troy has revealed himself. Although, he never shouts when he's angry, he looks at me with a very intimidating stare that I don't care to live with. He opens his mouth with lies and said all the wrong things to me. This time he said, he will deal with Bay-Bay later. I'm asking myself what's going to happen later. What is he going to do to Bay-Bay? I didn't say anything more to him about Bay-Bay, I've said enough. I'm not even paying attention to him. I wish he would shut up and drop dead. He said, I'm the first woman he has let into his world and if I leave him, he will kill me and then kill himself. I am already numb from my other abusers in my other messed up world. I didn't argue with his threats. Intimidation and lies is all he knows and I've been letting him get away with it for my own selfish reasons, now it's over.

I waited until, he went back to work to get my charming revenge. I'm playing house, cooking, and cleaning in front of him so that he would think everything is alright. He's still suspicious. Why? He knows he's crazy; it's no big secret, not around here. He knows that I know he's crazy. I hadn't experienced a lot of things when I first met Troy, but I know crazy when I hear it. I didn't know if he would cross the line and he has, more than once. Now I know what a bad relationship is like. I can't get out of his life fast enough. You can't save a sick person that thinks they know everything. However you can save yourself.

I won't physically fight. My son is with me. My strategy for leaving is, treat him like he's smart and make him feel like he can do anything to me, I'll never leave. I'll love him hard. When I leave, I'll leave him wanting more. I'll leave the house spotless; he will miss me more when I'm gone. He will never see it coming; he will realize what he lost. That's how I got the name 'Smooth'. My smooth revenge will hurt him even more to know that I outsmarted him. I should have been gone, but it's hard to leave my first.

That morning, I moved out for good. I smoked one of Troy's joints in bed, and then got up. I got Little Man and myself all dressed up for the occasion. I was leaving hell and going home. My plan was to call my mother and tell her to get my brothers to come and move our things out. It was a hard call to make, but I had made it. In all my planning, I forgot the most important thing. What am I going to do with Bay-Bay? Would he expose me like before? I was seriously about to panic.

Little Man got up crying. Children know when something is not right. I was used to getting high and partying with Troy. I'll take three hits off his joint and I'm full. We, would eat until, we fell asleep. I never smoked an entire joint alone or tripped that high alone. I never had to do something as sneaky and daring as that. And that today, I was doing both. Why was I feeling like Troy is working with the FBI and they're going to break down the door and arrest me for growing marijuana? I kept going to the door and window. I kept hearing the door bell and we don't have one. I'm wondering if Troy really went to work and feel as if he's watching me.

Sweet freedom that came with a bad case of paranoia. I'm paranoid and I don't know that it's the weed yet and I thought, 'I must be going crazy'. I don't know what's happening. I planned to clean out Troy's closet to make sure I wasn't leaving anything behind. Instead, I find myself searching, looking hysterically for something, I didn't know what! Opening up shoe boxes I've never opened before. In the right-hand corner of the closet on the very bottom, I opened up a shoe box and made a shocking discovery. A book called, 'Devil Worship' with pictures of demonic faces and the chapters read how to cast evil spells on people.

The box had different types of drugs; mostly weed and pills. He works at a prison and has access to a lot of drugs. This is too wild. I hate it when my mom is right. I'm holding proof that he practices witchcraft, just as she said. I'm freaking out, throwing the book back in the box. Why did I smoke the whole joint? I tried hard to pull myself together, but wasn't any use. Falling to my knees I cry out, "how could he do that to me?" And feeling everything in my life has gone wrong and I may die soon. I know I smoked too much and shouldn't have opened that book to see the demons staring at me. I thought they were after me. I ran around frantically holding myself. That evidence scared the pee out of me. I was scared to leave the room and had to go in one of Troy's marijuana plants.

I couldn't believe what was happening! There's not enough soil in the pot to soak it up and sat right out in the open. I opened the window and picked up the plant, "I solemnly swear that no one will ever know I'm standing in a third story apartment, pouring urine from a marijuana plant out the window."

Suddenly, I heard men arguing. I was too panicky to open the bedroom door and look out. God please help me to feel normal again, so I can get out of here. Just when I thought about hiding under the bed, the voices got louder. I recognized my big brother's voice. I got up off of the floor and opened the bedroom door. Bay-Bay had the front door open with the safety chain still on the door.

He's shouted to my brothers, "You better leave, or else."

He was a mad man. He is going to fight, not one man, but three men, to stop them from taking me away. My male cousin, D.Q. Jr., had showed up. Little Man screamed, hysterically. My mother had told my brothers that something wasn't right between Troy and me. When they heard screaming, they were ready to kick the door down. I understood what was happening, but couldn't think of what to do; I was tripping hard. When that front door came open, I came down off my high fast! The love I had for my brothers, and my cousin, made my high history. I didn't want to see them fight. I ran up to Bay-Bay.

"These are my brothers, they're here to save me, Bay-Bay."
I explained fast. He still didn't believe me and pushed me behind him. He thought that I tried to run off with another man.

My brother Moe-Joe stepped in, "Look, man, this is our sister. We don't look alike but check out the ears. Family has the same ears. Jamaica is our sister and we come to take her home, where she belongs, don't try to stop us. Man, we don't want any trouble and we don't want to see anyone get hurt."

My other brother, Cool, and cousin, D.Q., had his back. Things got quiet; everyone had a chance to take a deep breath. After that, my cousin, D.Q., and Bay-Bay helped us move my things out. Bay-Bay actually has this down-to-earth smile on his face, as though he cared about me and he didn't like the way I was being treated. He wanted me to leave and wondered what took me so long. I thought how sweet freedom felt. What a relief. I'll never go back.

My brothers and the rest of my family thought everything was okay because Little Man and I seemed fine. They didn't know my life and theirs had been threatened. I don't ever want to see Troy's face again. I just want to be over and done with him. Troy is a vengeful person. I know he's coming after me. He's spiteful and it's hard to get rid of him these days. He has talked me into anything in the past, he's my weakness and I am his.

Right now, it's good to see a smile on my mother's face again. My dad looked me in the face and shook his head. He's hurt and has every right to be upset with me. I never said I was sorry and I regretted that. I know I can't stay here long, guys are after me and I can't be here when they come. I don't want to get approached anymore. If I let all this anger out, who knows what will happen. I'm tired and I'm already having morning sickness and have scheduled an appointment to get it taken care of. I'm looking for a place to live, somewhere where Troy and all my other enemies can't find me.

Lady Dee stepped up with a proposition. Lady Dee was a super star. She was famous for singing in the 70's; she performed on TV, traveling the country alone. She's a recording artist and had a hit song and album, 'Midnight Lover's Blues'. She was on the cover of magazines and performed with a lot of famous people. She never talks about it, she lives in the moment; working as an Airport Manager. Dee and I talked. She explained, I can move in with her. My responsibilities would be babysitting my three year old nephew (I named Money), cooking, and cleaning, and I wouldn't have to pay rent or bills, while looking to find something of my own. I didn't have to think about it, my sister and I get along.

Troy called to try and get me back, but it's too late. I answered the phone and, surprisingly, he did all the talking. A week had gone by and I didn't hear from Troy. I had plenty of time to recover from my hospital discharge.

> "I can't believe you left me after everything I tried to do for you and Little Man. I tried, Jamaica. I did my best. I'm not good enough? You know I love you. Don't you know how much I love Little Man? He's like a son to me. You two are my life; you're my world. The day you left, I came home from work and my world was gone, my reason for living. I can't live without you two. I'm coming to get what's mine; you're my family. You belong to me,

now. This is where you belong, this is your home. I got to see you." he pleaded.

"No! Troy don't you come here ever again. I don't want to see you anymore, it's over.

"It's like that? You could leave me like that? I have been giving you time to miss me and you're telling me it's over?" he kept asking.

While he gave me time to miss him, I had an abortion. The baby was his. I didn't want him around but I could never tell him that. I felt horrible and empty on the inside. I had to do what I done. I know he'll make me feel worse; he will never forgive me and he will make it harder for me to forgive myself. My body feels better now. I had a rough time when the hospital released me. My four sisters came to pick me up and we had to tell B.J. that I got a different type of surgical procedure. If she knew about me, she would cry and call me a baby killer. She's very emotional. She takes everything hard and I feel bad enough. I'm laid up trying not to listen to Troy's lies once more. I couldn't believe he opened up expressing his feeling outside the bedroom.

Even a crazy man can make sense when he wants what he wants. I am impressed. I wanted to run to him.

He said, "I'm coming over and you better let me in or else."

He made his point. Here we go again; he didn't stay smart for long.

"Or else what?"

"I'm going to kill your mom and dad."

It took about twenty-five minutes for his crazy self to get to my parent's house. It's 1:00 in the morning. Instead of going to the front door, he walked around to the back of the house, standing in front of my bedroom window.

"Get up and let me in."

Now, he wants me to let him in my parent's house, to sneak in bed.

"No way! Go home."

"Not without you. Do you want your mom and dad to die tonight?"

"No! Do you?"

He explained to me how he was going to kill them. He gives me nightmares. I did not leave the house for two weeks. I never want to go outside again. For what? To fight guys off me or fight for my life trying to keep Troy from killing me?

An old friend stopped by. His lust is not my desire. The day I decided to go out, the doorbell rang. I looked out the window and it was Troy, not my Troy, an old friend I knew that used to pick me up after school sometimes. He's six years older than me; he's a fireman. We have kissed a lot, making out, but that's all. Either he has heard that I had a baby or the rumor is going around that I'm giving it away. Right now, I don't know if he has heard anything. I don't know why he's here. I opened the door to welcome him. He walked in, acting anxious.

"Sit-down. Are you alright; would you like a class of water?"

"Yes, thank you."

As I turned my back to walk into the kitchen, I turned around and he looked at me like a pervert; hoping I still wanted him the way he wanted me. He started coming on to me and I wasn't impressed. Now, I know why he's here.

"Please leave," I said.

"Not until, I get what I came for. I've wanted you for years, you know that," he said.

"Didn't you get married?"

"That has nothing to do with us. I've waited for this moment with you."

He grabbed me and then kissed me. I wouldn't let him kiss me in the mouth, though. He touched all over my body. He tripped me on the floor, ripped off my clothing and was about to force himself on me until, I screamed his name.

"Look at me! Look at me, Troy!"

He looked up and saw tears streaming down my face. Mucus ran out of my nose, all over my face. I wore a horrified expression. He saw that he was hurting me and something clicked in his mind. He began to cry.

"What am I doing?" he cried, repeatedly.

"I'm sorry Jamaica. Are you alright?"

He fixed his clothes and then left out of the house, walking fast. He never looked back. When he sped off. My father pulled up and saw that he was upset. I was still messed up. I couldn't keep it a secret like the others, I had to tell him. My dad was hurt; he jumped in his truck and went after Troy. When my mom got home, I told her what happened before my dad returned and she got upset with me. She blames me. She remembers Troy and I used to mess around. She believes I was sleeping with him way back when. She expects he's coming back for more of what I had already given him and feels that now I've got her man mixed up in my nasty mess. That's the very reason why I haven't told all along. How can I, when my mother passes judgment, I'm guilty. My dad found Troy and talked to him. Troy apologized to my dad. Troy was not my desire and he wasn't my next phase. He's never treated me the same after that, like I was going to lose sleep over him. I know he had heard the rumors.

I'm having a hard time falling asleep lately. Every night, like clockwork, my ex, Troy, calls me, or he's at my window terrorizing me, his threats have become my bedtime stories. He thinks there's something he can say to get me back. I would lie up and listen to him bully me, until, I fall asleep. Time for me to get out and have some fun. My girlfriend, J.J., called and asked me to spend the weekend with her to get away from everything. I was at her house every weekend or she was at mine before I moved in with Troy.

We were too young to get into nightclubs. We would drive to the air force bases and party. We partied all the way there and stayed until, closing. When I got back to her house in San

Mateo, I'm crazy stressed out. I had already told her about me leaving Troy. That's all I told her. I didn't want any more gossip to get out. She had heard the rumors about me and believed them, too. I didn't speak up for myself; I couldn't talk about such things with her. She hadn't experienced living with a man. We would go to the store and get what we wanted, take it back to her house and pig-out on junk food and lots of sodas in the daytime, hanging out in her bedroom laughing all day watching the Carol Burnett show, The Monsters, and Good Times with Janet Jackson.

Days were simple and fun when I didn't talk about my life. At night, we partied with her friends. J.J. and I had fun with the guys on the base. They travel all over the United States picking up the latest trends and dances and taught them to us. I would cross my legs while sitting down at the table and guys would stuff numbers into my high-heel shoes. I never called or gave out my number, we weren't sleeping with the guys, and we were just there for the party. We're California girls and never wanted to leave California. At the end of the night, we would leave them, and take the party back to J.J.'s house and practice those moves to perfection. Some nights, it would be six of us girls together turning out one house party after another with all the latest moves. This time, I didn't have as much fun. I'm young and restless. Too young to suffer this pain, and because of the way my life was going, I needed to get away.

I craved affection badly, my mind was on overload. I felt all messed-up; no guy can fill Troy's shoes in the bedroom. Before Troy, I was living two different lives and both worlds collided together and blew-up. I didn't clean up the mess mentally or physically; I didn't deal with my problems, I swept them under the rug and ran off to start a third life with Troy. I never talked to anyone about my two worlds coming together and blowing up. Now, I have left three worlds behind. That's crazy, who can keep up.

Everyone thinks I go around sleeping with boys. I've only had consensual sex with one guy and that's Troy. Now that we have broken up, I feel like my life is disconnected from all humans. I can't act out what I feel, I got to hold my head-up in public, not knowing that's what many people do and was a statistic I didn't know. There wasn't any sign of Troy when J.J. and I got back to San Francisco. I went to my parent's house to pack. I had made my decision to move in with my sister, The Lady Dee. I packed everything and said my good byes.

For my family, the white picket fence cliché was hereditary. It spread from one generation to the next, but the big white house with the picket fence wasn't inheritable. As a sixteen year old girl, I had an abnormal passion to meet a man and have an undying love. When I heard them use the phrase, "white picket fence," it meant, find a man with money. I tried all my life to find intimacy and happiness with someone that fits that description. I tried my best to fall in love with a man that could make the 'white picket fence' happen for me.

It wasn't the white picket fence or a man but I felt good to be out of my parent's house again. I got out of my car, opened up my trunk, filled my hands with clothes and headed one step closer to independence. I was almost at the front door, savoring the taste of sweet freedom, when Troy stepped out of the bushes, looking as he hasn't slept since I left him; as if he had been living in those bushes. He looked really bad. He had gained about six pounds, in his belly alone. I can see him for what he really was for the first time. I was speechless; his appearance looked nasty.

> "I'm not going to let you get away with tossing me to
> the side. I am here to make it equal. We've got to equal-
> ize the situation," He said.

He reached out and grabbed my hair. Pulling me down to the ground with my things falling all around. Troy was out of control. He pulled me in the opposite direction of my sister's house.

I dropped everything. I got up and fought him. I got away from him and then ran. I made it to the front door. Troy was right behind me, stopping me from closing the door. The entire time I thought, he ambushed me, like something you would see in the movies.

Chapter Four
My Guardian Angel

I ran into the house and was almost at my bedroom door when Troy grabbed me from behind.

"Let's make it equal; we got to equalize the situation."

He dragged me back down the hallway backwards to the front door. He had an excessive compulsive disorder and continually repeated himself.

"We got to equalize the situation."

He was clearly having a nervous breakdown. At that moment, I saw a giant shadow on the wall in the entryway. Troy and I looked up at the same time. It was Toby, my third to the oldest brother. Toby loved making people laugh, but this situation was definitely not a laughing matter. He stood tall and strong like a bodybuilder in Dee's doorway; his shadow on the wall looked like a super hero. He was my guardian angel that day, standing there looking down on Troy and me.

"Man, I can't let you treat my sister like that. She doesn't want to be with you anymore. Let her go and leave."

He only had to say it once, and Troy let me go and left. Toby helped me up, and he had the family trait smirk on his face that all the men in my family possess.

"Jamaica! What have you done to that man and what does he mean by 'let's make it equal'?"

I couldn't answer his question. I didn't know what Troy meant. Maybe he was saying to me, you have taken my life and my world, now I'm going to take yours, and then we will be equal. While I unpacked, Lady Dee, my friend JJ, and Toby laughed loud and heartily, saying "Let's make it equal. We got to equalize this situation," I wasn't laughing as hard because of the look in Troy's eyes. He let me know that rejecting him was a wrong move and our fight was far from over. They didn't know he had threatened to kill me.

As I finished moving in, I couldn't help but think of the good times. I missed him and the way we were before he lost his mind. I imagined what I could say to convince him that it was over. He would never accept the way I lived my life; he would hinder my growth. Some people stay in bad relationships because they're in love with the way things used to be. I don't want to be one of those people. I'm feeling a revelation and wondering what's next for me.

The doorbell rang and I answered. It was Troy. He had calmed down and began acting normal. He thought that Toby may still be here. I hadn't given him my phone number. He wanted to take Little Man and me out for dinner. I said no, and he let me know he was at the hotel around the corner if I needed him. As I struggled to make it through the night without reminiscing, knowing I would call him over, I reached the final conclusion that Troy and I were history.

The morning after, I got the Cadillac ride from hell. Today, I expected Troy to come back. I got dressed and waited for him. He arrived and had cleaned himself up and had changed his clothes. Little Man and I left out with him. I never would have taken Little Man if I had known that he was in any type of danger that could cost him his life. Troy had to stop following me around. I wanted to talk, to find closure, and he wanted me to see his new place. First, we had to go to his old place because he wasn't finished moving. When we arrived, he packed up the last car full of his things and left us there alone. He was gone so long; I went outside and played with Little Man.

I was outside waiting for Troy, and his neighbor walked up with drama, talking loud and acting nosey.
        "What did you do to those two guys?"

"Who are you talking about, Troy and Bay-Bay? Why is it any of your business?"

"I never in my life witnessed two men fight and breakup like two women. Bay-Bay was crying and whining. Troy threw Bay-Bay's things off the balcony; clothes, stereo system, pots and pans, dishes; everything went flying."

I thought that this man told the truth. It sounded like them, but I had never seen them fight.

"Are they both in love with you?"

"I don't know what happened between those two; they love each other like brothers.

"They fought over you," he said and then turned and walked up the street.

I already felt bad; now I felt worse. Troy must really hate me. I know he blames me behind my back for their break-up. They met each other on the beach in Miami, Florida, when they were teenagers and have been together ever since. Now they don't have each other anymore. I can't let them find out I know what went down. Troy returned, and we hung out, riding around in his Cadillac with Little Man sitting up on the armrest between us. We stopped at a red light at a busy intersection. We were in front of the shopping mall, and people were everywhere doing what they do. A yellow car drove through traffic, going full speed, ran the red light and hit us head-on.

All I saw was an obese woman under the wheel. She got out of her car and turned her back to us. I was one of many eye witnesses to her four humongous butts fighting each other for room and board. She reached into her back seat. People ran for cover. As she turned back around she had a rifle in her hands. I was able to identify who this woman was, walking towards my side of the car. Everything was in slow motion, and I had a rifle pointed at my head. It was Troy's stepmom. She hollered and cursed.

"Get her ass out of the car now, Troy!"

I sat there looking down the barrel of a rifle.

"Troy, what have you done? Do something! What are you waiting for; she's after me?" I yelled.

Troy blew his horn, hoping he would create a diversion, but no one else blew their horn. It was completely silent. Everyone waited to see me get my head shot off. Troy backed the car up and then forward. He hit her with the car and knocked her down in the middle of the street; he whirled the car around and drove up the street. He was almost out of her sight when he decided that he wasn't going to run from her. He was going to deal with their problems, right now.

"She doesn't want to kill you; she wants to kill me in front of my son!" I screamed. "Are you crazy?"

Little Man was in shock.

"Troy, take us home, deal with her later."

At that point, he had tuned me out. He pulled the car over and waited. Here she came again, speeding up the street after us and ran right into us, again. This time her colossal butt got out of the car, and she still had the rifle in her hand. Troy got out and went after her, to stop her before she got to me. Troy protected me, and she was mad about that. She stood in the street shouting.

"You better come get your man; he's been sleeping with me anyway. He's been doing me, every night."

She turned the rifle around, held it by the barrel, and tried to hit Troy with it. Finally, Troy lost his cool, took the rifle, and beat her down with it. He left her laid out in a daze on the ground with her rifle. He got back in the car, but I couldn't stand the sight of him. I was sick. I threw up because of what I had heard. I had reached my breaking point. Little Man thought I was going to die. I couldn't calm him down and didn't know where to take him. I held on to him, rocking.

"I'm not going to die. I'm alright."

I jeopardized everything for nothing. On the way home, Little Man went to sleep, and I tried to put it all together. When I left

Troy, he cried on his stepmom's shoulders. They seduced each other at their weakest moments and became lovers. Both of them laid up and got fat together. I didn't recognize her, she had gotten so big. Misery loves company. He knew if he went to her with a broken heart, she would mend it, and he would end up sleeping with her.

Now, he thought we were back together. I'd never go back to that crazy nonsense after this. After today, I was over and done with him. I never saw his new place because he'd been living at her house. She must have followed him earlier when he took his things to her house. He had been with her all the time he begged to get back with me. Troy's father was going to kill him. Troy took me home. I went to my parents' house where Little Man could feel safe. Troy called, but I wouldn't talk to him. He knew he had turned that lady out and got her head messed up over him. I almost got my son killed today. I jeopardized both our lives. I had to regroup.

Everything moved too fast. I had to get rid of that man, but my aching heart wasn't able to stay away. Have you ever needed someone that was bad for you and you were desperate enough to do anything to save him or her from himself or herself? I couldn't live with Troy's, 'If only I had money'. I couldn't live on his words, for they didn't represent me. Troy couldn't be trusted. I couldn't live on good sex alone! There would not be any more rides from hell. Troy was sick and he had everyone around him sick. Troy was history.

Shocking news, shocking visit. That night when I left my house, I didn't see Troy anywhere. I went out of town to J.J.'s house for two days. When I got there, she told me that Troy and Bay-Bay came to her house to kick-it. I was in shock. She told me that they took her out as if they wanted to get to know her better. I don't know what Troy was up to, but J.J. said that she set them both straight. Before I left her house, I called home.

"Have you seen Troy; has he called? Has he come by asking for me?"

They all said, "No" but as soon as I got back and got out of my car to walk to my door, Troy ambushed me again. This time he put a gun to my back, to stop me from fighting back, and told me to walk. Someone let him watch one too many cowboy and Indian stories when he was growing up. He pushed me into his car and kidnapped me. He took me shopping for clothes but wouldn't let me try anything on. Then he took me to a hotel. He beat me again.

> "That's what you get for running. I got to beat you every time you run to show you whose boss. You won't run from me again."

He continued explaining to me that he knew how to beat a woman without leaving any incriminating marks.

> "That's why I never punched you in the face."

But I thought, 'a hit is a hit'.

> "I'll never get arrested so don't try me. It's my word against yours."

He threatened to shoot me the entire time that he talked, in case I tried to get away again. There was nothing sweet about Troy's gangster dreams. His lovemaking was stronger this time because it was forbidden love. He took me against my will. Troy thrived on danger. He felt like he was at the top of his game. He felt powerful having me in his arms. He felt like he had won, in spite of the fact that he was being reckless. He spit his best rap in my ear, well into the night. In those moments, I knew that I was ruined and would never have a normal relationship. I knew, I would search for another lover like Troy for the rest of my life. As perfect and unique as his lovemaking was, his mental state did not connect to his physical capabilities. His word was supposed to have meaning and promises and were supposed to last forever.

I couldn't give up on trying to get away. I wouldn't be his prisoner anymore. Reality had set in, and I was more afraid of him than ever. There was a gun under his pillow.

He laid there dreaming up homemade ghetto gangster flicks with my life. What was I doing there in his crazy world? I had existed in that misery for a reason. Although in the reality of my reality, I had always felt we were put here to be someone's guardian angel, and I might be his. What other reason was there for me being there?

All this running was not my lifestyle. On the third day when I awoke, the thug had left the building for the first time, and his things were still there. I had to move fast; he was coming back soon. I looked down and noticed a diamond ring on my left hand, ring finger. In case the threats didn't work, the bribe would. That was his sick logic. I called my cousin Dwayne. He was somewhat familiar with my situation, and I let him know where I was.

"I'm on my way," He said.

I couldn't call my mom and dad and holler kidnap. I had run away from home many times to be with this man. My cousin picked me up. I took everything Troy had bought for me, but the ring, and ran. He knew how badly I wanted a ring, so it was hard to leave it behind. Troy couldn't afford that big ring; I knew he had robbed his old lady who happened to be his mother-in-law.

I was not going home. That would be the first place he'd look. We drove around until, dark. Dwayne told me it was time to party and took me to my first player's club where the freaks really came out at night. I found a seat at the bar sitting there drinking and listening to wanna-be players and laughing at their rap. They were a disgrace to the players club. I danced out onto the dance floor alone, and my body began to move under the influence of the three deadly combination; pain, alcohol, and drugs.

My dance had gone from innocent to erotic and I was on fire. I escaped my captive, I was emotional, and I felt dangerous. I had plenty of company when I danced my way off the dance floor and back to my seat at the bar. With men all around me, not knowing how to approach me, one man stepped up and took the seat next to me. He didn't ask, "May I buy you a drink?" like the others; he told the bartender to move the other drinks and he helped him. He was a player.

"Is that straight Tequila?" He said.

"Yes, Tequila shots. I'm a big girl; I can handle it."

He ordered two of what I was drinking.

"Are you drinking Tequila, too?" I asked.

"No, I don't drink."

He opened his mouth and let loose the beast in him. I braced myself. His rap was intelligent and well put together. His game was tight. He was definitely a pimp, so, I called him Player. I thought to myself that his rap sounds like letters from guys in prison. They had a lot of time on their hands to read. Player, had that dictionary rap, but he messed up and got nasty with it. I wasn't going to take off my panties and put them in his right pocket or his left, and I wasn't impressed enough to hang around. Yes, I was in a nasty state of mind, but he wasn't my next phase. I wasn't going to waste my time listening. That's what got me in trouble the first time with Troy. As I got up to walk away, he started talking normal. We laughed at his attempt to blow my mind. He cleaned up his conversation and promised that he would stop trying to run his game. He was the first pimp that let me judge his rap. He had a different rap for every occasion. On a scale of one to ten, they were all a ten.

"The one you tried to mack me with wasn't my game, but don't change a thing. If those words don't attract a freak, it wasn't meant to be."

I small talked, but wasn't interested.

"The rap I laid on you wasn't created to get a freak. I gave you my best, created to turn you out and make you mine (prostitution). If you would have done what I asked, you would be."

He made his point. That was how I started my quest to find the best player with the best rap in the San Francisco Bay. He asked me to go outside and smoke a joint in front of the club. We stood outside talking, and all of a sudden we were targets in a drive-by shooting. As I'm laid up under the front bumper of a truck scared to death, I realized my power as a woman, it came as clear as day. I could have had any man I wanted. I walked into the club tonight and all eyes were on me. I had drinks waiting for me on the bar. I turned away, letting them know that I wasn't interested. Men stood around me, waiting for me to choose, and no one got upset. That night, I realized I had the power of choice. I made Troy do things differently; he knew I had him completely whipped. That was it! Troy didn't want me to know my power as a woman, with the power of choice. The shooter wasn't identified. I believed that it was Troy. He could find me anywhere. I had to run for my life, until, I had outrun my enemies. Never tell an irrational man, "Make me fall in love with you."

When I got home, Lady Dee said her boyfriend Carl was coming to town this weekend and brought this brother, Thomas. He was a college football star majoring in law. I had only seen pictures of him; he was always away at college. If he was anything like Carl, he would be charming and fun. The brothers arrived, and I couldn't believe how sweet Thomas was; he didn't talk as much as Carl, and I liked that. Carl played a lot, and Thomas was serious. We were laid back together; it felt right. He knew what he wanted and took his time getting it. He was totally locked in; tonight was all about me. His concentration alone was mind-blowing. We were having such a good time that at the end of the night he didn't want to leave with his brother.

Carl laughed uncontrollably at Thomas because Thomas didn't want to leave me. So, Carl left, going back to The Sac alone.

Thomas and I were hanging out in Dee's room alone with the door open. We were getting to know one another better. My youngest brother, Ray Jr., was in the living room with Lady Dee watching TV. Troy knocked on the front door, and they told him I was busy, to go away. Troy was being persistent, trying to bully his way into the house, but they stopped him.

There was no back door so when he left we thought he was gone for good. I heard something in my room and got up to check it out. Troy had climbed through my bedroom window trying to get to Thomas. I was angry about that, and I had never been so embarrassed. Not only had I been keeping my life a secret, I had been keeping his craziness a secret from everyone, too. I had let this hardcore thug into my life, and now I couldn't get him out without him blowing everything for me. 'The wild cat was out of the bag'. I had to leave Thomas in the room by himself while I went into my room to try and calm Troy down. He was a walking time bomb in my life once again, believing that I was his property after I had left him twice. I had told him that it was over, and he still undressed me. He knew I had company. All he wanted to do was lie down with me, and I let him.

He talked to me. He told me how he felt.
> "I turned you out. I know you want it all the time. I knew it wouldn't be long before you would start wanting to sleep with other men. I was right feeling that way and can't stand the thought of you with anyone else. That's why I asked you to marry me. I want you. I'm here for you when you need love."
> "I want a normal life," I said.

While he and I were in the act of love, his performance got loud. I tried to make him keep his voice down. Everything that's good to you is not good for you. We were finished making up for lost time and Troy wouldn't leave; instead, he went to sleep. I got up and went back into the room with Thomas. I sat on the floor in my sister's walk-in closet and cried like a baby while Thomas watched me. Troy and I had left our mark on each other. It was too much for me to handle mentally. Our craziness had been exposed. Our love/lust for each other had been exposed. Out of everything he had done, I wanted him in my back pocket. I couldn't have my way anymore. His insane ways were no longer my secret and he was no longer my lover. Troy couldn't handle our love, and I couldn't handle breaking up. I felt no one understood what we were going through.

Lady Dee came in and explained things to Thomas. She knew I was too embarrassed. I had a problem with expressing myself to anyone because of the abuse I had endured. I sat there while she told Thomas how Troy and I had been in a long-term relationship. She told him that Troy had been a father to my son, and it was hard for him to except that it was over. We both felt bad that Thomas had to see what was going on between Troy and me. Maybe if I tried to explain to Troy one more time that it was over, he would get it. It was important to make the right decision the first time around when choosing a mate because you could never go back. I wanted to keep Thomas, but I knew that I might lose him. I was devastated right then. The next day everyone was gone except Troy and me. I expressed to Troy that he was the reason we weren't together.

"You have no idea how to make me fall in love with you."

I didn't make my point, he made his. He took a gun out, put it to my head, and pulled the trigger.

My Rude Awakening
Post-it!

To All Yes Men
When a woman says,
"Make me fall in love with you," She means, you must earn her
love by knowing how to create a comfortable environment.
Romance her with episodes of imaginative excitement (Gifts
wouldn't hurt) where we could relax and build a positive, loving
relationship.
To a woman, Make means: create intimacy. Intimacy means:
closeness, understanding.
The confidence that we don't need outsider's opinions, just two
private hearts, with private conversations.
To a woman, Make doesn't mean: control, force, intimidate,
threaten, bully, terrorize, rape or beat.
These are negative things that tears down a relationship.
Get help!

Call 1-800-799-7233, a 24-hour National Domestic Violence hot line. They will talk to you and give you a local number for help.

Men and women express feelings differently. He didn't know what I meant when I said, "Make me fall in love with you." When I heard the gun click, I went into shock and lost my voice. The trigger got jammed, as he tried to shoot me. Troy picked up his shoe off the floor and beating me with it, until, my voice returned. He told me that he was going to get his gun repaired, and that he would be back to finish the job and then, he left. Lady Dee came home, and we called the police. They arrived and told us to get a gun for protection but not to use it until, Troy was in the house.

The policemen laughed, as if something was funny.

"You only got one chance to pull a gun on a man. If you miss, his pride won't let you live. Don't point it at him unless you're going to use it. If you shoot him before he gets in the front door, grab him and pull him in. You got to shoot him in the house. That way you won't get convicted. Come to the station and get a restraining order, it may keep him away. When someone decides to kill you, there's really nothing one can do to stop them," the policeman said.

While both policemen walked out the door, I told the police, thanks for nothing. I thought why they couldn't shoot him and get it over with? I had no idea what to do next. The police were my only hope. When he said that, 'hope' blew up in my face, just like everything else. I was too young to die. Why was Troy tripping so hard? Why didn't my parents say things like, "A woman has the power to drive men insane?" They told me everything else but that. I remembered them saying to keep my dress down, and I couldn't do that. If I was going to die soon, I was not going down without a fight.

Chapter Five
My Death Wish

I was in a dangerous situation. I was in a dangerous state of mind. I was on my way to my other sister BJ's, house to talk to her husband Robert and his stepson, Rob, Jr. I arrived at her house and was upstairs talking and playing around with Rob, Jr., who was home that night from college; his best friend Bow was there, too. The doorbell rang and my brother-in-law answered it, and it was Troy. He told Troy to get away from his house; that he was messing with the wrong family. Troy broke through the door. Robert, Sr. went for his gun, Rob, Jr. and Bow went after Troy, and Troy ran after me. All of us ran up the stairs into different rooms.

Troy ran into the room with me. He closed the door behind us and locked it. Rob, Jr. and Bow plead with me to open the door, but I guess I didn't move fast enough.

"Pops' got his gun. He's going to kill Troy. Rob Jr. said. I can't allow Pops to get involved. Bow and I will take care of Troy. Since he's bad enough to break through a man's door, why is he hiding behind a woman?

"Hey, fool, you're going to die tonight! Why don't you come out and fight a man instead of beating up on a woman. Fight like a man!"

"Troy won't let me open the door!"

"Kick him where it hurts and open the door. Let us take him outside and teach him a lesson. When we get through with him, he'll never bully you again!" Rob, Jr. yelled back.

Troy struggled with me. He threatened to hurt me and tried to stop me from opening the door. Right before my eyes, Troy had a reality check; I got a human reaction out of him. He started pleading for me not to open the door, telling me that two against one wouldn't be a fair fight. Now, he knows what fair means! I wanted to let them beat the crap out of him. I couldn't stop thinking of what would happen after the beating. Rob, Jr. would go back to college, and Bow were nowhere to be found. They couldn't protect me when Troy comes back for revenge.

After being in the room for hours. I had Troy believing that I was on his side. I opened the door, and everyone backed off. They didn't push the issue; instead, they grabbed the issue, took him outside, and handled the problem. They beat Troy so badly, I didn't hear from him. It felt good to finally get some rest. I didn't want to get the people I loved caught up in my fight. I would rather have died than cause someone else to get hurt or die. Troy was not bluffing, kicking in another man's door.

Trust me, when a man tells you, "If you make me mad enough, I will kill you." That man is telling you what to expect, if you make him mad enough. Don't take his threats lightly by laughing in disbelief. Start planning your strategy to handle your defense.
I got myself into that situation, and I world get myself out. That night, Robert, Sr. gave me a gun and showed me how to use it. He loaded the gun for me, and I was ready to use it.

Church folks were people too. The particular public said church folks run to church when they get caught up in their problems. One night, while driving across town, I thought about my son. If anything happened to me he would never know my story. No one would. I hadn't told anyone that Troy wanted to kill me. I let Troy and all these other guys take advantage of me and get away with abusing me. I didn't want my son to grow up hearing about my abuse. He deserved much better than that. I deserved better. Reflecting back, I made a conscious decision to run away from the church, but now I missed it. I had fun, but I missed my friends, uncles, and aunties, nephews, nieces, and all my cousins, and the good times. The next night I went to my parents' church. Before I walked in I made the transition from one world to the next.

I didn't want anyone to see my pain. I had to go correctly. I was all dressed up, even put my girdle on, out of respect. I didn't come to repent, for my heart was too hard. I had some unfinished transgression to complete. My mother didn't raise no hypocrites. It's funny to me, when I hear people say, church folks run to church when they get caught up in sin. Here I was, I could end up killing my lover. I planned the worst type of sin and it was always best to repent rather than follow through. If everyone ran to God when they got into trouble, instead of taking the law into their own hands, the world would be a better place. The joke is on the people that say that.

Everyone doesn't feel remorseful. I am sitting in the service watching my family, listening to my dad and brother jam on their guitars. My dad wasn't just any guitar-man. He drew crowds from miles around, coming to hear the gospel soul sounds his famous guitar threw down. He would pick those strings and make his guitar shriek and holler. Some say he made his guitar speak with the Holy Ghost. He had a southern style. That's what they came to hear; that's what his fans loved the most. I thought this may be my last time seeing them pick those guitars, and my last time seeing everyone else I love. My other brothers and sisters are singing in the choir and beating the tambourines—they tossed one to me. I beat it and made it holler and then tossed it to someone else.

I felt happy and safe in church with my family. All the while, I'm trying to get the strength to deal with Troy. In reality, I'm embarrassed before God and too ashamed to pray for help. I feel like I let Him and everyone else down, for wishing He would give me the strength to put Troy out of his misery—He did it for Samson. The music was stop and go. The people were up and down and I got an unexpected surprise. Troy walked in, ignoring the ushers standing there to seat him. Troy struck a pose at the door until, he spotted me. Then he approached and sat next to me. He's missing the whole concept about who God, Jesus, and

Mary is. He thought something crazy, like, 'Would you look at this pathetic bunch of losers'. Men like Troy probably don't believe in God. They come to church to pick up women. To them, a woman in church is fair game. They're lost and need something or someone to believe in. They need someone to worship and tell them what to do.

Troy already thinks he's "The God of all creation," coming in here thinking he's my savior. He has threatened my life, I don't know how many times. What is he up to now? It means so much to a church girl when she can convert a man. I don't know if I or the beating converted him. I believe it was the beating. I've never seen him in church. All I've done is convert him in bed. I hope he can forgive me for loving him too hard and blowing his mind. I hope he feels remorseful for hurting me...

I called his bluff. He's all dressed up and that caught my attention, and everyone else's too. Troy dressed up for a totally different reason. Troy's here to mack his best game on me. He wants my love bad and I can't help myself. I'm really turned on by his bad boy image. He knows I like it when he acts gangster—but not here. This is not the time or place. He's messing with my head impersonating, 'The Mack'. He idolized that movie and he's putting on a show for me. Troy is sick! Although, we're not together, it feels good to see his face back to normal after the beating. I had hoped maybe the madness was over. He opened up his jacket and showed me his gun. My dad was up talking and Troy told me to get up and walk out, and then threatened me again. I can't believe he tried an abuse tactic in church. First, he intimidates me at both my sister's homes, now, the church? Hasn't he any shame before God; the man doesn't even acknowledge God's house.

> "I'm not going anywhere with you," I whispered, trying to keep a pleasant expression, as I looked around waiting to be judged.
> "I'm a preacher's daughter—respect that!"

89

"Do you want me to take my gun out and start killing people; starting with your parents?" He mumbled. I looked him in his foolish eyes with a secure stare.

"Go ahead and do it, Troy."

Troy sat there a moment. Then he stood up real slow as if he was waiting for me to stop him. I can't lie. I almost panicked when I saw the gun. I wanted to freak out and yell, "He's got a gun. Everyone run for your life." I just sat there and played his game. I called his bluff that time and he understood that I'm on to his devious ways and he left the church. I had hoped he was gone for good. What did Troy say? What did he do? After that service, we had another service to go to. Troy followed. When we arrived, Troy didn't come in, he waited outside for the service to end. He's only here to destroy my life. I can't see him but I know he's here and could be watching my every move. The service was over and people were talking.

Good-hearted people, they hug and kiss one another. After the service was over, I was about to make it to the front door to leave and then Troy became visible. He stood at the front door of the church looking right at me. It was just my luck. I heard a man's voice calling my name from behind. I recognized the voice, it was Gabby and I knew he was coming to hug me. Troy doesn't have a heart, he would never understand that church folks hug and kiss one another. I started signaling to him to warn him not to. Gabby thought I was playing and grabbed me anyway. Troy walked up and said, "Look, man, I heard her tell you not to hug her." Troy forced him outside and I saw Troy telling him off and I hoped he wasn't threatening him.

I stood there thinking, Troy expected everyone to understand, no means no! But him; he was the exception to the rule. Gabby jumped in his car and hit two other cars getting out of the parking lot. I thought, the only thing that could have shocked Gabby that bad, was Troy showing him his gun. Gabby hadn't been around that type of ignorant mentality before meeting Troy. I felt bad for Gabby. I wanted to ask him, "What did Troy say, what did he do?" I couldn't say anything to him and he couldn't say anything to me.

These days the good in Troy is skin-deep. He can only lie and pretend to be a good person to everyone for so long before the bad boy Troy surfaces and has a complete mental breakdown. His superficial side emerges and exposes the ugliness within. After the breakdown, blackout, setback, whatever, he normally goes back to fantasyland acting out a phony nice boy routine again, hoping people accept him as normal or it's no big deal that he has many faces. No one wants to ride a violent merry-go-round that never stops. Troy has lost touch with his dreams. If he can't be phony, living in a make-believe world, he doesn't know who the hell he is at times.

He's crazy all the time, nowadays. At this point, I know he's going to kill me. Right now, I feel like the walking dead. I think he's living in his car most of the time. I know he's not working because he's a full-time stalker wanting to live in my back pocket. He keeps finding me—he shows up out of nowhere in the strangest places. He intently watches my every move. He's convinced that I left him for my baby's father or a church boy—but I don't have anyone because of him. A phony, that's what he is, he keeps telling me I'm going to die. I wish he would kill me now and get it over with.

Post-it!

Every morning, I wake up and ask myself, is this the day I get murdered? As I look back over my life, I find that I haven't accomplished anything. Yet, my spirit is hopeful and tells me to fight. I couldn't respond physically. I gave up all hope. I was too exhausted and embarrassed to fight for myself or ask anyone for help. I felt as if no one cared. I believed everything that was happening to me was somehow my fault. I have been running away from my problems for too long. It's time I faced them one by one. I must take my life back. I've got to face Troy and anything can happen with him. I hope no one is around when fate goes down.

The situation is out of our control. I want to stop feeling like I am on the run all the time and something bad is about to occur. I won't let Troy stop me from living my life. I don't know when he's coming after me again. I'm going to enjoy my life and live it

92

up every weekend. Little Man and I love the beach. Together, we build sandcastles and get our feet wet running away from the waves. We listen to seashells and throw rocks in the water. We feed the birds our food and then go to McDonald's to eat. I spent all day Friday with my son and did all the things he likes. I let him know that he is the most important thing in my life.

Thomas has been writing from college. I haven't had a chance to write him back and he will be here tomorrow. I want everything to go smoothly—there can't be any interruptions this time. I'll party hearty with Thomas, live in the moment, and enjoy myself as much as possible because tomorrow is not promised. It's Saturday morning and Dee and I are getting ready for our dates. We're cooking and cleaning. I can't wait.

Thomas is everything a woman wants in a man. I wish I had met him before I met Troy. I'm not ready, mentally, to move on—I will enjoy him while I can. The brothers arrived and we were ready for whatever. We knew we were in good hands. All four of us jumped in the car and went out to a nice quiet place. We had drinks, good conversations, and excellent company. I messed up and drank too much.

I'm on a sexy high. Somebody passed the joint to me and said it would mellow me out—wrong! I laughed too much, I talked too much, I tried desperately to keep up with the conversation—but I don't know what's going on. The conversation on the way home was hot—joking about how we felt and what we wanted to do next. They thought I was happy. I laughed on the outside. Thomas didn't know I had to get high to make it through the date—to deal with the pain. I thought that he may not want to see me after tonight's behavior. I didn't act responsibly for my actions. The only thing about the night I'm proud of was, after I got wasted, Troy's name didn't come up—not once. I don't think about Troy when I'm with Thomas, so, I know I still have some sense left.

We got home and I invited Thomas to relax in my room. I didn't want the night to end. His body was a knockout. I felt alive in his arms. Thomas had a specific body language that made me feel privileged for every moment he and I was together. His manner and style was patient. He had a whole lot of love and affection for women. I'd never been with a guy that loves to love women all the time. I feel like it's my birthday. Is this the man that's going to love and cherish me and send me to bed singing 'Happy birthday to me' every night? You only run in to this quality of a man once in a lifetime. He's confirmed it. I'm going to die soon. After that night, I couldn't face him again. I wanted him to be mine so badly—but I didn't want to mess his life up with drama. Although, I deserve to be loved, I wasn't ready for love or to love Thomas the way he deserved to be loved.

Chapter Six
A Thin Line Between Love and Murder

Watch out for those thin lines. Our true nature is love. All human emotions fall under love and hate. I have witnessed that hate runs as deep as love. What separates the two is, love has the power of authority over hate. A sick mind, wouldn't know that fact. A sick person can't see thin lines. Their sickness is not strong enough to detect and separate the love from the hate. Troy can't see the power of love. His strongest emotion is hate. He can only see pain. A person like that can kill everything around them and then, kill themselves. He has crossed the line. He hates me and he wants me to suffer; he's my nightmare. Because he has declared war, I know he's somewhere plotting how he will do it.

Troy's home address is in hell. We all left out that morning. When I returned home later in the evening, Troy was in my room sitting on my bed and my bed sheets were pulled back. I hadn't changed the sheets from last night.
"You haven't any right to be here." I said.

I got angry and he got angrier. Heaven forbid, I get angrier than him. He has to top everything I do and every emotion I have. Anyone can get mad and act a fool, stable people don't act that way. I'm indispensable and he knows that, but that don't mean a thing when you're facing a crazy person that wants you dead. Troy can't stand how cool I am right now; he wants me to be afraid. I won't act a fool, and I want be his fool.

I got my gun out of my closet. I pointed it at him and he took it from me. He pointed it at me and pulled the trigger. There aren't any bullets in the gun, he had found my gun and emptied it out. He threw my gun onto the bed and showed me the bullets that were in his pocket. I told him to get out and don't come back. But before he left he had to have the last word.

"I know what you've been doing. If I can't have you no one will, you're not going to be with anyone."

He turned and left. If you asked Troy where he lives, he should say 666 Fire Pit Lane, in hell, because he wants to be a bad person, and he lives in misery.

Looking back, I knew that Troy had a legacy of problems. Troy's troubles were bigger than what I could see. It's him against me, life or death, he has become my biggest problem. I'm spending this weekend with my parents. Friday night, I cooked dinner for everyone. We sat down at the table and enjoyed each other's company, reminiscing about old times. I'm cherishing every moment. I tried to accept death mentally. How does one accept death? My spirit won't acknowledge it and is telling me it's not my time, don't give up, fight! A person has to be on the highest ego trip in the world to take someone's life away from them and their loved ones. It's such a selfish act to take your own life or someone else's because you can't handle life or have the one you love.

That's why you should always ask questions. Act as your private detective. Troy never talked about his parents. He never calls his dad on the phone; that's not normal. I should have investigated sooner. I found out a lot when I started snooping. My mind hasn't settled yet from what I uncovered in his closet. I never confronted him about drugging me to keep me there. Some people have a legacy of corruption and need to be on medications and locked up, locked down, or locked away; whatever fits his problem. I'm suffocating. Facing up to the evidence that he's going to kill me. My mom asks me to go to Friday night service and shut-in with them. That's when you consecrate yourself to a Divine life. You pray for power for the purpose of conquering unwanted spirits. They stay in the church all night fasting and praying.

I said, "No, but take Little Man."

I knew what I was doing. Troy knows where my parents go on Friday nights. I know he's watching. I can't put it off any longer.

Tonight is the night. I want it to be him and me alone. It's going to be ugly. To have a human hate you so bad is suffocating. The thought of him trying everything in his power to take my life has suppressed me. The fear alone shuts down your body and the anger is eating away at my mind. I am so weak, I don't know who I am anymore. I thought I was too young and too cute for any man to kill me.

When my parents left, I broke down, thinking about all the bad luck and the relentless attacks of abuse, that I have to die this way. What did I possibly do in my life that was so wrong? I am alone, no one knows my despair. I'm at a disadvantage and the results may be the loss of my life. All my life, damage has been done to my mind, my body, and soul. I have drawbacks, set-backs, and issues, plus I'm a lover, not a fighter. If Troy feels like his life is over, why kill me? Why doesn't he kill himself and get it over with?

I got an urgent knock on the door. I looked out the window. It's Troy with his back to the door, making sure no one is looking while he's scheming.
    "What do you want Troy?"
    Troy cried.
    "My father is dying, I need you. You're the only one who cares," he said. "You're the only one that knows me, Jamaica."

I thought, 'he's crazy'. I know him. I have loved him and he treats me bad. Now, he has reached a new low. Is there no end to his illness? Now, he's lying and using the only parent he has left. He shows no sign of having a relationship with his father. For all I know, he can already be dead, I've never met him and he's begging me to open the door. I ran to the phone and called my mother.

"Don't open the door, it's a trap," she said.

"Mom, I can't help myself, he needs me. I got to open the door."

"Don't open the door. We'll be home in the morning."

I hung up the phone walked over to the door and opened it. As soon as the door was opened wide enough, Troy put his gun to my head.

"Step out of the house and lock the door. You'll never see this house or your parents again."

I thought, "Fine! OK. Shoot me and get it over with. I don't want to see your face anymore." I am helpless. I can't express my anger. I can't talk to him. How will I be able fight him for my life? He's a crazy man. He has kidnapped me for the umpteenth time. I can't look him in the face and call his bluff, he's not bluffing. This is real. This is it. I'm going to die. In the hotel room, I had a near death moment. Troy drove twenty-five miles to a dark hotel. I thought, 'how many numbers of women has he killed? Will he add me to his list'? We walked in the room.

"Take off your clothes and get in the shower. Leave the shower door open."

He watched me take a shower for the last time. He walked over to the towels, picked one up and handed it to me.

"Lay across the bed," he said. He took the gun and rubbed my body up and down with it. Troy acted even stranger than his usual strange behavior.

Later he began to say his good-byes.

"I'm going to kill you first, then kill myself because I can't live without you."

I hadn't said a word from the moment he put the gun to my head at my parent's house. I haven't anything more to say to him. He doesn't deserve to hear my last words. In the room, my soul doesn't belong to me anymore. It belongs to Troy. I am waiting for death to happen.

A Higher Power entered the room and calmness fell around us and I felt more powerful and confident than ever. My God given authority and power that humans possess, gave me the strength to look Troy in his face. I witnessed Troy's condition with my own eyes. Troy's face had taken on the form of a demon, I saw in his book. Troy's voice changed and he spoke a different language.

Troy didn't know what was happening. Although killers will lie, I believe it when a killer says, "I don't remember committing the murder. I don't know what happened; I blacked-out."

I was having a near death moment. My life passed before me with two revelations. As time froze in the room, I was taken back to when I was four years old at home with my mom. Everyone else was at work or school. I'm following my mom around the house imitating her, doing my version of helping her clean. Every day at twelve noon, my mom would stop cooking and cleaning and went down on her knees to pray. I would join her, and everything she promised God, I would promise Him.

I was too young to remember making those promises. God doesn't forget promises and He had revealed that my mom taught me to pray for what I wanted. I promised Him that I always would. My second revelation, as my life passed before me, I was seven years old, my sister Dee was fourteen, we were in church service. Dee got sick and wasn't responding. My parents came over and began to pray for her life. I stood there as this seven year old child prayed to God for my sister to live and finally she spoke. My past revealed the knowledge to save my life from Troy's murder-suicide attempt and I was guided away from death's door; it wasn't my time to die.

This incident was memorable. I witnessed what happened to Dee with my own eyes. Dee had died. I was too young to fully understand why it was meant for me to see. That night in the room, I understood the power of God. We all have the authority my parent's had. Human authority controls power over any other power here on earth. When you understand that, and believe that you can handle anything in life, you can conquer life's situations. My parents are believers. I have to believe in my prayers like I did that night, praying for my sister without a doubt or any hesitations, or else Troy would kill me, and then himself.

I was alone with my enemy. I didn't have any other choice but to stop, listen, and learn. Before all this happened, my pain tried to tell me that God was making me strong in all life situations. Life's revelations come when it's time for us to grow. Seeing that my entire life had prepared me for this moment, blew me away in that room. Everything came together like a chain reaction. I wasn't lost in that moment. I was challenged and made to remember who I am and where I come from, and I had to represent and I didn't hesitate. I began to pray with authority, alone with my mom and dad, as my intercessors praying all night at church. My prayers got louder, with conviction, until, I passed out. When I woke up, I was on the bed. Troy didn't have the face of a demon and he was no longer my enemy. He was himself and sitting in an easy chair. The gun was lying in the corner by the door. Troy picked up his gun.
"Are you ready to go home to be with your family?"
I answered a simple, "Yes."

I didn't have words for Troy or to express at that moment. We are all individuals. We go through different experiences that are meant for us to learn. Mind blowing miracles happen to save us from ourselves and others. No terminology could express my feelings, Troy didn't say a word. It's obvious he's alright. Both of us are trying to take it all in, I was still playing it over and over in my mind. I got back to my parent's house and went to sleep. I awakened happy to be alive, but I wasn't ready to commit to the person that I became in that room. Being that strong person in the room was the person that I was taught to be. I didn't understand that I had found myself in that room and being that

100

person worked for me. 'If it isn't broke; don't fix it'. I wasn't getting it.

I needed to figure out if that was the real me. I wasn't convinced I was searching for something else; perhaps a different way of life than my parents. I had breakfast with my parent's. I talked to my mom about the night before and they left for the day. Dad took mom to see her Optometrists Dr. Smith, she complained that her eyes was runny and blurred. Little Man and I were there alone. I heard a knock on the door, looked out the window and its Troy. I opened the door and he walked into my parent's house for the last time. Troy had come to say goodbye, he's moving back to Texas, his hometown.

"Please don't hate me, Jamaica Gold," he said and walked out of my life.

I had to write about my first love in my journal. It was one of the hardest experiences I ever had to write, but I had to get it out.

Goodbye My First Love

You discovered my innocence.
I was young and beautiful.
You felt my texture was soft as silk.
Far as the eyes could see,
at the peak of love, you asked me
to be yours. I said, "Yes,"
and you became my weakness,
my husband to be.
I trusted you with my life.
We were the best of friends
as well as lovers.
I was soon to be your wife.
You told me
I was everything
you wanted in a woman
to be happy.
Seeing I was a warm person
with class and style, looking at me
you were watching your sun rise.
Your soul felt love and, for the first time,
you laughed and you smiled.
I said, "Yes" for years
and didn't realize it.
Pleasing you made me happy.
It was what I wanted to do.
I agreed all those times
because it was something
I believed in. I wanted to believe in you
I want you to know we had those things
in common, we both were grown.
I wasn't trying to live up
to your expectations, I had my own.
Outside of our bedroom world,
my life you tried to control.
I disagreed for the first time
and you hit me.

You went crazy when I said
"No,"
Then you tried different ways
constantly to destroy my
loving soul.
I was no longer satisfied or content
because I found our love wasn't heaven sent.
I was miserable and confused
when I discovered I had been used and abused.
How could you hurt me after all the love I gave?
Why do I feel guilty?
You're the one with the problem!
I'm the one needed to be saved!
You told me that you needed me
that you were sorry things happened
that way.
You told me
you would never again lay a hand on me.
Then you begged me to stay.
I was still too in love
to see it was all a trap
to win control, to drive me insane
so you can capture my passionate soul.
You told me I had a peaceful
love that was easy going and forgiving.
Loving me was the perfect dream.
You hoped that moment
could last forever.
But that was just another scheme.
I felt like a child again
trying desperately
to jump off a merry go round
going full speed up and down.
I was definitely aware
leaving could cost me my life.
You tried to take mine
many times before.

You told me I would never
be happy without you.
I took no time to argue the point.
I had no life with you anymore.
I stood on my own two feet,
boldly talked up to you, anticipating,
preparing the moment I walked out the door.
Now I'm happy
being free from your bondage and threats.
The bond is broken.
You can't force me to love you.
I'm not your token.
You always protected me from
the world's confusion.
Now,
I need the world to protect and
keep me from your delusion.
Goodbye My First,
Sweet, Bitter, Love.

I should have been happy. But instead, I felt abandoned and immediately went deeper into depression. Later, I began to realize that I've been too busy running from him to notice it's been awhile since I've run to him to comfort me. I've been handling my problems on my own. I convinced myself that I am strong enough to make it through my life's disappointments. Face facts, it wasn't my time to die, but to learn from my past mistakes. I've been given another chance to live and move on. Some people come into our life and stay forever. Others cross our paths for us to help. While another will show up to teach whatever it is we need to learn to get to our next level. Some make it, some don't. The people that never learn are left behind and they're not all bad people just, slow. We call it bad luck. Troy came into my life when I needed him the most. Companionship needs common ground. He couldn't live on my level and neither could I live on his. He couldn't catch up and I wasn't going backwards for the rest of my life.

From the beginning, Troy and I began falling apart trying to force a relationship that wasn't meant to be forever. Our time together is over; people have to know when to say goodbye. I got the second chance many women don't live to see. Right now, I can't grasp all there is for me to understand in order to move on. I'm relieved he's gone and I have to take it one breath at a time these days, like an addict coming off drugs.

Today, I got up to drive Little Man over to my parent's for his father to pick him up. Afterwards, I got ready to leave my parent's house and there's a knock on the door. I looked out the window, "Oh my God! It's Bay-Bay. What's he doing here?" I open the door and he is standing there, looking lost without Troy. We definitely have something in common. We missed the good times the three of us had, thinking it would last forever. We lived together in an era that every song that came on the radio was a hit love song. The words to the songs had a positive message that brought us together.

Living in the ghetto was fun. Every person, place, or thing was a trip. We were forever tripped out on weed and tripping hard about love. We were young, beautiful, and hot. We enjoyed one another's company before things went wrong. We loved the way we each looked in our clothes. We never got into any trouble with the law. We had our own law and that broke all the rules for love. We were in our own cool world before it blew up. Saying goodbye was not easy.

When we are young, we don't know ourselves. We can't see ourselves the way other people see us. We see that we're inadequate; we see our failures, faults, and weaknesses. When looking at ourselves in the mirror we see our inner insecurities. In a nut shell, we are able to see our fears. You don't really start to appreciate beauty until, you're much older, because then you're happy to be alive. You've conquered most fears and are able to look in the mirror, ignoring whatever doubts you have left about your appearance. You stop reacting to life's frustrations, disappointments, and insecurities. You've learned to take the bitter with the sweet. You work on your looks to stay young and live life to the fullest, instead.

Somehow, some of us find comfort in our features. We know and accept who we are from the inside out. The one's that never grow up, never stop reacting to insecurities and never appreciate how they're aging. I am happy to see Bay-Bay; I needed a crutch. I need to talk to someone that can feel me. I'm one of those people looking for the next person to make me a better person and that doesn't work for long, if it works at all. I have gone through more experiences with men than my friends. I can't talk to them right now. Things went further than I expected and Bay-Bay knows where I'm coming from, he was there. Bay-Bay knows to come clean with me. He knows what I want to hear and, couldn't wait to tell it. He told me everything that's been happening, more than twice. He said, Troy was run out of town by his father. I know he didn't make that up, because I saw it coming. Bay-Bay and I sat up all day and night reminiscing.

We started out at a Chinese bar & restaurant. We drank in the bar. We moved on to the dining room of the restaurant and ended up at a hotel. I played his game and he played mine, right into each other's arms. Being with Bay-Bay made me feel closer to Troy, although, they are two totally different men, like night and day. Bay-Bay doesn't like how Troy treated me, but he's the only one who knows how Troy really felt about me. He's my witness that Troy tried to change his life for me. Troy and Bay-Bay were also guilty of looking for someone else to make them a better person. Although, Troy and I didn't make it, Bay-Bay will always show me love and respect. That's why I answered his curiosity for me that night. Bay-Bay wanted me and I felt the vibes long before I looked out the window and saw him earlier today. Bay-Bay had lost a friend that was like a brother to him. Somebody was going to pay, and Bay-Bay had come to collect. I felt that we both were getting back at Troy. We both loved Troy and he wasn't able to handle life and pushed our relationship with him too far. We loved each other for one night, that's all we needed. We gave each other something to remember the way we were, lived, and loved. He dropped me off the next day and walked out of my life forever.

I knew that all men like Troy can dish it out, but can't take it. The whole experience of knowing Troy left me a lot more knowledgeable about men and myself. I know how to separate the men from the boys. After Troy and Bay-Bay, I started telling men how I expected them to love me. Unaware that they felt less than a man when they weren't experienced enough to deliver. I started telling men the same lies they told, unaware, I would make them cry.

I gradually started rapping to men using their lines. If you can't beat them join them. That's when I found out I could beat them at their own games and tactics, it was too easy. It wasn't my plan to be a player, it was an invitation, and I was game. I looked for love in all the wrong places. Men thought that I was being too forward. They were getting choked from my smoke. I wasn't getting attacked by men anymore and I was still depressed.

I stopped having to fight them off physically. I was dogging them mentally. I didn't realize I was being abusive. I had been hurt and I was angry with men. I have a death wish for any one of them to put me out of my misery, fast. It doesn't matter whom. I've been in a war with abusive men, a shock therapy kind of love affair resulting in offensive earthquakes and after effects to the mind, shaken, but alive. I have someone in my life that keeps me rational and stable. Without him, I would flip out at any minute. I'm in yesterday's pain and I just want to run away from everything and everyone. I won't leave the people that love me, I won't leave my son, to grow-up believing that I left because I didn't want him. Children always blame themselves and none of this is his fault.

The reason for leaving would be, I'm tired of living and dealing with the liars and pretenders. I'm letting it stop me from concentrating on me and mine and being a better person. When Little Man and I spend time together, I talk to my son and I teach him a lot. He is my little star and entertains me with the funny things he does. Every night that we're together, he tells me he loves me. I didn't teach him to say that and I miss that when he's not here. I can't stand the silence. I create poetry and I write in my journal. I write about his life which keeps me way out of mine, he keeps me sane. I don't let him see I'm depressed and it's scary. I don't know how long I can hide my dark side from him.

Little Man's World

Looking in your eyes
Listening to you talk
I am in another world, your world.
You bring happy feelings to a confused world.
When times are hard, you make me smile.
You always know to put your arms
around me giving me a big hug and kiss
every night you never forget to say
"Good night, Mom! I love you"
I realize I have you to raise
All your questions to answer.
Son, being a little person is not easy.
I feel like I want you to know everything
and no one will hurt you.
But no one knows the changes of life
how they're going to hold on to the laughter
and pain.
As you grow, remember to cherish
the love I gave and you'll never give up
your love for life.
Love is the key, Son.

I called over to Mom's. I wanted to speak with Little Man to let him know, I am coming to get him. Mom answers. I'm sitting in the bathtub, soaking, talking to her on the phone, feeling broken down and I start to cry.

"I can't do this alone."

She takes a deep breath.

"Many women that have a man living in the home are doing it alone," she explained.

Little Man never knew how much I hated his dad but I had never told anyone. I didn't get Little Man caught up in our mess. A woman will keep secrets because she feels she has to make everyone happy and she forgets about herself. I put Little Man first. His dad wasn't mature enough to do that. When you have a son, it's not wise to put his father down and tell the child all his father's problems and mistakes or say he's nothing but a loser, or whatever, without telling him the good qualities and attributes. Your child may not be strong enough to rise above hearing his or her father's mistakes and become something in life. When it's a girl, it could hinder her from having respect for men and developing trust in a relationship. All children need someone to look up to, don't destroy that. Sell them a dream and let them dream it. Some families are cursed with jealousy, where the adults talk against other family members, competing and comparing, teaching the child to look up to them only. They go to great extremes to get their children to like them best. When you make them think you're the better parent or adult, your child has no one to turn to or look up to when you make a mistake or fail.

I'm far from perfect. I taught my son to love family, allowing them all to have a loving relationship with my child. I want him to have a family of people to run to and get support from, that love him most, when I let him down. If you don't do the same, the relationship with your child may suffer the consequences in the future. I couldn't take my anger out on Little Man or his dad, but I did take it out on other men, left and right.

Chapter Seven
Bad Girl Behavior

My bad behavior got wild and crazy. What helped me to see myself for what I had become happened one night when a new friend Parker called and asked me to celebrate his birthday with him. I promised that I would, but I spoke too soon. He got to my house on his birthday, and I was entertaining an old friend. Dressed in a skimpy outfit with money stuffed in all my nooks and crannies. I answered the door with Diana Ross,' 'Private Dancer' playing in the background. I had been dancing in the middle of the floor for hours. My date sat on the sofa watching me. We drank and smoking marijuana, having fun, escaping from the madness.

I had double booked. I hadn't forgotten, but I was hoping he had forgotten his date with me. I had hoped I would get stood-up by him when someone more fun came along. The birthday guy was excited and ready to party when he walked in and saw my first date got all the action. What can I say? First come, first served; the early bird gets the worm. I turned the birthday boy away. Before he walked out the door, I made a sly remark.
>"Come back tomorrow, I promise to show you a good time."

I didn't actually think he would. After he left, my date joined me in the middle of the floor. Dancing was all I had. I would close my eyes and lose myself, not caring anymore about who I hurt. I was a private dancer, dancing for the money, one man at a time.

The next night when the belated birthday boy arrived, we were having a good time, until, I wanted to see more of what I was dealing with. I told him to strip down and make tender love to me because that was how I liked it. I came across too strong. When I said make love to me, he got quiet. I looked down and noticed he wasn't aroused anymore. I didn't know that it was possible for a young man to have this problem.

"Don't I turn you on, birthday boy?" I asked him seductively.

"Are you crazy? Yes! I have never been with an experienced woman. You're the first. What if I let you down? What if I'm not good enough?"

The entire time he talked, tears streamed down his cheeks. I scared tears out of him! He brought my high down; I felt like a dirty old woman, and we were the same age. I was on a bad girl high, feeling good. Now, I felt really bad, and that left me thinking. I took him by the hand and sat down.

"You're beautiful just the way you are. It's not you, it's me."

I told him; something a guy would say to a woman. The entire ordeal helped me to understand why many men say what they say and do what they do. Are you ready for this? They have feelings! They've been hurt and they're lost in the pain, too. They don't have time to nurture yours. They're trying to survive the game, which allowed life to push them into dogging women out. Sound familiar? I won't be a part of that statistic.

I apologized to my birthday boy.

"Forgive me. I would appreciate you for being a sensitive gentleman, if I wasn't so messed-up right now."

I felt terrible for him and hoped I hadn't hurt his pride as mine had been hurt. It would be too bad for the next woman that he would encounter. After I rocked him to sleep, I sat up thinking about everything that happened last night and tonight. I know this is a sign for me to slow down. Right there, starting then, I would be celibate. I went from celibate to promiscuous.

Ask me how old I was? I was club-age. The Ship is a restaurant on the marina where I had been hanging out with my friends. At night, it turns into a nightclub and we would have to leave. The night I turned twenty-one, the guard held up my ID at the door and announced my birthday to the crowd. I couldn't believe he broadcasted my business like that. I yelled to the crowd.

"I'm club age."

They couldn't send me home to mommy anymore. I took my parents there for dinner. I wanted to impress them, and let them know where I was clubbing, "Right?" I thought, I took them somewhere they haven't been. They never dined at any restaurants on the marina before, or so I thought. Anyway, there's this really long road you drive up, to get to the marina. It feels like a crazy but fun roller-coaster ride. For fun, picking up speed has you flying out of your seat. We laughed.

When you sing, it makes your voice sound funny. I sang, "Row, row, row your boat." I tried my best to get them to join in, but they didn't roll like that. I wanted them to experience the valet treatment. When he walked out to park our car, my dad really enjoyed that. I enjoyed my parents' southern style, and I impressed them after all. I paid the bill, and we left. They both felt a little better about my nightlife.

I received a call later that night; from Benny Gee, I had met him while playing tennis at the college. He was from the dirty south, living in California on a football scholarship and trying to make it to the pros.

"I'm not asking you for a date; I just want to hang with you on the weekend. You know, walk, talk, and feed our faces." He doesn't know many people here.
"Yes, I'll hang."

He was younger, but just for fun, I decided to go. Getting dressed for my young date took me back to when I was a little girl, hanging-out in the neighborhood. Boys would ask me to go to the playground, and I would ask, "You got ice cream money?" I wanted to ask him the same thing. He seemed so young.

He picked me up in a hooptie. We started the non-date driving around talking and listening to music. We walked around the mall eating junk food that he paid for. I'm hooked on Blue Chip cookies; I had to have them every day. I expect cookies on every date. After we'd had dinner and cookies, my non-date and I ended up at my house. I let him get comfy on the sofa. I had to be cautious who I let in my house. Boys will be boys. I control how far the date will go. I have learned that there are different types of guys. Some guys are laid back and waited for me to make the first move.

Some assume sex; that's if they get their foot through the door. Another type, if I let them stay later than midnight, they start to assume that sex is on the menu and an offer to stay the night. I hadn't met the boys who got sex and then left. I had problems getting rid of boys. I was into cooking and kissing. Girls like to make out; guys think making-out is a tease. Guys want sex, period. It doesn't matter what time it is, in their minds there's always time for sex. I wanted to be friends with boys. I was the let's-be-friends type.

I never met a guy like I was dating that night. I didn't know any males with the, 'let's have a non-date.' Trying to get out of paying for a date and wanting sex at the end of the night. A woman doesn't owe you sex, whether-or-not you buy her dinner. That may work wherever he comes from, but, trust me, in California, guys are bold and most had their game on, but I had never gone out with one who doesn't want to pay. California men asked for what they wanted or took it. My date found me attractive, but he couldn't ask for it. The reason why he hasn't approached me sexually was that he doesn't have the California game that I was use too.

114

I haven't approached him because he wasn't aggressive; he was being a nice jerk. He wants to lie in my bed and have sex. When a man is serious, he talks; when he's attracted to me, he's patient. When I'm ready to take it to the next phase, he's satisfied. My non-date was emotional like a girl. His feelings got hurt when he heard the word "No." I refused him because we don't know each other, and he doesn't express his feelings with words. For fun, I showed him my skills. I went into my rap.

> "Baby, I love whole heartedly. Until, you feel me, I will keep undying love for you to me. True feelings run wild and free, captivating the back of my mind, hiding fantasy sex dreams of the day you tell me, 'baby you're the one for me.' Turning hidden dreams of sex fantasies a romantic reality."
>
> "Did you make that up? Let me hear more. A woman has never rapped to me," he said.

I wasn't rapping to him, I was pretending to be a man rapping to a woman, and he didn't get it. I said, goodnight to my non-date before twelve. He still wasn't ready to leave me, he wanted to hear my rap, and I wanted to hear his. I was spoiled. He wasn't telling me where he was coming from. I got up and took him by the hand to walk him to the door. His comfy time was up.

Regaining self-worth is liberating. He stood up and started a make-out marathon. He was too late. Our non-date was over. Benny tried to force me down on my sofa. I snapped, picked him up, and threw him to the door, shocking both him and me.

> He yelled, "Girl, do you know what you just did? You picked up a two hundred and forty-pound football player! You're cock-strong, girl! You're cock-strong!"

That was my defining moment. I felt empowered. He looked at me with a serious expression on his face trying to figure me out.

> "You can tell me what happened. Someone did something really bad to you, huh? I'm sorry I scared you. Come here. I wasn't going to hurt you," he explained, holding me in his arms.

"I'm a long way from home, and I don't want any enemies. I can't let trouble cause me to lose my scholarship. We cool?"
"Yes, we're cool."

After that night, I sat home contemplating, "Did he
want me to give him private lessons? Maybe, he wanted
me for his sex toy. Did he choose me to lie up with;
keep his belly fed until, he got through school?"

He wasn't going to run me crazy. Remember, how Troy treated
his older woman? He stole her ring and put it on my finger. That
messed me up from getting with younger guys. He came by a
couple of times after that, but I never let him in. I didn't know
what he was after. He was a fish out of water that needed to go
back to the dirty south. He wasn't my next phase.

When you can't read a guy, keep your distance. If a guy does
not confess feelings of love, but is trying to have sex, he's up to
no good.

I got just what I needed from him, when he allowed me to manhandle him. Thank God, he took it like a gentleman. The whole
situation helped me regain my self-worth, which I felt was gone
forever. Benny Gee made it to the pros, and many nights I sat
up watching him. I was thankful, and I knew our paths crossed
for a reason.

I had been liberated. Whenever you've been treated like an animal, sooner or later you learn to fight back. When you have
been lied to, lied on, and looked down upon by abusive men,
especially your baby's daddy, it affects every aspect of your life.
I don't care who you are. I was robbed of my womanhood. I
wanted my self-worth back. I don't know how long it would
take, but now I know that I could fight back, I wouldn't let any
man take my body again.

I missed having a man. I hung out four nights a week at the players' clubs and listened to their distorted minds. I was all about a party. I literally didn't have anything going on. I was non-stop recreation and entertainment; that was my recuperation since Troy left. I fall through the door, and all eyes are on me. I don't wait to be asked to dance, I get up and start my art of dancing moves and let the boys fight over who's going to win or lose a dance. I danced until, the last call for liquor, until, the last dance of the night. I closed my eyes and slid my body left to right; letting the music carry me through my pain.

As long as I moved, I felt alright. I danced like I live my life, one step forward and two steps back. I danced fifteen records straight, going in circles, like my life, not knowing where my head was at. If I sat down, my table was filled with drinks and my head filled with misery and strife. I missed Troy's face. I kept looking for his features in the crowd. I missed having someone in my life who knew how to make mad, passionate love to a woman and keep sexual fantasies alive.

I lied to get rid of a man, not to get one. Another reason I was celibate was the hostility that I had towards men. In the club, my cold shoulder kept me celibate and stopped altercations. I danced off aggression. I would go home soaking wet. The next day my voice was gone, and I could barely move my fingers. I hung out with girls my age, and we lived for the after-hour clubs. That was how long it took to make up our faces and put our blue jeans on. We helped each other to pull them up; one pushed in the booty, and the other zipped them up.

We were party chasers. We went across every bridge in the bay area, from Reno to Los Vegas to L.A. and back. We were all in the same boat, learning how to handle guys and how to discipline the way they acted. We thought up all types of lies to get rid of them. That's what we felt we had to do. One night in L.A., I gave a guy JJ's name, as JJ stood right there. I lied about my occupation, and then gave him the right phone number.

I laughed and said to JJ, Coco, and Nicky, "He's cute, I can get into that."

We laughed because if he does call, he's going to find out that I was a liar. I was learning the ropes. My sister, Jazzy Black, and her girls were older and more experienced with handling guys. I know, because Troy and I used to party with them. Now that I'm older and still single, I couldn't wait to go clubbing with them and learn the ropes. Knowing what to say and how to say it was important. Being sarcastic with a crazy man could get you hurt.

I'll never forget, one party night in particular, while dropping off Little Man, I had a conversation with my dad.

"Dad, I'm going to Union Square where white people clubs and mixed crowds are rocking with 'Donna Summers' back to back."

Dad said, "Stay out of San Francisco Square. It's too fast for you; someone may hurt you or you can end up dead."

"Dad, if that happens, it's my time to die."

I hugged him and drove off. I wondered if he knew that was the drug talking. That same night. I was in a club in Union Square having fun until, I told a black guy, "You're not my type. I don't want to talk or dance with you. Bye-bye." He followed me around the club, mad and calling me yuppie names. He kept interrupting my conversations with white guys while talking loudly and crazy. The white guys sat back and watched me dance, but they wouldn't rap to me. I was dying to hear if they had a rap. At the end of the night, the crazy guy followed me to my car, blowing off steam. I stopped when I got to my car and gave him my final refusal.

"No, you can't make me give you my phone number, go away!"

He went off, and his reactions surprised me. He acted as if I owed him something,

"Do I know you?"

"Oh, now, you don't know who I am?"

"Did I stutter?"

He pushed me onto my car. I unlocked the door and got in the driver's seat. He grabbed my hair so I couldn't close the door.

"You gave me a wrong name and number at Freaky Monday's in Oak Town. Now, I want the right number. I've been hearing your real name all night, Jamaica Gold."

Some Oakland guys are crazy, always domineering and bossing you around. They were so dramatic. I pulled off slowly not to hurt him, but he acted a fool, running along with the car, trying to pull me out by my hair, while still asking for my number. I put my foot on the gas and picked up speed. He had to let go or die. Just to shake him, I stop hanging out there for a minute. Being sarcastic with a crazy person is not a good idea.

Party! Party! Party! Every woman deserves her moment in time. I started going out with the older crowd; they're more laid back, without as much drama. The first night we went to Jazzy Black's college dance with her friends. They couldn't believe how laid back we were and how we quietly checked things out. As if dancing wasn't my thing. I got on the dance floor and turned it out, one older guy at a time. My personality adapted, and my anxieties disappeared. I enjoyed moving to the spirit of an older crowd. The very first night with them I tried to pace myself while drinking. Every time my sister ordered a drink, I ordered a drink. By the end of the night, I was drunk, but still in control, as she got more and more sophisticated.

I stopped dancing and studied how she worked the room. She looked beautiful as she captivated the room with her unique manner and elegant glow, as she danced the night away. She was a natural. I named her, 'Sophisticated Drunk'. Jazzy Black partied the same way she lived her life, like an educated woman.

That alone kept the trashy men off her. Her style intimidated them. She had her moment. It was her time to shine. Some women miss their moment. Some will never feel the high of capturing the attention of a room. They haven't experienced what power the true essence of a woman can achieve, or what it's like to be admired by everyone around you. Some women are fortunate to have looks and brains; their moment is on the job or in a classroom. Some are fortunate to have looks, fortune, and fame and enjoy life in their moment. I have danced in my moment, with eyes closed or eyes wide open. I've thrown my hands up, and I have captured the moment. I have chosen the finest man in the room and he has chosen me. I have danced until, the dance surrendered to that moment with no regrets. I have cried happy and sad tears in my moment. For some women, their moment may last for just a season; for others a lifetime. Whenever I have a moment, I cherish it because I don't know how long my moment will last.

I know my style, but I had to perfect it. I couldn't wait to go out with Jazzy Black again. I was working on my image. First, I envisioned all the women whom I admired in my life, keeping in mind their different aspects. I wanted perfection that would catch a different type of man. To me, two people who are the same are boring. I like it when opposites attract, when they're both positive people. My sisters and the women on both sides of my family are sharp dressers, and they had their styles. I like ethnic styles and designs. I was ten years old, the first time I walked into my brother, Cool and his wife Angie's, house. It was mind blowing. I thought I was in Africa. It was everything I had envisioned Africa to be in my mind and more; it was me. From all these people in my life, my distinctive style evolved.

The more I perfected my style. I influenced ethnic class into everyone's life around me. The next time Jazzy Black picked me up, I was Jamaica Sensation, African style, baby. I couldn't wait to get to the club and show off me. As soon as we walked in, we went our separate ways. I thought to myself, okay that's different from partying with girls my age when we would babysit one another. I didn't get a table with Jazzy, I danced straight onto the dance floor. The men formed a circle around me complimenting my every move, one dance at a time.

It was standing room only. I couldn't see a thing. The ladies found me when it was time to leave. I wasn't hard to find. Jazzy looked for the circle of men, and there I was, in the middle, lost for time. Men followed us as we exited the club, and I was about to panic. Jazzy turned around and said with confidence,
    "She came here alone, and she's leaving alone!"

She got rid of them without wasting anyone's precious time, Jazzy Black had skills. That stopped men dead in their tracks. That's what I needed to see and to learn: how to stop things from getting out of hand. All I wanted from men was love and respect, for them to recognize, I was somebody who was there to party. It is what it is, you understand? I want to allow my expectations to feel free to explore life. I want to feel alive and safe enough around men to finish school and go to work like a normal person. All I needed was space to let Jamaica shine.

Chapter Eight
Surviving the Abuse

It matters to me that I am what I am because of rape. My welfare and my confidence in myself and people in general were destroyed. I knew I was a mess. I worked hard toward having more faith in myself; trying to trust in God and myself first and then a man. I wanted to find love within myself so that I would deal with my future problems better than I did my past. Will I tell my man the truth about my past or keep it a secret? I'll never lie about it; any man I love won't make a liar out of me.

My future will be a challenge. If I tell men about my past, will they be man enough to handle it by keeping it private? Or, will they use it as ammunition, throwing it in my face whenever we argue? Most men don't hear the word rape; they ignore and reject that part when dealing with a woman who has been abused, and that's a fact. Instead of listening, they're judgmental in their thinking that other men will see you as being weak and easy. They'll see you as someone men can take advantage of. It may bring out the abusive side of them, and that's important to discover in the beginning. If I'm going to tell him, I'll tell in the beginning.

At the end of the day, all men want a woman who knows how to keep other men off her. Isn't it sadly ironic rape is committed every day by abusive men? Yet, in spite of it all, these types of men want to blame you for everything when we know most things that go wrong in their relationships are because they are immature. With all respect to a good man, would you please reach out and help the abusive men be a true man? A strong minded man will face his problems and try to solve them. A weak mind will blame it on the rain. He'll continue to pee on a woman's leg and tell her that it's raining. At the end of the day, a man has to know how to handle his problems and his woman.

Here's the difference between men's and women's logic. A true woman looks at a situation and sees the whole picture. She thinks before she leaps. A weak man can't see the forest for the trees, yet he leaps from one tree to the next. This type of man is on the path to destruction. He's a dog, hopping from one tree to the other. He's not just hopping trees; he's either knocking them up or chopping them down. Either way, they're damaged goods. He leaves a trail of dead trees in an abused forest. In reality, this is a man's world.

This type of man has hound-dog syndrome. He has created nations of abused women with unwanted children. That's not bad logic, that's having no logic at all, in a man's world. The issues I have with these men are countless. The issue I have with the logic of weak minded men is their weak minded double standards. A madman's logic is raising hell one minute and "baby, let's make love" the next, or, "let's make a baby." The two just don't go together.

Two heads are better than one. One and one, equal two. If you don't give a hundred percent, you and I don't add up. If you can't give but fifty percent, you can't be my better half. Men who yell and holler are not truly loved by women. You can't love a person who's mad and complaining the entire time saying, "I'm a man; respect me and treat me right." They haven't any intention of treating you that way. It doesn't cross their minds that they have the wrong concept of being a man by wanting you to understand when they can't do any better. When the tables are turned, their understanding goes out the window. Their women have to be perfect. They can make all the mistakes in the world and never apologize—but their woman's supposed to know better.

I hate it when a man says, 'I love you' to get what he wants; and, only heartless individuals propose marriage to get sex. Women dislike the way you lie about the weather, when the only thing you truly own in life is your word. That's the only thing that can't be taken away from you; gain knowledge of telling the truth. A grown man doesn't have to answer to anyone, therefore, he doesn't need to lie.

Honesty is the best policy to get women. If you respect that about yourself, you would earn respect for whatever you do or believe in. Just believe in something that makes you civil. Make sense when you speak your mind or don't say anything at all. You're searching high and low for women that better tell the truth at all times; as long as it's not the truth about you. You can't handle the truth about you. Without a foundation of truth, everything you build will tumble and fall because of lies. You have too many issues. If you don't change, your doomsday is coming.

Face who you are. You have a long list of things that you will never own up to; important things that you will always deny. Women go in and out of hospitals every day because of abusive men like you. They are there for many reasons. The biggest one of all comes from you not knowing how to make love to women correctly. You refuse to face it or ask questions to learn how to handle a woman according to her weight and more importantly your size and weight. You deny cheating on a woman that has been faithful to you. Allow yourself to become a man. Own up to everything that you deny.

What do you deserve out of life? Abusive men take what they want and deny its rape. Rapists deny that they don't wear condoms and deny their children who are born out of rape and that doesn't have anything to do with romancing a woman. Abusive men... take notes. Women are trying hard to have romance. When a man loves his woman, he's not in a hurry. He befriends her while he learns her wants and desires; while she learns how to love him like he wants to be loved. It takes two. True love is a teacher; let it take its course. The next time I fall for a man, his first impressions will tell exactly who he is and exactly what he wants. I mean business. Boys that cry with insecurities are wasting my time. A man handles his business and keeps it to himself. A man loves to love a woman all the time.

For a woman to say she's in love, she's saying something. A woman's love is meaningful and runs deep; she wants a deep loving man. When a woman speaks her mind, that's powerful, don't take it lightly. To a woman, words mean everything; she won't say it unless she means it. That's why she has to believe in her man. She wants her man's words to be rooted in the vessels that hold his heart together. She falls over and over in love with not just your major heart, but also the heart of every part of you—the heart of your eyes, the heart of your smile, the heart of your heart, the heart of your hands, the heart of your manhood, and the heart of each step you take toward loving her. She doesn't fall completely, until, she finds every heart of you worth the fall.

Understand, for a woman to fall in love with a man, she has to fall hard to be true to her nature. When she falls completely, her true nature doesn't compare her past to her present. All her feelings of being loved, her sexual moments like size and performance, are voided from her life. In her mind, there is a clean slate she waits for you to fill. Romance a fresh new love into her life; surrender to her while you have her undivided attention. She feels like she's in love for the first time. Handle her with care. Leave the past in the past—she's caught up in the present, keep her caught up. In her heart, you're the one she loves. The other men are memories of her life that belong to her to cherish, or not. When a woman falls completely, it's no joke. When she says, 'I love you' that's God's favor on your life. It's not luck, you're blessed.

Only when a woman falls completely, she'll open up. She will let love rapture her. Loving you until, your curiosity of her is content enough to rise with confidence and passion, not cheap lust. Its romance she's advertising—she doesn't sell herself cheap. She will give you her all to make you salute to the shapely center of her world. Give her what she needs romantically and she will keep you at attention by bringing out the best of your real nature—the true man. She's just an ordinary, compassionate woman that can make you evolve and fall hopelessly down on one knee. The next time I find romance, I hope to fall in love over and over. I dream that he's going to love me right back. My man will be for me.

Throw Down

YO righteous love
YO courageous, brave love
Filled with devotion and trust.
Won't you dare? Throw down affection!
Free desire! Show me different!
Teach me something nice—be bright!
Tell me something pretty. Go ahead, surprise me!
Take me somewhere interesting. Touch me tenderly.
Say something clever. Pick me up! Carry me!
Let me enjoy YO strong arms.
Caress me. Talk to me. Laugh with me.
Let me know your true feelings.
Do something exciting and thrilling
That will warm my heart.
Be my friend! Tell me my love.
The sky is the limit—THEN!
Trust me to love you
for who you are.

Lady Dee came home from work.

"Let's take the boys to my job's basketball game tonight."

"Alright, let's go."

I can't wait to see this guy she likes; he's older and I'll bet he's
the pretty boy type. She's been dying to ask him over—and
hasn't. This way, I can see all the guys she works with. We got
the boys ready—hopped in the car and rolled. When we arrived,
we walked into the gym. I smelled the aroma of men before I
got close enough to check them out. I like to sit up high in the
bleachers. Lady Dee likes the bottom; we compromised and sat
in the middle. I sat down in her world. These people see her as
much as I do, and sometimes more.

I watched the game as the game watched me. The guys were
showing off their skills. I noticed that I stared one guy down. He

127

appeared gorgeous. He was tall; his skin looked like caramel candy, as mine does. He had a hard body. He had to lift weights, or women, one or the other. He was doing something to keep fit. His eyes were beautiful, staring me down, looking as if he wants to get to know me better. After the game, the guys walked over and introduced themselves while playing around.

The winners bragged, of course. They were all perspiring, with towels in their hands, wiping and rubbing themselves down. The one I wanted was Romeo. He's the one I chose for me. I like the way he takes control; he talks a lot—I know he's not shy. The first thing I noticed about him was that he seemed to be a leader and the most popular; the other guys followed him around; everyone liked him. Could this be the man that will fall hopelessly in love with me and be devoted to me only for as long as we both shall live?

Lady Dee lives in the moment. I got to meet her friend. He was tall, high-yellow and masculine looking. He wasn't there to play ball, he was there to mack my sister. He was dressed like an old school pimp with a sky-blue suit, sky-blue shirt, and it was unbuttoned down the front, showing off his chest. He had a sky-blue wide brim hat on his head. Everything matched his sky blue Cadillac. Lady Dee better think about it—here we go again. Blue was a player. He must be a smooth talker to land Lady Dee.

We returned home. While having a midnight snack, Lady Dee told me her job is hiring. It was a summer job. She invited me to her job to fill out an application. My sister, Sassy Girl, got hired last year for the summer only and I have a good chance of getting the job. I told Lady Dee to tell Romeo I liked him and called it a night. The following day, Dee came home from work smiling.

She walked straight to the dinner table and sat down as always. Of course, I had dinner ready because she comes home hungry every day. Sometimes she doesn't speak to me; she comes in and starts eating. I had her spoiled like that. Both of us can throw down in the kitchen. My favorite meals to cook are spaghetti, seafood gumbo, Chinese and Mexican. The boys like my spaghetti and want it all the time, along with my virgin piña coladas. Lady Dee's favorite meals to eat and cook were Rice-a-Roni, string beans, salad, and fried pork chops or fried chicken wings, soul-food style. Our cupboards are filled with her favorites.

At dinner, "I filled out an application at your job today."

"Mom, you know how to work."

"Yes, taking care of all of you is work."

Everyone laughed. The boy's asked to be excused.

"That's good, I'm sure that you will get the job. The guys asked about you. Romeo thinks you like his friend, Monte. He said, that you talked to him the most."

"He must be joking or really naive about women. I didn't look at any of the guys the way I looked at him. I made myself obvious looking him up and down; he knows that."

Dee and I continued talking and eating. Right after we finished and I cleaned up, the boys came in from outside and wanted desert. Two weeks later, I went for an interview and got the job working at the San Francisco Airport. My other jobs in the past were part-time, too. I never had a real job—but working nine to five every day is a start. I began working, weighing one hundred and twenty-five pounds. I had promised myself that I would get serious about working when Little Man turned five. He was old enough to start school and he was excited, too. I got the job! First, they hired me for the summer and I didn't get to see Romeo a lot because they had the summer workers in the warehouses.

After summer was over, the airport laid off the summer help. Two weeks later I was hired on as a permanent worker; my first real job. I worked hard and got the low down on the people I worked with. Learning what my job consisted of—now that I'm actually in the airport, getting trained as ticket master for United. Lady Dee's friend, Blue, couldn't wait to turn his friends on to me. I don't know what their jobs were, besides walking around and talking, making sure everyone was working. I saw them walking by looking all day long. Bring them on—let the games begin with player number one. Blue introduced him as a hang-out buddy of his that doesn't work at the airport. His name was Johnny, his name wasn't important. He won't be in my life long.

That night, Johnny walked through my door, clearly dressed too old for me. Plus, he was ten years older. He took one look at my behind and said, "Wide as the golden gate bridge. I got to take good care of you. I want you to be my sweet, young thing." We left out together with him saying how fine I was and that was the only nice thing said all night. The first thing he said to me in the car was, "I'm married and you are going to be my plaything. My marriage doesn't concern you." It was all downhill after that. He treated me to a steak dinner. We left the restaurant and rolled up to a cool little nightspot.

Verse: The player's club, old school style.
It was an older crowed where the music is rich and mellow. They played lots of slow jazz to minds moving fast. The men are suited-down, matching from head to toe as their styles filled the room. I'm in another phase with laid back, sharp-eyed sharks— their eyes are glued to my behind, checking it out from top to bottom. I'm all a gaze as I notice there are two women to every man, as we case the joint for a table. I hope his expectation for himself is not to be some big time player. If so, he doesn't fit the bill. Not with this crowd. If two women are required, he's minus two. Billy Preston said, 'Nothing from nothing leaves nothing.'

Verse: Look at the Black women in this place!
They're simply a work of art you can't help but recognize. The Black woman's style is her signature. She's certified. It's not just

the beauty of her face and the way her butt fills out her dress. It's not all in her words and the way she expresses herself. It's definitely in her stare. When she stares you down, her attitude becomes her; all her admirers are aware. A Black woman's signature is her cold blooded stare. With a heart of gold and eye contact she can tame any man, any time, and anywhere. It's not her intent to intimidate when she stares. When it happens, it happens. Her number one talent will always be the flair in her stare. The club was nice; it's old school style.

My date had a problem that needed my attention. We ordered drinks and after my second, I hit the dance floor with plans to hypnotize his mind. When I walked off the dance floor, I was ready to mess his head up as he has messed up mine.

"So, what's going on with you and your wife, why aren't you together—you want to talk about it?" He got upset, like I care.

"Don't you ever mention my wife again, you understand. My wife is a good woman. She's this and she's that, and you're going to respect her by keeping her out of this."

I'm thought to myself, "This..."
This doesn't exist he's crazy! He had to be on some type of drug. He's insinuating that I'm not good. He called me a tramp? He thinks I'm that young and naive that he can talk to me like that? He thinks he can get away with the sick mind game he's playing? I know just how to play him. I'm going to teach him a real good lesson; correct his mess. It's time he reaches his turning point and treats a lady with respect. I got your tramp, sucker!

Once a woman knows her power, beware. She's a hard woman to beat if you try and take her on mentally—unless you're a genius; you can't out-think her. You can't always take her down physically and either way she will be a challenge. Most men look at all the wrong things when they are looking for a woman's best quality. You get lost in her looks. You get caught up in the way she moves and other sexual abilities that she possesses. You overlook the best part—the journey into her mind.

A woman's strength is in her mind. Stop looking at the package; study the eyes. If she likes what you have to offer, they will lead you straight to her mind. Follow the pathway that she lays out for you. In time, her eyes will lead you to her heart and the eyes don't lie. It works both ways for men and women. You got to detect if the eyes are saying love connection or manipulation conquest—detect the next move before it goes down. My eyes have been telling him all night that I want to take his manhood and destroy it.

We have to fight hate everyday of our lives, and this is one night I was fighting a losing battle. I told him to take me to a hotel. He took me to a prostitute hotel and I went into a prostitute state of mind. I was in an unfamiliar zone. I was in unfamiliar territory but I got comfortable real fast. I was living on the edge and that edge had me high, I felt wild and crazy. I started rapping hard and dirty to the old fool. He doesn't even know how crazy-mad I am right now. It's a bird; it's a plane; it's, 'Super Dirty Sister'. I put him under a spell with naughty words. I nicknamed him, 'Dirty Old Daddy' because, another dirty old fool told me when you call an old man, 'Dirty old man' it turns him on and makes him try harder.

I'm scared of myself right now. I'm out of control. I'm acting out the instincts of an insane woman. I don't know what I'm going to do next. Right now, I understand how hate takes over people's minds. When you let hate build up in your mind, you are giving hate a brain to think. When you express hate with words, you are giving hate a voice. By keeping it alive in your mind, you are giving hate a life in this world. Hate feeds off of your power—you allow it to exist. You allow it to breathe, to survive, and become powerful enough to make you check out mentally. When hate has all your energy, it takes your authority, completely, and controls your mind. Love is our true nature, it's internal. We have to fight hate everyday of our lives to stay one step ahead of the game.

Soon as I walked in the door, I had doubts. I wanted to run back out and just keep on running, until, the hate I felt for this man was gone. I needed to run, until, the throbbing pain in my heart stopped. It wasn't too late to run but I didn't. I set the scene, I made my bed; now was the time to lay in it. I ripped off my clothes, then his. I pushed him onto the bed and I raped him; the same way I had been raped. I manhandled him, dogged him out. I was an animal; as rough and tough as a woman could be with a man.

He yelled, "You like to do it!" and using the 'F' word over and over.

That's when I realized rape is a woman's point of view (except a man that has been raped by another man); it had only one meaning to women. This type of man I'm with, has no point of view—rape doesn't exist. In his mind, it was good sex and I gave him his preference.

How was I supposed to know? He wanted me to kick his behind and treat him like a little girl? I wasn't street smart. I've been sitting in church all my life, with a girdle on. When I, as the victim of abuse, was finished doing my damage as the abuser, I dedicated it to his sick mind and told him to take me home. I was exhausted. He got up and went into the bathroom and passed gas for four minutes straight. I grew up with five men and I never heard anything like that. His old butt set off bullets, missiles, and bombs. And, just when I thought he was done, I heard a finale of grenades.

I got home. I knew that I had humiliated myself and I felt bad. I got ready for bed and as I laid my head on my pillow, I heard Lady Dee's man laughing, loud and hard. My date had gone home and called back to gossip about the date. I thought that he was too old to kiss and tell. I laid there trying to figure out why I acted that way—I lost it. What's really going on? My abusers rape me with a violent spirit that has become a part of me growing stronger and acting out; this was the second time. The first was when I picked up my two-hundred forty-pound non-date and threw him across the room. I'm losing the war on fighting to keep my sanity.

Before falling asleep, I felt like a monster. Maybe, I should lock myself in my room so that men of the world are safe. I hate him. He didn't know it was a set up. I never want to see him again. It would be a wise move on his part to never show his face around here again. Tonight, I found out why some uncomfortable person came up with the name, 'Old Fart'. He was a waste of my precious time. I don't even understand what Blue's laughing was all about. All I know is, I had humiliated myself.

Early the next morning, the doorbell rang. I answered it. When I opened the door, I couldn't believe my eyes, it's Old Fart from last night with two big suitcases in his hands. I'm standing there feeling like Bubba in prison after he has raped a guy and finds out later the guy liked it and he follows Bubba around begging to be his jail mate. I went off. For the first time, I said exactly what I felt, with authority. I cursed him out and felt like a pro. For once, I cared about my feelings, not the man's. I told him, I never, ever wanted to see his face again!

By that time I had awakened dead. Lady Dee and her man, Blue, had made it to the door. Old fart was in shock and I wanted to kick him while he was down. I didn't—because I knew he would have liked it. I turned and walked away from the door. He saw his friend, Blue, and broke down crying. I stood in the background thinking, 'I beat him at his own game'. This went down better than I planned.

If I got to fight, I'll do it my way. Blue helped the player that just got played carry his suitcases back to his car. Lady Dee came back into the house, looking embarrassed for what I felt I had to do. I noticed she was holding her laughter back. Lady Dee was cool like that—but she doesn't condone what I had done. She got to understand I had good reason. She knew I had never acted that way before.

"Jamaica, why did you do that?"

"Because I had to, I didn't say that he could be my Sugar Daddy."

I couldn't tell her that last night he talked to me like he was my trick, like I was his whore or something. I was too embarrassed; he hurt me. I didn't have all the answers. The mental abuse that I had suffered with Old Fart got me ready for every old pimp trying to hustle the game. I carry myself well. I'm me, a quiet little church girl. That's my image, that's what people see. The bad girl image is fake—she's my veil and protection. I perfect her to protect the real woman that I'm trying to become. I have to fight men off me my way.

I went too far to get this man. It was all worth it. I had my moment when we were standing in my doorway and it hit him that I really wasn't turned on last night. I didn't mean all those sexual things I said. The sweet names and the flirting were all lies. When it was all said and done, I didn't have any regrets—that moment was priceless and I witnessed it with my own eyes. He felt the rape. He felt violated, like a girl. I believe he knew he had been used and abused by a twenty-one year old, church girl that he thought was an easy hustle. He can't deny it, I have witnesses. And, I believe I punked him-up. He's going to laugh about this when he grows up.

What hurt the most about that day was, I held back physical reactions. I wanted to unzip his suitcases and throw his clothes all over the ground and step on them. I wanted to take him out! But you can't go around killing people—it's unsanitary, it's not humanitarian, and it's against the law. He had gotten to me. An extreme dislike for men tried to take over my heart and soul; it was killing me. Too many women have been through what I had done to him. We know what it feels like to be used like that. The lies, the deception hurt so badly when trying to live them down.

I don't want to ever use my power in that way. I don't want to be the kind of woman that entices men to love her to take over their mind and destroy their pride. I knew I had a long way to go before I could surrender to the true woman within me and love me, and fall in love with a man deeply. Whenever I think about how he talked to me, I cringe. The way he tried to intimidate me makes me sick to my stomach and also to think of what could happen to our young people. What if I wasn't experienced or wasn't taught to know better and warned of these types of men. He may have gotten away with using me and putting me on the streets. It happens every day in the world we live in.

How dare, he! A man like that is why parents are terrified. Blue came back into the house, laughing. Blue knew I don't bother anyone. I'm in my little world showing love and taking care of everyone. He wouldn't have believed the whole thing if he didn't see it with his own eyes. I did what I had to do.

I've been going to the airport basketball games. Romeo is taking his time to get to know me. I like that. We're building a friendship. One night, Lady Dee and I got high before going to the game. I kept hearing the doorbell and running to door asking, "Who is it.?" Lady Dee started tripping on a picture of Ray Charles she had hanging over her bed. She said that she could see his eyes through his shades. She got up on the bed and demonstrated to me that the right eye was going upward to the right corner, and the left eye was downward in the left corner. She had me sitting there for the longest time, trying to see his eyes, and finally when I got good and high enough, I did.

We left out for the game. When we arrived there Lady Dee got paranoid and didn't want Blue to know she had been smoking. Some of the guys walked out of the gym, coming to get us and asked why we weren't coming in. That got Blue's attention and here he came. Just about the time Blue got to Dee she was straight. He brought her high down being nosy. I went in and watched the game...

I got to work the next day. Romeo was waiting for me. He's a machinist and works on planes. He's very dedicated and serious about his job. Every morning before he starts work, he stops to talk to me. Today he's still hyped about winning last night's game. All the other guys on the team came by to speak; they like to see Romeo and me together. Romeo talked loudly,

"Mind your own business and leave ours alone."
He told me they're all dogs don't trust them; they act nice around nice girls.
I thought to myself, 'he must really like me'.

"You want to go out with me?" He asked me out for the first time.
"Yes, I'd like that."
"Do you have anything special that you want to do with me on our date?"
"No, I want you to plan our date."
"Let me put it this way. Is there anything you enjoy doing that you want to do with me?"
We looked at each other blushing and laughing.

"I like to dress up in a dress and high heels. I like men in suits and I like going to concerts; hanging out in nice restaurants and clubs in Union Square. I like going to the movies and spending a lot of money on junk food and snacks."
"Alright, all that sounds good; we got that much in common but you didn't mention my all-time favorite, Sports. How can you leave out sports?"
We laughed, blushing again.

"I like sports, although, I don't know much about them."
"I'm going to set things up. I'm going to make our first date special, I'll let you know when. Bye-bye, for now!"

I got home and I was feeling good. Blue and Lady Dee were there. Blue is up to his old tricks again. He had planned for us to go out to dinner with another hangout buddy, his name escapes me. He stepped up and wants a taste of this alleged bad girl and he's up for the challenge. I guess he thought that I needed taming. Bring on player number two. When I say player, don't get me wrong. I meant the next contestant, like old men playing a childish game. He walked inn and I took a glimpse from behind the bathroom door and saw he looked too old, too short, and he was another pretty-boy type, and that's not me.

I like tall, dark, masculine, men. Before we went out, they were drinking while Dee and I were getting dressed. They're 60 year old men, the ones that think they're players—dress like pimps and drink like fish. I don't think they know what the word player really means. I hang out at the player clubs where some of the most proud players in San Francisco make an appearance from time to time and on occasion.

One night, Lady Dee and I dressed up alike in our tight, brown, tweed suits with the suede patch on the elbows. Remember those? We had our manicures and pedicures; we were styling long human hair wigs with our hair mixed in to look natural. There was a big party going on that night. The popular player's club was celebrating the young and hot new owner and it was our first time there.

We didn't know what to expect. We walked through the door and everyone greeted us as if we were super stars. We were followed into the ladies room by a woman that was all over us. She was asking our names and if we were sisters. Her job gave people a club name and spread gossip about you around the club, making the night more interesting. We walked out of the ladies room with new identities 'The New York sisters'. No telling what else she put out, because the ladies and men were in our faces and we were treated like V.I.P.'s and given the best table.

This one guy was too arrogant and pushy. He was up in my face asking all my business.

> "Back up off me. I'm on the dance floor. Do you mind?" I said.

He went to Lady Dee, mad, and asked her about me.

> "Who does she think she is? She doesn't know who I am? She acts like she makes more money than me. She acts like she drives a more expensive car then me."

I walked off the dance floor. Lady Dee told me what he said— we laughed. I thought it was cute but I still wouldn't dance with him. He stayed in my face telling me off and it was good stuff. He was pouting, and sulking like a baby so I put up with it.

> "Look I own this club. I've had every lady in this club. My motto for women is, 'Easy come, easy go'. I get whatever woman I want. That's for sure."

I had a hard time holding my laugh in because he wasn't going to have me. After that night, I went back without Lady Dee. Danced my butt off but not with him. I wanted to hear his rap so I talked to him. I heard him out just to see if his rap was as good as he looked. He was the owner and really was a professional boxer. He thought I knew who he was and that I was playing hard to get.

He went into his zone and macked his best rap.

> "They call me Boxer, the boxing strangler; the player that hit like a storm. Players are entrepreneurs; we're smart and intelligent. I drink but you will never catch me drunk. I'm always sober and up front. I work hard to take care of my women. I pay for my life style." he said.

He went on and on trying to impress me with words and I listened.

> "A player got game but I don't play. My rap is not a game, it's a way of life. Accepting my lifestyle is your choice. There's only one type of player but many types of pimps. A player loves women. We don't abuse wom-

en, we invest. You become my woman you become a part of a family of women, if you pass the test. You accept my lifestyle, I might take you out and spend five thousand dollars or more on you; it depends on the night. I aim to please. I'm the real deal, baby. When you love a woman right, she will take care of you and give you everything she's got and everything a man needs. Players don't have anything to hide from his women, he's open and up front. I take care of my own and everybody's happy." He said.

"You are way to head strong for me."

In Blue's car, Blue and his friend are still drinking. This can't be good. We got to the Mexican restaurant and they were drunk. We were seated and served chips with green salsa and red salsa dip. Lady Dee and I set them up pretty, knowing the green is unbearable. We told them to taste the red because it's the hottest but to eat their chips with the green. We didn't know they were going to pig out on chips and dip. They were stuffing chips and green salsa dip into their mouths so fast, they weren't reacting to the hotness of the salsa; they couldn't feel anything. They were too drunk and didn't have sense of feeling.

We sat there and waited. Both of them jumped up at the same time and they couldn't talk but used sign language, wanting to know where the men's room was. There were police officers sitting in the bar and they were laughing hard at these two drunken fools. They laughed from the time they left the table drunk and came back sober. When we got home, they stayed up talking about it and I went to bed alone.

One cute guy came to work, parked his car in the airport parking lot, and shot himself in the head over a woman. We found out that his father killed himself over his mother. Another guy killed his girlfriend. We knew we weren't going to see him any time soon; didn't want to see him. As fast as I got the news, he was back at work, walking towards me. I started having flashbacks. I wanted to take off running. He had a smile on his face and said he wasn't convicted. The girl's family testified against her, that he had to use self-defense—she was a mean person. He looked like he could kill somebody for no good reason. I like being here but I don't talk to everyone.

Romeo stopped by the job to see me. He came by to tell me he's working a double shift and wants to have lunch together. At lunch he told me he has our date all planned and when it's going down. I'm ready for this date, I can't wait. On date night, he picked me up and took me to meet his family. He left me alone with his mom and she told me that he has a twin.

"Leo come here meet your brother's new girl."

He ran up the stairs, "I've been dying to meet you. You're all he talks about. Now I can see why. You have any sister's?" His mom interrupts.

"You have made a man out of my son. You're his first woman and he has bought an entirely new wardrobe. He didn't even own a pair of dress shoes. He's an athlete; he likes brand name sport gear and attire. He told me that you like men in suits and that you like to dress up and go out. The entire time she talked, I said to myself, 'that's cute he has a twin and they're both mama's boys. I know she's telling me all this be-cause she doesn't want me to hurt her son'."

He walked out of the back with flowers and candy. He was the real deal. Romeo had made everything right so far. As we left out, he opened doors for me. Thank God chivalry is not dead. I thought, 'finally I got him to myself'.

"Where on earth are we going? You're looking so good in that suit; you clean up well," I made my point.

"Thank you, so do you. We look good together, don't we? We're on our way to my best friend's house. You're going to love Joseph and Cheryl. I've known Joseph a long time. I have a lot of respect for them as a married couple; they're both smart, intelligent people." As he went on talking, I realized that our first date is a double date. We arrived there and I thought to myself, 'Romeo likes to brag about people in his life, what has he bragged about me'?

We rolled up to a big yellow house, walked through the door and they did everything but bow down to me. Romeo is right about these two, they were a lot of fun. I felt better about sharing him. I can't see anyone but Romeo. They're in love and can't see anything but each other. First, we went to Pier 39 on the helicopter ride over the bay, then to dinner. We arrived at a seafood steak house and sat down outside on the pier. I liked the view. I looked at my date, we looked at each other and then looked out at the ocean while having a drink.

"Are you having a good time?" He whispered in my ear.

"Yes, are you?"

"Yes, and I knew that I would."

I thought, 'yes, yes, yes'. After dinner we were alone and he didn't ask me to be his. He told me I was his first woman and I assumed he meant all his other dates were girls. He tried to be straight forward as he went on talking with enthusiasm, being very open with his feelings.

"I like you and I'm having some serious feelings for you."

"I want to be your woman. I am serious about getting to know you better."

I knew our first date was the start of something big. I wanted to be happy but I was not happy. I wanted to be free but I didn't feel free. I wanted to just be me but I'm not me. I'm so far from me that I feel I'll never find me. Usually, life gets worse before it gets better. I asked myself, 'can life get any worse? Have I learned what I'm supposed to learn in order for me to grow'? If I'm not at the place I'm supposed to be at in order for me to find myself; that means life is going to get worse. I'm still asleep. When we are asleep, bad things happen to awaken us.

When we are lost, hard times helps us find our way back to where we started from so that we may go forward again.

It's the cycle of life. We got to keep going in circles, until, we get it right. Hard times prepare us to be fighters but even born fighters get knocked down. Everyone that gets back up is not in his or her right mind. You can get back up, lost, and never be the same again. You can get back up and never grow, never find your purpose. I know who I am. I just can't get to me. I don't know what roads to take. I don't know how to prepare for the trip.

I'm freaking out. If I don't have a plan, I don't have a future. I've gotten back up on my feet after being knocked down—mentally and physically. Sex had been my life support, without it, I would die. I got to break this story down and make my point; knowing I was not alone. Most grown people and teenagers are on life support and looking for someone to save them with the act of sex. I wanted to love myself. I needed to feel me, my heart, and my emotions; the love I had for me. I want to be happy.

I went to work and Romeo was waiting for me.
>"Do you want to go out with me and some friends?"
>He gave me a kiss on the forehead, "Yes."
>"I'll come by and pick you up on my off day."

When I got home, I took the boys to the movies, then to my parent's house. I then went home and went to bed. Later that night, Lady Dee and friends came in. I didn't even get up. I was in my room with the door closed and there's a knock on my bedroom door.
>"Who is it?" Blue's friend, 'Hot Salsa'. He walked into my room.
>"Can I crash in your bed until, Blue is ready to go? I'm wasted." He asked.
>"Yes, and stay on your side of the bed."

He laid down on his back and exposed himself. I saw something unbelievably huge. The shadow on the wall looked like a baseball bat. I jumped up and turned on the light. I couldn't believe my eyes. This is not humanly possible. I turned the light back off and got back in the bed turning my back to this freak.

"If you think I'm going to straddle that, you're crazy. I still got to catch a husband with this."

He laughed himself to sleep. My friends Coco, Nicky, and JJ came over feeling good. They'd been club hopping all night and ready to mess up some man's head. For some reason, that lead them here. They gave Lady Dee pictures of them that were taken at the clubs and told her to show them to me. Hot Salsa looked at those pictures and jumped up and ran to the living room. I laid there half asleep. I heard him telling them that I said his bat was too big. I know he tried to impress me when he exposed himself. Now, He tried to impress my friends by talking about it. He was impressive. We were buddies after that. I liked him because he told the truth about what happened behind closed doors, like a man that has self-esteem should.

Chapter Nine
Romeo, the Crowd Pleaser

It was Romeo's and my second date. I was always excited about our dates. I went shopping to buy a new outfit. While shopping, I met a guy that asked if I wanted to model clothes at a new club. I told him that I would come to the club and check it out but couldn't promise anything. I went home and then I got dressed. Romeo arrived with friends. We picked up even more friends and then headed to the player's club. Romeo sat at our table with his legs wide open. My chair was placed between his legs. I sat sideways. I watched him and I watched the dance floor. Everything went fine until, my rival, the pro boxer, walked over to intrude.

He flirted with me every time he saw me at the club, as if I was there for him. He walked right up to our table, bent over and whispered in my ear.

> "Hello, my love. I'm not going to bother you for a dance tonight. You're looking better than I am tonight. I just left the gym and I'm on my way home. Would you care to accompany me?"

He paused, while waiting for an answer. Yes, taking me home would make him happy, but Romeo is my man. I didn't say anything; I didn't introduce them either and he gave me a very passionate kiss on the cheek. I sat there indicating I was with a date. Actually, as he walked away; I swear a love-jones sensation had fallen over me and I was lost for words. I lost track of time; I had zoned out. I couldn't think whenever he was around.

I had every excuse in the book. His words were intended to make me feel like I belonged with him and I did. He took his time with me, slowly running his mind game, training me to want him more and more. I didn't know what to do with that boxer; I kind of liked him. He was luring me into the fast life that

I knew nothing about. I knew who I was there with and ignored his whole seduction and tried my best to hide what I felt before looking into Romeo's eyes, but it was too late.

Romeo noticed I was exposed and he realized my curiosity for the man. I disguised my lust with shame and dropped my head. That was when Romeo jumped up to go and fight the guy. Romeo's friends followed him outside and the boxer was gone. Romeo's friends consoled him as teardrops fell from his eyes. They came and told me he was angry and wanted to fight the guy over me. I got up and went outside to say to him that I was sorry, and I let him know the guy was the owner of the club and a pro boxer. I pleaded for him not to say anything. I didn't know what else to say.

I made him feel worse. I laid down one of my mother's lines for all it was worth.
> "It's a thin line between being a coward and having the wisdom to walk away."

He was upset with me because I didn't get the guy out of my face. How could I tell him that I had been playing mind games with a pro boxer that was named Boxer by his adopted parents? We had sexual magnetism, battling to see which of us can seduce each other the longest before giving in to our mental rapture and getting physical.

He was misunderstood and had been fighting to find love all his life. He thought like a fighter; he studied his opponent and didn't hesitate to take them down. It was my first mental seduction, a sex war of the minds going on between us. Since I had given him a chance to rap to me, in his mind, I was as good as his. He was a yes man. He was accustomed to getting what he wanted. Boxer was the ultimate player and that's what attracted me to him. He would only allow me to tease him for so long. He didn't allow me to waste his time, nor his efforts. Sooner or later he was going to have me.

He told me that he had a strong game to get women. He said his rap was not a game; it was a way of life and he was proving to me he was a man of his word. He wanted me; and I blamed me; I hated me for somehow being responsible. I went outside because I didn't like the way I handled the situation. And, to prove to myself I wasn't interested in what Boxer was offering. When you're doing things that make you hate yourself, you've got to fight to save yourself. When your abuse has been publicly exposed, everyone knows why you're like you are. When you've been keeping your abuse a secret, you're alone and people think you're doing things a certain way because that's who you are. I had to fight the fact that I was turned on by a player that I perceived was the ultimate bad boy.

Some people need help and some have to be told that they're going in the wrong direction. They need to be taught and guided through every step of recovery to free them. I've been taught, and I knew better. I had been misled by yes-men and I needed to heal, I didn't want to go backwards, I wanted to go forward.

MISLED

Something happened
That misled you as a child
It invaded the depths of your soul
Now you've hidden it away, never to be told
It left you bitter, broken-hearted and
Afraid.
You're an adult now and with it comes
Responsibility to accept your past
For what it is and go on.
Don't let it hold you down
With guilt and shame you wasn't the blame.
Although you were damaged and torn apart
Keep the faith. Pain exists to make us strong.
Don't hide in the dark let the strength within
Guide you on.
There's a scar on your heart
That you've had to learn to live with
It will always remain.
Unless you change,
Live your life to the fullest
Make yourself happy within.
Never look back on that
Broken-hearted
Anger, fear, or shame
Strive to reach your goal
Success belongs to you
To cherish and appreciate
More than others do.
Hold your head high.
Tell the world you're stronger than most.
You've had to work harder to become who you are
In life you will go far.
Be proud of where you come from
It made you what you are today.
Although it was rough it
Molded you in a very special way

I wanted to conquer the world. First, I needed to conquer my life. I wanted some alone time with Romeo. I made him feel he wasn't man enough for me in front of his friends. I felt I didn't satisfy him, either and I wasn't enough for him.

Every time we went out, we were never by ourselves. He was a crowd pleaser; and he had to show off his toys and his women to other men. Whatever his case was; he felt in control in a crowd; he was funnier, and more content. To him, being alive meant proving his charm to both sexes; he was a performer. I don't know if I could ever get him to say, "I do" because he was bored with two.

I had planned to get my own place, maybe then he would come around more and spend some quality time. Romeo seemed like a good man. I just didn't know if he was a forgiving man. I was taught, when there's a problem in a relationship to pray for an amazing grace. Grace gives the power to go on and continue pleasing each other in a pleasing manner. Grace allows you continue to give love when it was unearned and inexcusable. Grace gives the power to apologize whether you're right or wrong and the power to forgive over and over again, until, you get it right. I apologized and I hoped Romeo had enough grace in his heart to forgive me.

Forgiving

Forgiveness is a choice,
To stay with a love that has really hurt you.
It takes time to heal from a broken heart.
You can heal better in the arms of the one you love.
Love your one love, in a lifetime, hold on to it.
Only the person who broke your heart can mend it.
If you chose to say, I forgive you.
You have chosen to live with the painful memory
And to never bring it up again.

People choose which vibrator device to love. They buy vibrators to own control of turning an electric buzz off and on. No matter what; they'll get their way in that sexual relationship. A vibrator doesn't fill the void. It gets the job done, but could become a love-hate relationship, like some human relationships that don't have a variety of foreplay. The same old thing gets boring: it doesn't love you back, nor does it talk, kiss, caress or cuddle afterwards. Yet the fear and the anger of being hunt makes some believe the vibrator is your destiny.

As humans, we can't buy people as devices and call that true love; and you can't choose true love because they may not choose you. It takes two complete hearts brought together as one to be soul mates. It takes harmony to let destiny take its course. First, I needed to take control of my life and stop trying to control men. When it came to relationships, I was angry with men that I couldn't rule. And the fear of being hurt again kept me angry and out of control. I felt that I could love a man right and I knew I would be faithful if I could find the right man that didn't fear me.

It was graveyard shift. Romeo stopped by to see me and gave me a forehead kiss. It seemed routine, as if we were now buddies or something. I wasn't expecting things to jump back to normal and wondered if they ever would. Was our love strong enough to last? I needed him to love me. That morning, when I returned home from work, I couldn't go right to sleep. Instead, I created poems in my head and that always helped me fall asleep. I got up and cooked and I fed the boys and cleaned up my mess. I watched TV with them and I went back to bed three hours before time to go to work that night.

I sat in my room with the door closed. I felt blue and someone knocked on my door. I thought it was one of the boys, since we were the only ones home.

"Come in."

The door opened and in walked Dee's man, Blue, with nothing on but his underwear.

"What do you think you're doing? I know you're not a sleep walker."

"I'm getting in the bed. I got sick at work and Dee gave me her key to come and get some rest."

"She didn't tell you to get your rest in my bed. Get out!"

He exposed himself and sat down on the bed.

"If you don't get out right now, I am going to scream for the boys. I know you don't want them to see you in here making a fool of yourself."

He got up and headed for the door.

"Don't think for one minute that Lady Dee's not going to hear about this."

I warned him and he didn't believe I'd tell. The next time I talked to Lady Dee, I sang like a bird. I thought for sure I was never going to see his face around our house again.

Lady Dee told me she wasn't ready to let him go.

"A man is going to be a man; some will try you. You handled it like a woman; you put him in his place. When a man gets out of line, a woman stops him in his tracks. I'm proud of you for doing the right thing because people always blame the woman in these types of situations. Women should respect each other's territory.

Listen to me, men have a way with words and will have you to believe that you're more woman than any other woman. They'll say, you're younger, better looking, and

151

smell better. They'll look you in your eyes and smile, then say, 'she doesn't understand me the way you do', and it's all lies."

I knew I hadn't given Blue time to use those tactics. Not him or any other man was going to come between my sister and me.
The next time I saw Blue, he looked at me like I stank. He wanted to win against me so badly. He had the nerve to tell me I wasn't a woman because I snitched.

"I thought you were a woman."

"I thought you were a man."

"If Dee believed you, little girl, why am I still here?"

It was over and we never brought it up again, ever. After that, I moved out of Lady Dee's house into my first place. It was Friday, midnight, the last night of swing shift. We received our pay checks at 12:00 A.M. and everyone was going to the bar to cash their checks. We called the bar, 'Airport Bar' because everyone goes there before and after work. Some would stay all night, leave there in the morning, and go right back to work. That night, I decided to go with a group of women that I worked with every day. We cashed our checks at the bar. We had drinks and partied a little with the guys and when we left, they followed.

We led the party to a little hole in the wall club filled with bay area bad-boys that hung-out on the streets and would often chase me, demanding me to pull my car over, as if they're the law. That night they were hanging-out in front of the club, corroborating about a dance with me before night's end. I acknowledged the ones that were in my face but never promised them a dance. I walked into the club, ready to unwind. The girls and I were having a good time when Blue walked in and ordered a round of drinks for everyone.

The latest song played, 'More Bounce to the Ounce' and the women choose men they wanted to party with.

"That's what I'm talking about," I yelled.

Those women were aggressive about everything; they didn't play when it came to getting what they wanted. I sat and watched them turn the club out. Blue walked over.

"Hello Jamaica, how's Dee doing?

Their relationship was going through some changes that most relationships go through at some point. They were having some guideline technicalities and their system was on the blink. Every relationship creates its system and theirs was broken down; they had to compose them-selves and back away.

Blue was lost without Dee, he was not as happy as he normally was and I didn't know what to tell him, "You have made your bed, now lie in it," wouldn't have made him feel any better, but I was tempted. He knew he was wrong and could lose a good thing. We were in a club and instead of dancing; I listened to him complain about how he had messed up. I thought to myself, 'Dee probably gave him an alternative test. One of those, let's get married or break up tests; see how you like being without me deals'.

Yes, I did say test, not game. Tests are allowed, within fair reason. A man better come to the table with some tests also. A yes-man doesn't like it when a woman puts her foot down and exposes the test. The relationship had been all about him, up to that point; about his wants and desires. A woman's determined to win over her man; she'll say to her man, I have given you the best of my love and this relationship isn't going anywhere. A woman assumes the man loves her because he's there. When his actions are saying this is as far as we can go, the test begins.

It's a woman's business to find out where she stands. She's not withholding sex on purpose just to make him suffer; she's suffering, too, being without her man. The test was real. It was her life, it was her body, and it was her test. She wanted something to offer the man that wanted to marry her. A woman will tell a man to take some initiative, test me, turn me upside down and check me for fleas. Whatever it takes to convince her man to move forward, she's game. She will ask her man, "Are you ready to go all the way in this relationship?" When a true woman said, "Let's go all the way," she's seriously talking marriage, not sex. She wants her man's love documented and acknowledged. She wants papers on her man and his word. A man's honesty fills her emptiness and her craving, night after night. That's why she needs to know the truth about how he feels. When a man doesn't feel the same, his time is up. Next!

I couldn't take his wallowing. I had to speak aloud.

"Blue, everything is not about you. Understand, when a woman is being true to her nature, she can't lay up night after night, year after year, and never talk or plan a future together. A woman can't be creative in a relationship that's not going anywhere. She holds back, unless she wants the same things. You're missing out on so much love you two can both share as a couple when you let her assume she's yours. When she doesn't hear your words of love or witness your actions of a love connection between you, she builds the relationship on her assumptions, because you're there. She's there because she loves you. Her assumptions are pure, she wants you to love her. It's about both you and her. Can't you understand that? A woman needs something to sustain her in order to keep letting you amuse yourself with her love and not laying any foundation. It is true, marriage is harder on the man? You will be the head of the house and family and it often takes longer for you to commit. Blue, I'm sorry to say, you messed up."

Overall, it's not easy on either sex. Dee was a strong woman and she carried the weight of a one-sided relationship by waiting until, Blue was man enough to step up and confess his love and carry her and bear the load together. The separation test usually works if he was the one. The test was supposed to leave him

154

feeling that he wanted more than the two of them had before the test. Blue didn't know how to separate the relationship from the world, or Dee from any other woman.

"Blue, women believe that since we know what we want, men should know what they want too, so, come clean. You're using the cop-out system with every excuse in the book. What's really going on? Are you mentally wounded from your past and her past and everyone else that you've known to have had relationship problems? You have been exposed. You have deep trust issues. You need time to deal with that. Get over it and grow up!"

"Well, I asked where she expects the relationship to go."

"Really, Blue? A women falls in love with a man that can meet her halfway; discuss things and come up with solutions."

While Blue and I talked, I stood up. We both walked over to the bar to order another drink. A guy appeared out of nowhere and put his hand on my right arm.

"I've been watching you all night. This is my song; I have been waiting to dance with you on my favorite song."

"Have you noticed I'm not dancing? I'm talking, take your hands off me!"

He wouldn't let go. He had my arm and pulled me to the dance floor. I pulled in the opposite direction. I snatched my arm away from him and fell backwards into a barstool but caught myself before hitting the floor.

Blue cursed at the guy. He looked Blue up and down, and took two steps forward and got into Blue's face.

"Blue, I'm not scared of you and you're not going to stop my action!"

He cursed Blue out. I came here with five women and when I looked back at them, I saw five gangsters. They had left the dance floor and made it back to their tables to arm themselves. I stood there speechless as I watched them kick off their shoes, take off ear-rings and reaching into their handbags for weapons. They brought out: guns, knives and mace, all to fight one man as they shouted to Blue and me.

"Let him try something! We got your back!"

Life is all about those thin lines. Blue had to use wisdom that night. He didn't want us women fighting. He surely didn't want blood on his favorite blue suit, hat, and shoes. He grabbed the man's right hand and a cool sounding chuckle came out of his mouth. Blue shook the guy's hand.

"Look, man, we don't need to fight in front of these beautiful women. We can settle this like intelligent men."

Blue saved the night. I guess he was some kind of man. The following day. I told Lady Dee about everything that went down. She didn't have much to say about Blue. She was just happy that I was alright. I guess I was right about the test and it was over between them.

"Your sisters and I are going out this weekend,"

"You all are going out without me? I have two nights off, and I'm living for the weekend."

My first night, I was out with my sisters, BJ, Jazzy Black, Sassy Girl, and Lady Dee. We walked into the 'Player's Club', dressed like money. I had on a one-of-a-kind copper silk suit that Dee bought when she traveled the country singing. It hugged every curve on my fabulous body. I had on black, silk, after-five shoes. I borrowed Jazzy', black silk, after-five clutch purse. We had the best table in the house, right in front of the stage, and dance floor. I was up close and ready for action. I gave eye contact to one very tall gentleman; amazingly good looking and well dressed. He styled a copper colored suit; go figure. A man came between us and I wanted him to move but instead he walked up to me.

156

"May I have this dance?"

He wasn't wearing a suit and I felt that I looked too good for him.

"No thanks. I'll pass."

Like he cared that I had good manners.

I looked right past him, as he tried to block my view. I was saving myself for that one man I made eye contact with. I thought to myself, 'I want him to ask me to dance.' As I thought to myself, I don't know who you are, I don't know where you come from, all I'm concerned about is letting you know, I am here for you. I'm your party tonight, sweet thing. I felt good to be alive. There were many different dances out and I had practiced every one of them and had them down to a tee; the Worm, the Freak, the Dip, and the Bump was still bumping. The D.J. put on, 'Brick House' and every woman in the room felt he talked about her but I knew for sure, he talked to me.

The D.J. put on, 'Got to Get Off'.

Jazzy Black yelled, "You ain't never lied."

The handsome man dressed in copper walked over to me.

"May I have this dance?"

I recognized his voice and tried my best to keep my cool. There's only one man with a voice like that.

"Yes, I'll dance with you, boyfriend."

My table was already on the dance floor. I stood up and started to move. I thought I was going to out-dance him, but every dance I did, he did. We danced together like we were born lovers. I mean, dance partners. A slow jam started and we didn't miss a beat. We were in each other's arms.

"What's your name?"

"Jamaica Gold."

"Do you know who I am?"

"Yes!"

"Is this your first time seeing me in person?"

"Yes, your voice is distinctive. You're the D.J on my favorite radio station, the best on the bay."

I had listened to him for years on the radio. When I got home from work every night, I poured myself a glass of wine, lit candles, and relaxed to his bedroom voice. He helped me fall right to sleep. Listening to him on the radio, I pictured him to be dark and handsome. In person, he was that and more with a masculine face, short haircut, and a thick body. We danced four records straight and ended up in the middle of the floor.

On my way back to my seat. I heard Jazzy Black hollering Lady Dee's name and the crowd was loud. Lady Dee was on stage with the band beating a holy fit on their tambourines. I was afraid she was going to toss it to me. The club had gone straight sanctified. I thought that we were the only church girls there, until, I heard other women in the club saying they wanted to go on stage for the longest time. They got right with Dee and the band. I sat down at my table and listened to my sister's.

Lady Dee told them who she was on stage singing in all her glory, converting people, telling her story. Dee's background singers were BJ and Sassy Girl with their voices humanizing on the big stage. Jazzy Black was on the dance floor making men backslide as her body glided. I notice that the D.J. had struck a pose beside me and let everyone know not to mess with me and it never crossed my mind that he could be a player, he was so polished. Everything on his body glowed. I thought, 'was Boxer bold enough to come over and seduce me with words and bully my date as usual'? My dance partner sat beside me and we had a nice, but loud, conversation. I enjoyed yelling to him.

We walked back out onto the dance floor. Our second dance, more people had come onto the floor and there wasn't much room to dance. I stood in one spot and danced the dance called, 'The Worm' around and around in a circle until, everyone joined in. I thought, 'I was dancing circles around my partner' and when I looked up, he was gone. As I looked across the dance floor and through the crowd, I spotted him. He was dancing circles around the entire dance floor, pointing at me. It was exciting. I never saw anyone do that; he had his style and I had mine. Could this be the player that will turn his back on the game and promise to give up other women? Will he fall madly in love with me and be devoted to me only for as long as we both shall live?

We walked off the dance floor. I daydreamed while we enjoyed each other's company. Boxer walked up and I was stunned; I didn't see him coming. He asked me to dance to a slow jam. I danced with him for the first time. He held me in his arms as a man would hold the most beautiful woman he had ever seen. He caressed me as a man should and I melted. As I looked into his eyes, I forgot who I was or where I was. My heart, felt an electric shock that moved through my entire body, slowly. My mind thought, 'The man wants me bad'.

"Leave with me?"

"I can't live your lifestyle and I won't change mine for yours."

"Don't go back to your table, come to mine. Let me buy you a drink?"

He let me go and I went back to my seat and sat down. He took my breath away. The D.J. waited for me.

"Is there something going on between The Boxer and you?" The D.J. asked.

"Nope, he has too many women after him."

That night, the D.J. asked me to be his dance partner and then he invited me to the dance studio at the radio station. He told me that we could practice different routines for events around the bay. I was thrilled that he asked. I told him that I had to think about it. Before the night ended, he invited me to the player's club house party of the year and handed me an invitation. I said, 'yes' and accepted the invitation. I couldn't wait to dance with him again. I left the club that night soaking wet for the last time. I was too cute to put my coat on and the next day my voice was gone.

I had laryngitis again. How was I supposed to go out with my man tonight? I went to my mom's house and let her doctor on me; gargling all day, until, Ray Jr. came to take me running. He almost killed me running up hills. We ran up a hill so steep, I was falling back down, until,, he hollered, "Swing your arms or else you won't make it up." Did he think I was supposed to know that fact? Do I look like an athlete? I caught a bad cramp in my leg and he didn't stop. He told me to run it off or else I'd be in unbearable pain. I already thought I was dying and I couldn't scream for help without a voice. When we were finished, my clothes were falling off. I had lost two pounds. I couldn't believe he worked me that hard. I'll be ready for him the next time.

On our way back to our parent's. I told him about meeting the D.J. and he begged me not to meet him at the radio station. He said, 'he's a player, don't mess with him, he's out of your league'. When we got back to my parent's house, I asked my mom if I should go. I knew she had to pray on it and would change my decision. I wanted her to talk me out of it. I've been straining my voice all day talking. I thought if I gargled with Scope mouthwash and drank some down, it would make my voice come back quicker.

I went home and got dressed for my date. Romeo and his twin Leo picked me up. My voice hadn't returned and I was limping from a cramp but I went anyway, hoping to have a good time. Romeo knew I had lost my voice but had planned to introduce me to some of his relatives. They knew we were on our way so he couldn't back out.

"Let me do all the talking; just nod when I say nod."

He was joking but I didn't think it was funny. I was going to look bad. This is what I get for not staying my butt at home. When we arrived, I smiled and nodded while Romeo told them my business. He told them that I've been partying hard and that's why I can't talk. We left there and went to eat pizza and drank beer. I had wine and some of Romeo's beer. We sat-up talking, laughing and watching a big screen TV. I wasn't intoxicated, when my stomach started to boil. I felt dizzy and told Romeo I needed some rest.

On the way back home, all three of us were in the front seat and I was in the middle, when I began to get really sick to my stomach. The music was loud. We had the windows down but I wasn't in a window seat and I had to throw-up bad; I couldn't hold it down. It was coming up to my throat, and into my mouth so I couldn't say, pull over.

I don't want them to know I was sick they're going to think that I'm a drunk. I opened up my purse and threw-up in my purse and they didn't see a thing. They were high and had been drinking, so they couldn't smell me. I could have gotten away with anything. I was proud of me. That was ghetto brilliance; a fabulous idea. As I regained my sanity, I looked down with a shocking discovery. I remembered what purse I was carrying and I panicked again. I had ruined Jazzy Black's favorite antique purse. I was the walking dead. Jazzy Black was going to have a ghetto rap sheet when she's finished with my behind. I'll get hung for this one; and she may get life.

When we pulled up to my house, I was as sick as a dog. Romeo got out and helped me out of the car. I faked it all the way to the front door. As soon as I got to the front door, I put my key in the lock and rushed inside. I didn't look back. I slammed the door in Romeo's face. I left him outside waiting for his goodnight kiss and smooches. On the inside, I stood with my back up against the door, hoping I still had a boyfriend. While he stood on the other side wondering if he still had a girlfriend.

He thought I was mad at him for drinking and driving. Later, he said, 'I brought his high down that night'. I never told him what happened and why I wouldn't let him kiss me on the mouth. What made me sick to my stomach was the mouthwash I drank, mixed with pizza, wine, and beer. It all turned toxic in my stomach...

The next morning, I had tonsillitis and I had never been so sick in my life. My throat was on fire. It hurt so badly, I couldn't walk. I had a high fever and my bed sheets were cold and wet. My mom came and had to keep changing them for me. I'm going from burning hot to freezing cold. I couldn't eat or drink. I couldn't do anything but spit in a jar for a week. I will never leave a club soaking wet. Cuteness doesn't turn death on, or scare death away. I knew I was dying, or I had died and went to hell.

I gained my voice back and it wasn't a very exciting moment. I dreaded making the phone call to Jazzy Black. I had to get it over with. I'm so embarrassed. I called and I told her. I said, "I'm sorry, Jazzy." I washed it out but hated to give her purse back. It was an antique and she wanted it back. Now, I'm her slave; cooking and cleaning, running errands, at her beck and call.

I had time to work on my first apartment. Everyone called it, 'the patio' because all I had in the living room was a wicker blind hanging on the patio door, patio furniture, and plants. The birds loved it and flew in all the time. My brother's took me to pick up my furniture from three different stores. We returned and they helped me carry it into the house. I went to work and was kissed by Romeo. I told him about my brothers helping me. Romeo came over after work. He fell in love with my apartment which I designed to look like an African jungle. Our lovemaking was very tender and was convincing that he could be the one; everything felt perfect to me. Maybe to him it was a bored-to-death kind of perfect and he liked excitement.

There wasn't any drama between us, we never fought, or argued. It seemed as we were made for each other. We talked a lot and expressed our feelings. We had a lot in common. I was an exciting woman and I didn't feel that I gave him what he wanted. I wanted him to come over all the time and get to know me. I was used to men who wanted to lay up under me all the time. I started assuming again and that meant Romeo was not saying what I wanted to hear. Our needs were not being met in our relationship.

When we met at work the next day, we spoke and went separate ways. I ran into Lady Dee coming off graveyard shift. She was not leaving. She was working overtime that day. We did that sometimes coming off graveyard, since the boys were at school. Dee and I stood in the worker's lounge and listened to Dale; he was an old-fashioned cool guy, as in... still living in the 1960's. He told us about the limousines business he owned. He drove on the weekends. He said his business was doing well; trying hard to impress us. He promised to have his limo pick us up and take us out on the town.

He spits when he talks. Lady Dee and I ducked spit and laughed. Every time we said something to him, he would answer, "I heard that." So, that was what we called him because his conversation's was basically, "I heard that."

Guys walked by and called Dee and I twins because of our big butts. Romeo walked up excited about the party him and Joseph were giving. I told him that I was coming over to see him after work.

I returned home from Romeo's house and called Coco, Nicky and J.J. to see what they were doing for the weekend. I told them about the player's party and they said let's all go, and have a good time. We weren't taking Lady Dee. One night, we taught her the dance called 'the Worm' then took her to the army base dance contest with us. We had tried to win 'The Worm' dance contest for the longest time. She went there and won the contest and danced like she taught us.

The weekend came and my three girlfriends and me met up at my house and headed to the player's party. We took Bayshore freeway and headed for South Beach. We rolled up to a huge mansion on the water and I thought, the D.J. must have money. We walked into the party and Mr. D.J. was happy to see me. He immediately walked over and spoke to us. He led me away from my friends and introduced me around the room as Miss Buttersworth. I didn't know what the name meant; I just went with it.

The D.J. walked into the middle of the room. He held up my right arm with his right hand in mine, and twirled me around as if he were showing off his queen and thrilled to be my king for the night. He started his dance routine. His sexy moves were electrifying and smooth. We danced, gently flowing together, as if we were alone; just the two of us. I loved dancing with him. He had to be the coolest guy I had ever danced with. Every dance he did, I did and people gave us applause. We danced to many records.

> I needed a drink and to rest. I stopped and said, "Thank you for the dance."

I walked into another room to the bar and he followed. We ordered drinks. He picked up our drinks off the bar and carried them to his seat. I followed his lead. As I sat down next to him, my eyes gazed at a dark corner and saw Boxer. I was relieved, I didn't have my drink in my hands. I would have dropped it.

I pretended Boxer wasn't there. I sipped my drink and talked to D.J.

> "Thanks, I needed a drink."
> "You deserve a drink after that performance. You're body motion speaks a language just for me and that's rare. I want to hang around as long as you allow me the honor."

D.J. sat close to me giving me his undivided attention, smooth talking me. He complimented my outfit and hair and then Boxer walked over and asked me to dance.

"Miss Buttersworth, dance with me?"

"I asked D.J. to excuse me. I stood up and Boxer took hold of my waste and led me to a private terrace where we could hear the music and dance. He wanted some alone time. Boxer was ready to make his move.

"I want you tonight. I won't let you go, until, you say, yes."

"How would I look leaving with you? D.J. invited me, not you."

"I asked him to invite you. I named you Miss Buttersworth. How else was I going to get you to my house? Come with me, let me show you something." He took my hand and led me up the stairs and down a large hallway and then stopped.

"There's my room and here's yours. Let me take care of you Jamaica?"

He opened the door. The room was beautiful. Lavender and gray with a white leather sofa; it was my favorite colors. We walked into the room and he opened up the dresser drawers one by one to show me, they were empty.

"I want these filled with lingerie, beautifully made with the finest silk, from all over the world. I would buy for you only."

He walked me over to the bed, "Lie down in my bed I want to see how you look in bed."

I sat down on the bed and crossed my legs. Boxer took my shoes off and placed them in the empty closet.

"I want to fill this closet with the finest clothes and shoes that money can buy; anything you desire. I aim to please. I love your style. I want to see more of it. I want to see more of you, Jamaica Gold. I told you, I get what I want, people do what I say. I got you right where I want you. Say you'll stay with me tonight?" He was so full of himself and I let him kiss me on my face a couple of times before I asked him,

"What about my man?"

"You can have any man you choose."

I walked away from him. I couldn't believe what I was offered or the words I heard coming from his prefect lips. I couldn't believe what I felt and I couldn't give him an answer. I had to test him to see if he would let me walk away. I put my shoes on and left.

I went back to D.J.'s table and sat down to finish my drink and breathe. I let him know, I couldn't be his dance partner because I work rotating shifts. I could see he was very into his art of dance. I wouldn't be able to make rehearsals or performances. I found all three girlfriends and we went to the ladies room and snooped out his player's pad and then, we left.

That night when I returned home, I didn't listen to my D.J. I put on my girl, Tina Marie. I laid there and wondered where my true love was. I had Romeo, but not where I wanted him. My bed was empty. I was laid up lusting after those fine players at the player's party and thought about what Boxer had to offer. I never had an offer as temping as his. I really wanted to explore his world. I wanted to hang out in his crib, lie in his bed, talk dirty, and bare all. Just to mess with his mind, exercise the power of my sexual fantasies, and walk away. I didn't have time for that other stuff he was rapping about. I loved everything about a player in the bedroom. Other than that, I wouldn't want anything to do with them. I went to sleep thinking neurotic, love-sick thoughts to myself.

The next weekend, I headed to Oak Town. Oakland California, It was party time and I picked up my cousin Retha and we went to check out a new after-hours club. It was ladies night, free additions of course. There were more men than ladies. We found a table and ordered drinks. The club was large and the dance floor was huge. You couldn't see who all was there. A guy danced over and asked me for a dance. I walked onto the dance floor and had so much room; I took over the entire floor. I danced until, I had the dance floor to myself. I danced record after record. The men took turns as I out-danced them all.

I went to my seat and the men hollered, "Don't stop". Ree-Ree laughed at the reactions I got. A guy walked up and introduced himself.

"Hi, I'm Mark. What's your name, baby?"

"My name isn't baby, it's Jamaica."

"Jamaica, you want to go outside and smoke a joint with me."

I knew better than to walk out of the club with a stranger. I did it like it was the thing to do. You don't have any fear when you feel the worst had already happened to you. Although, the worst would be losing my life doing those types of things. I continued to do crazy stuff and it never got me anywhere.

It all started when I was younger. My family and I would attend church conventions at hotels; The Hilton, The Hyatt Regencies, and The Marriott. Our parents would participate in church. And, a group of us, boys and girls would get together and party in the hotel rooms. Then we'd walk up the street to hang out on the corner and smoke weed. We never got caught.

I stood outside with Mark, in front of the club while he went to his car. He returned with the biggest joint I ever smoked. I remember taking three hits and I left him outside alone. I went back in the club and danced onto the dance floor. The weed had me. My moves captivated the room. I could have danced all night. They turned the trip lights off and shined the spotlights on me. I felt like a star.

I went back to my table and Ree-Ree was in a panicked state of mind, begging me to stop dancing.

"You're leading men on. I'm scared. How do you plan on leaving with men wanting you this way?"

167

"Relax, I do it all the time. I walk away. If they follow me, I tell them I'm here for the party, not a man. The show is over."

We stayed until, the club closed. As we began to walk out, we had a crowd of men behind us. They wanted to party, have sex, one or the other. Who cares! I got rid of them all, except one.

That night, one hard head kept following me; the guy I smoked the joint with. He refused to get out of my face. I may have kissed him when he blew smoke in my mouth. I didn't know the correct way to do it and guys always kissed me when they blew smoke in my mouth. I didn't remember what happened outside.

Mark refused to leave us alone. He followed us to our car. Ree-Ree was driving and needed gas. He followed us to a gas station. He stepped out of his car and walked up to ours. He laid down his rules.

> He threw another one of his joints in our car window, "I'm going to spend the night with you both. Smoke on that, I'll see you when we get to your place; you should be good and ready for me by then."

We both were hollering out the window.

> "We have a man at home!" He still took off after us...

The long car chase seemed like forever. Ree-Ree worked in Oakland and knew it well. She cut through alleys, flew up and down hills in residential neighborhoods, and he was behind us in hot pursuit. He thought we lived in Oakland.

"Forget his foolishness, I'll take the freeway and lose him."

Ree-Ree made a quick U-turn, did some donuts and got on the freeway headed to San Francisco. I looked back and saw all the headlights on the freeway and panicked.

> "Ree-Ree, now, there's a lot of cars chasing us!"
> "Stop smoking that joint; it has you hallucinating."

168

Mark didn't follow us onto the freeway. The entire drive home, my cousin talked about the chase and she talked about me. I was smoking Mark's joint, and laughed.

When you are born to be in the spotlight, it follows you wherever you go and whatever you do, weather the spotlight was good or bad. You're going to stand out in the crowd. Someday, I will accept my true purpose and live up to my gifts and talents. I will find my true spotlight and be proud of my accomplishments.

That morning, I returned home tired. I wanted to go straight to bed. Lady Dee called and said she was sick. I went to take care of her. Romeo called that night to talk about his party. We all got together; Romeo, Joseph, Cheryl, and me. The party was a surprise for Leo. We had dinner and a meeting to discuss a theme, we all agreed on, 'Ring My Bell'. The party was named after the number one hit song. We were going to pass out bells at the door. Cheryl and I were going to watch the furniture and the men were in charge of keeping the party under control. The food would be catered.

After the meeting was over, I called a meeting of my own. I told Romeo that I was pregnant and his response was that he was okay with being a dad. I knew he would be a good dad, but I decided later that I would have an abortion. He went through the entire procedure with me, along with Joseph and Cheryl. I didn't tell anyone else; no one knew about the first. The entire ordeal helped me to see clearly. I knew where I stood with him and I got protection after that. I won't need to call any more meetings with him.

The night of the party Romeo acted strange. Everything went down as planned. Everyone said it was the best party they had ever attended because Leo was actually surprised. My older brother and sisters came and had a good time. I enjoyed myself, but something wasn't right with Romeo. He kept me with him all night. I danced every song with him. Then he and Joseph switched partners. I danced with Joseph and Romeo danced with Cheryl. I don't know if he was showing me off to his friends or didn't trust me. Later, I found out that he watched me because he didn't think that I was strong enough to party, after my ordeal.

After that night Romeo thought he was a player. I called him on my lunch break to ask, how he was doing and he was talking about another woman. He said the woman was at Leo's party. He said her name was Stacy and she had been hanging out at the airport bar seriously coming on to him. She liked him out of all the other guys and had been buying him drinks. He told her he was already in a serious relationship. He was clearly turned on by her whole seductive flirtations and I thought, 'here I go again'. He was going to cheat on me, if he hasn't already.

I was born at night but not last night. There is a woman that kept coming on my job looking at me. One day, I went by Romeo's house and she was there. Romeo said, she was Leo's friend. Leo didn't say anything; he left the room and left her sitting there alone. He didn't want anything to do with Romeo's games. I know she was there for Romeo. I know why she had been watching me and she was crazy if she thought she can take my man. I was going to make him choose in front of everyone.

I called my sister Sassy Girl and asked for her help.

> "Romeo is cheating on me, here's the plan. I'm going to the job's party. I've never been to one before and no one expects me to show up. I want you to come with me to drive my car home after the party."
> "Girl! How are you going to get home without your car?"
> "Watch me! I'm going to tell Romeo that I'm riding with him."

She was shocked and she didn't think that I was smart enough to put two and two together. She surely didn't believe that I would confront him in front of everyone. We arrived at the party, and my womanly intuition was right. There they sat at a table together. Romeo caught sight of me and jumped up and ran onto the dance floor, without Stacy. He danced to the music of a live band, acting like a groupie. He was making a fool of himself. Sassy and I walked over and sat down at the table behind theirs. He stayed on the dance floor until, the party was over. Everyone that knew what was going on thought I was clueless to Romeo's games. After the party, as planned, I walked toward Romeo but he made it to me first.

"Jamaica, I'm surprised to see you; you're looking nice."
I thought, he was more shocked than happy to see me.
"I want to hang out with you tonight."
"OK. Mrs. Lady, I'm ready, let's go."

Things heated up in the parking lot when Sassy caught up with us to say, 'bye'. Romeo, Sassy, and I walked toward his new car. Romeo and I held hands. Two of Romeo's friends, Monte and Joseph, jumped in front of the three of us to get Romeo's attention. He wanted Romeo to notice his other woman that stood at his car waiting on him. Romeo let my hand go and walked away from me. Monte and Joseph started talking to me to stall me. I tripped, because people were stepping up and working harder than Romeo to save Romeo's relationship.

When I reached the car, Stacy was upset.
"Romeo, what's going on? Is everything alright?" I asked, all innocent-like.
"She drove her car, now she wants to ride with me."
Stacy started talking loudly and showing her true colors.
"Romeo, tell her who I am, you've been telling everyone else. Tell her where you've been every night this week and every other week before that. Tell her we've been sleeping together. Why don't you tell her where you obtained the money to by our new car, Romeo? You bet-

ter tell her something quick! You can't talk now, huh? This is our car; you're going to ride her in it, right in fount of me? It's not going to happen."

Romeo opened the passenger door for me to sit in the front seat. Stacy jumped in and raised the seat up for me to sit in the back seat. There was a crowd of people standing around Romeo's car, including Monte, Joseph and Sassy, all waiting for Romeo to choose between Stacy and me.

> Joseph walked right up to Romeo, "Don't let these women put you on the spot and make you choose, send both of them to their cars and deal with them later."
> "No, Joseph, man, everybody knows that Jamaica is my woman."
> "Joseph, who do you think you are to tell Romeo what to do and how to run his game?" I said.
> "He's my friend; I don't want him to lose his job over a woman."

It wasn't like Romeo and Leo to manhandle a woman. Monte walked up and grabbed Stacy out the car and pushed her out of my way. She stumbled and hit the ground and Monte stood over her cursing her out.

Everyone hollered at Stacy. Monte sounded like he had been sleeping with her, too.

> I said, "I don't care who been sleeping with who, when it comes to who's the best one for Romeo, everyone chooses me, this is my man!"
> Romeo hollered at me, "Jamaica, get in the car!"

Sassy held me back. She didn't want me to do anything crazy.

> "Don't holler at me because you can't control your women." I shouted.

I sat in the car. Romeo got in the car and drove off.

172

"Yeah, I'm on to your little game. You're sitting over there laughing because I chose you. I know that you were making me choose, Jamaica. She and I are friends and we let it go too far. She always hung around the guys and me trying to buy our attention. I'm sorry."

He apologized but I wasn't buying it. Romeo wasn't making sense to me. I refuse to believe Romeo would stop seeing a woman that bought him a car. I was going to keep my eye on him. I'll get to the bottom of his mess. He sounded promiscuous to me. I was onto something and that was why I had to follow him around and he didn't have a clue. On my off night, I drove to Romeo's house and parked up the street from his house and new car parked out front. At 12:00 A.M. He walked out his door alone. He was definitely up to something. I followed him down town San Francisco. He rolled up to a sports bar and stepped out of the car for valet parking and then walked inside.

I sat there for one hour. I watched him walk out of the bar. He was not alone. He was with a white guy and they were too busy talking to notice me. Romeo didn't ask valet for his car; he sat in the guy's truck and they drove off together. I drove off after them and ended up at a club. I paid the cover charge and walked in and a guy met me at the door.
      "Hi, I'm Drake."
      "I'm Jamaica."
      "You're welcome to sit at my table?"
      "Okay." I followed Drake and sat down.

Romeo and his friend sat at a table alone, talking. It looked like they had a lot to talk about. The guy I sat with told me that the club was a gay club. I had figured that much out but still, I needed to hear that from someone else.
      "Are you gay?"
      "No I'm straight, that's why I asked you to sit with me."
      "Are you gay?"

"No I'm straight. I'm into men." We laughed and asked each other why were we there.

"It's live!"

"I heard a lot about it. I like mixed crowds and wanted to see for myself." I came up with one excuse after another as to why I was there.

At that point, I was not making any sense. Drake didn't seem to care; he was just trying to hold a conversation. Romeo and his friend sat there cuddled up, enjoying one another's company. I started getting really mad, until, I couldn't take it any longer. After my third Screaming Orgasm, I forgot that I was spying on him. I stood up and walked up to Romeo's table holding my drink in my hand. I stood there looking at him with rage in my eyes. He looked up and couldn't believe that I was there.

"Romeo! You're leaving with me right now!"

"Romeo, man, handle your woman. Why do all your friends tell you what to do and run your business? You better handle your White boy." Romeo stood up in shock. He couldn't think of what to say to either of us. Romeo was high, drunk, and speechless. He thought he was hallucinating. I think he was waiting for me to disappear.

"Jamaica, why are you following me?"

"Are you my man or not? I need you to come home with me, now!"

"Can't you see, I'm talking?"

"What; you'd rather sit here with a man than be with me? What are you doing in a gay bar?"

"Jamaica, this is my business go home."

"I'm not going anywhere without you."

"Go home and wait for me."

"No!"

Romeo grabbed me by my arm and we walked over to the bar.

"Look, give me the key to your house. I'll come over after we leave here."

"No! If you don't leave with me now, don't bother coming to my house, ever again." I threw my drink in his face.

"That's the last orgasm you're going to get from me." Romeo's friend rushed to his side.

"Romeo! Is everything alright"

"Are you gay?" I asked. Then Romeo stepped between us.

"Which one of us are you defending?" I asked.

"You are out of line," Romeo said to me.

I lost it! I beat Romeo in his chest. I was hurt because Romeo defended him and he never introduced us. I reacted from reflex. Everyone looked at us. Their expression was as if this happened there all the time. I was another dizzy woman in denial that her man was gay. He threw me over his shoulder and carried me out of the club and put me down.

"Go home and wait for me. I'm not going to talk here."

"Talk about what, Romeo? Romeo, what? Why won't you talk to me?"

I couldn't understand why he wouldn't leave with me, what was wrong with me? I went home and sat there. I cried myself to sleep and I won't accept Romeo being anything other than my man. He spent the night with that man. Why would he do that? I couldn't cope with that. I couldn't make sense of it all. For the first time, I came out and admitted to myself that he was gay but I needed to hear him say it to truly believe it, as if seeing him wasn't enough. I was about to lose my mind. What little I had left.

I couldn't face my life or Romeo's life or why he didn't come to my house until, 4:45 A.M. Romeo picked me up off the sofa, cover and all, and carried me to the bedroom. I was crying my eyes out, 'Wildflower, Let Her Cry for She's a Lady', 1972 hit song by Skylark came on the radio. It made me cry harder. My D.J. was right on time with that one. Romeo laid me in bed and undressed me. I started ripping off his clothes and he was putting them back on. I begged him to make love to me, once more.

I didn't want it to be pity sex. I knew Romeo cared. I wanted him to make passionate love to me. He acted as if he was dirty and didn't want to contaminate me.

"Romeo, talk to me. Baby, tell me what's wrong?"

Something was killing him on the inside. Everything about his actions was telling me that he was confused about who to love and couldn't choose. Romeo wanted to have his cake and eat it too; he wanted to please everyone. What do you call that?

Our lovemaking was strong and more passionate than ever before. I knew he felt what I felt that night. I could see love in his eyes. We enjoyed our goodbye love but he couldn't tell me that it was over. He didn't want to hurt me. We cried ourselves to sleep. He left without saying goodbye. I felt there was someone else in his life, stopping him from having a serious relationship with me.

I called Romeo on my lunch break. Leo told me that Romeo was in the hospital in ICU (Intensive Care Unit). I left work and went to the hospital. The hospital staff wouldn't let me see him and said I wasn't allowed to visit. I looked right at him. I watched him through the glass window in his room. I saw Romeo laid out on his back and hooked up to several machines.

I asked his nurse, "What's wrong with Romeo; why is he here?"

His nurse wouldn't tell me what was wrong and asked me to leave. Three days later Romeo called and told me that he had tried to kill himself.

"Why?"

"You know why."

"No! I need you to tell me why. How did you hurt yourself?"

"Pills! Jamaica, you know me. You know me better than anyone and I need you to help me get through the emotions that I'm feeling. I don't want to give in to my desires. I want to fight what I'm feeling. Will you help me?"

I wasn't strong enough to help him but I couldn't say no.

"Okay, I will." I still hadn't heard him admit that he was gay; maybe he wasn't. We were both in denial.

Things like, being gay didn't happen in our world. It certainly didn't go down in my world. Being gay didn't happen to people like Romeo. Back then, it wasn't on TV. Romeo being gay couldn't be happening. I went to Romeo and we prayed together. If Romeo had been turned out by a man, it may be too late to save him. As far as I knew, he hadn't. I kept hanging out with him hopeful he could stop wanting men. I noticed changes in his personality. I noticed a difference in his behavior; he was gradually coming out.

He started trying to be me. He studied my type of woman. He was attracted to my type of man. One day that we were together, he hit on a man that was hitting on me. We shopped together and we bought a pair of shoes alike. Romeo moved in his first apartment and fixed it up similar to mine. He cooked the first dinner I prepared for him at my place, and invited me over for dinner. I couldn't take it anymore.

I made myself feel better. I went shopping for clothes at the mall and for fun, I test drove a new car at one of the car dealerships. The salesman gave me his best sales pitch. He talked me into test driving sports cars. The next thing I knew, I was in the office filling out an application to buy. I couldn't sleep and went to work sweating bullets; it still hadn't gone through. I dropped by after work and I had the car.

I put five thousand down and drove off the lot. I rolled in my apple red, custom Corvette, designed to look like a spaceship.

My dream car I always wanted that I felt I never could afford. I was totally infatuated with the car, like everyone else. The experience of driving up the street was crazy. People were running after my car. Men were running red lights to catch me.

I drove to Lady's Dee's house and Dee drove off in it alone and she returned and threw the keys at me. She said she had been chased all over town. Every day Dad came home from work, I would be there picking up Little Man and there would be a different car blocking his driveway.

> "Girl, what are you running at my house? First, I come home and there's a police car out front. The next day, it's a fire truck and a motorcycle after that. Today, there's an ambulance in my driveway. I thought someone had died."

The ambulance driver stood right there, like he wanted to know, too.

> "It's the hot red sports car, Dad" What did he expect from me and my red Corvette?

The day came that I had to face that my Romeo was gay. Romeo traded in his car for a black car like mine. He and Leo picked me up for a dinner date. We stopped at the bank and Romeo stepped out alone. Leo reached under the seat and pulled out some letters and put one in my hand. The letters were addressed to 'Oh Romeo, oh Romeo'. I struggled, trying to open the envelope. I rushed to get the letter out. I opened the letter and began to read.

It was beautifully written and I thought, 'wow', this is a woman madly, deeply in love. She sounded like they were meant to be together. With all of their different positions and the intense passion of missing each other, I was surprised Romeo and her weren't living together or married. It was pages and pages of pure ecstasy. It had me on cloud nine. They had the love affair I've been looking for. When I finally got to the bottom of the last page, I saw a man's name. I guess my mind didn't know how to react, so it simply didn't respond; everything in me went numb.

Romeo was gay. He walked out of the bank and I was gone. I sat in Leo's lap when I opened the car door and left. I walked up the street alone and did not care where I was going. The love letter was embedded in my hand and I was getting the hell away from Romeo. Romeo didn't know what was going on. Leo ran after me and held me in his arms, telling me he was sorry and felt I had to face the truth sooner or later.

I saw Romeo running towards us. I began ripping the letter into pieces. I saw a trolley bus picking up passengers and I broke away from Leo and jumped on the trolley. After that day, I hid what Romeo and I was going through from the world. I didn't see or talk to Romeo at work or at home for two weeks. He called and asked to take me to dinner. I said yes! I felt that he was the only one that can reach me. I was hoping that he would have a miracle up his sleeves and wished for him to say, 'wake up', this has all been one big nightmare.

We didn't speak a word in the car, we waited to see who would break the ice first but no one did. We arrived at the restaurant and ordered our food. Romeo talked about the weather. He blamed all of his problems on the rain. I had hoped he hadn't planned to destroy my life and he had successfully completed doing just that when he confirmed he had come out of the closet. I died of a broken heart and asked myself, what more could he bring to the table. He looked into my eyes and told me that he sleeps with both men and women.

I tried to digest that Romeo was still sleeping with women. I thought about how bad I wanted him, while he went on turning the knife in my back.

> "My man understands what I am going through and my woman says she will be there for me, no matter what. She'll accept me for who I am."

Then he actually opened his mouth and said, "There's nothing better than sex with a man and then sex with a woman." The entire evening was for him to rub his gayness in my face. Romeo bragged and he was clearly proud to come out of the closet.

He hates me because I couldn't handle it and he had asked me to help him fight it. I don't know what went down since then but it seems someone had turned him against me. Romeo had been turned out by a man and I felt that I had been lied to and double-crossed. I had been used and abused all over again. When he dropped me off I went into the house and didn't come out.

I remembered crying for days, the days turned into weeks, and the weeks turned into months. My job called and sent mail-a-grams and telegrams to my home. I wasn't washing myself and I wasn't talking to anyone. Little man stayed at Dee's house. No one in my family knew Romeo turned gay on me. I couldn't bring myself to tell them. I was hurting for Romeo, too. People are going to treat him differently, laugh at him and talk about him behind his back. I couldn't stand the thought of someone hurting him but I had hurt him. I wasn't strong enough to stand beside him. Right then, I had to save me and it took three months to do that.

My emancipation came the day my dad brought groceries over. He told me to clean myself up.

> He enlightened me, "Prayer will always be the 'IN' thing. Praying would never get old and it wasn't an old person's role; praying is for everyone, young and old. You need to be more responsible; now that you are old enough to pray for strength for yourself."
> All my life my mom had said to me, "I'm living on someone else's prayers and don't know it."

That day, listening to my dad, I was reminded again of my promises to God. So much had happened in my life, I didn't know where to begin praying. I cleaned myself up, sat in my car, and drove to my parent's house.

I put the key in the lock and opened the door. I felt faint from the lack of food and suffering and the stress from allowing another man to totally drain me. I walked over to my mom, baring it all. I sat down next to her on the sofa and placed my head in her lap. I broke down when my mother started talking to me.

> "Jamaica, my beautiful baby girl; what is it? You can talk to me. I'm your mother."
> "Mom, it's not me, Romeo is gay." I cried.

She reminded me that I wouldn't listen. Then came her, 'I told you so' speech. When I first described Romeo to her, she exposed him and she told me to take my time to get to know him better. She explained to me that there was nothing I could do for Romeo.

> "Wish him well and go on with life. You have a child to take care of. Someday love will find you and when it does, you'll be ready for it. Sometimes in life, real love comes along and catches you by surprise; a true love captures your heart and helps you realize you're ready for love."

Mom prayed for me that day and when she finished, I felt better. We talked about her eyesight being bad in both her eyes and that she was going blind. We called a family meeting. Moe Joe handed her the money for her operation and she turned him down. She explained that even with one operation she would need more and still gradually go blind.

That night when I went home, I spent some time with Little Man. I knew I had lost sight of who I was and I needed to hear it from someone else. My mom was that person. I wanted my son and me to have a man in the house so bad. I was sick on the inside. I just could not see what I was doing anymore. I couldn't understand why I didn't feel complete without a man.

I had saved up money, thinking Romeo was the one. The plan was to combine our money and start a life together. Instead, I bought my car. I felt like Romeo decided to come out, than to run from an already-made family that he wasn't prepared for. Romeo said, I was his first woman and he may have meant I was the first female he had sex with and he still had some experimenting to do. I blamed myself. I didn't have anyone to reason with or to help me make sense of it all. You can only tell your mother so much. And now, she had her worries, too.

You can't talk to anyone about wanting a man when there's only so much you can say to people before they stop you. The first thing I would hear was, you can do it by yourself. I knew that was true but I didn't want to do it alone. I didn't want Little Man to go without. I felt I'd never be good enough for my son without giving him a father.

After taking three months off sick leave, I went to work and everyone stared at me. They tried to figure out if I knew that Romeo came out of the closet because I was acting like everything was alright with Romeo and our relationship. They wanted me to be angry and talk about my Romeo behind his back. Where did they think I had been for three months? One lady employee told me that Romeo didn't work there anymore. I asked myself, 'was it my problems that cause him to act this way'?

Was this my fault? I left him but that was after the letters. He made a choice that I couldn't live with and I knew I couldn't share him with men and women. I wanted him all to myself. I cut off all communication with Romeo and that hurt him worse. I did it to save myself. I was celibate once again. Men tried to get my attention but I was not interested in anything serious, other than hanging out.

My brother Moe-Joe bought a house boat and he threw a party on the boat. I met a guy named, Boss. He came aboard like he was God's gift to women. His looks were flawless but his game was lacking. I could see right through it. He was clearly a yes-man. He was worse than everything I tried to get away from. His profession was hustling women. I got sick of listening to his lies and I wasn't amused by his game.

> I walked away from him, "Don't walk away, I'm your present, take me home and unwrap me, and play with me. I'll be your biggest toy."
> "I'm so over playing with toys; I need a man. You're welcome to come home with me if we bring your brother along."

Boss and I both stayed until, after the party and when the three of us went to my house, I opened a gallon of wine that he knocked back all by himself. I went to bed and they stayed up talking for the rest of the night. I came home from work and called my brother to talk about Boss. Who was that guy? I wanted to know more about him the day after I met him. I didn't remember much, only that Boss had taken an interest in me. Was it love at first sight? When I talked to Moe Joe, he said that Boss and his twin brother were liars that owed him money. They're womanizers looking for someone to take care of them. While we were talking, the doorbell rang. I answered and it was Boss standing there with his suitcases. In the past, I had been one of those people that jumped from one relationship to the other, without working to better themselves.

> It was time for me to grow up, "Boss, what are you do-ing here?"
> "I don't have any place to go."
> "What happened between you and your brother?"
> "He and his woman put me out."
> "How did you get here?"
> "My brother dropped me off."
> "Boss, I'm sorry but you can't stay here. I'll take you back to your brother's."

"He's not home and I don't have a key."

For that moment, I let him in my house but my mind was made up. I told him to keep trying to reach his brother on the phone.

"I was nice to you for one night and now you're trying to take advantage of me, Boss, I don't even know you. What's your problem, why don't people want you around?"

"How do you know that? You've been asking about me?"

"Yes! Did you think I wouldn't?"

He went on talking. He started out saying, how people don't understand him nor did anyone believe in him. He acted like I knew him best.

"Because of my good looks, I was spoiled as a child. I grew up on the laps of beautiful women and I would put on a show. I was always the center of attention. Women kept my pockets fat with money and as a result, I learned to use my good looks to get my way. I like aggressive women but I have a short temper with them. Jamaica, you're my first nice girl. I know I won't have a problem with you."

"Boss, yes you will. You take 'nice' for granted and I don't want to see your bad side. I've been there and I've done that. You have an anger problem and you need to accept that for what it is. Stop making excuses and blaming everyone. Everyone gets angry about something. All of us have been hurt by someone in some form or fashion. You have to learn how to own your emotions. You're responsible for your anger, not other people."

Boss was clearly a yes-man and I couldn't take the lies and the deception anymore. Thanks to Blue, that allowed me to be straight with him. I started telling the men in my life the truth about them.

"Boss, I see you as the kind of guy that would have other women in my house when I'm at work. I see you as a man that will steal from me, without any remorse, like I owe you something. You just said you've been taught to get paid by women. When those same women stopped giving you money, you went in their purses and took their money. Am I right?"

"Yes—but!"

"No Boss, it won't work, the answer is, "No."

Ultimately, I knew he would bring me down, so I decided not to waste my time.

"Boss, you are a grown man. You can't go around acting irresponsible forever and intimidating women when they say, 'No'. That's how children act and you need to deal with the fact that you hate women because you found out that every woman is not going to sit you on their lap and give you money. Playing on women with your fine looks will not work anymore, you're getting older; now what?"

Pretending to be him, I stood up to demonstrate how obvious his game was. I wanted him to see how he walked into a room, flexing his muscles and putting on a show for the ladies.

"You don't need to put on a show, your presence is the show. You have the look and the body; you have it all!"

I laughed at him and he laughed at me. He told me his business ideas and they actually were pretty darn good. To learn how successful he could be wasn't impressive, he was depressing. We sat on the sofa talking and he then exposed himself.

"I never had to ask for anything."

That was just sad, he couldn't get me with his looks and charm so he relied on his size and performance but he won't be performing here. When I saw him, I thought that he had a large load to fall back on when he couldn't charm his way.

"Put that away, I made the point that we don't have anything physical going on, not even a love connection. Women are not turned on by men who do that."

I was never turned on by men who did that. There was a time when I laughed but it wasn't funny anymore. Boss turned me off. I was not into perverts. That man had serious problems and I was going to listen to my brother and my true feelings.

> "Boss this is not about how good you look. This is about real feelings hidden away in your heart and soul. You need to let somebody in; let them know you have feelings. You're getting older. Honesty is the only way you're going to find love and be loved. See, some people will never change. Some are so busy trying to get their way they forget to grow up with compassion."

I drove Mr. Boss back to his brothers, I wished him well. He didn't have any respect for women and he wasn't going to be the boss of me. He was a fun guy. I was hoping that he would make a change. Not long after that, he died of AIDS. For some, AIDS is the ultimate wake-up call and some people get a second chance.

After Boss' funeral, I jumped in my car and drove off. I drove to the lake and cruised around, flirting with whomever. I parked outside of the lake and watched other cruisers as guys hollered and blew at me. A tall, dark, and handsome man rolled up and jumped out of his jeep. When his feet hit the ground, I panicked. He had shorts on and his personal business was hanging five inches below the shorts.

He could clearly see that I was scared of him. I was teasing men and didn't think they'd bite.

> "Calm down, you need to go home and put some clothes on. What do you expect when you're out here dressed like a freak? You're going to catch a freaky boogie man with a three-word demand, "Take-me-home" and he won't take 'No' for an answer."

He made a monster face at me and I sat back in my car and drove off. To get away from the boogie bears, I decided to cruise the inside of the lake. I planned to drive right through and go home. While cruising, I saw Boxer jogging. He was working-out with his trainer. He saw me and asked me to pull over.

I hollered out of my window, "No! I'm on my way home."

"I'm nothing to play with, Jamaica. You never gave me an answer. I can end it, you know. Who do you think you are? You think your car looks better than mine?"

He was in the middle of the road hollering. He scared me. He was too demanding. I was tempted, before he started to yell. He sounded too much like Troy, wanting to equalize the situation. All I wanted to do was wipe the sweat off of his firm body, lie in his arms, and cry. I would love that pretty man so sweetly; he wouldn't be worth a dime to his other women.

I was tired of going through things by myself. Boxer was no exception. He was the bad boy I was fighting to stay away from. I knew what he was all about, and he was not typical. He was a die-hard player. I never knew what to expect from him. He was still tripping on who had what. Why is he so mad at me? That night at his house, did he expect me to fall into bed when he manipulated everyone to get me there? I was ending it by never going back to the player's club; not in this lifetime.

When I returned home, I was depressed and I was in a crying state of mind. That night, I put on Natalie Cole's, 'I'm Keeping a light shining in the Window', 'I'm Catching Hell', and 'Annie May'. Next, I played, Stephanie Mills' 'Feel the Fire', and 'I Need the Comfort of a Man'. I couldn't listen to those two without crying my eyes out. I was crying about my mother's eyes, and my pain. I wanted the loving touch of a man and couldn't find it. I was sad that Boss didn't get a second chance at life, as I had.

I wanted an honest man in my life that would lay my head on his shoulder and talk to me. He would make me feel better just to have a shoulder to lie on and listen to a man's voice calm me. I wanted a man that looked for one woman to love! One set of fingerprints on my body to feel clean and deserving of love. I believe, when you're worthy of being truly loved, it will come. I don't want every Tom, Dick, and Harry groping me. I felt that life hadn't found me worthy, and so that night, I entered a new phase.

I had found that, honesty was not the best policy. Men thought I was lying when I was telling the truth; calling me smooth Dr. Suez. For whatever reason, all this time men had thought I was playing them. Dealing with the men I dealt with, I found out that an honest woman didn't exist to most men in this world.

I had looked death in the face many times and lived. I felt brave because I had dodged a bullet like AIDS and I felt invincible. Plus, the drugs made me bold; I was high on marijuana most of the time. Trying to save one troubled man after another was hopeless. There was something seriously wrong with the men I tried to revolutionize and they said the same thing about women.

I gradually started rapping to men using their lines. If you can't beat them, join them. That's when I found out, I could beat them at their own games and tactics. It was too easy. It wasn't my plan to be a player, it was an invitation, and I was game. I looked for true love in all the wrong places. I needed to go out with my sister's but they were all busy.

I couldn't help but think about the last time I went to a concert. I had so much fun with my four sisters. We all went to see 'Frankie Beverly' and some more groups. We danced the entire concert. When the intermission came, my sisters and I needed to stretch our legs. We decided to walk to the other side of the coliseum to scope out men. While we were over there, we saw a tall, handsome guy crawling up the stairs. He reached the top and then threw-up. Then he started trying to crawl up the walls. He didn't notice us standing there. We went back to our sets. The music was jamming. The concert was in full swing and our hot bodies were moving in the California night heat. The evening was almost over and we were breathless. At that point we were resting and eagerly waiting for them to sing their last song, 'Look at California'.

> "What's going on, ladies?" We all looked up at the same time to say hello and recognized the man face. It was the guy that was crawling on the other side of the stadium.
>
> "Hi!" We said all at once.

We glanced at each other at the same time trying not to be obvious we were holding our laugh in. The music started and we jumped up and started to scream. He was cute so we played it off and let him join the party, as if we didn't know he couldn't hold his high and was lost most of the concert.

I'll never forget, 'Frankie Beverly,' and I'll never forget him. The night he and I went out together, we were both high. I was having sex without contraceptives, playing Russian roulette. I was suicidal. Unfortunately for me, I was searching for a man to fill the void and I didn't want but one man that could get the job done. I was talking street-talk I picked-up while hanging with the wrong crowed. Hopping in men's laps, talking about the first thing that popped up, hoping he'd have a conversation.

I dropped lines like, "I'm looking for some biscuits and gravy," and didn't even know what all that meant. I wanted plenty enough sex and drugs to put me to sleep. One of my biggest regrets was being that type of woman and I didn't know getting rapped was what put me in that state of mind and keeping secrets kept me there. I blamed Troy for my sex addictions. I craved the perfect lover. I couldn't live down the way he made love to me. When I was younger he was my sleeping pill. I was spoiled and well-seasoned. Living up to my bad girl tags and being labeled as a hag, I needed to feel everything a man had to offer in bed.

That night at my date's house, he couldn't perform and tried to knock me for his problem. He blamed me because I wouldn't do all the things he needed to make him stand at attention.

> I told him, "Hold up, wait a minute now, I don't know about all that stuff you're asking me to do to you. When I asked for gravy did that mean put it in my face? It isn't what I wanted. You need special help, a professional, maybe a prostitute, or something. I don't think you have enough money to pay prostitutes for the time it took for you to get aroused and at attention. Two virgins won't do you a bit of good."

He finally told me that it was the drugs he was using. All I knew was, I'd never again ask another man for gravy. Unless, I was holding a KFC biscuit, mashed potatoes, and a piece of meat that was finger licking good.

Chapter Ten
The Silent Breakdown

I had been moving too fast, but still, I wasn't going to miss the unforgettable party on the bay. I was non-stop drama, all about, 'where's the parties been' and wasn't listening to my body. Throwing everything over my shoulder, and telling myself I can get over my craving, and my addiction for men. I had a man friend coming to visit me from Santa Barbara, California. I met him one night when my cousin, Ebony, and I went to a club on the Santa Barbara army base. He looked good and everywhere I went, he followed. For me, it was lust at first sight.

Ebony said, "Look at that tall drink of water."

"That's not water, that's a tall mug of hot chocolate with marshmallows on top."

His name was Cody and his teeth were big and white. Cody had a smile that lit up the night and he worked there on the army base. He and I became friends and he would fly to see me every year on his vacation. That year he came, he stayed at a hotel. Cody felt safe with me and ran to me to get away from other women. It's true that opposites attract and birds of a feather flock together. Cody was a good hearted man that was chased down and seduced by women. We were compatible as friends and hanging out together was fun.

He detailed my car and helped me paint Little Man's room. He was an easy going man and the smallest things made him happy, like ironing his T-shirts with starch and making them look new. He didn't get out much, so every year, I surprised him with something new and special. That time it was tickets to a singles cruise on a yacht called, 'The Championship' in San Francisco Bay.

He and I went shopping for the event, I dressed him in white and I had on a simple white dress with the back out. As we boarded the vessel, we were happy to see that we looked as good as everyone else. We didn't stand out other than the fact that we looked appropriate. We got everyone's attention as we stood talking to the host. She led us downstairs, where we had cocktails and dinner.

We headed upstairs, excited to enjoy the festivities. The live entertainment was George Benson. We listened to his jazz band music as we rocked and swayed on the bay. Everyone was ready to party and to have a wonderful night. A young lady came over and asked Cody for a dance.

"Excuse me, Jamaica, it's time for me to groove."

"OK, have fun."

Cody, his white suit, and partner, danced into the night. It was a singles party and Cody was fair game. I headed downstairs to freshen my drink when I heard a man call out my name. I turned around to answer the call and it was Boxer. I wanted to jump overboard but before I could say a word, he walked up and kissed me in the face.

"How do you like my yacht?"

"I love this yacht. I didn't know who it belonged to. I'm just here for the party."

"Come with me; let me show you around."

"Well, I'm kind of with someone."

"Don't worry about him, he's being well taken care of."

"Boxer, did you set this up? How did you pull this surprise off?"

"Jamaica, we're together. Does it matter how it happened? Come on; you're in good hands; you know that."

He escorted me to the Captain's quarters. I walked in and felt like I was in a dream or a nightmare; we would soon see.

"What are you drinking?"

"Champaign."

"Here, try this, it's Cognac," he said, as he sat down beside me on the sofa.

"Jamaica, why are you afraid of me? I only want to get to know you better. I like you. And I go after what I want. It's how I live my life; this is who I am."

"You're telling me, all I have to do is sit back and listen and you'll stop the sexual mind games of manipulation, I don't know what to call it, what else you might want from me?"

"I want all of you. I organized all of this because I want to make love to you. Tonight is our time and I know you feel the same way as me."

For the first time, he tongue kissed me and I tried to think of a reason to stop him. I attempted to get up but I couldn't leave. I couldn't think of anything to say or do. Boxer had worn me down; he took my breath away. At that moment, I wanted him as much as he wanted me and it was then, I began to put it all together. Boxer sent a guy to my job to sell me tickets. The tickets were three hundred dollars each. He allowed me to talk him down and he sold them both for a hundred dollars. Boxer and I made love that night and stayed together until, the party ended. He looked into my eyes and said all the things I needed to hear.

"Jamaica, don't leave; stay. I'll ask my driver to take Cody to his hotel."

I stayed with him and we made love once more and talked the rest of the night. That morning during breakfast, Boxer gave me back the five hundred dollars for both tickets and said his good-byes. On my way home, I thought it was official, I was his high class prostitute.

Later that evening, I still had last night on my mind and Cody called and said he had a good time last night. He asked to buy me dinner and I dressed up and met him. He didn't go into details about his night and I didn't mention mine. I made sure that he had a good vacation and then it was time to say bye-bye. I couldn't wait for him to leave. My head was messed up from the night before. I couldn't stand the thought of me making love to a serious player; a hard core pimp, or gangster. I didn't know what hell he was. What were his plans for me?

I felt I had made a bad mistake by sleeping with Boxer. I cried for weeks. I didn't seek help for my need for the wrong man. I continued picking up more men. 'So many attractive guys, so little time', I thought.

One day after work, I went to the beach to jog and to run off steam when I saw a gold custom made Corvette parked in the parking lot. I thought it was someone I knew and to amuse him, I fell over the hood of the car and stumbled up to the window on the driver's side. I looked inside but it wasn't him.

I was embarrassed and apologetic. He thought I was hilarious and continued smoking a joint, and then put it up to my mouth.

"Get in, you've earned it. You want a hit off this joint?"
"No, thank you."

I answered to both the Joint and the invitation to get in. He was clearly a yes-man. I thought about, what I was going to do about Boxer perusing me.

"Sorry, I thought you were someone else," I said, as I turned and walked away.

During my jog, I ran into Drake, the guy I met at the gay club. Turns out, he was a lifeguard at Golden Gate Beach. He had been sitting on his watchtower watching me make a fool of myself the entire time. As I jogged, he joined me, until, I became tired and he walked me back to my car.

"May I come home with you?"
"No," I'm going to my parent's. I love my parents and they love me."

Drake was tall, dark, and handsome with a hard body shining in the California sun. Standing in front of me, he casted a large shadow. I was hot and needed the shade. Right off, I could see that Drake wanted to be a player and thought his innocent charm could persuade anyone into loving him, no matter what. He was what I tried to get away from, except he seemed harmless. He mentioned that night with Romeo.

"I'm so sorry about how we met. You deserved to be treated better than that, but, you and me? We were meant to be."

Drake was convincing and I loved that about him. I took him home and introduced him to mom. Mom had a way with people; they would spill their innermost secretes. I went to freshen up and put on more make-up. First, I heard bumping and then I heard the out cries of a man in pain. I hurried to the living room and witnessed Drake rolling on the floor. He told my mom that he had a sex addiction and she tried to pray it out of him.

Sex was the only thing I was interested in, from him. That night because of prayer, he might be free of his addiction and I would never know if he was any good. At the end of the night, I was still interested and wanted to know him better. I took off my gold chain with the floating heart charm and placed it around his neck. I took him to his house and dropped him off.

When Drake was ten years old, his father died in service, so I picked him up for the Veteran's Day parade. We were in the house getting ready to leave and his doorbell rang. When he answered the door, it was a woman.

"What are you doing coming to my house without calling first?"
"I didn't know I had to call, the door is always open. Now, all of a sudden you have house rules. What's going on, who is she?"
"None of your business. I don't have to tell you anything, this is my house. You seem to have forgotten that,"
"Are you asking me to leave?"

"Yes, please!"

"Well, I'm not leaving! You're my man! If you don't want me anymore, put me out!"

She slapped Drake in the face and Drake stood there and took it, like a man. She reached up and snatched my gold chain off his neck and broke it. I picked up the chain first, then went after my floating heart charm that rolled across the floor. He picked her up and threw her across the room in the same direction that I walked. As she was airborne, in mid-flight, she hollered,

"He's going to kick your ass this way, too!" She flew right past me and landed on the floor.

I picked up my charm and went outside. I wanted to give them time to talk, say goodbye, or fight, whatever! She came out of the house, wildly, and walked up the street to wherever she came from. Drake apologized all day to prove that she was his ex. At the end of our date, I went back to Drake's for a good time. I knew it would be our last night together.

Alone in his room, I wanted revenge, so I took a tampon from my purse and put it in the top hankie pocket of his father's army jacket. I left the top of it sticking out like a cigar. The jacket hung on the wall above Drake's bed. I knew that Drake would continue to see other women and would continue to do so as long as we allowed him to.

After that night, Drake called.

"That was a cold-blooded move you made on me. When the other woman saw that tampon, she had to face that her and I were over and she left, mad. I couldn't do anything but laugh. You should be happy; you won. I'm all yours. Come over, let's celebrate!"

He sounded like we were playing a game of chess. He thought he was a stud but to me, he was a joke. He kept calling, wasting his time; it was over before it began. Next.

Lady Dee was married; she married a pilot she met at the airport. My cousin, Ebony, came up for the wedding and partied with me that night. She was under age and we tried one club after another and couldn't get her in. We were walking away from the last club about to give up when two guys walked up behind us, suggesting that we follow them to an after-hours club.

They were wearing nice suits and driving a Mercedes. I didn't know what their faces looked like. They were checking us out as we were leaving. We arrived at the square and stepped out of the car. They walked up to us, introduced themselves and then escorted us into the club. One walked in front of the other, as the first guy passed me up for Ebony. I was able to see what the second guy looked like.

I felt like dancing to the beat of his stride; he was just walking. I was going to make him mine, even though I was infatuated. His look was beyond gorgeous. I asked God to let him be the one. I wanted that man.

"My name is Anthony and you are?"

"I'm Jamaica Gold."

"I love your style. You're wearing that dress and the dress is wearing you. We shouldn't have any trouble getting in the club the way you look. Besides, the owner is my friend. Have you ever been here?"

"No I haven't."

When Anthony and I got through the door he said, "There isn't one table available. Excuse me, I'll be right back."

I waited right there for him while he talked someone out of their table. He returned and the music was insanely loud. It was the perfect time to get close. He whispered in my ear.

"Do you mind sharing a table?"

"No!"

We sat down and immediately the women were drawn to him wanting to dance with him. He rejected them fast. He gave me all his attention. I couldn't help but notice the women staring him down. It was worse than the women that stared at Boxer. They gave him the eye and every other turn-on expression. They offered him drinks and anything else they hoped he wanted. I had never witnessed such behavior from women before. I could have sat up and watched all night! I turned down men, too, while waiting on Anthony to ask me.

"Why aren't you dancing?" he asked.

"I'll dance with you."

"Let's dance."

Anthony was a smooth operator. On our way to the dance floor, he held my upper right arm and eased his hand down to my waist.

"I wanted to dance with you and I saw you turning everyone down. I didn't want to be turned down; not by you. I want to see you move in this dress and I want to see how the dress moves you."

I felt special talking with Anthony, so we danced to every song together. At the end of the night, I played hard to get because he ignored women giving him attention and flirting with him. He looked for a challenge and instead of giving him my number, I waited for him to offer his. I called and he wasn't home and he didn't return my call. Two weeks later, I was at the mall after work, inside a phone booth, talking on the phone with Drake. He begged to get me back.

He said, he and I were meant to be and he couldn't live without me. Drake used those same tired lines, trying to entice me to come over. I saw Anthony step out of his Mercedes wearing a brown suit, carrying a suitcase, walking towards me.

"My, my, Mr. Businessman."

I thought he would recognize me and he walked right by me. He ignored me like I was one of the women at the club the night we met. I hung up the phone on the past and ran after my future. I was not going to let him get away twice.

> "Excuse me, do you remember me; I met you two weeks ago and I followed you to the square, remember?"

> "I remember, you look different."

> "I know, I had my hair down that night. I usually have my hair up in French-braids every day for work. People say I look different with my hair in braids."

I made a fool of myself, going on and on about my hair. I told him about my job when an African guy that had been watching me walked up and interrupted.

> "Hey, sister, if I took you to Africa, you would be an African queen?"

The oldest African come-on line ever.

> "Why I have to go to Africa to be queen, what am I here?"

> "An American," We laughed.

Anthony and I walked away and the guy just would not leave.

> "Hey, man, if you're going to live in this country, you have to speak the language and understand what it means. In America, no means no; there isn't any explanation for the word no," Said Anthony.

> "Thank you," the African said, and walked away.

I was impressed. I gave Anthony my number and said my good-byes. That day he ran behind me.

> "Do you have to leave? Come over, let me show you where I live. Let's hang out. I'm on my way home. I'll change my clothes and we can go to happy-hour, have a drink, and then dinner, whatever you want. What kind of food you like?"

> "Good tasting food."

> "I'll take you somewhere you'll love. Wait right here. I must deliver these papers."

Anthony returned. We walked to his car.

> "Get in; I'll give you a ride to your car," He drove me to my car.

"This is a nice Corvette. This is not the car you drove the night we met."

"That's right, I was driving my sister's blue and white Cutlass Supreme. She used my car to go on her honeymoon that night."

He gave me directions to his house to make sure I'd make it. I looked at the directions.

"You're a rich kid, huh? Do you live with your parents? Only doctors and lawyers live on these hills."

"Both my parents are doctors," He said, in his calm, dignified voice.

We arrived at Anthony's house at the top of the hill and I saw an incredible home that sat three stories high. Upon entering, I noticed a waterfall in the large entry hall. I had never been in a home as big and beautiful as that one. To the right, was a large room with an exclusive pool table colored gold and white. To the left was a sitting room. Directly in fount of me, was an extravagant stairwell with a view of the first floor. His mother stood at the top looking down on me. He introduced us. She was pretty and looked young. We talked while he changed.

She showed me the house, Anthony returned and we left to go to dinner. In the car, he told me that he was a lawyer. He was at the mall handling a lawsuit. His favorite hobby was shooting pool and he was undefeated. On the way to dinner, we stopped at two different game boards in two different sports bars where he could see who had signed up to play him on a certain day or night. By the time we got to the restaurant, we were good and hungry. It was an upscale sandwich shop downtown with a view of the bridge. I let him order for me because he wanted me to taste a particular hot sandwich; steak and cheese with onions, bell peppers, and mushrooms.

While we ate, the conversation was relaxing, he was easy to look at and he felt the same about me.

"Have you ever been to a bathhouse to rent a Jacuzzi room?" He said.

"No."

"Would you like to go with me sometime?"

"Yes, I would like that."

At home, later that night, Sassy-Girl called and invited me to go with her to her boyfriend's birthday party. I said, yes, and asked if I can invite a friend to meet us there. She said, yes, and I took down the address. The next time I talked to Anthony, I told him about the party; he was going to try and make it, but he wasn't going to make any promises.

The night of the party, I was excited to wear a tight, blue and green striped dress; my hair flowed right. I was ready to see Anthony and party with him some more. I wanted Sassy-Girl to see how the women fall for him. I arrived. I met her new man, Ramon. His sarcasm was funny and I liked his style. Every time I looked at him and Sassy, I smiled. They looked cute together. I thought the house party was at its perfection when they hollered, "The roof is on fire, let it burn."

The front door opened and everyone started to chant the name, Russo. I thought, there can only be one character that called himself Russo Esquire. He could walk into a party and his entrance alone would turn the party out. He'll be happy to see me; we go way back. When we were both younger and moving fast, we had a wild fling. It ended when we were still hot and heavy for one another.

There was Russo, dancing through the party like the ghetto superstar that he was. He danced up to the birthday boy and offered his best wishes. He swaggered and strutted and showed off his skills, checking out the women while performing his male mating dance. Then, he spotted me. That was when the roof caught on fire for me. He picked me up and twirled me around.

When Russo put me down he locked his arms around me and held on tight.

"We're going to party tonight," he said, singing to the beat of the music.

We talked while dancing. We haven't seen each other since I was young. I first saw him when I was eighteen, walking to the mall from Troy's house. We had not officially met yet, until, I recognized him at this club, called, 'Freaky Mondays'. He approached me for a dance.

Russo was tall, dark, and fine and one of a kind. He looked mannish that night with all that hair on his face. We were having fun when three white people, two men and a woman walked into the party and straight to the kitchen. They boiled water and scooped and mixed from one dish to the other. I watched, thinking they were caterers. They put everything on a tray and carried it upstairs.

I could see, it wasn't food they were catering but something else tempting. I continued to party and Russo left me and went upstairs behind them. When Russo returned in a good mood, I was dancing with someone else and he cut in and held on to me again.

"Do you trust me?"

"No, why?"

"I want to make this our night. I want to turn you on to something new. But promise me, you won't do what I'm about to show you with anyone else."

On our way upstairs, I thought, 'Have you lost your mind?' Since I had been abused, I made decisions with an abused mind. I made bad decision and used drugs to forget about the sexual abuse. I needed to get revenge on Anthony for not showing up for the party. On top of that; I tried to forget Boxer. I couldn't understand, how I reached the point of letting him make love to me? I can't get him out of my mind and everything else that was wrong in my life. I was out of control and hid my depression, obsessions and all my demons from every one.

Sassy-Girl doesn't know that I'm high as a kite on weed and she would really freak out if she knew what I was going to do; drugs with Russo. When we got upstairs, Russo was all over me assuring me that he won't let anything happen to me.

"I have tested the drug, its good quality. I know these people, they only have the best."
First, they passed us a dinner tray that had lines of white powder.
"What do you call this drug?" I asked.
Reaching for the tray, he said, "Cocaine."

We were standing there waiting for our turn to inhale the Jeannie bottle with water at the bottom. When it was passed to us, I didn't know one end from the other, I was ready to try it. Everybody there did what they do and it looked as if they were having fun. My conscience kicked in. When you don't listen to your conscience telling you no, don't do it; you could end up in big trouble; because then, you want to drown out your conscience and your pain with the ultimate high and you could overdose. I tried to get high enough, so that my conscience couldn't reach me. I didn't want to feel reality, nor my emotions for Boxer.

Russo took a hit and demonstrated for me how it was done, and then passed it to me. My first hit overwhelmed me. I felt rich and I believed that I was the most beautiful woman alive. I had it all. After the second hit, I felt smart and important and I asked everyone.

"What is your occupation?"
It was crucial for me to know. After the third hit, I started rapping to Russo in my mind, so I thought. I always thought to myself, except that time I talked out loud and dirty. When I realized that I could hear myself, I couldn't stop myself. I wanted to put my hand over my mouth, but the worst had been said. Russo

had set me up. He knew I was going to feel that way. If looks could kill; Russo would be dead.

"Russo, I've had enough; I'm going downstairs."

Russo caught my hand.

"Jamaica, don't let the drug control you; your fine. You only expressed your feelings for me; you're still in control. Trust me, if you wasn't, I would take you home. This is our night and it's a party, relax, let's have fun."

When we went downstairs everyone knew what I had said to Russo upstairs. Everyone started chanting his name again.

"Now, I know why they chanted, because they knew his game." I thought.

After the party, I told Sassy-Girl that I was going with Russo.

She asked Ramon, "Is Russo a nice guy?"

"She's in good hands," he said and smiled; when he should have said, 'No'. Russo's a super freak, you'd better stop her.

Russo and my high-self went straight to a hotel. That morning, I awakened with my dress hanging out on the balcony. My undies were hanging in the doorway, leading into the bathroom.

"Why are my things hanging out to dry? Did we get caught in the rain?" Russo laughed.

"You got in the shower with your clothes on." he said.

He left while I dressed and then came back with my favorite breakfast. I was surprised he remembered what I liked for breakfast. We ate and talked about old times and couldn't believe we were in each other's life again.

The following weekend, Russo called. I talked for a minute and then we planned a date for the following weekend. I had plans to go to the bathhouse with Anthony that night. Jazzy Black called and told me that James King was back in town and wanted to see me. I was shocked. I haven't seen The King since he asked me to marry him. He had kept in touch with me through letters but I never wrote him back.

I felt bad about him and me and how we didn't make our relationship last. I felt that he was over me; he had been married three times; so it was safe to see him. Everything that we went through was old news and I answered, "Yes, I'll come." Anthony called and I told him what was up to and that I had to go see an old friend. I also told him to give me two hours for dinner and then page me on my beeper.

King looked good and he said I looked the same. He had a look in his eyes that let me know he was still very much in love with me. I was uncomfortable and ready to leave when I first arrived. After two hours of talking about old times and how the three of us used to hangout, Anthony beeped me. I told King I had to leave. I said my goodbyes and left.

Anthony was waiting and I didn't miss a beat; I drove home and jumped in the car with him. First, we stopped to get something to drink. He was exhausted from work and I was exhausted from play, so we couldn't wait to get in the hot tub. We walked in the room undressing. I stripped down to my bikini and stepped in.

> "Is this your first time? I'm sorry to tell you this, baby girl, but you're not supposed to wear that in here. You need to take off that bikini. You shy? Let me help you with that thing." He helped me take off my bikini and tossed it, "Now don't you feel better? We came here to relax."
> "I was relaxed with my bikini on and I know there isn't such a rule about wearing one."

We talked and laughed and I loosen up a little. We didn't have a love connection, but the night was still young. Later, we were at Anthony's house and we were laid back enjoying each-others company. The doorbell rang and in walked the answers to my questions. She was Anthony's ex-girlfriend, little and gorgeous; with hair down her back. The two of them looked as if they made the perfect, rich couple. Between the two of them, I wondered who left whom? She didn't go to him; she walked over and acknowledged me and introduced herself as his ex. She wanted to know my story and I wanted to know hers.

When we finished talking, we both had gotten what we wanted. Well, I didn't get all the answers. Why would a woman let a man like Anthony get away? I needed information so I wouldn't waste my time trying to get with him. After hearing their conversation and watching her walk away, I had an AHA! moment. Instead of Anthony coming to the party, I invited him to that night; he went to her party and she had a new man. He'd rather be with something old than with something new. He still had feelings for her; he may be in love and can't let go. After they straightened things out, she left and he was ready to drive me home. I was stood up for his ex. And now, she had ruined our date. It seemed every single man I met was attached and that sucked.

I thought he liked me more than that. I was feeling like the rebound woman when I returned home. I wasn't going to lose any sleep over him. Jazzy Black called to tell me the scoop on King. She told me that he was upset that I left so soon. She said that James King scared her because all he talked about was me. And that he had an obsession with me.

James King seriously wanted me back. Jazzy doesn't know that he had asked me to meet him today and spend the day with him but I didn't go. After hearing what she said, I'm glad I didn't go. I knew what James King wanted. He was my first boyfriend and I was a virgin when we were together. King never made it to second base so he will always want me.

I opened the door to leave and James King called. He was upset because I stood him up. He said that I hurt him again just like I hurt him before. He was crying, so I started to cry. King said that he's been all over the world and he couldn't find anyone with my big eyes, nose, teeth, and lips. I couldn't listen any longer. I felt bad that his life had been affected by my bad choices. And, like everything else, I swept it up under the rug.

One weekend later, Russo called. He announced, he was ready for our date. I told him I was leaving and tonight I'll be home alone, then gave him my address. Russo showed up as I was laid out on the sofa eating all my favorite snacks and watching Boxer fight on TV. He had a one-track mind. He thought about sex with me; where, when, and how he would get it.

All I kept saying was, "Russo, don't. Russo, stop."

He was all over me. He found my comfort zone and I zoned out. The good thing was, I taped the fight or else I would have missed Boxer knock the guy out. I had a selfish craving that would allow me to shut out everything and everyone. That night, I chose Russo to forget my worries about James King. I wasn't the one to help him. He wanted me and I didn't feel the same way. We were just friends. My life was about me feeling good with the best lover that I could find while fighting the painful secrets of my past.

I wanted to be in love. I wanted a man that had more to offer. I wasn't myself. I had a war going on inside me and it was good versus bad. I was choosing to do wrong over right and using one man to forget the other. I was mad at myself for being with Russo. I knew what he was all about. I was mad at my pain and the drug kept me from healing, so I swore off men and drugs and was alone.

Four months later, I was on vacation for one week. I walked out of my job and Boxer's Rolls Royce was parked next to my car. I walked up to the car but he wasn't in it. His driver was there to bring me to him.

"I don't want to leave my car here."

"We'll take care of your car; he wants to see you now."

He opened the door and I stepped in and gave the driver keys to my car. The driver drove me to the marina. I was escorted up the docks and onto the yacht.

Boxer waited. He watched my every move. He had that look on his face. It was a very familiar look. Oh no, I thought, 'here I go again' he was in love with me. Until, that moment, I thought him and I were playing a player's game. I walked right up to him and gave him a kiss that said, 'I love you, too'. He took hold of my hand and we started to walk.

> Boxer was being sincere. He opened up and talked to me, "Why did you kiss me that way, and why did you love me that way the night we made love? Are you playing games with my head? Say you love me. You can't say it, can you? Look, Jamaica, all I think about is that night. I've never been loved like that before. Since that night, I know what it feels like to be loved by a woman. Don't play with my intelligence; you made love to me that night. Who are you Jamaica? I want to know where you come from."

He fixed us a drink. We sat down in a little cove on the deck and I began to talk.

> "I'm a preacher's daughter. My father is the pastor of one of the largest churches in the Bay. I've been taught to love hard and I love deeply. You brought out the best in me. The passion you brought out of me was the declaration of my love and faith. The depth of the two consumed me. Boxer, I felt guilty. As strong as our love was, I felt condemned for loving you that way. Considering my lifestyle and yours, we're from two different worlds. I can't say, 'I love you' because it sounds good. It seems like we should get our lives together and collectively cherish the love we felt that night. If we don't hold onto it, we're throwing it all away. It's just wrong to say, 'I love you' and go back to doing what we do. I need a mature relationship. I need a man that's about taking it

to the next level; you know, love and marriage. I need conviction from my man."

"Jamaica, we brought out the best in each other and I don't want to lose our love; it's more than a good feeling. Your luscious glow and style brightens my world. Your looks are so delicious to me, girl. Your lips are so kissable and I want to cuddle next to your body. I want you all the time, Jamaica Gold."

We couldn't hold back any longer; we were in each other's arms.

At the height of lovemaking, he said, "Save me, Jamaica Gold, I want to be saved."

Hip-Hop was jamming, 'The Ghetto' by Too Short. Grandmaster Flash and The Sugarhill Gang 'Don't Push Me', Cause I'm Close to the Edge" was slamming; it was the 1980's and my first time hearing rap music.

"What do you know about this?" He popped in a Nat King Cole tape.

Boxer was my age and I didn't know anything about Nat King Cole. I was an old movie buff and had heard most of his songs watching classic films. I didn't know that I was listening to a black man. I was holding that player close to my heart thinking, whatever that feeling was it sure felt good. I didn't really understand his way of love, but his manner had changed. He had calmed down and let me see the softer side of him. Could this be love? Before I left, he told me that he was in and out of town boxing and didn't know when he would return.

I was on my way to Anthony's job. He was partners with two other guys. They had their own law office. Him and I were downtown San Francisco in and out of court all day. The women made complete fools of themselves and he acted like it wasn't happening; he could have cared less. I enjoyed him because he was smart. He knew what he was doing. He knew exactly what he wanted and I felt that he wasn't making me feel like he wanted me.

At the end of the day, Anthony acted like it was all in a day's work. To me, he was a good man. We went to my house and while we were sitting, listing to music and talking, 'The Drake' called and said he wanted me back. Drake said, one night he was drunk and crying over me; he and his friend drove to the San Francisco Bridge just so he could write my name on the bridge to prove his love for me.

> "I don't believe you for one second. You're still drunk and you must have dreamed that. We are not together because you wanted to be a player, so go play."

Anthony and I left out for the evening. We went to the beach and parked. We sat up, talked and shot pictures, until, late night. We went to the club and his best friend was there; the guy he was with the night we met. He introduced me to one woman after another while they were trying to get him away from me.

He never left nor took his eyes off me. When we left the club we were both turned on and wanted to be together. When I took him home, he asked me to come in and took me right up to his room. I gave in to what I was feeling. The first time we were together, it was just sex. That night, the sex positions were like the ones I read about in Romeo's love letter. They seemed like something two men would do with each other and the passion was missing.

Anthony wasn't emotionally connected with me and he wasn't affectionate enough. He didn't touch or feel my curves. He didn't kiss my lips or caressing my body. He was going through the motions. When he tried to cuddle, I didn't know where he was coming from. We weren't making a love connection, just some really good, old fashioned, down-home sex. I couldn't use him to keep Boxer off my mind. I needed to know more about Anthony. I knew he was hiding something.

One day, I called Anthony's house. I told him that I had a picnic basket filled with food to see what would happen.

He said, "Alright sounds good to me."

I cooked! We had fried chicken wings, potato salad, deviled eggs, and fruit. Anthony loves to eat. When a man says, 'yes' to a picnic and actually goes through with it, he's into you. What's even better is, when he plans it and shows up with food, wine, and a frisbee or kite.

I drove there and he wanted to drive my car. We stopped for wine and ice, then headed across the bridge. He wanted to go to the lake in Oakland. I thought that he would take me to a much more secluded spot where we can be alone. Going to the lake where everyone hangs out let me know that we were only friends.

I laid out the tablecloth and I put the picnic basket down and proceeded to have a picnic. My sports car stopped traffic as usual, plus, I looked good. He couldn't just kick back and enjoy the attention; he ate and then he was ready to go. We packed up our picnic basket and left. Of course, I thought that we were leaving to go somewhere else and hangout but I found myself on the other side of the lake where fags hangout.

They were gay men that acted like women. They spoke their language, in their little world or so I thought. Anthony parked, and opened the trunk. He fixed himself another plate of food, poured himself another glass of wine, and sat back in the car. This beautiful specimen of a man sat there eating, drinking, and living it up; he couldn't stop laughing. I had never seen him that happy and content. Red Light! I thought he wasn't only gay, he was old-school, in-the-closet gay.

211

A woman would assume he was 'On the down low' gay. A man that would rather sit up and watch other men be gay was curious.

"Shhhh, do you mind? I like to watch and listen, isn't that the funniest thing you've ever heard?"

All I heard was, 'head this and head that'; head was echoing through the park and bouncing off trees. I must admit it was some funny stuff. Men were picking men up and dropping them off. Every time one returned, he'd gossip about head; what he did to his date and how he did it. Some picnic!

Anthony finally had an ear full and said, 'let's go'. We left the lake and as we drove up to the San Francisco Bridge going home, I saw my name written on the bridge. Drake wasn't lying. He had to be out of his mind drunk to do such a dangerous thing. Still, I'm not going back to him.

Anthony had other plans that didn't include me and asked me to drop him off at a friend's house.

He pulled up to a strange building and said, "Wait right here, I'll be right back."

He returned and said, everything was fine, goodnight.

Of course, I was curious, why he didn't say anything about who his friend was, so, I asked, "Who is this person that you don't want me to meet?"

"We're going to be roommates."

That's all he said! I don't know where he was. He didn't give me an address nor a phone number. I couldn't believe this was happening to me again.

The following day, Anthony called and said his car was being serviced and asked me to pick him up in the same place where I dropped him off. I gave him another chance to invite me up or let me meet his roommate. When I drove up, he asked to drive.

I moved over and he drove off. I sat there wondering, if this so-called roommate was a woman or a gay man. He wasn't talking.

"Can I use your car while you have your manicure, pedicure, and hair appointment?"

"Yes, as long as you make it back at 9:00 p.m. I'll be tired and ready to go home."

He promised to return on time. It was 10:00 p.m. and the salon was closed. Anthony was not answering his beeper. I stood out in the wind and rain and I just paid one hundred and fifty dollars for my hair alone. My hair was wet and I was mad.
Drake lives up the street, so I called him. I asked him to pick me up. I stood out in the rain soaking wet. Drake picked me up and drove me to his house.

"Take off your clothes and let them dry."

"No way, I'm not here for sex. Thanks, but no thanks, Drake. I'm waiting on my car. I saw your artwork on the bridge; you know you could have died doing that. What makes you act that way? What kind of drugs were you taking that night?"

"I wasn't taking drugs. I just missed you."

Anthony paged me and I gave him Drake's address. I sat by the window where I could get up and leave when Anthony pulled up. I saw him coming and I headed for the door. Drake headed for the window and saw Anthony driving my car.

"You can't play a player, Jamaica."

I stopped him dead in his tracks, "I'm not playing anyone. You and I are not together; we never were. I care about both of you and I don't want to see anyone get hurt, Drake. Stay in the house alright."

"I'll play your game, we were meant to be, I want you back, remember that." He kissed me on the lips and said, "Later!"

I left a 100% man that cheats on women with other women and I drove off with a man that could be gay and possibly living with

213

another man. On the ride home, Anthony was cool, calm, and secretive; he was not talking. That was his last chance to come clean with me about who he was staying with. He pulled up and stepped out of the car. I sat in the driver's seat and drove off.

Days later, Drake called and asked me if he should move in with three dancers that wanted him as their live-in bodyguard with free room and board. Drake was pimping.

"So, you're a lifeguard by day and bodyguard by night. Are they paying you cash, too? A brother needs cash money."
"Yes, when they get paid, I get paid."
"Well, I always wanted to know, does their job pay a lot?"
"Jamaica, you would not believe how much money dancers make in one night, so much they need a bodyguard. Should I do it?"
"Yes, it sounds like something you could do well. I know you're not telling me everything so I'll just have to fill in the blanks. I know you and you're a lover not a fighter. Now, you're a bodyguard with benefits?" He laughed.
"When it comes to taking care of women, I'm good at what I do. Here is my new address and you can come to visit. The old house is open if you want to use it. I know you like Victorian houses. You can move in and take over the rent if you wish. My lease is up in two months. Let me know something before then."
"I will. Good luck, Drake. Bye-bye!"

Anthony called and wanted me to come and pick him up. I said, 'No'. At this point, I don't know where his car was. He told me to meet him at the park. I smoked a joint, dressed in my sexiest outfit and jumped in my red Corvette, tripping off of my surroundings in the ghetto. I loved driving through the bay area and listening to the song, 'The Ghetto'. I had planned to tell Anthony our friendship was not working out and that I wanted more. I arrived before he did. I stepped out of my car and

214

leaned up against it. I stopped traffic and turned down every type of offer until one guy recognized me as a dancer from Boxer's club and pulled over.

He was the bouncer at the player's club that Boxer owned. He stepped out of his car to talk to me. He told me that Boxer sold the club to one of his older woman and that, rumor has it, he was getting rid of the rest of his woman to pursue his boxing career.

> "What are you up to Miss Lady? We haven't seen you around lately? Your absence has been causing quite an up-roar."
>
> "I'm breaking up a friendship with a guy that doesn't want to take it any further. He has me assuming crazy things. I'm tired of trying to read men's minds."
>
> "I'm single, give me a chance to make you mine. I won't have you assuming anything. You're too fine for any man to have you assuming. If I can't have you, I want your sister. If I can't have her, I want your mother. Hell, I'd take your grandmother you're so fine. It has to run in the family, I can't lose. I'd do anything to have you or be in your family-circle."

He went on and on talking and telling me what I wanted to hear.

> "I am standing right here, next in line. A man doesn't want to lose a nice woman like you. What if he doesn't want to let you go? If he gives you any trouble, you want me to handle it?"
>
> "Please don't; I care about him."

I should have kept my mouth shut. It was disturbing that I'm not satisfied unless I had men fighting over me and that was another thing I blamed Troy for. A man shouldn't have to physically fight to prove he loves his woman.

Unconsciously, I tested guys. I wanted to see if I can push them to the point that I pushed Troy. Troy made me feel I pushed him to the point of no return, but he was crazy all by himself. That day at the park, I was in a bad state of mind. That man could have hurt me and it could have ended up deadly. The bouncer continued talking. He talked about how a man treats a woman when he cares for her.

"If he cares, he's not going to let you walk away without a fight. If your man is for real I'll back off, I promise."

While he talked, I saw Anthony coming. He walked toward us with his signature walk. His body motions were foreplay. I felt him making love to me with every step. Awe, sooky, sooky Boo! His sexy smile was to die for. He seduced me with that plain ole' sex appeal I've loved since the night he pimped his way into my life.

Anthony was such a man in my eyes. I was such a romantic lush, I was nauseated. I was in love with the thought of being in love. The guy had never made love to me. Anthony's looks were irresistible. I couldn't help myself. I planned to say good-bye to him over the phone. As Anthony walked up, I was totally infatuated again. I didn't have enough sense to want guys that wanted me.

I was running around after gay guys. Trying to get them to fall in love with a woman. I didn't know that was what abuse could do to you, when you don't get help. The bouncer stood there as he said he would. Anthony stood up to him and got in his face.

"What's the problem man? This is my woman and my business; you have a problem with that? Don't try me bitch!"

The bouncer stepped back without any words expressed.

"Maica, get in the car." Anthony said, with his deep voice while pouting.

He gently squeezed my arm and led me to the passenger side of my car. He waited for me to get in and then he closed the door. He joined me in the car on the driver side and drove off. He drove to the other side of the park and then exited the car. He sat-down on the grass. I then exited the car and sat down next to him.

"Why are you playing games? Messing with one's emotions isn't like you. What I like about you is you don't play mind games with me."

I tried my best not to fall for him. But when he said, 'This is my woman', I knew he cared for me even if he wasn't in love and that touched my heart. I felt he was sincere. We sat there, talking about a lot of things. I still didn't get answers about his secrete home life, though. He controlled the conversation by doing all of the talking. He said he was going through some things at work, but with us, everything was fine. Later that same evening, I watched him play two sexy games of pool. He had done everything as a sexy and masculine man and I needed some alone time with my sexy date, Anthony.

I had him drive to Drake's old house, then I told him I thought about moving in and wanted him to check it out. We walked inside and Anthony snooped around. He was tall enough to see on top of the refrigerator so he found a picture of Drake purposely left there for his revenge. The Drake had retaliated with 'The big payback' and his vengeance towards me was for leaving my business for his other woman to find. He was so vain that he would leave a picture of himself.

Anthony had some nerve when he threw the picture in my face, he wasn't taking care of me sexually or financially. He was late that night and I did what I needed to do to take care of me.

"I picked you up at this man's house that night?"

I changed the subject, there was nothing going on with Drake and me. I called Anthony into the bedroom and I fell onto the bed. Pat, pat went my beautiful manicured hands; hitting the spot where I wanted him to fall. He fell onto the bed and we continued getting high on weed and had really good sex. Nothing had changed.

Anthony's sexy body was there but his emotions were not. I didn't have any idea that night would be our last time together as he kept-on talking about vag-hags (Straight women that hung around gay men) was he calling me one? I felt like I was being attacked. I became dispread to attack back. When he wasn't looking, I took his two empty condom wrappers and placed them neatly in his side coat pocket. The next time I heard from Anthony, he had lost his partnership at work; they paid him off and he walked out the door of his job.

Anthony never saw my revenge coming. I found-out by him that he had been turned out by one of his gay law partners; the same partner he had been living with. That same day, he came clean and he walked out of my life after telling me everything. Did he know I set him up? If so, he never said a word. Anthony left town for another job. I cried for a week until, I discovered I wasn't any longer crying over Anthony. I was mad about life in general.

In my depression, I tried to be creative and my many tears turned into poetry. I hadn't finished any of the poems, yet; they lived in my head and journal. I carried it around with me. I needed a certain poem to help me through whatever I was going through. I recited whatever poem to myself that went with the pain. If nothing came to mind, I would make something up on the spot.

> I cried so much, my favorite one to recite was, "In my hand flows a river I cried from loneliness. I captured my feelings in my hand and gave them love. No one had time to give. I didn't wipe them away. I caressed them and made them stay."

I didn't have a title for all of them. My motivation and interest in finishing them were gone. I wasn't trying to get them published. I had forgotten that I had talent. I was too busy chasing the dream of having a man love me.

Chapter Eleven
Promiscuous Sister

I was on a suicide mission. Promiscuous sister; that was me. People could push you into anything, 'When you don't stand for something, you'll fall for anything'. I didn't stand up for who I was. I had become what my abusers, and my so called friends and enemies said I was years ago; even though, I knew then, I wasn't that person. I was going backwards; and living in the past. I allowed those lies to create the person that existed.

The pain and the suffering had taken over and had pierced a hole in my heart and the wound was so deep and so severe, I was lost in that hole. That fabricated person that I was defined to be back then, was the only person I could identify with. I was that promiscuous girl. Lies don't die, they multiply, until, you out-grow them.

I didn't want to be with bad boys anymore and I fought my sexual feelings for Boxer. I visited different types of men that claimed to be nice guys. Nice men that lived alone, told the same story; all they met was women that brought drama into their lives and hurt them. First, I didn't want to listen. I wasn't going to sit up and listen, while they put women down, and by listening, I found out that's not what they were about. They weren't crybabies or womanizers; they were men that deeply wanted to be in love. I saw them as men that couldn't see they were attracted to those types of women; I couldn't get them to see that they have to mature mentally to find a stable and mature woman.

They were single men that were set in their ways. As well as single women that were set in their ways and living alone. How could two single people that were unchangeable compromise? Everyone felt comfortable in his or her space and didn't want to give up their freedom of boundary and privacy. Most single men and women wanted a mate, but everything had to be on their terms. It was impossible to find a compatible mate.

Either a man treated me like I was stupid, or he acted high and mighty and didn't listen to what I had to say. The guys that didn't have much to offer wanted to use me for what I had. The sweet one's had been too emotional and cried on my shoulder about life, in general. I would awake morning after morning alone and single and I couldn't take it anymore.

A woman has to take care of her. I had to separate myself from the bad boy who were freaks and wasn't ready for commitment. I had learned something bad about myself with each guy. I had to face that I had been attracted to those types of men and needed to grow up. I had to say goodbye to my past and move on. I didn't need any extra baggage.

My reality of dating bad boys had hit hard and I started having flash-backs, remembering being young and courting. I thought I had a boyfriend until, birthdays and Christmas came around. He would either break up with me or disappear until, the celebration was over and show up on my doorsteps like nothing had happened. To keep that from happening to me at this age of the game, they all had to go. They were just too predictable. What's the point? Next.

I gave up waiting for a man and determined to do it alone. I looked for some where my son and I could call home. I walked out of work one day on my way to look at more property for sale and Boxer sat on my car.

"What's going on stranger?" He gave me a big hug and kiss. Did you miss me?"
"Yes, I have and I've been watching you on TV."
"I have something to show you and I can't wait for you to see it."

I got into his car and we were in each other's arms. We rolled up to a big, beautiful house and the *For Sale* sign out front read 'Sold'.

> "What do you want, a condominium or house? Whatever you want; I aim to please."
>
> "I want a house with a white picket fence around it; and with a big backyard for Little Man," describing the house in front of me.
>
> "Get out, let's check it out."

We walked in and I immediately fell in love with the house.

> "It's perfect, but what do you need with another big house?"
>
> "It's yours, baby. Would you be my woman? I want to come home to you every night. Let's live together and get to know each other better."

I quickly said yes and jumped into his arms. Boxer and I designed it together. We went to a unique furniture store in the bay area so many times, they told us that they were planning to get a bed for us to sleep in on the showroom floor. I got one-of-a kind expensive furniture. I bought a new refrigerator, stove, and a new stereo system, plus my first washer and dryer.

Boxer and I were happy. We both were enjoying our new place. Little Man and I loved having him around; I was feisty and straightforward with him, about everything. When boxer was around, I felt safe; I exercised my strength as a woman. He was right; we brought out the best in each other. We bathed together, dressed each other. He's a romancer; our life was a love story.

Whenever he sat down on our sofa, I'd sit on his right leg and Little Man would run and jump on his left leg. Little Man liked to entertain Boxer by break-dancing. He would get in the middle of the floor and start break-dancing. He does it well. Boxer loved how cool he was and how he jumped all over him, showing him love. Boxer laughed.

"That's a happy little kid, I like that."

I left for work one morning. That evening when I returned, Boxer and Little Man had left a note saying, "I dropped Little Man off at your parent's for the weekend and went to the gym to play pool. We have the house all to ourselves. Love, Boxer."

I walked into my kitchen and looked in our refrigerator. Boxer had taken Little Man grocery shopping. I had pork roast, roast beef, lamb roast, ground beef, and chicken, crabs, shrimp, hot links, bacon, and I can go on. The man had filled up our liquor cabinet and bar; I can get used to this. He's got to be the man for me. Boxer called to tell me about their night.

> "Hi beautiful, I'm on my way home. Little Man was happy in the store, until, he got to the liquor and asked was I going to get his mother drunk with all that liquor and I told him, 'No'. He said, that's good, I don't want you to get my mom drunk. Then he asked, if I would call him, Mannie. He returned home and we had a perfect weekend."

The next weekend. Boxer went away for three days. On my two days off, I did some entertaining, having friends come to see my place and all I could think about was Boxer. When he returned, he took us to a restaurant that has his favorite dish on the menu. It's the most expensive thing on the menu, they bring you a whole lobster. The body is stuffed with lobster meat, cheese and potatoes. He told me that he had plans to take us to Tahoe, Nevada, the fallowing weekend.

When I'm at work, Boxer cooks and helps Mannie with his homework. I come home at night and the fireplace is burning and there is Champaign and roast beef finger sandwiches with fruit and cheese sitting in front of the fire and he's fast asleep. He gives me good loving and puts me to sleep wanting more. Our pad alone looks like Hollywood and when I saw that he wanted to take care of my son, I felt like a star.

223

It's the weekend. I awakened to Mannie getting ready. We were both happy campers getting ready for our trip. Boxer got up, got dressed and we were on our way. We played in the snow, we watched him box; working out at the gym. Mannie and I had front row seats. Boxer won the fight in the fifth round and won another belt; his forth one, and we came home. That night, I felt good; Boxer had changed my life. I wanted him to be the answer to all of my problems. I got what I always wanted. Mannie and I finally had a man in the house.

One night as always, Boxer put Mannie to bed and then came to bed and enlightened me that he was leaving me.

> "I'm moving overseas. I've been offered a lot of money to fight over there. I'm young and I would be a fool to turn it down. I'm leaving you the papers to the house. I'll always be in touch. You're my girl, you changed my life and this is home."
>
> "It takes a lot of guts to do what you do. You know how to walk away from what's holding you back. I respect you for that and I'm proud of you. I'll be mad at you tomorrow, but I'll love you tonight. You're always welcome to come back into my life."

We loved each other for one night. Boxer left his mark. What's wrong with me? I should have fought for him, but what was I supposed to ask.

> "What about us? Would you give up your life for me and my son?"

I felt I did everything right, except, as soon as Boxer left, I start tripping again, knowing having a man was not the answer to my problems. I come from a strong family of women and that makes me a strong woman; I know it's in me. I got to get over the fear of being alone and stand up and be the women that I know I am.

I was failing at womanhood. I needed the woman in me to step up and save me and be independent and express to all men that I'm no fool. Did Boxer see my weaknesses? Did I give the impression that men can walk all over me. And, is he coming back? My brain was going in circles without him in my life.

I didn't miss a beat. I went to work and turned on the charm. I saw Lady Dee talking to a pilot, he was in uniform and I love men in uniform. She called me over and introduced us. His name was Rick Rogers. He asked for my number. I didn't write it down on paper; I said my number out loud as fast as I could. I didn't think he would remember and wasn't waiting around for his call. The next morning, he called and asked me to dinner and a movie. Afterwards, we went to a quiet bar to talk over Long Island Iced Tea. The night went well.

Rick and I were dating; getting to know each other better was complicated. He's a friend of Dee's. Since Dee is my sister, he thinks I'm like Dee; he acted as if he knew me and that turned me off. Plus, we're on our third date and he hasn't made a move on me.

> "Look, are you going to make love to me or not?" I asked. I shocked him.
> "We haven't known each other long; I'm trying to take it slow," he said.
> I snarled, "Slow, we haven't had a first kiss?"

Rick wasn't ready to make a move on me. He thought I was letting him call the shots. My woman's intuition told me to keep my eye on him; he's up to something. He's an older man, he should know what a woman wants. I'm not trying to fall in love, but sex would be nice. Within communicating with my sister, Slick Rick knew what I was raised and taught to believe in.

Dee talks way more than I do. She had matured, she found her confidence, and she knew who she was as a woman. She preached to men about her faith and religion. She laid down the rules and now he thinks he knows how to play me. I believed while he wined and dined me, he was seeing someone else for sex. And trying to act all 'holeyer than thou' with me.

Slick Rick is a scheme artist. That wasn't a good strategy; he's getting us sisters mixed-up. The brother was confused and his game was weak. I like men that take their time, but he moved too slowly, if he wanted me. Understand, I always recognize game when it approaches me. I'm attracted to the game. I sat back and watched it unfold; I get a high off figuring it out. I'm going to enjoy this man's game as long as I can; until, his mess explodes and hits the fan.

On our forth date, Rick considered taking me home with him but he got cold feet and couldn't perform. This can't be good! He's an older man; ten year's older. I looked for him to try and sweep me off my feet and blow my mind the first night. Show me what an older man can do. Entertain me with a mad passionate roll in the hay, and love my pain away for a minute or two, maybe, if I'm lucky.

Instead, he was acting insecure. Rick was worried that I wasn't going to like his performance. Afterwards, I felt he got the job done and I was glad he was normal. He'll be alright, once he accepts that I don't mind our age difference. I had planned a dinner party. I invited him to my dinner party and went home.

I slept late the next day. After I felt rested enough, I got up, cleaned up, and poured myself a glass of wine to relax. I began to cook all types of seafood recipes. When I'm cooking, I am cool, calm, and collected. When I finished, I was pleased. Later that night my guests began to arrive; my sisters came to help. My cousins, friends, new neighbors, and people that I worked with showed up. They turned it out, Hollywood style. The party trays were going around with finger foods. We drank Martini and Rossi, while we dined, sat back, and enjoyed good times. I always feed friends and family well because I'm always happy around them.

I was unhappy that Rick didn't show. Red flag! He knew I had a dinner party and he was invited. Slick knows that airport personnel were going to be here and he wasn't concerned that one of them would try and talk to me. He knew the four guys that cater to me at work were after me. Every day at work, they buy me something to eat or drink. All five of us worked hard and played hard, but never in each other's playground, until, my party. They wouldn't have missed it for the world. All night, I wanted to make sure every move I made and everything I said would get back to Rick. Anyway, when the party ended, I was so out of it; I went and crashed.

I slept peacefully for two hours. Then, I got up and went to work. Everyone talked about how live the party was. One girl, Brenda that I normally talked with walked up and joined in the conversation. She told me that she was coming to my party, but her friend, Rick, didn't want to come. The other guys from work had already left, on their way to the party. I didn't tell her that I was dating Rick. At this point I didn't know who all was dating Slick Rick, or if he was anybody's man.

I needed more information. I wanted proof, to confront him before I expressed what I thought about him. I became Miss Colombo. Rick is an older man; he doesn't have a clue what I know about men and their devious games. I wrote the book on men and the games they play. He walked over to me and told me that he brought my lunch. I didn't say anything to him about his scandalous ways. I made him feel that everything was fine; like he wasn't a hound-dog.

At lunch, I saw Rick walking towards me. You would not have believed how young and stupid he thought I was. He walked through the airport, passing out hamburgers to female employees. I knew these were women that he had slept with. And, or,

ones he planned on sleeping with. These weren't just any burg-
ers, they're as big as your hand; expensive and he knew they're
my favorite. When he got to me, I didn't accept mine.

I wasn't going to get played. Not this time.

    "You can keep it." He had the nerve to question me.

    "Why, I bought it for you?"

    "If you're mine, your mine, and my man wouldn't walk
    through my job passing out hamburgers. You did that to
    prove to your other women that it's no big deal; all of
    us just happened to get one." He looked shock.

    "I didn't know you were jealous and insecure," he said,
    using child psychology on me.

    "Been there, done that."

That was the kind of stuff Blue would do.

    "I'm not a child; just take your burger and leave."

I went to his house after work to wait on him so we could talk.
He wasn't there, but his girlfriend Brenda was. I stood there and
watched her search his house for the ingredients for Long Island
Iced Tea, our favorite drink. She had the nerve to ask me where
he keeps it. He wined and dined her, too. I wanted to say, "Kiss
my ass, I'm gone."

She wouldn't have understood where I was coming from; she
didn't know about Rick and me. Instead of taking it out on her, I
left. I got home and I'm cleaning up, lounging around, and
watching Boxer Box on HBO. I threw a steak on my indoor grill
and thought about Slick Rick's hound-dog syndrome.

I got to work early the next morning. Slick and Brenda were
standing by the worker's lockers kissing and they were hot and
lusting for each other. I read their body language. They weren't
just making out, they were sleeping together, for sure. I didn't
disturb them. I went into the ladies' lounge, until, it was time to
start working. His girlfriend Brenda came in and looked at me
with a smile and spoke as usual. I snubbed her. I acted like she

wasn't even there and kept walking. She ran and caught up with me.

> "What's wrong with you? I've never seen you upset like this. I thought we were friends. I like you and I need to know, what I did wrong?"

I was quiet.

> "I'm not going anywhere until, you talk to me."
>
> I rolled my eyes, "Rick and I are dating."
>
> "What?" she said, in total surprise. "Jamaica, I'm sorry. I didn't know. How long you've been seeing him?"
>
> "Two months."
>
> "We have been messing around a lot longer and he's never said anything to me about you."

When she left, I knew she was headed straight to Slick Rick.

That day, at lunch, I walked to the lunchroom and I saw Slick Rick running to catch up with me. I continued to walk, and he stopped me. I didn't have anything to say to him.

> "Rick! Why are you and your girlfriend running behind me? Go run behind someone that cares."
>
> "What's wrong?
>
> "I won't let you play with my intelligence. I'm not your fool. I'm not as young as you think, Rick. Move, get out my face!"
>
> "You're going to tell me why you're not talking."
>
> "You're going to make me say it; I know who you've been sleeping with."

He looked at me with that dumb look that men get when they have been caught and thought they were getting over on you. I ran his entire game down to him.

> "That's why you weren't in a big hurry to sleep with me and the same reason why you weren't at my party. I turned you on to Long Island Iced Tea and you go and wine and dine her with our drink? I saw you together before work and your body language spoke loudly; she's your lover."

Slick Rick couldn't think of anything to say; he was in shock. I waited for his reaction; one second, two seconds, three seconds, four seconds past.

"I don't even know you. How in the world did you figure all that out? I guess I'm going to have to work really hard to get out of this one."

He tried to explain.

"It's over between her and me. It's been over. What you saw was a goodbye kiss. I've been trying to let her down easy and concentrate on us. You got to trust me, Jamaica," he explained from a mouth filled with lies.

Rick tried to redeem himself. Every weekend he took me to his cabin on the lake. I know that I am not the one. I don't want to be number two or three. I had become one of those women who tried to rush a man into relationships or marriage to convince herself she's the one. A man will let you know if you are the one. I thought, if I could get him to ask me to be his woman just maybe I will feel confident that he was serious about being with me. All the while, I tried to prove to myself that all these men don't leave me because of me.

I had lost touch with reality before I met Rick. Now, it was official. This was not a relationship. I'm denying the fact that I can't call the shots when he's not on the record as my man. I had to face what I was doing. I tried to make him pick up where Boxer left off.

"You don't miss your well until, the water runs dry."

I didn't want to accept that Boxer was gone and I was alone again; that would hurt worse. Slick Rick was dirty. He got what he wanted from both of us women. At the same time, he watched me act delusional about he and I being together. I wanted to stop her from having him. Then I found out that he was going hot and heavy with two other women; he didn't have time for love. Does any one of us touch his heart and soul? He was buck wild with women. I had nothing to fight with; and nothing to fight for, I hadn't made him mine.

I'm planning to end it before he does. I believed he was one of those men that lured women to his house just to take advantage of them. He's been wounded badly to have so many women in his life at one time or he's going through a mid-life crisis. Rick said his wife left him after fifteen years. Some men and women never get over getting left; and they grow old trying to prove they've still got it.

At work, I had been taking love notes off my car for two weeks. The notes have been on my front windshield and under my left window wiper. The last three days the notes have turned into love letters with pages of old love songs. I had been reading them and asking myself, what is this, high-school? Yet, I was curious; words are my thing; love notes were my weakness. I'm waiting for this poet to reveal himself. One day after work, a limo was parked by my car. I was happy because I thought Boxer had come back to me.

The door opened. The limo driver stepped out acting as if he's the second coming of Jesus; and it was The Drake. He looked flawless dressed up in a tux and thought he needed to flaunt. He reminded me of Boss.

> "Uhh. Jamaica! I told you, you and me was meant to be together. Your co-worker, the one you named, 'I heard that' is now my boss. I told him that I knew you and he wants me to show you a good time."

Drake approached me to take my hand, and helped me in, he watches my behind as he's holding the door to the limo. He drove me to a ritzy club up town. We walked in and he said, have a seat and a glass of wine to get the party started. He returned wearing a nice tan suit and walked me back to the limo and we both got in the back seat. Another driver got in the driver seat. The driver didn't introduce himself. He strapped himself in and we drove off.

> "My ladies named me Chocolate. I see you all the time. I'm always at the airport working, I didn't have the time to say hello." He said.
> "Are you the grown ass man leaving love notes on my car?"
> "Figure it out, use your imagination!"
> "Are you slow, I just did and I like your style Drake; and didn't know you had it in you," I said.
> "I've always liked your style and I'm glad you appreciate me, I meant every word," he said.

We went to dinner and then to a club. We talked about old times. He was still working for the dancers, except, he didn't live with them. He had bought himself a house. By the end of the night, the limo was filled with people. I partied so hard, I lost a shoe.

I've been taking a lot of naps lately. I feel pregnant and if I am, I've got a decision to make about keeping the baby and Slick in my life and all his baggage. I never let him stay the night and I don't stay all night with him. I wanted the comfort of my 'California King' sized bed and no man is allowed in Boxer's bed that he and I picked out together. I missed him so much and my depression and loneliness for him took its toll on me.

I felt bad, and it wasn't all about losing Boxer, it was the abuse, and the memories of all my men and the pain of having abortions, haunted me at night. I missed not having children. I thought about things as when I die, my only son will grieve alone. I'm around people all the time and I felt alone. I partied hard to exhaust myself to get sleep.

I went to work drained. First, the guys at work brought me lunch; then Chocolate Drake brought me lunch. I saw Slick coming and I hid two lunches under the counter. Slick had brought a lobster sandwich and I don't let lobster go to waste. At lunch I thought, I can't handle his life right now; he's too laid back; slow to make a move and he doesn't do tricks or foreplay. I still wanted to do wild and crazy things with my man.

Slick was scared of getting left by a woman. I'm one of his many women and he runs from making a commitment. I tried to make myself believe that I'm wrong about the slick games he played, but he's living up to his name. He made me feel like I don't look good enough or dress sharp enough to be his one and only. Who knows what he's up to or how many woman he had? I don't have the time to figure it out. I'm young; I'm only human. If an older man is lagging and there's a younger man interested, I can't help but be curious. I thanked him for the Lobster and I went in the ladies room to throw up.

I got home that evening and my breaking point hit me like a ton of bricks; immediately, I noticed a change because I couldn't think of what I normally did before bed. Days later, I began to notice that I had forgotten how to dress myself in the mornings. I couldn't set my alarm clock, I couldn't find anything in the house. I was lost from everything and everyone. I was having a hard time driving to places that I had been driving to for years. I didn't understand that I wasn't going to get better on my own and I wouldn't seek help.

I left work early one day sick. I went to Chocolate Drake's house to look for my shoe. His car was there, but he didn't answer the front door. I walked around to the back and opened the patio door. When I walked in, I saw Drake standing behind his bar with a mountain of cocaine and a big scale. The first thing that came to mind was, 'what is Drake doing with all that baking flour'? His nose was white and it was all over his face. Drake wasn't just a pimp and limousine driver, he was a drug dealer and user. He tried to explain that he was done dealing. I was sick and I didn't need any more drama; I was headed out the door.

He caught up with me and looked into my eyes. He placed both my hands in his.

> "Jamaica, stay with me. I'm going to fill these hands with diamonds, and then he kissed both hands.
> "Why would you do that? So you can take them when I'm fed up?"

I bet drugs had something to do with him owning that house. I got to get away from this Chocolate mess, now. I'm confused about who he was or tried to be. I can't bring my son into this situation. I took my shoe and left.

I'm in deep trouble on my job. I had anxiety for being late to work so many times. I had a hard time getting up in the morning. I don't have any more chances to screw up. I had found out that Drake was a limo driver, drug dealing pimp and dealing his drugs on my job. I've been going to work looking so bad, the people there thought Drake was my drug dealer. Everyone called Drake Chocolate and didn't know his real name. Rick heard about Chocolate and Me.

> Rick asked, "Why are you going out with a guy like that?"

He had the nerve to ask me that. At lease Drake got paid for being a pimp. Rick just used women.

> "Why am I going out with either of you? Anyway, I just found out and planned to tell him not to call me anymore."

Rick walked away mad. I went to Rick's house and I told him that I was pregnant. First he didn't say anything, he just listened.

> After I finished talking, he said, "I'm glad that you told me."

That was all that was said. I left.

I went to work the next day and got sent home. I was sent home for cursing out my boss who caught me sleeping on the job. I couldn't hide my mental stress any longer. He could have fired me on the spot, but he knows that I'm not usually that way. Instead of firing me, he took me into his office and put me on a three day suspension.

"Get it together. Whatever is troubling you is affecting your work," he said.

I hadn't been sleeping; worrying about what's happening to me, being absent-minded and everything keeps getting worse. I knew Rick wanted to talk to me. He wanted to know for sure about the baby and if it was his or not. That night, he came to me. Being with him felt good; especially, when I sat in his lap and laid my head on his shoulders. Everything seemed small, me, my problems, and my enemies. I wished I could make everything right in my life. In the past, whenever a man would do something or say something that I don't like, I moved on without telling them the real reason why. Plus, it hurts worse when a person leaves without giving you a reason. I don't like that Rick doesn't talk and he sees other women. He hasn't fallen in love with me. I guess I never thought that Rick or any man cared about me one way or the other to give them a reason for me leaving them. I don't even try to make relationships work.

You've got to love yourself before you can feel loved. It was hard to accept love coming from the opposite sex because of my past. I should have told Slick Rick how I felt about everything, but couldn't. Instead, I talked about Drake and how I knew him before he became Chocolate. I acted as if everything was fine between Rick and me; I wanted to enjoy time spent together. Meanwhile, our relationship wasn't working out, for either of us.

We loved each other for a minute. A minute is all we had. In that minute, I witnessed him care for me and I know that I cared for him. But, we weren't in love. What was it all about? Some people show love in such a strong way, they don't need to say it. Some people show love because they can't say it. Mostly older people are like that because they've been hurt a lot. Insecure people with low self-esteem need to hear, 'I love you' every day and all day long. Mostly young people will put you through that.

There was a generation gap between Rick and me. How do you say it's over? I didn't know what to say or how to say it and he wasn't talking either, so I guessed it was over. Rick rocked me to sleep on the sofa and then left. It was time for me to go back to work except, I couldn't remember when I was supposed to be there. I had gotten my work schedule mixed up. That was the day all hell broke loose on my job. Rick confronted Chocolate about me being pregnant by Chocolate. He beat Rick in the head and gave him a concussion. Lady Dee called and told me that Rick was in the hospital. I went to see Rick and he was mad and didn't want to see me. He told me that he can't have any more babies and he knew the baby wasn't his. He wanted revenge on Chocolate.

I've been sweeping my problems under the rug. I have a mountain of problems and don't know how to help myself. I'm still looking for someone to save me from myself. I felt hardship weighing me down. I can't do this thing called life. I couldn't go back to work for a week. When I got into the car to drive back to work and simply couldn't, I noticed I was stressed out and couldn't concentrate and forgot my way to work. I remembered to take the back roads but that would make me late.

I got into the car and drove to work. My head pounded with unbelievable pain and my mind was blocked. I wasn't thinking rationally. I was slowly losing my mind, for real, and didn't know it. I thought that I could snap back, like always. That day, I got fired for being late and not given any more chances. I went home and fell into bed. I didn't call anyone. I didn't want any man in Boxer's bed. Chocolate Drake kept calling. He wants me to snap out of it so him, my son, the baby and I can be a family. I told him that I wasn't pregnant, I was sick because I lost my job. He cooks, cleans the dishes, and mops the floor. He really does a good job cleaning the house from top to bottom. Drake vacuums my floors.

He's acts like he's so in love. I'm pregnant by someone else. In the middle of a breakdown, he and I went shopping for an engagement ring. I picked one out. He bought it and put it on my finger. By accepting his ring, I was hopeful and maybe it would stop me from hurting, but I was being selfish. I needed him to give me time to get over things, resolve things with Slick, and all the madness, and move out of Boxer's house; but most of all, get help for my breakdown.

He started planning our wedding without me. I knew I needed mental help and I wanted to get help, but Drake ran back and forth waiting on me and ignoring that I was sick. He would come over in the middle of the night to satisfy my food cravings and didn't ask any questions. He polished my nails, holds down three jobs and compensates for both our households. I felt so guilty for letting it go too far.

Chocolate Drake took me to concerts to cheer me up. I saw a lot of groups perform. He paid good money for seats in the front so I could dance in the spotlight. He sat there and watched me dance the entire concert. I had good times with him, but I used him to keep from being alone; I was scared. I knew I had to deal with him sooner or later. I've got to tell him that I need space. I need some alone time. I feel like I'm having a miscarriage. I had a constant pain at the bottom of my stomach.

Keeping secrets and lying made things worse. I couldn't live like this any longer and I couldn't tell Drake that I was pregnant and living in another man's house. I didn't want to hurt him. I got up the nerve and went to Drake's house. I told him that I needed time and space. Apparently, that was the wrong thing to say. In the real world, space means, it's over, it's just not working. He thought I wanted time away from him to get back with Rick. It was over between Rick and I; I had run Rick away.

Drake was so hurt he turned on me. I walked outside and he followed, yelling at me. His ex-girlfriend had warned me about his temper and violent behavior. I ran and jumped in my car, thinking he may get violent with me. He shouted.

"Why are you leaving me? How could you do this to me? Give back my ring!"

He yelled, over and over again, until, I took the ring off. I opened up the door and gave him his ring back and then, I left.

I went to the Doctor. He told me that I was three months pregnant. A week later, I lost Boxer's baby and my depression became worse. I couldn't dress myself in the mornings and simply didn't. The simplest things were too hard. I couldn't take care of the house anymore. I was playing with my sanity and had no idea you can lose your mind by not expressing emotion, but it was happening to me. I'm aware that I make bad decisions. I blocked out all intuition because I thought it was my mother's voice with all her rules, telling me what I should and shouldn't do.

I know right from wrong. I chose wrong almost every time. My mother is on me repeatedly; she will continue to try and run my life as long as I am incapable of surviving without a man. The thought of self-survival causes me to do desperate things. I'm alone again. I wanted a man to make love to me and make me forget. I wanted someone that would never leave me, no matter what.

I needed a friend for life. Someone that would be strong enough to hold me through my unfolding pain and never let me go, until, the pain was gone; a man that doesn't judge me; that can slow me down and tell me everything was going to be alright. I moved too fast for that to happen. I thought, if I slowed down my pain would be more intense and that I couldn't survive. I didn't understand what was happening and didn't want to go through it alone, but no one would put up with me like this. Actuality, I needed to get help on my own, but couldn't stop picking up men.

I lost my job. I thought my life couldn't get any worse. Until,, I went out with Drake; I told myself, the date was to give him closure. In reality, though, I was using him. Drake's place was the only drug house I knew that could supply the amount of drugs I needed. I planned to get high enough to put me out of my misery. And, I wanted to leave him on a good note.

I was scheming and he was too. Drake put a flesh eating fungus on me that I couldn't shake off. It was worse than any drug and felt worse than death. The doctors couldn't see it and wouldn't take x-rays to find it. They looked right at it and said it wasn't there. I hated Drake for doing that to me. I swore I wouldn't have anything more to do with black men, as I felt my body being invaded. A ruthless fungus was living and breathing on my flash, eating me alive. I was afraid to take a bath or shower, thinking it may spread all over my body and devour me. At night, I would wet towels with hot water and lay them between my legs, just to sleep. One night, while sleeping, I changed positions and the hand holding the wet towel ended up on my chest. The fungus followed the dampness of the towel and now lived on my chest. My chest turned red.

I covered up my chest. Hiding from the world, like a wounded animal. I thought the pain was going to burn right through to my heart. I thought that I was being punished to death by excruciating pain and knew I wouldn't be able to bear it much longer. I remembered something my mom warned me about once, regarding her medicine. She told me to never open the capsules because the contents are poisonous to the human skin.

One uncomfortable night, I'd had enough. I wasn't going to let Drakes revengeful attack be the end of me. I stumbled to my car and drove to my mother's house. I grabbed three of her capsules and then drove back home. In my bedroom, sitting on my bed, I opened the three capsules and rubbed them into the fungus on my chest with my right hand only. Screaming in unbearable pain, I laid there and felt the fungus dying like a savage with a throbbing vengeance; and, not knowing if I passed out from the pain, died, or fell asleep. I was out for the night.

The next morning, I was still alive and the fungus had died. Out of all the excitement, I forgot to put on clothes and my fingernails on my right hand, were totally gone. My chest was black and the layers of skin that the fungus destroyed, had dried, cracked and peeled and then fell off my body. I continued to hide my chest and thought it would never be the same again. In time, it healed and I was alone again to face everything unfolding in my life.

Unfolding Souls- Lyrics

Unfolding soul opens old wounds, unlocking the door to your secret life. Set free buried anger! All addictions unfold. Oppressions and obsessions unfold. Old dust has finally settled reaching its peak. Don't wallow in it. Don't stumble through it. Don't stagger around it. Don't try to climb over it. Speak to your mountain and tell it to move. Find where your strength comes from. You've got to search the heavens and the earth to find you. Discover what you're looking for. Searching for a voice strong enough to allow your story to be heard.

You got to represent your pride! Emotion has to come up deep down, from the inside. Whatever you find to work with, work with what you got; let your soul unfold. Life is worth talking about. You're alive! Living is all that matters, be proud.
Be proud to unfold.

Everybody needs to die, to be born again. Let them die to be born again. Everybody needs to learn how to live again. Let them learn how to walk again. Everybody doesn't live to learn over again, or get one last chance to talk and tell the story again. Everybody has a sad story to tell that hasn't been told. Everybody has to search to find peace of mind as we twist and turn through time. Everybody's turn comes around as our lives go up and down. We win when it's our turn to win! We lose when it's our turn to lose. Somebody's got to survive to be set free; somebody's voice is chosen to set others free.

You can't hold back your purpose or your gold. The world can't hide unfolding souls. Let the standing ovations carry you far beyond the mind games and the names that wounded you to the core. You were a victim of circumstances; you've earned your wings to soar above the crowd and all the rest. Fly over! Unfolding soul! Humiliations! Scandalous lies! Spreading rumors! Your mountain was just a test! Life is just a test to find out who you really are. You were born to be here. You are who you are.

Mom said, "Jamaica your hobby is going to dinner with men."

"Mom, I look for them to have values and principles."

"Yes, while you have stepped out of yours, like taking off clothes."

"I just want men to be accountable for their actions."

"Yes, sweetheart, while you are standing on the outside watching the world go around as if you're not human and your actions doesn't matter."

She said a mouth full. I feel, I don't exist to myself or to anyone else. I've lived my life as if I am invisible to others, so I don't have to be accountable. I've lived in denial, to keep from being hurt, judged or disliked. I'm running and hiding from my reality that I couldn't tell her or anyone else about.

Mom said, "Some people move forward and prosper, while some don't prosper at all. They stand around and watch, as they judge the people that go in circles. You don't like the spectators and let people hold you back."

I had survived many stages that an abused personality goes through. I made Drake use force with me. I really didn't want to sleep with him. Unconsciously, I wanted to re-live the rape over and over. I was addicted to pain. The only way I could be with a man is to make it seem like rape. I'm losing my craving for sex and my two personalities are fighting a war against each other. The good personality is getting stronger while the bad is getting weaker.

When a woman gets to that point of fighting and asking men to abuse her, she's in trouble. Some men will think, okay, she likes it rough; and will be too rough. For a woman to like to fight roughly before sex is not a preference. Pain is not foreplay; she's sick and needs to get help. I didn't want the act itself to be rough. Once he over-powered me, I wanted everything calm and easy. How would a man know I wanted love and affection? I was lucky Drake didn't kill me.

I was at another crossroad; the next phase. I was going through another process of healing from being abused. After Drake, I had excluded myself from physically abusive men in my life. Now, I had to choose between the mature good girl and the immature bad girl I was dementedly torn between because I couldn't say good-bye to the game of love.

I considered what I would do next? Reflecting on my life and feeling Boxer may ask me to move. To get away from everyone, I went to check out a new store in the bay area, just to pass some time. I planned to walk through and get an idea on back-yard designs. As I tried to get in touch with my creative side. I noticed that I was being pursued by a white man. I picked up something off the shelf and dropped it on purpose to see what would happen.

I kneeled down to pick it up. The man followed me and we looked into each other's eyes. His eyes were three different colors and seemed to be looking right through to my soul. They were blue-green with gold around them.

"Hi I'm Matt," He said, as he picked up after me.
"I'm Jamaica."
"I couldn't help but notice you walked through the door alone. I can help you find whatever it is you need. I'm a contractor and I know my way around this place. I would like to walk around with you if you don't mind."
I didn't respond, yet.
"I'm a good guy. I don't go around following every woman I see. I'd like to get to know you, is all. Can you talk?"
"Yes, I talk."

A white man had never approached me in all my years of clubbing. I tried to figure him out. He rushed me like a man, he wasn't obvious with his game like a player, he didn't have a rap, but he had conversation. Before I knew it, he had asked me for my number. I gave him my mom's number. I knew that she would answer and expose him for who he really was. I'm sure she will let me know what he's all about. He called and it went down just as I planned. She talked to him and because he didn't ask her any questions about me or our family, she told me that he just wanted sex.

He left his number with my mom. I called and he asked me out on a date. We agreed to meet somewhere and I was supposed to get in the car with him. I pulled up and I saw him getting out of his truck with a bottle of wine and two wine glasses. I wondered what was going on. He had seen my car when I drove up and wanted to ride with me. He got in and I noticed a fat joint in his pocket. I thought, oh, we're going to have a drink before we get to where were going. I was excited to see where a white man would take me on a date. Assuming that he was going to take a sister somewhere I had never been, show me something different. Matt sat looking at me.
"Where are we going?" he asked, and got comfortable.

I gave him the benefit of the doubt. I took him across the San Francisco Bridge to the City of Berkley Marina and parked. On a clear night, you can see the San Mateo Bridge, San Francisco Bridge, and the Golden Gate Bridge. Before this date, I had dated a black guy that thought he was white. I was the first black woman that he had ever dated. He wanted to take me shopping for shoes, eat pizza and drink beer. Some white woman had him trained. I'm sitting here with a white man who tried to get what he wanted from a sister with a bottle of wine and a joint. Some misled black woman had misled him. I'm sitting here waiting for our date to start, and this was it.

The bottle was empty, the joint was gone, and my hopes are high, sitting at the marina on my first date with a white man. Now what? He moved toward me and stuck his tongue into my mouth. It laid in one spot with passion and gentle pressure. Then he gently started sucking my tongue. He changed the position of his head, mouth, and tongue and did it all over again. Then, he got really creative with his tongue in my mouth and everywhere else, the man took his time.

With my eyes closed, his tongue felt like I was with a black man. Matt knew how to kiss and I liked that. I never made out on the first date. What was I doing? His long, blond hair and beard felt soft, resting on my face. He was very experienced. I could tell he was used to getting what he wanted from women. His hands moved over my body in all the right spots. I was in white boy heaven; I went from don't, to don't stop. I was about to be converted, until, he spit his white man rap.

"I love the rhythm of a black woman's body when she's making love, there's nothing like it."

He had been turned out by black women. Black women were his play ground, filled with all types and sizes and Matt wanted to try us all. I wasn't anything more than a sexual attraction; a ride in his amusement park. He supplied the high and I was supposed to perform with rhythm and my black woman style. I was about to make music for his mind, body, and soul. I straddled his lap and was about to do just what he expected of me. I was going to blow his mind and his eyes were telling me to do it. Eye contact while having sex drove me crazy. I loved a man that could talk with his eyes.

I couldn't look him in the eyes after he said that. He made me feel cheap, and I didn't ask God is this the man that's going to love and cherish me for as long as we both shall live? As I dropped my head on his chest, there was warfare going on inside my head. His hard body turned me on. I wanted him badly, but my preference had always been black men. In the heat of the moment, I came to the conclusion, I loved black men more than I could ever hate them.

Black Man

I Choose You
To have and to hold from this day forward,
You can take my hand and together we will stand.
You've taken me through hell and high waters
to heaven right here on earth.
Let me be the woman to show you
a woman's worth.
I will never give up on you, Black Man.
I won't ever turn my back on you, Black Man.
My body is your playground and turf.
My rhythm, and my Black woman style was yours first.
My word is my bond that can't be broken.
Trust in me, I have spoken
as your friend, your woman, your wife
your love, your lover, to entice.
I am your world; I am your life.
BLACK MAN
You are the man
I want to call to bed
every night.

The war continued in my head. I had to stop and ask myself.
"Who am I going to be?" What's going to become of me if all I
want to do is blow men's minds? At some point in life, we
should somehow find the answers to our questions, and I'm at
that point. Matt brought back unpleasant memories and more
secrets that I kept from everyone. I don't care what was done to
me in the past, no more excuses. I can't be this bad girl any
longer; my mind blowing days were over.
The only thing I've been blowing is my life and that makes me
no better than all the bad weirdoes that have hurt me. I had to
face that I was this bad person that I didn't like. Within me, was
the better person? I can't let this gorgeous, young white man
hurt me; I'm right at the point of getting therapy. How do I
come back from a broken hearted love affair when my heart has
been broken by a black man and a white man? I'm sure that

there are women that have overcome this same type of heart-ache that I felt I wouldn't make it through.

I wasn't strong enough. I couldn't do it just for the experience, anymore. I had experienced enough for a lifetime. That night with Matt, I was a big tease, as I came up with every excuse not to have sex. A fascinating attraction was going on and we ended up talking, and lying in each other's arms. It was meant for us to talk, that's all. I was hung-up on what I thought a white man should be and he wasn't the man for me. Matt thought that he gave me what I wanted. He was guilty of putting all black women in the same boat.

I've been stuck on what a black man should be and haven't found the one for me. Most of us are trapped in a mind frame about what we have heard and believed to be true. We judge each other's race, without knowing one's personal intelligence. Color hasn't anything to do with who we are on the inside and true love hasn't any color. After that night, I didn't hang out with Matt anymore. The man was trouble. I could feel the danger; I tried to get away from what he was all about. I had to work on me.

I got home and hit the liquor cabinet. I drank so much I couldn't see straight. I laid in the tub, when I heard someone in the house, but I was too drunk to move. Whoever he was, he stood tall standing over me. I thought to myself, finally, someone is going to kill me. At last, someone is going to put me out of my misery. I passed out or he killed me, one or the other, I was out like a light.

The next morning, I awakened to the aroma of grilled steak and eggs and I got sick all over again. I got up and saw suitcases that belonged to Boxer. I ran back to the bed and played like I was asleep. He had come home. I was mad at myself for not being strong enough to live without him.

Why was he here? He walked into the room and laid down next to me. He put his arms around me and kissed me on my shoulder.

"Jamaica, I had a house filled with women and I didn't know what love was. You taught me what love was. Once I found it, I felt that I could do anything and I have done something about it. I have established a life that I am proud of. You were raised in a family that taught what love is. Baby, why can't you love yourself?"

I wasn't ready to answer any questions. Boxer had a lot. He got up and began to pace the floor. I thought it was cute. In reality, he'd had enough.

"Jamaica, I'm asking you questions and I'm not getting any answers. I want to know, why you asked me to kill you last night. What's going on? I was attracted to you because of the fight in you. I've never worked so hard to get any woman the way I worked to get you. I came at you bold; you said I was too headstrong. You wouldn't give me the time of day, your number, or address. Hell, girl, you wouldn't even dance with me in my club. You made me work Jamaica and that's what you got to do to get me. Live and strive, baby. That's my motto for life. I know you want me, but you can't live your life through me. When we met, you said for us to get our lives together first, then come together and build on the love that we're feeling. Look around you; I've been your bread and butter. I have given you all my love, what are you giving me? Look at this (he picked up my panties off the floor). There's no other woman here, just you. I let each and every one of them go, for you. And, what have you accomplished? There's no proof of you building you or us. I took your words as the ultimate challenge and I'm holding you to it. No one has ever talked to me that way. Your words are what's keeping me focused on my livelihood. I have held up my end of the bargain, now you got to hold up yours. I'm a fighter, Jamaica, in every aspect of the game of life; that's what I do. I can't love someone that doesn't fight for what they want. You don't want to live and you won't tell me why. I need to know why the woman that I'm fighting for wants to die."

Boxer stood over me waiting for an answer.

"Did I ask you to love me? I didn't ask you to let your women go. Why did you come back? So I can watch you leave all over again? Why don't you just leave now and get it over with? Get out, Boxer! I don't need you! I was fine without you!" I cried.

"You want me to leave, I'll leave? You know where I am. I'm in town for two weeks. Since you won't talk to me, talk to someone. Do whatever you need to do. Just get better for you and Mannie. I'm working; I'm not walking out on you, Jamaica. But I won't be your crutch either."

I always know the right things to tell people. I don't listen to myself when talking. Boxer was right; I needed to hold up my end of the bargain. Men had told me lovely things before, but they were all talk. Boxer wasn't all talk; he tried his best to show his love and I couldn't see it. I wanted love, but I couldn't feel his sincerity because of my pain. I had been living in it too long.

My son's dad and all the men that raped me, hated me. They made me feel like I didn't deserve to be loved. It's hard to live that down. It's harder to allow someone to love you when you don't love yourself because you've been mentally and physically wounded. Boxer came along and said, I'm worth fighting for and made me remember that I am worth fighting for.

I'm so confused. Does he mean that this was the love I've been waiting for? I hated him for coming home and finding me that way, and, for loving me and making me see myself. I felt like he deserved better, and I tried to run him away. I finally went to the doctor for help. At first, the sessions were hard because they don't say much, you do all the talking and hearing yourself was supposed to show you what a pathetic human being you were. I guess the doctor feels that alone should be enough to make you straight.

I got more depressed in the beginning. After every session, I felt as if I'd never go back because I made such a fool of myself. I wouldn't let them put me on medication. Some people need medication and they should take it. I wanted to get better on my own; I knew I had it in me. I told the doctor what mom said and how I felt about myself. I never talked up to people to express my true feelings. Pain is my true feeling. I didn't want to take my pain out on anyone. I never talked back, not even to my parents. I run and hide because hurting people's feelings hurts me worse. When I speak up, I tell the truth and people don't want to hear the truth. The types of people I'm hanging around don't expect it or accept it coming from me, when I'm doing what they do. They'd rather hear a lie or nothing at all. I don't say anything at all.

The doctor was just there to listen. I was there to figure things out. When he had my problem good as solved in his mind to get to the bottom of the matter at hand, he would throw in psychological sayings like, "The grass always looks greener on the other side," or, "A bird in the hand beats two in the bush."

The day the doctor asked, if I believed in a higher power, our sessions were over. That's parent talk, I turned him off like a waterspout. But he had already worked his psychologist education on me and brought me back to my family tree, which had been my backbone that I hadn't owned up to.

I needed to accept who I was and how I was raised. Again, I thought a white man was going to give me a new conception or a different perspective on life than what my parents taught me. I finally got it. I was searching for something I already had and won't use it. My values and principles and my spiritual perception is what's been keeping me alive and safe through all the madness in my life. That day, he helped me to see who I was and believe more in where I came from, so I'm getting there. I didn't talk to my family about my breakdown or share with them that I was seeing a doctor.

My family knew I had been injured. They knew I was going through something heart-wrenching and they didn't have all the reasons why I was sick. All of them felt that whatever the case might be; I would get through it and didn't want me to give up trying. As a family, they didn't treat me like I was stressed out or sick; it seemed like they worked me harder. At one point, I thought for sure they had a bet going on to see which one of them can run me the craziest the fastest. All my brothers and sisters had been there for me. I had no excuses for my present reasoning. There wasn't anyone abusing me anymore. I appreciated them wanting to help and Boxer for telling me to get help, but I had to do it alone.

Chapter Twelve
Where Do I Go from Here?

Change doesn't come easy. At first, I wasn't living. I was a stranger to myself, an alien to others. Day in and day out, I wasn't doing me; until, one day, I bought a magazine and took it home. I wasn't reading it, instead, I flipped through the pages and rubbed the sample perfumes on myself. I got to the page that read, 'In the Spirit', by Susan B. Taylor, and I began to read.

Susan's column was spiritual. It sounded like she was reading my mind. I thought to myself, this should be me. I got angry with Susan for no good reason. I tried to make myself believe that I didn't use my God given words and talents to help people and God has taken it and given them to Susan. The truth was, she's actually using her God given talents to reach people; something that I was born to achieve also.

I broke down hard for being jealous. That stubborn denial that my mother said I was living in, collapsed. The wall I had up, came tumbling down. I was ready to take my place in this world. Understand, I was born to help people get in touch with their spirit. But first I had to get beyond my pain and get in touch with mine. When no one else could reach me, God used Susan B. Taylor's 'In the spirit'. The gifted words He gave her spoke to me. I ignored my family's spiritual insight and still, He got my attention. That day I prayed until, my mind felt a transformation taking place; my unhappy tears dried, and I cried healthy tears.

My anger turned into positive anger. I got out of my own way and snapped out of hindering my growth and maturity. I had been thinking more about what other people thought of me than what God thinks. Giving Him what He wants is the only way I'm going to find me and have what I want. Where do I go from here?

First, I tried to live through Susan B. Taylor. I couldn't wait until, the next issue of the magazine came out to read what I felt about life and what I had written time after time. I wanted to meet this person that seemed to have my thoughts. Her education made her point of view sound so clear. I understood every word. I didn't know that was Susan's picture at the top of the page. I was reading her column for months before I made that connection.

One day, I went to see my mom. She had lost her eye sight and called all her children together. We were sad and really didn't know how to handle the news. Everyone left but I stayed there with my mom. With my magazine in hand, I got in bed with my clothes on. I was fed up with not having a life and living through Susan B. Taylor's life. I was fed up with watching my mom and she didn't know if I watched her or not.

Mom was fed up also. She was sick and tired of listening to me flipping through the pages of my magazine. She knew that I was lost and told me to go out and do something about it; figure it out; go to the library and ask questions and don't leave until, you get answers. Before all the rapes, I was totally into me and I needed to find that person, again.

I got up, got dressed, and went to the library. As usual, I checked out the biggest book I could find. I like to look book smart, but I'm not going to read it. I hadn't read any book, cover to cover, to get a sense of accomplishment. I had not dressed up in a while, so I looked good. I had my little suit on, clutching my big book, like I had a sense of direction; looking real important, shaking and faking on my way out of the library and I ran into Nicky, my girlfriend, she had graduated college and is now running the public library. I saw her and broke-down crying.

"Jamaica, stop crying before you start me to crying. What's wrong?"

"I'm lost, I want a life and I don't know where to start. My spelling is so bad, it's holding me back from doing what I do best; writing. I want to write."

"Go to the computer center behind the library. Come on; I'll show you."

I walked through the door and the computer changed my entire life. I signed up for classes. I started school and began my life all over again. I read books. I read other people's autobiographies and I felt a sense of achievement and self-worth. After reading what some people had lived through, I was happy to be me. I had a journal filled with poems and a book of poetry in my head that needed editing. I learned to type my thoughts down and click spellcheck.

As I built up my life, my confidence grew. I felt motivated again. I was ready to create something. When I got affiliated with the computer, the first poem I brought to life was, 'I Gave My Soul'. It helped me through so much sadness. So, this is from me to my readers.

I Gave My Soul

In my hand flows a River
I cried from Loneliness.
I captured my feelings
In my hand
and gave them
Love.
No one had time to give.
I didn't wipe them away.
I caressed them
and made them stay.
In my hand
flows a Sea
I cried from Sorrow.
I captured my sadness
in my hand
and gave it
Affection.
No one had time to share
I didn't throw them
away.
I caressed them
and convinced them
to stay.
In my hand
flows an Ocean
I cried from Despair.
It was up to me,
Alone, to care.
I took my life
In my hand
and faced it.
No one loves you when
you're down.
At that point,
I turned my life
Around.

I never let
one tear of emotion
touch the ground.
I wouldn't let them
get away.
I caressed them
and made them stay.
In my hand
flows a Volcano
of Love.
when it erupts,
it will make a
powerful sound.
The world will know
of the talents
I hold.
In my hand
I discovered
A Book of Love
that gave me
peace of mind
and taught me
to pray.
In my hand
flows great Rivers,
mighty Seas,
raging Oceans
of Strength.
All the Power
I caress
I gave my soul
to the Creator. For He holds the
world in His Hands.

The weak have the power to become strong. Some humans let other people trash their lives. Don't let them lead you into mischief and destruction, you are somebody. Some people feel that life sold them short and they suffer with shortcomings. Life has taken advantage of them while they remain at a disadvantage. For some, life has made a positive example of them at their weakest moment, in difficult situations, and has taken them from rags to riches.

Some people say. "What's the use," and give up on life. Not knowing if they don't fight, their present conditions will make a negative example of them in their future. That is not life's plan. We were meant for something greater.

Read this poem. Let it lead you back to the light of living. At my weakest moment and my worst rape, I created the beginning of this. Now, that the dark clouds had been lifted from my life, I can see the sun shining and could end this poem with a positive goal. For the first time in my life, I looked forward to the future.

Born In The Light

I was born in the light
Raised to take over
Where my ancestors left off,
Taught to be proud of who I am
Until, I was introduced to the dark side.
I was blind to the fact that I didn't belong.
Fascinated, it all was so different
And wild. I wanted to fit in,
So I tried to live in darkness.
I wasn't aware I could never be happy
Trying to be someone else.
I was too modest and too real
To live in darkness where there wasn't any truth.
I was abused in more ways than one, badgered
And pushed too far.
I was lost from the light and couldn't
Find my way back.
I was pushed off the edge of the mountain
Of my accomplishment. Darkness stood there
Watching. As I was falling, I saw everyone
Around me for what they really are
And noticed the sun doesn't shine
On their faces.
I hit rock bottom.
That's when I became aware of myself
And who I am. I am the light that
Forced them to see themselves
As fools that despise wisdom.
They live in constant fear of darkness.
Some will never see the light.
Some will never accept God as the way,
The truth and the light
In all of us that believe in him.

One day, I got home from school and began to draw. Mannie had never seen that side of me. He thought he knew all there was to know about his mother; he was in shock and happy at the same time. Boxer couldn't believe that I had done the drawing either. The next time he returned home, he brought art supplies, sat down and watched me draw my first pictures. I had so many pictures and poems, I started setting up art shows to stay encouraged.

I called family and friends to attend my first show. Boxer was out of town boxing. People from school showed up, the news reporters taped a publicized commercial for TV stations. The more I accomplished, the more confident I became. I sold out and felt alive.

I majored in philosophy. My favorite professor's name was Dr. Bill Hill. He made a difference in the way I perceive life. The specialty stores carried my work. I produced work for one hundred stores just being me. I write and create what's in my head; my work is a natural talent, I had found me. People were coming to me for advice about love and sex. Now, that was using my brain, they're hopeful that I could help them sort out this mess called life. I talked to people my age that are going through things that I went through when I was fifteen, sixteen, and seventeen. That's how I began writing books. I write to help people fall in love. In all my breaking down in my past, I kept it private. Now that I tell my story, people look up to me for not running around crying on shoulders. People that thought they had me all figured out, found out they really don't know me. Old men friends and rivals came out of the woodwork trying to get close to me again. I sent them right back into the woods.

People I grew-up with felt like I had deceived them. I never let anyone know my creative side because I couldn't give one-hundred percent. I couldn't express myself because of the pain. I was lost from myself all that time. I let people feel whatever way they wanted. I didn't owe anyone an apology. Now, the possibilities are endless. I had purpose and integrity. I was alive again and I had a mature life.

I was around positive people. I had found myself and nothing else mattered; my depression was gone. I was able to see that I am somebody with potential. Boxer was in and out of town and it didn't matter. I was going to make my life work with or without him. I was hanging out at coffee house rap sessions where people get up and express words or poems, just to get it out. Businessmen were in my face wanting to invest in me, but they wanted me to move in with them first.

They were older men, established, with plenty of money to throw around, using their homes to get young girls. Slick said things to me like, "Your car would look good parked in my garage," and "Come home with me and make my house feel like a home, give my house a womanly touch."

Dealing with men like Old Fart's got me ready for their foolish games. I already had a man and I wasn't his investment, he cared. I was about my business. I was doing the school thing again; I was doing so many things right. I just wasn't up to failing at anything; I couldn't face losing Boxer. I live in his house; he comes and goes as he pleases. The better I got, the more I felt his love for me. It was time for life to challenge his motives.

My first real test of clean living came one day when I went to my parent's house and there was a knock on the door. I answered and it was Troy. I hadn't seen Troy in years. I thought he was dead. We just stood there staring at each other. I had flashbacks. I didn't know if he was there to kill me for sleeping with Bay-Bay, or if he came in peace. I just stood there, waiting to hear what he had to say.

"Can I talk to you for a moment?"

"Troy? We don't have anything to talk about. Why are you here?"

"I'm not going to hurt you, Jamaica; I want to share my
testimony with you about that night in the hotel."
I thought, 'I got to hear this'.

He was going to kill me and now he has a testimony. We sat out
on the front porch. As I listened, I noticed that Troy was a broken man. He wasn't the same; he doesn't have game, any rap,
or swagger. Where's the pimp costume? His clothes are plain
and boring. Where has he been? What happened to him? He's
acting unfamiliar. It's just weird. I felt that I never knew this person. I thought, 'This is a test'.

Troy went on and on, until, I felt his conviction.
> "The prayer was powerful and it brought a miracle into
> existence. God rescued me that night. I walked into that
> room with a mind to kill both of us, but that violent atti-
> tude left when I walked out of that room. I wasn't sure
> what had changed about my life, but I knew it was
> something big. I realized later my lifelong problem an-
> ger was gone."

What Troy said was mind-blowing. I heard him out and to hear
that both our lives were spared? Troy, my aggressor, and I, the
victim that had survived his abuse, left us speechless. Mom had
been listening through an opened window. She opened the
door and began to talk. God granted her the moment she had
waited for.
> "You two are the reason I'm blind. I can't see because of
> your selfishness. You didn't care how your decisions af-
> fected others. And Troy, your obsession to kill my
> daughter kept me up nights. I prayed long and hard the
> night you took my daughter from this house. And, I
> prayed and asked God to spare both your lives. You
> have life because I sacrificed mine. I gave my life for
> you."

She unfolded the burden she bared for us and closed the door. No words could express what we felt. We had cried together before, but for different reasons. Those tears of mine meant, 'How could I let that happen'? The tears coming from Troy were 'I'm so sorry I treated your mother and you that way'. That day, he told me he would always love me. Why was he back in my life? Troy being here was so incredible and unreal. Both our human minds couldn't comprehend the importance of the encounter. That was the day my mother got to speak her mind and Troy and my tears were remorseful tears.

Still I couldn't release myself. I couldn't tell him what I went through that night in that room or how I felt about my mom going blind because of us. I didn't want to bond or connect with him again; not in any way form or fashion. That left him alone to face it.

Afterwards, I felt good that I was over Troy. Mom said the Power of God works through humans, through intercessory prayer to heal people. And, sometimes it takes more power than our mortal bodies could bear and could leave the human body injured; and that's why she was blind. In other words, she sacrificed her life and negotiated with God and he used her as a mediator and spared both our lives.

I was proud of how I handled the situation with Troy. I listened to my intuition. I didn't act excited to see him and I didn't talk much. I didn't want him to get the wrong impression. He asked if I could ever love him again and I told him no; let's leave the past in the past. I brought out the worst in him and if I did it once, I may do it again. I told him to find someone that doesn't know about his past and the person he used to be; she can love him for who he is today.

All of us are on earth to save someone. First, we must save ourselves. Help someone become a believer; that's the most important reason our lives exist. I ran to Troy and he couldn't save me, so I had to save myself. Today, I'm still trying to break that habit. I don't want to feel I need to run to anyone, but it's good to have someone to run to. You remember your fist love even if it ended tragically. Troy broke my heart because he couldn't handle our love mentally.

For the first time in my life, I understood why our relationship went down that way. Life has taught me that when I listen, life gives me answers. There's a higher power at work in our lives. We think our life is about us; all we can see is our wants and needs. We all have a job to do here on earth. I went on with my life. I wasn't comparing men to Troy and our sex life anymore. I was comparing men to Boxer and hoped he was the one for me.

My 25th birthday was coming up. I want to mark the moment of getting on with life. Boxer arrived in town.
>"Send an empty limousine to pick me up and bring me to you," I said.

I didn't say anything else, I left the rest up to him. When the limo arrived, I walked out the house styling a black and white leather suit. All my neighbors were outside watching, giving me applause, gathering around, complimenting me. Mission accomplished. I felt like a star. The driver opened the door and I got in. Everyone stood there and watched me leave.

I didn't know where I was going. I was relaxing, talking on the phone to my mom, drinking a glass of wine, listening to music, and watching TV. I turned everything on and had the sun roof open. I realized that I was on the Golden Gate Bridge; first time across in a limo. I was happy. The driver rolled up to the Sr. Frances Drake Hotel. I had seen it before, but had never been inside, I took a deep breath and I was ready to shine.

He stopped right on the red carpet. The door man opened the door for me. I got out and I was escorted up the red carpet into the hotel. The third guy escorted me to the piano bar and there was my date, 'The Boxer', it was definitely my *Pretty Woman* moment. He sat there with fabulously wrapped gifts all over the table. I greeted him with a big smile, hug, and kiss.

First, I got my birthday card. It absolutely blew me away. On the inside he wrote.

"Love isn't easy; it's deep awareness, the beginning of our foundation. You've secured us with your sweet and sexy creations. My heart and soul wishes you a very happy birthday. My body will be your biggest present birthday night. Love Boxer."

I opened my birthday gifts. He ordered Margaritas and Tequila shots on the side. This was a Margarita Moment, perfectly planned. He was perfect; just what the doctor ordered. It was a love connection. My gifts were a complete set of White Diamonds perfume. Each piece was wrapped separately in four boxes to look like many. I opened up the fifth box and it was diamonds, a tennis bracelet!

"Thank you, my love, I love it.

"I aim to please," said Boxer.

We walked into the hotel restaurant. We dined on a five-course meal and then went up to the room for birthday desert. That night, we went to see George Wallace and my face hurt from laughing so hard. When we left there, we went to an after-hour salsa club where they gave lessons to beginners and we caught on fast. We had big fun out on the dance floor; it was exciting. We got home and the party didn't stop. That morning, Boxer had to leave town.

I was hyped about my second book in the stores. I was on top of my game. I put *Sister-to-Sister Talk* on my first T-shirt. I made a collection out of it: T-shirt, book, bookmark, and poster. The idea for the book came about when I was exploring my options trying to find me. I worked downtown San Francisco. While standing on the street on my way to work one day, every woman that walked by me didn't speak but every man spoke.

I got inspired. I began writing this book in my head, talking to those women, asking what's up with that. Some of us can walk by each other every day, all day long and not acknowledge each other. They can tell other women about your stylish fashions and everything you had on, from your hair down to your designer shoes; if your makeup was flawless or not, and not speak to you. Are we that familiar that we ignore each other's faces?

To me, she was saying we don't acknowledge ourselves with love, honor and respect, but we are looking for a man that will. Let's talk and learn from each other and pass it on to the next generation.

Sister-2-Sister Woman-2-Woman
Lets'-Talk

Talk to me sister to sister, the forsaken image of my ignored being. I am one of many righteous women reflecting you, when I
look at myself in the mirror. Yet my likeness walks by me on the
street as if I am not familiar. Speak to me, women to women. I
exist, as a part of you that you haven't taken the
time to get to know.

Notice me, ask me how I am doing, and encourage me to have a
nice day. Love me, whether we are feminists or anti-feminists,
must we insist on getting along like politicians? Government
can't ignore us to any further extent. Let's not overlook each
other to any degree or time spent.

Recognize who you are, know where you come from, that's your
first responsibility as woman.

Education is the only way to face the reality. Woman to woman,
sister to sister, throw down the barricades. Because we are born
fighters, the war cries never cease. We are fighting to keep our
men; we are fighting to get away from our men; we are fighting
to save our men. We are fighting to seriously maintain when
confronting the series of changes and differences in trying to
keep our house a home.

We are fighting for our sons and daughters; we are fighting cor-
porate discrimination in society.

We are fighting, defending the lives of our people. Yet we are
struggling with our own little wars within. Still we are fortunate
to have our own identity, living independently, but we are still
alike, with unfortunate anxiety; living in the same shadows
of shattered dreams.

Showing the world and each other integrity. Joining forces we
have nothing to lose, but respect for each other we will gain.

Talk to me, my sister, face to face, sister to sister, race to race,
not just about our men, what they have and have not done, let's
talk about us; let's discuss the backlash epidemic, women who
have turned their backs on their sisters,

266

demoralizing our progress like society does.
Let's talk about what we can do for ourselves as liberated sisters
who have been led to the water, and can't drink unless we look
a certain way, or be certain size, or have certain
fashion. Led to the water to wait in line for second best. Led to
the water to be placed in society as sex tokens. Our identity has
arrived, but our equality is often denied, or excluded.
Together we can set ourselves free mentally. Together we can
learn how to achieve our goals. We have the power within us.
Let's be real; let's be intellectual; let's be loyal; that is our cus-
tom. Let's be proud to be women. I am you.

To my Sister, the Confused and Unconscious Waiter.

Who has no intention in finding work, assuming Mr. Perfect will
one day come along? Sister to sister, a man that has something
to offer a sister, wants a woman with expectations in life, not an
idealist sitting up polishing her fingers and toes waiting for
someone else to make her happy. Or, if you are a sister with very
high expectations in life, making your own happiness, he could
feel intimidated. Look out! Men like to wine and dine all types of
women. When he meets you he places you in a certain class of
women; judging you by profession, rank, or social group. Then
he makes his decision: sex toy, money investment, or wife. If you
are serious don't give him sex until, you know his intentions. Un-
less you are playing the same game, then you deserve each
other, two wrongs don't make it right.

To my sister, the Egotist.

Who despises me and thinks she's better. Stop judging me, sis-
ter; stop accusing me, and stop abusing me. Don't live wrapped
up in yourself. Look around you and see the same essence is in
me. Don't live stuck up with your nose in the air, our noses are
equal. Look me in the eyes; get to know me, and love me sister
to sister. Learn something positive. Stop degrading yourself.

To my sister, the Gold Digger.

Who married for money and not love; thinking you could find happiness; hoping you could beat the odds; manipulating, scheming, and undermining your man, sister to sister, look out! You are deceiving your way right into bondage. There aren't any witnesses behind closed doors. A man knows when he's loved or being played for a fool. Don't volunteer to make your life a living hell; your life is what you make it!
You're not going to break him. He's going
to break you, from your treacherous lies.

To my sister, the Apprehensive One.

Who has a good man, but is avoiding marriage because of fear. Fear is of the Prince of Darkness, come to destroy you and the love in your relationship. No one knows if their marriage is going to last; go to a marriage counselor, live strong, and make that move. There's a man shortage, sister, and you are neglecting yours with your skeptical attitude. Good men are hard to find, don't
let him get away.

To my sister, the Timid

Who's going through a divorce? Failure in a marriage attacks the heart that numbs the soul, which breaks down the body, inch by inch, until, you croak. Get him and the marriage out of your system, fast. Take two laxatives, you'll feel better in the morning. Take your life back, sister. When you get to the point where you can laugh at my humor; that's the day you will know you have the ability to live again.

To my sister, the She-Devil.

With a bad attitude. What is your problem? Must you live nasty twenty-four hours a day? When you put out bad vibes, that's what you get back in return. As you humiliate people you lose your identity. That's why you're evil and stressed out; it takes a lot of energy to hate. Don't live negative, there are still some nice people in this world. Find yourself respect; fall into some-

one's arms and be loved. Your pain is too obvious, you are hurt-ing. On the inside you are unhappy.

Three months later, the dead has arisen. I came home one day and there was a message from Troy on my phone. He tried to reach me; if it's important, he'll call back. The next morning he called and said he needed a ride to get his clothes from one point to the next. I don't know what's going on, but I got to find out what happened to Troy. Something has destroyed him; he's acting like he has had a severe break down. He's dead on the inside.

As I dressed in my best clothes, I thought about when Troy and I were together we had dressing up in common. That's still how I roll. I jump in my red Corvette and bounce. I don't even know where I'm going. Troy doesn't give me an address. He told me the street, but it's a long busy street and a lot of people hang out there. He gave me a landmark and I pulled up to the spot.

I didn't see him anywhere. I only see an overweight, homeless guy that sat on the ground. I watched him get up. He had on dirty clothes, a do-rag, and some other mess on his head. He had on the entire homeless costume. I thought, 'go away'. As he got a little closer, I thought, 'no way'. The man had blankets, trash bags; and everything looked filthy. He mopped around my car and then came towards my window. As this deranged man got closer, my shades drop off my nose, my mouth flew open, I was in shock.

Am I hallucinating? I'm not tripping; I haven't had any drugs since my breakdown. "Oh My God!" It was Troy, exposed as the overweight toe-ragger I met one day in front of a liquor store. How that story came about. After casing San Francisco Bay players clubs and hanging where real live gangsters are born and raised, I found the best one liner rap ever. That rap came from a toe-ragger (a homeless tramp) sitting on the ground leaning up against a trash can. He was in front of a liquor store with a do-rag tied around his head, dressed in the entire home-less costume. As I got out of my car, I walked toward him.

"Say, baby!" He said.

"What's up? I said.

"What's your name?" He asked. I lied and answered, "My name is Sue."

He rapped his best line, "You don't have to sue me, ba-by, I'll give you everything I own."

He knew darn well, he didn't own anything! I thought.

"Is this nobody the one that's going to sincerely love and cherish me for as long as I shall live?"

Picking him up that day would have been too out-there for me. Still, I wondered why our paths crossed. I believed they crossed to let me know I could be impressed by this person who I didn't even recognize as a human. I didn't see him as a man that used to have a job or money. I didn't think of him as someone's son, husband, father, or boyfriend that's loved by anyone.

My family reunion wasn't my first time meeting Troy. I didn't recognize him then because he was skinny and well groomed; now, he had traded in his pimp costume for a homeless one. He was overweight and looks used and abused. I didn't know what to do, breakdown and cry or get the hell out of there or just take off like I never knew him.

He got in my car and smelled unbelievably bad. What am I sup-posed to do with a homeless man? He's ruined his life. How could this happen to a man with his talents?

"You never saw me like this have you?"

"That's the first thing you asked me? Let's talk about how I lost my virginity to a toe-ragger, a tramp, a bum. Look at me, Troy! I'm not only in total shock, I'm hurt. You just blew a hole in my romantic story about losing my virginity."

Yet another secret I must bear. Now, I know why he gave me that sincere apology for abusing me. He knows how it feels to be mistreated. He's sleeping in the streets for a reason. Troy was on a guilt trip about the past; he couldn't handle what my mom told him and thinking he's being somehow punished because of his present situation. He brought me down, and I should have brought him down. I couldn't stop staring. I had never been that close to someone that lives on the street. I'm still stuck on the fact that I was once crazy about this homeless man. It was mind-blowing, but I consoled him.

"Troy, I made a choice to be with you and your abusive habits and I'd hoped that you would change. My mother made a choice and sacrificed her life for yours. Troy, whether you believe it or not, you have a second chance at life, take it."

I dropped him off and sat there to watch him solicit money, standing in front of a restaurant that feeds him well. It was very unpleasant to witness. Troy was a two-bit hustler and he had just hustled me for a ride across town. As I drove off thinking of him drifting his life away, living on the street, this is the thought that came to mind...

Our Purpose In Life

We all have wondered and asked ourselves
At some point in life who am i,
And why am i here?
I believe long before we were conceived
Our lives were mapped out and planned.
Our parents were carefully chosen,
Our purpose in life was thought out
With patience and understanding.
Our personality was created,
That every one of us would have our
Own identity.
There's a lot of us that don't know
We all, big or small, have a
Purpose here on earth.
Many of us have had to really
Examine our lives to find it.
Others have searched and searched
And have not given up.
The rest knew, right from the start,
And have accomplished great things
In life.
Life is so real and too important to run
And hide when times really get hard
And we can't seem to find our way.
Our lives have been decided.
We're the ones keep stumbling along the way.
There are multitudes that have gone astray,
Drifting day to day.
We all have been given this chance
To do our best in life to find our purpose,
To achieve our goals and complete the job
God assigned to us.
If God can work so hard for us, is he asking
Too much of us to carry out his plan?

The first time I read that poem in public, it was my art show at the college. I was happy to be able to put life in perspective and everyone enjoyed it; except one woman that confronted me, angrily.

> "What about the crack babies, were there lives planned? Where do they come from?"
>
> "The crack babies came from the multitudes of people that have gone astray, the drifters. Yes, God has a plan for everyone."

She wasn't about to spoil my natural high. I was happy that people sat back listening to my perspective. I made sense, that's all that matters. In spite of everything, I was listening to my parents.

Boxer came home. Mannie and I drove to his yacht and after a long day of cruising, we fell asleep on the ocean. That morning, we had breakfast on the yacht and I fell in love with Big-Rig, the chef's homemade, fried biscuits.

> "Do you mind if my chef, Big-Rig, stays in our pool house for three months?"
>
> "I don't mind at all; he's funny, he makes me laugh and he's getting along well with Mannie. He's always saying he's in love with Mexican women; he's not into black women. I should be safe until, he gets on his feet."

Big-Rig and I talked. I told him, if he cleans up after himself, Boxer and I felt that he wouldn't have to pay rent for three months. We figured that's enough time for him to do whatever. He offered to be our butler and I said, yes, if it's alright with Boxer. It was a deal; and having a manservant would be nice. I had tasted his cooking and it was good. On the weekends, he catered parties. I knew he was clean, he always smelled good. It will be nice to have a man around the house.

My butler moved in ready to work. He had a night job baking for a restaurant popular for their hamburgers, breakfast, and deserts. He comes home with five different types of pies every morning that he baked. Big-Rig cooks my breakfast before going to sleep. This morning my four sisters showed up in lingerie and P.J.'s for breakfast in bed.

My butler put on a show for them. Big-Rig's specialty was homemade pan-fried biscuits. He knows I love them and he served us plenty. While eating the best biscuits in the world, I had my best conversation. I had my sisters laughing about Boxer telling me how delicious I was. Then, he asked me of all people to save him. They said to expect them back for the four-course dinner and more Boxer stories.

My sister's arrived at 7:00 p.m. Big-Rig served homemade soups, salad, and grilled steak for the main course, plus home-made desert. Every night, he cleaned the kitchen and all the rooms and he sweeps and mops and goes to bed before going to work. Things were perfect. I was served three meals a day.

My butler became too interested in me. He was too informal with me. He stopped dressing properly. He kept asking me to go with him to fly his kite and I loved flying kites, but I turned him down. When he asked me to go with him to watch the sunset, I'd had enough. I knew that was the kind of things that lovers do. He's coming on to me. What was going on in his head? Was he tired of living? Boxer would kill him! Big-Rig and I were like family.

I couldn't wait to be home alone. I snooped in his room trying to find his journal he's always writing in. I found it under his bed and began to read. It sounded like a story about us.

I called the sister clan over and Dee read it out loud.
        "Girl, he's talking about you.
        "I'm her Big-Rig butler; I call her bossy lady. She's a wild and crazy oversexed boss lady. I serve her in the nude,

the woman likes it hot! I give her what she needs on the spot," Dee stops reading.

"It's getting too vulgar," she said.

"It's time for him to leave," I said, to my sisters.

"It's just a journal, let the man dream. Don't mess up a good thing," Jazzy said.

"Show him the door; he's gone too far," Sassy said.

"It's better you put him out than Boxer," B.J. added.

I got home one day and my bed was made. My clothes hamper was open and my dirty clothes were missing. He broke the two rules I gave him. Rule one. Stay out of our bedroom. Rule two. Don't touch my hamper. I told him I would clean my room and wash my own clothes. I went downstairs to the laundry room and my clothes weren't there. I ran back up the stairs and into my room and my clothes were folded and put away neatly in my dresser drawers. He's been here smelling my things. I'm living with a pervert. He knows my personal business. Where is he? I was furious.

When he returned home, I reacted, "Your three months is up buddy. Boxer will be back soon and he's going to hear all about you and my underwear drawer."

He started telling me how much he wanted me from the first time he laid eyes on me.

"You're not my butler anymore. Get the hell out my house! Go to your living quarter. The guest house, now!"

The following night, when I returned home, he was laid out in Boxer's bed with another woman.

"Get out! Get your things and leave our guest house to-night." I mean it.

He showed his guest to the backdoor and returned, "I have slept with all of Boxer's women. What makes you think you're any different?"

"Boxer doesn't love those women like he loves me; you got his leftovers. I'm his alone. Don't no man share me. I love him and you're going to respect that. You call

275

yourself a friend; respect that he has changed his life, and respect this house. Don't bring other woman in our home. Grow-up and stop taking advantage of friends trying to help you."

He walked away.

"Big-Rig, come talk to me. What's up with you? Why are you invading my private space? Are you wearing my lingerie on your head when I'm not home? Answer me!"

He stood there looking like he couldn't help himself. He was doing his best. I don't know where he's going and I don't care. My butler moved out that night. He wouldn't talk to me. I'll let Boxer deal with his behind.

I had a show to do at the coffee house downtown. It was huge and popular for networking. Everyone that's anyone walked through, or hung out. Once my show started, a man that had a table, scouting for a famous football team came over and bought two of my poems and carried them on the plane with the team. The coffee house threw a book party for me at the coffee house. Mr. Scouter showed up and said after the football team read my poem, 'Born in the Light', there wasn't a dry eye on the plane. He bought a book and encouraged me to keep writing.

I had been through too much drama with men. I still wasn't free to fly my highest, still, I was free from my sex addition with men. I had limousines, Rolls Royce's, Jag's, and Mercedes rolling up to the coffee houses to hear my words. One night, I turned it out with, 'The Pity Party Club.' Boxer was there that night. He had his spotlight and loving that I had found mine. I was handling my business and the people loved me. I told men, nothing's going on here, but business, and making money for me. I wasn't reacting to life anymore. I was enjoying capturing my youth and restoring my spirits, my mental health.

The Pity-Party Club
Emancipation

I'm unbound and mentally free
I don't have any more tears to cry for Mr. Sorrow
in my club meet. I demand this meeting to come to order
There will not be no more outburst from controlling old Mr. Pain
My life isn't no longer filled with his insane mind games
No Thank You, Sister
I don't feel like death warmed up for the main course
That's the woman that I used to be,
I'll never open up another bag of pity party chips for me
To drowned in my misery dip
and eat and weep and eat and weep
I don't care about The Small-Potatoes and The Big Dipsticks of
Ice Cream
Chocolate or Vanilla or The Mother-Rapping Mr. Hardship's
Child, I don't need any more biscuits and gravy on my lips
I'm no longer craving
I don't go off on my pigging-out, drunken high, pity party trips
I exercise to stimulate my mind
Survival is my everyday EMANCIPATION fun parties
With healthy foods like veggie dips that feed the brain; not the
hips
It's my celebration point in time. I don't need the Man trips.

I thought about coming clean with Boxer. He's waiting for me to answer his questions and I will, when I am ready. There is a continent between us, he's never here, but, he's the only man in my life and he make sense. I hope I don't wait too late to tell him how much I care. Love makes you want to communicate everything and I'm not ready, but I don't want to lose him because of my secrets. Love makes you want to run to that person and say, baby, this is how I feel and this is what I'm doing, and make them a part of your life.

Boxer and I have love. He helped me to realize the reason why I ran men crazy, by not speaking my mind. I don't want Boxer to think that I am playing with his intelligence. Every man I had ever been with, including Troy, told me after we had broken-up that I never expressed my feelings. I never used the L-word with them. Why throw the word around when men and women both have our definition of what love is? I had been caught up in assumed relationships for too long.

I allowed men to bring that behavior out in me. I hated men more and more. I'm not the kind of woman that talks for a man or asks him what he's thinking. I knew if he cared, he would share his thoughts, like Boxer does. For all those reasons, I just named, my priorities are straight with Boxer. I know he's a good man and I don't want to lose him. I've got to tell him that I love him.

Chapter Thirteen
My Soul Mate

Boxer and I have been going out a lot. He likes Bodega Bay; that's where they filmed the movie, 'The Birds', It's nothing but beach, souvenir shops, and seafood restaurants. We drive up the coast and stop at beach after beach. When we go, we play in the water, run, walk, and lay out on the sand. You can't eat on the beaches there because of the birds. One day, when we were there, tourists brought their picnic basket out on the sand and left it.

We tried to warn them by calling out to them, but the waves were high and they couldn't hear us. While they were in the water, different species of birds gathered from all directions. They fought over the food and devoured it to shreds. I couldn't believe how fast they ate the food. The birds opened up bags of chips, cookies, and sandwiches. Birds owned that beach. Boxer and I had the perfect time together when we went there. He finds amazing parks where we take pictures. We loved throwing Frisbees. He found nice places for us to hike. We dressed up to go to the movies and fabulous restaurants. Our time together was pleasant. I kept falling in love with him over and over again. Talking to him was my favorite thing to do. I loved daydreaming about him; when I was with him, remembering significant times like that one night at the player's party.

His house was so clean; I bet J.J. that he had a maid. I had to find an excuse to snoop and we went looking for her. He only showed me one room; there was something very suspicious going on as to why he didn't show me his room. J.J. and I went cloak-and-dagger on his butt. Two can play this game, well three, I had an accomplice. We snuck into his master bedroom and it looked like a totally different person lived there; it was a clean, but messy, mess.

I walked into his master bath, opened up his shower door and I stumbled across a scary, but nice discovery. He has an obsession. I saw some pictures he had taken of me on the dance floor at his club. They were bent up and had water damage on them and the ends were curled up. How long did he think they were going to last in the shower? When I looked back on those times, I knew he has been real from the very start.

He was sincere when he talked to me. Fear kept me from accepting his sincerity. Boxer was one of a kind, but a man, still. When we're walking, he talks about his past and future plans. He had hurt a lot of women, who wanted to be the one, to be with him. The entire time he talked, my thoughts ran wild, "I'm the one. I'm the one." He's my Mr. Right; I'm crazy about that man. I felt he was my destiny. I was happy. I had a life and I felt worthy of love; I'm hopeful that this is it.

Boxer came into my life fighting for my love. He told my friends that I was his soul mate and I didn't think he meant it. He shared things with me.

> "I've been looking for you all my life and you have been looking for me. Now that we're together, our search is over. I tried to impress women with my money. I want you to be impressed with who I have become; it's all because of you."

I've heard these things before and it was hard to take him seriously. He was a player. I even had Lady Dee to talk to him.

> "He's a keeper; he has wanted you since that night at the club when he got mad at you for snubbing him."

I think we have something special. We belong together; this feels right; it's comfortable. I couldn't compare him to any other. I can't fight him any longer. It doesn't matter what your soul mate has or doesn't have. When you're connected mentally and physically, you're fighting a losing battle. I didn't know what to do; if he's the one for me, he will be mine in the end. The problem was my secrets. Most women with secrets can't tell men the whole truth, or be straight up front because of the way most men are. The ones with hound-dog syndrome do their dirt with as many women possible, then back track and start all over again. Some hound-dogs retire, some don't. Die hard man-whores look for a heavenly angel to settle down with or marry.

I'm Boxer's angel. I saw how his face lit up when I told him who my dad was. If I tell him I've been raped, he'll say he doesn't want a woman that's not a fighter. If I tell him that I slept with two men since we've been together. It's three-strikes-you're-out; he's never going to trust me again.

He won't understand my pain. When he left the first time, I thought he had left for good. It was just a test to see if I would go on the rebound. I couldn't handle losing a man like him; he's special. I've given him a chance to romance me and he's won my heart. He kept me in the mood. At times I just sit up and hold him. His love taught me that men liked to be held, too. He has communicated all the right things.

He brings me giant gift baskets. My favorite had a big teddy bear holding a giant Heresies Kiss in it. Champaign, chocolate hearts, and peanuts. He gave me a credit card and the sky's the limit. Boxer had business meetings at different shopping malls and centers looking to open a chain of stores for me that we would run together. I never had a man to love me with that much to offer.

He read the bible every morning. He would eat breakfast and then drink coffee while he read the newspaper. At night, he'd kneel at my bedside, to pray; thanking God for me; he wanted to keep me forever. I needed to talk to him. I needed to be free to love him. I need to tell him my secrets.

So, one night. When we were home alone, I cooked all his favorites. I bathed him, and while I rubbed his muscles down, I got emotional with my massage. I made love to him with my hands and we began to talk about our love.

"Will you love me this way always, Jamaica?"

"Yes, baby, always."

"Do you know the night I fell in love with you? It was the first night you came into my club alone. You walked up to the bar and ordered a virgin drink. You handed the bartender the money and he said, 'the V.I.P. Booth got your tab'. You looked over at the booth to thank them. That's when you did something that blew us all away. You noticed they were dumping their ashes on my hardwood floor. You picked up two ashtrays off the bar, walked over to the V.I.P Player's table and placed one on each side of their table. You said hello and thanks for the tab. You stood there as their mouths opened, and one by one they gave their best lines; you listened to what they had to offer. You said, 'No thanks' to their speculated propositions, 'I'm just here for the party.' I knew I had to make you mine. My bartender said, "Player, that woman's looking out for you. I watched you strut your stuff out on the dance floor alone. Do you remember the song that played?"

We both sang at the same time, 'Cat Fish Makes My Nature Rise'. He told our story. I jumped up and grabbed him and start-ed to dance. I believe, I got my man singing and dancing. We were happy in our little paradise.

Boxer was good and relaxed. It was time for me to unfold. I started my spiel.

"Bad rumor's spread fast and I was attacked by boys at differ-ent times and I couldn't always fight them off. The attacks caused me to have low self-esteem. When you left me the first time, I thought that you were gone for good. I went on the re-bound with two guys. I don't want to be with you if I have to keep secrets. How was I to know that you loved me like you do;

guys come at me with every line in the book. I am trying to come clean."

"Jamaica, your skeletons got baggage," He jumped up and left the house.

I walked around his house moping, acting as if I had lost my best friend. Days went by before I admitted to myself that he was my best friend. It's been five days now, he has moved on, I know it. I called him and he wouldn't answer the phone and that made me go to him. I needed closure and so did he. I needed to get him out of my system; maybe then I will stop moping and move forward.

I arrived. Not knowing if I would be accepted or not. My soul mate had clearly had a breakdown. I knew he was upset because I took five days to make up my mind to come. They were five hard days for both of us. I had been calling him every day and expressing love for him on his answering service; his voice message wasn't playing and it usually did.

I sat down on the bed with him. He was on one side of the bed and I was on the other. He seemed like he hasn't been able to relax at all without me. I laid beside him, reached over and I linked my big toe around his and I was on top of the world, our world, the most amazing feeling I had ever felt. We knew it was meant to be, but how do we find our way back to one another? Ignoring hardships, we reached our peak before we began the climb.

I needed him and he needed me. That night after we made amazing love, I tried to talk to him and he said that he wasn't ready yet. I left and didn't hear from him. That evening, I got home and picked up my mail and there was a letter from a movie producer wanting to turn one of my books into a movie; both books had become best sellers. I got a letter from Troy stating he was in college and wanted me to come hear him speak.

I got a letter from Thomas. Informing me that he now stands as Judge Thomas; and he wants to see me soon. I went back and forth between the two men. I knew what Thomas had to offer, and I couldn't bring myself to lovemaking with Thomas. Boxer, my soul mate stopped calling me altogether because of having a friendship with Thomas. Any woman or man that has been torn between two people knew how I felt at the time.

The next day, I went to hear Troy speak. He talked about his past addictions and relationships.

"I wished that I could take back my past and start over again. Wanting to go back; that's what kept me from healing and moving forward. I'm telling you students to get it right the first time because you can't go back. Life goes forward, not back. When you've messed up as bad as I've known, you can't go anywhere but forward since you've burned all your bridges."

It was a good speech. I told him.

"I'm happy for you. Our paths crossed for a reason. Our season has passed. Our journeys have taken its course. That day would be goodbye, forever."

Back at home, I needed to choose and fast or I could lose both. Boxer tried to go back to his player ways and moved in with old Flo, the woman that bought his nightclub. Evidently, she took care of him, but I knew it wouldn't work out he was not that man anymore. I started to have dreams of her licking the wounds that I had inflicted on him. I felt him trying to give her the love that was meant for me. I needed to make clear decisions; so I moved out of Boxer's house.

I left everything. I gave back furniture, clothes, credit cards and Jewelry; the complete house except our bed and my wind-chimes. I gave up the big White House; and the fairytale cliché, to let him know that it wasn't the money I loved; it was him. I needed to show Boxer that I was strong and didn't need him for a crutch anymore, but I needed him. Everything I am is because of my mom. And Boxer, he was man enough to tell me to get off my butt and make it happen.

I bought a big brick house. I had out lived my childhood dreams. My life had gone beyond the white picket fence and me waiting for a man to buy what I needed. I had money and I wanted it all. I wanted The Boxer! Breaking all connections with Thomas, all I needed was a plan to get my fighter back. In true love relationships, you got to give up everything that comes easy and commit to love. (That means give up all other men that want to do for you. Say no to things that fall into your lap as gifts, and under your dress as sex.) Those things come easily; true love doesn't come easy. An honest man doesn't want any other men doing things that he wants to do for his woman.

I felt Boxers love was fate. He was my future. Boxer didn't know I wanted him back, but he was about to find out. Everything he did for her I deserved. I helped make his success, not her. No other woman can love him the way I have. I know I have a man worth fighting for and I'm going to get mine. I knew he waited for me to fight for our love. I went to her club and caught her in the act with her husband. I called Boxer and told him.

Boxer called. He wanted to know if I needed help getting settled in my new house. He told me, between his new woman's mind games and my secrets, he had moved out of her house to be alone.

> "She used me to avenge her husband, Jamaica. She played me like she was a man. She made me realize, you changed me. I didn't flinch when she lied and said she doesn't want him, she wanted me. I never wanted her. You hurt me and I was mad at you. There's so much I want to say to you that I should have said when I had you. I'll arrive in Cali Friday and I'm ready to talk. Bye-bye."

Don't be quick to believe a married person. You can get your head messed up really badly, getting involved with a married man or woman. Even if they're separated, it doesn't matter; it's not worth your life; stay away. Some marriages go through a lot of deep heart-wrenching emotions with wicked amusement and challenges. Some people's marriage gets down right dirty with payback war games and revenge.

When you're young and naïve, it's easy to be tricked. Some married people will tell you anything to pull you into they're mess, use you up, and leave you hanging in pain. It's respectable to them, and you, to stay out of the problems of a broken marriage. They don't know what's going on or what the outcome will be. They get desperate in wanting their mate to work towards having a good marriage.

One may leave to get the other one's attention. They will go to an extreme extent to get the other one to mature into a responsible mate and human being. This woman had Boxer laid up in her bed using him for bait to catch a no-good-lowdown cheating fish, her Husband, and he still had a key.

Thank God it's Friday. I couldn't wait to see my man. I hired movers and they had been working around the clock. Boxer arrived.

> "Welcome home sugar. Come with me, let me show you around."

That was something he would say. I took him into the master bedroom and opened up the courtyard doors, leading to a huge closed-in patio.

> "Look at all the wind chimes you have bought for me from all over the world. Come here, look at our bed; no other man has been in your bed. Doesn't it look good in here? Come let me show you the downstairs; that's the best part. You got to close your eyes for this one."

We walked downstairs.

I said, "Cover them up now, Boxer, no peeking, and don't open them until, I say so."

I placed him in front of the big double doors and opened them up.

"Okay, you can open your eyes now. Surprise!"

He stood in his own complete gym with a state-of-the-art boxing ring with his name on it. My man was moved to tears. My man was home and I wasn't ever going to let him go again.

He took me in his arms.

"Thank you, baby; I've missed you so much. I still want you. I love you and only you. I'm sorry for not telling you that before. Before we make this official, there is something that I need to confess. Come sit down and listen to what I've been keeping from you."

I sat down in an arm chair.

"Do you remember that night I came home and you were in the bathtub drunk? Well, you told me your secrets that night. I hoped that you were just talking out of your head from the liquor. It wasn't until, the night you sat me down and told me your secrets that I had to face the truth. You must have gone through hell and I wasn't there to save you and I feel for you deeply, but I hated you for being a victim."

I sat there looking up at him. I waited for him to tell me that we were over and he was never coming back. He continued.

"Then you told me about your two men and I had to leave. It was my first time hearing about the men. I thought I knew all your secrets. Jamaica, I never trusted you in my home, after you told me, I doubted you more. I hired my chef to spy on you. I told him to come on to you, but not to touch you in any way. He said you made him feel like a little boy getting caught with his hand stuck in the cookie jar."

"Boxer what is it? What did he say?"

"He said you asked him does he wear your panties on his head when you weren't there. Most importantly, he believed that you loved me after he went topless and you showed respect for my house. Baby, I'm really sorry, but there's more, I recorded your confession in your drunken state. Don't hate me, baby, I did it all for love. You need to hear you die to be born again. You're alive and all that pain is dead."

All I could say to myself was, "Oh, God. Oh, God. Oh, God."

Boxer hands me the tape. I walked over to the stereo and popped it in.

"Boxer is that you?" I asked, in my drunken state.

"No, it's not Boxer. If I were him, would you tell me your secrets?"

"No, I can never tell him my secrets; I hate my secrets. I hate myself for keeping secrets from Boxer and everyone. If Boxer knew my secrets he will hate me too. They're bad."

I had to walk back to my chair. I couldn't bear the pain I was hearing and I didn't want to hear whatever he had heard me say. The tape continued.

"What are your secrets? I promise not to tell Boxer."

"Mannie was conceived out of rape! He raped me, he hurt me; he hurt me really bad. Why did boys hate me? Why did they laugh at my pain? Why did they keep coming back again and again? Boxer never hurt me; he loves me and I did him wrong. I thought no one would ever love me or want me."

I sounded confused. I cried my eyes out.

"Who laughed? What did you do wrong to Boxer? Tell me what it is!"

He demanded to know. He interrogated me.

"I've been with..."

He interrupted.

"Who? Who have you been with, a man? Is there someone else? Dammed! Who? I'll kill him!"

"I did Boxer wrong. Just kill me, go ahead, please kill me and get it over with. I can't live without him," I said in agony.

I heard Boxer in the background praying.

"God please, I'm pleading; take her pain so she can feel my love. Help us!"

That was enough. Before I heard the tape, I couldn't see what I did to everyone I loved and what I was putting them through. After I heard Boxer's reaction from seeing me in that condition, I finally got it. I walked over and turned off the tape. Boxer stood there watching me. He didn't think that I would ever forgive him.

How could I not forgive him? Hasn't our entire relationship been about forgiveness? I knew the man standing in front of me. He held my hand and neither of us ran away. Boxer was right; as painful as it was. I needed to hear the pain I had unfolded for years. And, I wasn't finished, so I unfolded some more. I told him how I felt, right then and there. Surprisingly, the words came easily.

"Boxer, I'm not surprised that you did all that. Now, I understand you tried to find out who's this woman you had fallen deeply in love with. I'm sorry for everything I've put you through. Having heard the tape; you were hard on me and I'm embarrassed, but I wouldn't expect anything more or less from you. Boxer, I know who you are. You do everything hard; you work hard and you play hard. The most important thing about you is what swept me off my feet, and that's the thing I love most, you love hard. Baby with you, it's all or nothing. I never expected true love from you or that you would fight for me this way. You can't love a person without knowing them first and now we know each other well."

As I talked, I was no longer afraid.

"Boxer, that night you found me in my drunken state, you saved me from myself. Now, we must save each other. I want to share everything. I was pregnant with your child and I lost our baby."

He fell to his knees in front of me. He threw both arms around me, holding me while crying.

"No Jamaica! No, sweetie, I'm sorry, I should have never left you here alone. I should have taken you with me."

"No Boxer! Listen to me, this wasn't your fault. You can't blame yourself. You weren't my baby sitter. I needed you to leave me. I had to get better on my own. I'm happy that you still love me. No more secrets we've been afraid to share. We both are living examples, people can change."

Boxer proposed marriage to me. I said, 'yes' and we were married. If more men and women knew forgiveness, we could forgive ourselves, our lovers, and the ones that hurt us. If we could change ourselves, we can change the world by helping to heal the world from painful secrets. This world would be much healthier and rich.

Boxer was a perfectionist.

"I must call my lawyer to protect us. If another man puts his hands on you, I can avoid hurting him and going to jail for life. We are going to sue every man that raped you and let the world know that Jamaica Gold is mine."

After the honeymoon, my soul mate was back on the road. We would talk all night while he rode or flew. He sent sexy, Victoria Secret nighties for me to wear when we talk. I thought that was sweet. Jamaica had a man sending lingerie in the mail. I wanted to give him something cute and sexy, too.

I got an idea to record a tape. Rapping and singing to him while he travels the dark, lonely highways. He could pop in the tape and play my voice over and over. One night, at three o'clock in the morning, in my sexiest voice, in my sexy green nightie, sitting on the floor in our room looking out onto the deck, I recorded a love tape. I had love songs playing in the background.

Story's Player Love

Stormy brought a breath of fresh love to the air
Like a pleasant wind breathing a love song.
He walked into my life as a quiet storm
He blew in all the right places.
My Stormy,
He was someone I could talk to and depend on.
He was always there to protect me.
When I'd walk into the wind and rain,
He would be all around me, keeping me warm and safe.
Stormy was Powerful
Sometimes rough when he was angry.
But when he turns to me he was gentle, so soft and convincing.
I open the door for him and let him into my life.
Stormy had that player love
I celebrated lovemaking with him
I knew we would last forever when we made love
Stormy was real, a soothing sensation
every woman wants to feel,
Motivating my mind, soul, and body
Making me high, being so free, the motions of
Stormy's love satisfies me.
Listening to his beautiful very together
soft thoughts I love to hear,
Touching me smoothly being sincere.
Capturing my mind,
Loving me with all his might,
His wild Thunder awakens my life.
Hailing hot ice over my body,
Melting into soft puddles of comfort,
That became a part of me
I was stuck by lighting.
Caught up in a love storm only stormy can bring.
Real love like Stormy's is forever.
It doesn't change, come and go like time or weather.
It comes to stay even if our time together lasts for only one day.

I read what I wrote in my journal on our wedding night, "Boxer, I'm so happy my mother taught me to be polite and to always answer with "Yes, Sir or Ma'am," Get the attention that I deserve in life; "Take it like a lady,"
Things will work out like they should. Express yourself as a lady would. Say excuse me "Mr. or Mrs.," And sound like a lady sounds. Walk right and keep my feet planted firmly on the ground and everything will be alright. If only she could have seen me now on my wedding night.
I started to sing a song that I wrote and sang on our wedding night. The song came to me that first night that we were intimate, lying there in his arms, I never felt so loved, wanted and needed.

Feeling Good

Feeling good just you and I kiss, there's nothing stronger than lover to lover. Our love fit's like a glove. Fun and laugher brings rapture to rapture.
Feeling good, just you and I. Feeling good, just you and I
Feeling nice, just you and I touch there's nothing warmer or enticing, enticing,
Our body motions talk saying romantic things were thinking, mind to mind. Opposite attraction without rhyme or reason sees the moment now is our time.
Feeling good, just you and I. Feeling good, just you and I.

My Reward

My Man, My Man
My Weakness
My Baby Fully Grown
My Warrior
My Statue of Gold
My Rock to Please
My Joy, My Strength
My Nourishment to Grow
My Love, My Lover

My Super Natural High
And Low
My Man, My Man
My Heart of Emotions
My Lust, My Desire
My Nature to Rise
My Irresistible Pleasure
My King
My Sugar Boo
My Reward for life

Day Dreaming
With my eyes closed I see your face so clear
Wanting you next to me laying right here
Thinking of good times we've shared
Knowing you miss me when I'm not there
I don't feel bad about dreams I have had
Imagining
Seeing your face so clear
Bringing back thoughts
When your presence was really here.

Everything in my life was new. I had never before done anything like that. The tape was wild and turned out perfectly. He was totally blown away. He let me be me. I had his love and he had mine. Finally this is the man that's going to love and cherish me for as long as we both shall live.

One beautiful Sunday morning Boxer returned home safe and sound and we went to church together. I was in for the shock of my life. The shock struck as I first walked in, looking for a seat where I could see the most of what everyone came to see. I looked up and saw Troy sitting in the pulpit dressed as nicely as me and all of my rapists sat around him, cool as they could be.

I looked to my right and saw every man that I had dated and their faces were elated. I looked to my left and there were my

293

babies from my abortions reaching out for me. I ran up to the altar and I realized, I stood on a mountain peak with my sex addictions and bad habits beneath my feet. I stood in my anger and pain; all the guilt from abortions moved me to shame, the depression, the enemies, the revenge, and the blame. I had prayed for forgiveness and I meant it from my heart. The bad choices of my life were confronting me with a new start.

My secret past exposed. All my business was in the streets. What I'd done in the dark had come to the light and everyone came to see. Before God takes you to the next level, he's going to keep testing you. Not to convince Him you're ready, but to convince you, you're confident and ready for Him to unveil the past and reveal the future.

God heard my cry for help all my life. It was the prayer I prayed that day after reading, 'In the Spirit' that got through to Him.

> "God take my life! I give-up! I hand you my dirty mind, my body, and my soul to take, let your will be done for my sake. Take my broken heart. I can't bear the ache and the pain any longer. I don't want you to give any of them back until, my soul is forgiven and I'm clean and sober and all the scars on this broken heart are removed. I can't re-live them anymore. I want my pain to be over. I want my life to be happy and whole. Never again, will I need to unfold. I want all of me. Only with a new heart do I have a chance to live clean and free."

That's when He answered me. That Sunday every memory of every person around me was wiped clean. As a hard rain fell down from above with the thunder and lighting and washed my sins away, never to be seen again. Troy and Boxer were the only men from my past, left standing.

I ran into Boxer's arms. My soul mate was the one for me. Troy began to vanish before my eyes. The look on his face meant, "I really did love you, Jamaica. It should have been me," and said his goodbye.

Boxer began to vanish too. I watched his muscle shrinking down to size as I stood there alone. I heard a voice preaching in the distance.

> "When you're stubborn and bullheaded, God can send someone into your life that's so bad it will make you a better human being. That bad person's purpose on earth might be your soul mate and you'll have hell to pay if that's what it takes for you to wake up. Wake-up and call on God! Let him help you find your way. Wake-up! Wake-up!"

I heard someone calling my name and laying down the rules. The voice became louder and louder. I felt pain in my arms and they were going numb. It was my mother pinching me in Sunday school.

> "Children sleeping in the Lords house is a sin."

Then she made me repent for daydreaming and put me on punishment for falling asleep in church again. She picked me up and I wrapped my arms around her neck with my legs around her waist and I laid my head on her shoulders to fall asleep to continue to dream.

Chapter Fourteen
Set Free Buried Anger

Our lives unfold happiness and sadness every day. Unfold means, give details of, open up, clarify, make known, and let go, to free you. Most of us unfold pain because we haven't experienced happiness. I realized that I must write this book because I am the voice for many women that unfold their secrets and pain behind closed doors. Most women that allow themselves to unfold privately are sick and need help; they're either too proud or too ashamed, it's not ladylike and, for many women, it's not safe.

Society places a label on women that tell. I'm proud of myself. Everyone doesn't see the answers to their past mistakes, revealing what they did wrong. Whenever you find the answers to your problems, you have a story to tell and you should tell it. Getting it out is a part of the healing process; seeing your pain to the end. Everyone has been around darkness or experienced living in darkness, but everyone will not see the light. When I die, it won't be because my dark secrets haunted me to death. My secrets haunted me to happiness.

What's so amazing about life? Your mind has to be mentally ready to write a book like, 'Unfolding Souls'. I care about what people think, but I wouldn't let it stop me. I needed to unfold pain out loud to be happy. Taking each word and laying those Into place to write this book and lyrics came from my heart, it was dying to be set free; my mind felt it. I had to listen to my emotions, recognize and hear them. Most of all, to get emotional enough to write it down on paper for people that need to hear my mind of emotions, take it or leave it. This was my time to talk and tell my story.

People may call Jamaica Gold's life many things. She was naive and gave the wrong people more credit than they were worth.

Her story wasn't about hating men or getting revenge. Jamaica's life unfolding was about the process of finding love within. She discovered love and conquers her anger, fear, and pain. She progressed to help heal men and women from there abusive past. When you have gone through a season of pain like Jamaica, torture would have lasted a lifetime if it wasn't exposed. Accept it or not, if you've been abused, you need help.

Not in my wildest dreams would I have thought that life would give me a voice and to create a character to speak to the world about abuse. No one wants to talk about. People, that's been abused want to talk. Although, I don't speak for the people that haven't been, it's hard to sit back and watch others go through what you've been through and they don't have anyone to talk to. My voice was chosen to express to those people to talk, sing, write, whatever it takes to help stop the pain, do it.

Pain made me who I am today. I tell people that their pain is creating something in them that is so beautiful and unique. When you're in pain it feels like someone is carving your body with a knife, but the end results will be your true sculpture. Just hold on and stay out of trouble; the pain of abuse doesn't have to last always. In spite of the violence and prejudice going on in this world, there is a pure and powerful spirit moving and are drawing us together and you are meant to be a part of that loving union.

I didn't have to dig too deep for words. My everyday thoughts brought up reason after reason and I wrote it down and you can do the same. When it's your time, you will sit down and write. What's so unsuspected about this book is talking about the reckless past and young despair no one knew about. They were confused times and the story was complicated and filled with misunderstanding. My brother Silly Willy would drive me to school, fussing about me dressing in his car and putting on my sister's make-up, I wasn't allowed to wear. He kept stopping on the brakes and my mascara would be everywhere but on my eye lashes. People thought because I was a church girl, I really didn't know how to wear makeup.

I hung out with cheerleaders. I was their dance choreographer and able to ride on the bus back and forth to games, and that's when my first rape took place. The night I got pregnant wasn't a date. One game night, after a big win, I went with the team to celebrate; it ended up being another night I could have died. We were at a team member's family home. I was set up, I was told that the girls were using the upstairs bathroom.

Taurus took me upstairs. I got to the door of the bathroom and he grabbed me. I start fighting him hard to get away from him. The music was loud and no one heard my scream. He was close behind me and I couldn't close the door fast enough. He pushed me in and closed the door. We struggled in the bathroom. I fell into the bathtub and hit my head. I bit my tongue and bled. I tasted my blood but continued to fight. He wouldn't stop and made it seem as we were having fun. He grabbed me out of the tub and I fell to the floor.

I was exhausted when he dominated me. I didn't believe I could get pregnant from getting raped. I thought the act itself was earthshaking; emotions that had special meanings. That morning when I returned home my mother knew that I had lost my virginity by listening to me pee; discovering my physical body change. She gave the speech to let me know she had the wisdom to detect the change, but didn't know that was the condition the rape left me in.

Three months later, I went to school and suffered the same abuse, but worse. After the second time, I started making decisions with an abused mind like many abused people experience. My secrets were kept to protect the ones I loved and to stop my son from being hurt by those same people that hurt me.

Secrets can push you into a lifestyle that's unfamiliar. All women, girls, and boys that have been through rape don't make the same choices; everyone's circumstances are different. I got tired of being abused and I fought back. If nothing else, abusive men taught me to fight back.

I used abortion for contraception. I wasn't having abortions because I didn't want any more babies; I was sick, living with the trauma of the past. Feeling that my pregnancy was going to be another bad experience all over again, I couldn't handle any more babies but that's no excuse for the lives I'm guilty of taking. Some victims have stubborn behavior; no trust or belief in anyone. It takes time to heal from abuse and some people never heal.

It's important to talk to a doctor. Talk to yourself while in the process of healing. Say things like, "The person that caused me to be sick is sicker. I won't have anything in common with them. I need to get well."

Back then, I didn't have words to stop anyone from going through what I went through. Now, I can say that when you're hardheaded, you're going to go through more heart aches that makes life worse.

If you're thinking that you are strong. You feel you're strong enough to take being abused without help; you're wrong. If you don't seek help, the healing process will take longer, if you heal at all. Your pain is going to cause your actions to get you in some kind of trouble. I was taught to control my anger as a child and it became a problem for me when I needed to speak up and protect myself.

I didn't know what to do with my anger. I didn't express my anger. I held it in and it turned to hate, then pain. Being taught to control my anger, helps while speaking up and putting my foot down. Control demonstrates wisdom and it's the greatest gift my parents gave me. The Holy Bible was the very best gift. When you hate people. You're giving them too much power over your thoughts. All you can think about is your hatred for them and you're missing out on life. Your enemies have taken over your mind and sooner or later your life will suffer big time. You have allowed them to ruin your relationships; your rivals are all you talk about. You have let negative energy drain you and you are draining everyone else's around you.

Holding anger in, drains you. Get anger out by talking, writing, singing, sports, work and school. People that caused you to be sick will turn around and call you crazy to your face; you got to make your life better on your own. Enemies try to keep you confused. In their immature mind, they won't allow you to grow and mature. I broke away from that mold, I did mature. You have to find you and your style, yourself. Ten years later, they're telling the same old lies and those same old rumors. As a result, they held themselves back from growing. You can't treat people wrong and think life is going to treat you well. What goes around comes around. Sooner or later, people see you for who you really are. Let your light shine, no matter what. You've got to face your past. The person, place, or thing you feared most will hunt you down. As a church girl, I feared pimps and players when I had a near-death experience and survived. I did gravitate to them. I was attracted to danger and people with different characteristics than mine, my complete opposite. I was drawn in, but because of my values and principles, I wasn't buying what they were selling, until, Boxer. I was tempting death, playing sexual mind games with a player. I had a death wish. I was lucky to meet a player that wanted change. You might not be so lucky.

When I had a nervous breakdown, I needed answers. First, I went to my mom, I got the answers that I wanted from her; and then it was dad's time. I went to my dad and I guess he was ready to talk. I was ready to listen. At that point, they became the best mom and dad, and friends. From talking to my parent's, I got to know them better as well as myself. For the first time, I noticed my parent's at their best. My parent's always did their best.

I came up with reason after reason for being the person that I was, but as I got older I couldn't blame anyone, any longer. I had passed that point in life where I could see everyone for who they were and what they were doing wrong, but couldn't see myself; the point many people reach and never advance. I knew who I was.

God had to get me to the point where I could see myself. It wasn't easy. Every time He revealed things to me, I would throw it out. He would place good people in my life to make me see myself for who I am and I would throw them out. I had to hit rock bottom before I finally got it and it hit me like a thousand ton of bricks; I couldn't bear the person that I was another second.

I couldn't bear the anger, guilt, and shame. I was carrying that stuff around in my head and it was attacking my mind and weighing down my body. Some mornings, I had to say to self, "You got to get yourself up because no one else will."

I wasn't aware of how much there was until, I started writing it down on paper. Once you see it in writing, you're forced to face it and you've got to put in hard work to find your way out. Every adult individual has to be accountable for their actions. When I stopped blaming people and really listened, I heard what my life told me; the answers started to unfold. If life doesn't give you answers, go looking for them. Find out what makes you tick so that you can discover what all of us are supposed to discover. Peace of mind exists. Living without drugs exists. Waking up every morning feeling naturally high exists. Living in the moment exists. Facing that life is beautiful and hard. When you hide, you won't make these discoveries.

I Will Not Hide

I Will Not Hide

My mind unfolding, my mouth expressing
Words to all Mankind. My soul does not shelter the misery of
pain;
I don't fear life any more I've paid the price of misery and fear
To remain sane. I will not hide the pain I have endured
People don't need to understand my anger; I must understand
and set it free. I've paid the price of anger to the utmost degree
I will not hide
I allowed myself to be mentally bound long enough.
Our ancestors were mentally and physically bound;
They didn't have the freedom of choice. Love freed their soul;
but they were forbidden to express. Not in words or on paper.
They were put through the ultimate test.
I will not hide
The love that was passed down to me that brought them
through over three hundred years of slavery. For me to be here,
speak out or shout; I will not hide!
"The Middle Passage" (Slave Ships) was my rude awakening.
Cheers! To my Great Ancestors'
Who endured the ride, the slave Ships, and the Slave Masters;
Who really wasn't Masters at all. Hallelujah! Grandpa and
Grandma; Independence is My Civil Rights. I have the freedom to
express me; I say what I want to say. Freedom of Choice
to look people in the eyes and talk my talk. Write what I want to
write, sing and dance all night.
I ride in the front of the bus, or get picked up by my limousine
without a fuss.
Walk through the front door of any public building or restau-
rant; Yes! I am my Forefathers seed,
I am human, I am civilized; I eat human food; like anybody else.
I use the bathroom; I wash my hands, I exit through the front.
Above all the above facts; I have the freedom to vote, and free
mental slavery.
No matter what the struggle may be in my life; I must maintain
my freedom

handed down to me. Our ancestors paid the price so we could
live free
I will not hide; because they fought and died.

.

A Letter to All Abusers

WHEN YOU RAPE A MAN, WOMAN, BOY, OR GIRL, YOU'VE RAPED YOU

You are a man or woman that lacks dignity. You take away our pride and joy with your abusive traditions. I remember when my dad died; the pain was different from when my mom died. My sisters and I lost our natural common sense, while carrying my dad's wallet with the red rubber band around it everywhere. We had to go over everything twice and constantly back track on every decision. I felt like someone had hurt my feelings beyond repair. I thought my heart would be forever broken.

At family reunions, dad would get on the microphone and say, "If it wasn't for the father, it wouldn't have been no." Family is a man's pride passed on to his family. Fatherhood is where we get our most prized possession, our pride and joy, our livelihood. When he was alive, I found myself as a woman, through being his daughter. When he died, everything I believed about my life died too.

I had to find myself all over again. My dad taught me how to laugh, not how to cry. I had to teach myself how to laugh again, but it was a different laugh. I had to teach myself how to smile again, but it was a different smile. As time went by, as I grieved, I learned that when he died he had become a larger part of my spirit. He was still the apple of my eye. Today, along with the smile I taught myself; I wear and treasure a bigger smile, his smile.

My dad was a good man. I loved him more than life. He taught me to respect him as a man. He taught me to respect that all people are human beings and to treat them with human kindness, until, they give me reason not to. He preached about forgiveness. My dad was a leader. He wasn't perfect, no man is, but he took care of his family. What hurt so badly was, that once you have been taught what love is by two parents expressing how love works, love will never turn to hate. I wasted my life trying to hate you and I don't pity you. Today, I can love a man faithfully because of him and mom.

As family, we celebrate a man's courage. You mean the world to us as the head of this family; you are our father. That's why Father's Day exists. You are all the man we have in this world, to value and trust, created in the image of a higher immortal, God. You are God in human portion, given the authority to teach us right from wrong. In case you didn't know, a man's position here on earth is to teach his family to believe in a higher power and give us a solid backbone. A man's job is to protect the family and keep it strong.

You're the welfare of men, women, boys, and girls. Not just for your race, but for the human race. You make us complete. When you rape your seed or a woman God has given you to love, honor, and respect, you destroy that bond and yourself. You leave your abused man, woman, boy, or girl nothing to live for. There's no other man to look up to when there is no other man quite like you. Our faith in having a relationship with men is gone.

All we wanted was to be strong like God made you. Now, we have nothing to believe in because of your weak display of sin. Your victims are lost from themselves, to be found by strangers to build us up or tear us down. I've had a good man. I've had the best lovers, and their love and money could not mend me because of abusers like you who hurt and offended me. Who's going to pick up the pieces of our miserable lives?

We don't have an identity. When we are lost from man, we are lost from ourselves. No one knows who we really are. Why do you abuse over and over, then you leave your victims time and time again to find them? Why do you destroy yourself and your seed every day? You abandon your victims more and more. Can't you see that your life is a vicious circle? The mental and physical abuse needs to stop, right now!

In spite of everything you have done uncivilized, you have been living without shame in public light. At night, human emotions haunt you because you're human; you're conscious of your crimes when you're alone, you can't sleep from the headache, heartache, and mental pain of guilt. It's sad that some abusers don't have any regrets. You are a man and that's supposed to mean something, where is your pride?

Life is not a game. We look at you and see the form of a man. You were created strong enough to carry the weight of the world on your shoulders. Instead, you've been our downfall. Everyone has their cross to bear and we bear yours and ours. I blamed everyone and you're the blame. It was your hate that I felt and bared, not mine. I had to wear it and bear it. The sex drive was yours, not mine. I had to feed it and suffer the sick craving and the sick perverted arousal I felt, it all came from you, my abusers.

The cravings you felt was misread. They were not a command for you to go out and rape, abuse, and kill your seed. If your spirit wasn't corrupt, you would understand that your craving is a human emotion that comes from your true spirit (the person that you really are without the sickness) seeking to find the love that is in you. Created in the image of God and spirit you naturally crave peace; every man needs to possess his own peace. It's the only way you can have peace of mind in this world.

You can't find peace of mind abusing your family and others. We're all a part of you. Finding God's love within you motivates a man's true nature to grow and create peace in his mind and in this world. A true man tries to save the world not destroy it, pick up your pride; find your true man. I've heard abusive men say, 'I'm not that bad. I know men that are worse'. Get help! Rehabilitate your mind and you won't compare yourself to the worst of men.

There are born losers out there that are not trying to do any better. Compare yourself to the best of men that's always working to become better. Be a winner! You can measure up to men that don't mentally or physically abuse. In a perfect movie, the truth always comes out in the end, where the bad guy gets punished. For me, though, there was no end, until, now. The anger that has lived within me and me with it, is gone. My abusers brought hate and pain into my peaceful world when they brutally took my virginity and my innocence away.

I missed my sweet sixteen coming out party. I missed my Snowball Dance and Prom, the excitement of being a teenage girl. I've never been to Disney Land. Instead, you brought dark clouds and left me out in the rain to die a slow death. I thought I'd never be able to enjoy another sunny day. Now, even when the sun doesn't shine, my world does in every way. So, the next time you throw the name bitch at me, it's going to backfire like a boomerang coming right back to you, I will not wear it or bear it. That's not my name or my character. You don't know me and you never have.

Some have apologized and I have forgiven them. The others will take their lies to their graves. Go ahead and deny what you have done; lie yourself straight to hell. You see, I will always have my ups and my downs, except your hate, pain, sickness, and illness doesn't live here anymore.

A poem I was asked to write for a friend. 'Fatherhood' was written for an abusive husband that was forbidden by a restraining order that kept him from his wife. He had completed anger management, still after his hard rehabilitation the order against him hadn't lifted. Unfortunately, for him, he had lost the right to see his son and daughter. Something many abusive men and women are going through.

Fatherhood

I wish i could see you
So i can show you all the things
That i have learned about
Fatherhood.
I know now,
A father's love cannot be explained from afar
Love is a hands on action word.
I know now,
A father's love cannot be replaced
There is a special space in your heart for everyone you love
Just know there is a special place for me.
I know now,
A father's love cannot be denied
You came from me and our bond will always be.
I know now,
A father's role here on earth
Is to keep the family strong
Children need to be taught by example
To distinguish right from wrong.
I know now,
And i thank our father in heaven
For watching over you.
Please forgive me for my absents,
A parent intentions should be to raise you with imagination,
And sell you a dream that will give you a strong foundation.
I can only say keep the faith;
And love your mother and father
And never give up on hope.
I know now,
Children look to parents, to learn how to cope.
I love you more.

Help the Parents

Help the parents that have destroyed
Love and understanding in the home.
They're the ones that have lost respect
and their children no longer respect them.
Put love back in the Home!
Help the parents who are corrupt.
They're the wild ones that say and do
everything in front of the children.
They are a bad influence in the home.
They are bad company.
Give them Wisdom and Knowledge!
Help the parents that are thoughtless.
They're the ones that deprive their children.
They think of no one but themselves.
Give them a thoughtful understanding.
Make them aware of the children!
Help the parents that hide emotions.
They're the ones who have become strangers
in their own home,
where they are rough and violent, unwilling to forgive.
Save our children from child abuse
Make peace in the home!
Help the parents use drugs.
Their behavior is no longer normal.
They're the parents that have lost control.
Help them say NO to Drugs!
Help the parents who are careless.
They're ruthless people, arrogant, lost and turned out.
They ruin life for their children.
Strengthen their minds and teach them that a child
has to be taught right from wrong!
With no self-esteem,
How will they be capable to survive the future?
With no morals,
How will they have sense to value their
lives as well as others?

Encourage parents that are unprepared.
They're the ones depressed and stressed out.
Give them tolerance and endurance,
to guide them through anger.
Parents need help before they hurt their babies, and after.
Help us all bring us together as parents.
To help one another listen and learn
how to raise our children.

Chapter Fifteen
Rap Session

Although, we accommodate the poor with good deeds, in this world, we respect the strong and cater to the rich and smart. The weak have to figure out how to become strong in order to get respect. So, it doesn't matter if you're rich or poor, when it comes to respect, everyone has to earn it. Time and work heals all wounds. I have matured, but someone has not. You're struggling with open wounds; open wounds smell with venerability you have a fragile disposition. Abusers can smell you coming a mile away.

I don't know who you are or how you were raised. I don't know if you were given a backbone to stand tall with morals that has values and principles. If you don't, get help to get out of an abusive relationship. You have to use everything you have been taught in order to find you. This book is about three people that achieved the strength to change their lives. When you become strong, people will cater to you.

The first thing Jamaica did was separate herself from the crowd. The people that judge you for your mistakes are judging your pain and that's not showing any human kindness. When you become a positive person, they'll bring up negative moments of your past, shoot you down and put you back in a loser's place, where they thought you belonged. Victims don't deserve that. They'll get that look on their face when you're talking, and everybody around you knows the loser impersonation expressions. They're the true losers, impersonating themselves.

When you're clean, you won't like who they are, and, they're going to hate you. A messed up person can't befriend everyone. Somebody has to be on their hit list at all times. Don't let their ways and insults hinder your healing process; lose the losers. Get with women and men that show you love and the respect that you now deserve; the ones that encourage you to do better, as I did.

I don't have a mind to go back to my old habits. When you're stuck on failing, it's because failing is old and familiar; maturing is new, and new can be scary and exciting. That's why you have to listen to your intuition, and to positive people, to become more familiar with new and exciting surroundings to feel like you fit in and to have fun.

I was determined to do my thing. I wanted power and respect, but I wasn't making the right decisions or doing the right things to get it at that time. When you're hanging around the wrong crowd, you're telling all your business to people that you have nothing in common with. They don't know how to respect people's privacy; they don't have compassion or concern for your feelings.

Building relationships takes mature thinking. They haven't learned how to keep people's business to themselves. How do you think they can understand your problems when they can't follow any conversations long enough to comprehend one? No one has ever sat them down to teach them how to listen and they haven't taught themselves. That's why their restless users and abusers. You find yourself repeating the point that you're trying to make and explaining things to them that they don't understand.

Their thoughts were everywhere. Their nerves without any foundation or backbone; they struggle the hardest to survive in this world. They don't believe in anything or anybody. But they will try to convince you that they believe in you, just to know your business. Every time you talk to them, they believe in something different; so their life is always changing for the worse. They can't keep up with life or themselves and they try and hold you back. Why are you still with them?

They don't need anybody, that's what they're always saying when angered. Everybody that wants to be somebody needs somebody. You need a strong foundation in order to establish something. Be strong and don't settle for anything less. Be committed to achieving your dreams.

The day I stopped using any type of drugs. I chose drugs to numb the pain and stop my stress from the past and present. There is nothing wrong with getting professional help to change your habits. I got help because I wanted to stay sane for my family and for me. Drugs don't help you stay sane, drugs drive people insane because you're always looking for drugs. It's difficult to face what you're doing, feel regretful, and move forward.

Drugs make you deny reality. That's the hard part, you need to be sober to recognize that. People have millions of reasons and thousands of excuses for their drug use and believe they need them every day to get by. When I was using, I never heard anyone say they loved it. We just assumed that they liked it because they did it. I had addictions because I couldn't let go of the past. I had been hurt and blinded with anger. I couldn't forgive.

I held everything in. I carried my cross for so long, my brain couldn't think to tell me to forgive. I wrote this book because my thoughts are healthy and clear enough to tell you that God doesn't want you to bear your cross, but learn to let Him take it and move on. Stop thinking about your next high and be aware of my thoughts and feelings. Now that I'm sober, if I hear someone say that they love it, I wouldn't believe them, I've been there.

Using drugs feels as your living in hell. No one chooses to live in hell, unless you are in yesterday's pain. Maybe you've wanted to be someone else your entire life and don't want to face your present. "Face it. You are who you are." I didn't want to face my problems. I wallowed in them, because I didn't have a plan for the future. Getting high gave me something to do. As I got older, getting high on weed wasn't high enough, knowing I had not planned a future. I tried something stronger and that didn't fill the void. Yet, it occupied time.

You're holding on to pain because you are addicted to pain. You feed your pain addiction with drugs. I wanted to check out of here on my highest highs. I hate drugs, drugs hate me; I hate the high. I thought drugs were supposed to make me forget who I was and what I ran away from. I found out that drugs were unreliable; at my highest moments I couldn't forget or forgive.

Drugs are deceiving in many ways. They make you think you're smart when you're doing dumb things. Drugs brought out who I really was on the inside. Myself, and everyone around me knew I was a church girl with some serious drugs in my hands. Drugs are not the way you want to live and they're not the way you want to die. I wouldn't recommend using it for a slow death. Coming down off drugs hurt so badly, it made me want to live.

I would pray to God, please let me feel normal again. Then, get high the very next day. I kept trying to get that first high I felt with Russo. I was just getting hustled by a powdery substance that doesn't have brains, I did. Drugs talked to me and I listened when it was me all along. I was insane. I am human. I have a human's brain, instead of using it, I was wasting it.

Drugs were not something I wanted to celebrate in public. I used drugs to hurt myself, but I couldn't identify with it or accept the suffering that came with having a drug habit. I was suffering enough. I used drugs alone, separating self from whomever. I would use alone. I didn't want the image of being a drug user, it's ugly. Humans are better than that. I didn't know how to get drugs. Most times, they were given to me. When I was ready to stop, I knew if I told my family I was using, their disappointment and their shock alone would cause me to never use drugs again. That worked for me. I stopped cold-turkey, just as I did with sex.

When you've had enough, you've had enough. I stopped using right after I used up all the drugs I had in my possession. When I told my drug counselor, she said I was a drug user; I had a habit, and I got help before it turned into an addiction. An addict doesn't care who knows about their drug use. Drugs don't save you, they destroy you. Looking back, I feel that I've never been addicted to anything, but the pain of being abused.

My parents gave me something to fall back on. They gave me something that I can never get away from; their faith, love, and prayers kept me alive. Drugs couldn't drown out their prayers. Today, I am living on my prayers and I don't want people to hurt anymore. This book is tough love because I care. I care because I know how it feels, looking and hoping and wishing for someone to save you from self.

I wrote it for men and women that can relate to any type of abuse and substance abuse that tear you down on the inside and rip you of all humanity. My secrets that I have unfolded may help someone to find the answers that they need to heal. As humans, we must improve. We must strive to be better before we can enjoy our purpose and how special life really is. When you're drowning, you can't see your way out. The people I am trying to reach have given up on themselves.

I've gone to extreme magnitude to reach those people. Maybe the contents of this book measures up to their present misery, and misery is the only way I can reach them. This book is personal because I meant for it to be. Understand that these things are happening and it may be happening to someone you know; a friend or a family member of yours. Abuse can be hidden many ways, disguised with countless personalities.

Drinking was one of my personalities; drugs was another, but my family never saw me drunk or high. They didn't know about the drugs. Understand that everyone that has been abused are not users; it may not take everyone's self-worth. You may not feel like you owe men something. You don't have to let men use and abuse you to feel wanted. And maybe, you may not have a sick craving for sex. With this book I feel like I will reach the ones that do.

The person that I'm trying reach, you know who you are. My assignment was to reach into the darkness to pull you out. I can't force you out; you have to be ready, willing, and able to take my hand. Understand, the sex will always be there, the drugs will always be there, the party will never stop, but the party is over for you. The only way that you can start the healing process is to walk away from it all. Take someone you trust by the hand and walk out, give up the game before it takes your life.

I wanted to see my way out. Prolonging my miserable life playing with fate, I wanted to know that there was a way out and look up the road and see freedom, but I wasn't ready to walk up that road. I knew I had to crawl before I walked and didn't want to go through the healing process without the drugs. I wanted back the time I had lost. I wanted to make up for lost time with my son, friends and family.

I want my beauty back. I want to look like I used to look. Understand, you can't make up for lost time but you can't pick up where you left off. You've got to go back and start over. Many abused people die from some type of addiction. Most of them don't choose to die, they wait too late to get help. I know who I am today, I am a free woman. My soul has unfolded pain and I have nothing, but happiness to unfold; I have a voice in this world I'm proud of; forget the spectators.

My favorite line in my book comes from my song, "Everybody doesn't live to learn over again, or get one last chance to talk and tell the story again. Everybody has a sad story to tell that hasn't been told." Since the beginning of time, life has been about taking risks and making sacrifices and many of us don't. Young people are dying, angry over stress and heart break. Let go of your anger before anger takes your life. You've got to forgive.

You got to unfold your pain. It doesn't have to be publicly. As long as you know the world is unfolding and you are meant to be a part of the healing taking place. Let go of fear and step out of the box holding you back from living your dreams. You're stronger than your fears. As humans, we are obligated to unfold every emotion good or bad; play your part. Today, I choose my parent's way of life, without the extreme rules. I've done my soul searching and I like the values and principles in this person that they taught me to be. What you don't know about me from reading this book is, I'm a dreamer.

When I was writing this book, I had many good dreams. My wildest dreams were about movie producers turning my books into movies. Sean 'Diddy' John Combs named his next fragrance after my poem, 'Forgiving'. All people need to learn to forgive. In one of my dreams, Mary J. Blige sang, 'Unfolding Soul'. She sang as the world unfolded happy feelings and there wasn't any pain. In spite of all my phases, I thank God for giving me life and the mind to create poetry at my weakest and strongest moments.

About the Author

Oman McCullough-Fuqua was born and raised in the San Francisco Bay area of California.

A self-taught writer and poet, Oman is the author of three books, a collection of short stories, and greeting cards and is the creator of original art work.

She now resides in Indianapolis, Indiana, with her husband, LaMar Fuqua, and her two Yorkies, TABOO and CIROC.

www.ingramcontent.com/pod-product-compliance
Lightning Source LLC
Chambersburg PA
CBHW070216260626
47160CB00002B/574